MW00583546

ETERNAL DECEPTION

Published by Aspidistra Press

Created with Vellum

BOOKS BY JANE STEEN

The House of Closed Doors Series

The House of Closed Doors

Eternal Deception

The Shadow Palace

The Jewel Cage

The Scott-De Quincy Mysteries

Lady Helena Investigates

Lady Odelia's Secret

Dedicated to Bob, Laura, and Ally,
For putting up with me when I'm living in my head rather than in the moment.

ETERNAL DECEPTION

JANE STEEN

PART I

1872

1

UNFORTUNATE

"I know—*exactly*—what you are."

Mrs. Drummond, housekeeper of the Eternal Life Seminary, my place of employment for the last twenty-four hours, stood ramrod-stiff beside the large fireplace in the seminary's ornate library. The ring of keys attached to the belt at her waist, a symbol of her authority, caught a stray beam of sunlight as the clouds scudding across the prairie parted for a few seconds.

Two people flanked her: Dr. Adema, the seminary's president, and a Mrs. Calderwood. I wasn't quite sure what Mrs. Calderwood's role was, but she seemed to think herself important.

"We all know Mrs. Lillington's history, Mrs. Drummond." Dr. Adema's tone was gentle, and perhaps a touch ironic. "We were all involved in the decision to employ her, on Mrs. Lombardi's recommendation." The tremor in his hands, curled around a walking stick, betrayed his age despite the upright posture of his tall, gaunt frame.

I lifted my chin and laced my fingers together, determined not to show how weary I was. The five days' journey to Kansas had seemed like such an exciting adventure when Tess, Sarah, and I had left the small town of Victory. But bad food, little sleep, and an increasingly fretful baby had taken their toll on all three of us. The jolting of the cart along the rutted track to the seminary had been the final straw for Sarah, who had vomited on Mrs. Drummond's skirts as I was shaking her hand.

"Yes, yes." Mrs. Calderwood sounded impatient, an irritated gleam in her beady black eyes. She was a small, round woman, dwarfed by the two tall figures on either side. And this despite her efforts to increase her height by piling up her grizzled black hair in a style so tall that it wobbled as she spoke. "It is true that we were well aware that *Mrs.* Lillington"—she gave a small, sardonic smile as she emphasized my fictitious married state—"came from Catherine Lombardi's Poor Farm and is an unfortunate." She narrowed her eyes at me. "But I concede—"

Dr. Adema cleared his throat, cutting off the flow of words. "We were given to understand that Mrs. Lillington's, ah, predicament was the result of a single lapse of moral judgment," he said mildly. "It's hardly fair to label her an unfortunate. She was not walking the streets."

I felt my cheeks flame. At that moment, I would have almost preferred to be an unfortunate, as Mrs. Calderwood termed it. At least I could have faced them all down with the experience borne of being a woman of the world. To have them all staring at me and knowing that Sarah was the result of my own stupidity and ignorance—well! What about my cousin, Jack Venton, who had taken advantage of that ignorance? But of course, the only way I could have avoided the blame society inevitably laid on *me* would have been to marry Jack. I preferred keeping him in ignorance to entering into a marriage neither of us wanted. And I was not prepared to give up Sarah either.

"I concede," said Mrs. Calderwood, speaking a little louder, "that Mrs. Drummond has a point." She waved a small hand, tipped with little pointed nails, in my direction. "Not only is this young woman a person of demonstrably poor moral judgment, she is undeniably handsome. And she is a very *young* woman. In a seminary full of young men."

Three pairs of eyes considered my face and figure. I wasn't feeling particularly handsome, although I had done my best to make myself as smart and neat as possible. I was the picture of sober respectability in an unadorned black skirt and shirtwaist. My only ornament was the brooch of silver, jet, and pearl that Martin Rutherford had given me.

"So if I were plain or missing a few teeth, I would be more suited to my post?" I knew I was being impertinent, but I couldn't help myself. "I can assure you, Mrs. Calderwood, that having made a mistake once—and *only* once—and having suffered the consequences, I'm not likely to try the experiment again."

I also could have married Martin, I reminded myself. He'd almost offered, and he was my oldest friend, perhaps the only man I could ever have put up with day in and day out. But he had ambitions of his own and was even now building his dreamed-of store in a Chicago that was rising from the ashes of its great fire. And he had just as great an aversion to matrimony as I did.

"I promise you, Dr. Adema, that I have no intention of causing trouble with any male person in this establishment." I fixed my gaze on Dr. Adema's kind eyes. "I'm here to make a living for myself and those who depend on me. The deaths of my mother and stepfather have left me with few financial resources, but I'm a hard worker and skilled with my needle. You won't regret hiring me."

And if they sent me away, where would I go? To the Lombardis' mission? I'd thought it would be close by and I would be able to visit with Mrs. Lombardi, who had been so kind to me at the Poor Farm. But it was an entire day's journey away from this isolated place. My dream of an independent future was fast crumbling in the face of reality.

I stared at my interlocutors, refusing to be defensive about my past.

"I should have thought the matter out more thoroughly," Mrs. Calderwood mused. She linked her little fingers together under her chin and gazed at me, her head tilted to one side. "What will the boys' parents think if they knew that their sons' clothing—and, heavens, their bed linens!—are stitched and repaired by one whose hands are tainted with," her voice dropped to a hoarse whisper, "fornication? We have the reputation of this school to think of after all."

Mrs. Drummond nodded in emphatic agreement. A tremor ran over Dr. Adema's face that just might have been a suppressed smile. "I rather think the reputation of this school is my concern, Mrs. Calderwood."

I had heard of people bristling, but I'd never seen it done quite so unequivocally. I could have sworn Mrs. Calderwood's piled-up hair actually stiffened. "If my dear father could hear your cavalier dismissal of his generosity—"

"I am doing nothing of the sort, Mrs. Calderwood. Your family's money provided the land and the building, for which our denomination is most grateful. Gratitude, I may suggest, has been sufficiently shown by the role it has accorded your husband in the running of this school. Even so, I am its president, and the funds for the daily operation of the school come from the denomination, from our donors, and from the fees paid by the boys' parents." There was a hard edge to his voice that I hadn't heard before. "I assure you, I considered all sides of the question before agreeing to employ Mrs. Lillington."

"But look at her," Mrs. Drummond burst out. She was a

good-looking woman, tall and well built with a head of glossy light brown hair, clean and neatly arranged. Her eyes, large and green-gray in hue, fixed me with an expression of outraged anger. "How does she belong in a menial position in a seminary? She's all too clearly a lady. Look at her; hear her speak. Mrs. Lombardi completely misled me. I was expecting a humble penitent, suitable for a humble post. She is not suitable. Not suitable at all."

"I can sew the clothing and linens you need, order the necessary supplies, and keep good accounts of what I do. How much more suitable do I need to be?" I turned to Dr. Adema again since it was plain he was my best ally. "Please give me a chance; I have nowhere else to go."

And that was the nub of the matter, I thought ruefully, unless I were to throw myself on the charity of the Lombardis—for whom I would be a burden. Or return to Martin, and what on earth would a single man do with an unwed mother, a baby, and Tess, whom the world was pleased to call an "imbecile"?

"Furthermore," Mrs. Drummond continued, "she has not been brought up in a properly regulated household. Church attendance irregular, daily private prayer quite absent, Bible reading very irregular, strong liquor and tobacco in the house."

I opened my mouth to reply, and then shut it again. Mrs. Drummond had fired a series of questions at me while I'd still been trying to get my bearings the day before. I'd had to admit that I'd grown up in a household where God was respected, but which hadn't been an overly religious one.

Mrs. Calderwood joined in the attack, her eyes shining gleefully. "We explained to Mrs. Lillington that this establishment is run in strict conformity to the rules of our denomination, which exhort us to a godly life and forbid the consumption of liquor."

"And I signed your pledge of commitment in good faith," I replied. "I don't drink or smoke, and I'm perfectly happy to attend chapel and observe the Sabbath. Our church attendance wasn't really irregular—I simply told you the truth, that we occasionally missed church because of illness and so forth."

"But you—"

"And then again—"

Mrs. Drummond and Mrs. Calderwood spoke together, and Dr. Adema raised a trembling hand to enjoin them to silence.

"Jesus numbered a woman of ill repute among his followers—not that I'm saying you are such, Mrs. Lillington—and Scripture gives no indication that she ever erred again. If we turn this young lady away after bringing her all the way to Kansas, where is our charity? If we cannot forgive, how can we accept the Lord's forgiveness? Do unto others, ladies." His tone held a slight note of reproach. "We all have our weaknesses."

A faint pinkness tinged Mrs. Drummond's high cheekbones; Mrs. Calderwood merely looked truculent.

"Don't forget that we have the extra trouble and expense of three mouths to feed, not just one. That child will grow, and then there's Miss O'Dugan. Her capacities are not great—"

"Miss O'Dugan appears to be of excellent character." Mrs. Drummond interrupted with an alacrity that surprised me. "She is most fond of Scripture and shows great interest in the seminary. She's been asking me about my methods of keeping accounts." She feigned not to see my tentative smile of gratitude, but her face softened a little.

"Tess is helpful to me in many ways, and she's more astute than people give her credit for." At last, I felt I was starting to gain the upper hand. "You're getting two good workers for the price of one, you know."

"You will keep the child out of sight of the students," Mrs. Drummond said. I nodded.

"And you will remember that you only speak to the young men on matters that directly concern your employment," Mrs. Calderwood added. I nodded again, biting my lip against the retort that formed in my mind.

Dr. Adema smiled. "It seems we have reached some kind of agreement."

IT WAS A RELIEF TO REACH THE WORKROOM ALLOCATED TO US, even though it was cold and empty. The wood laid ready for a fire in the grate would not be lit, Mrs. Drummond had explained, unless it was really necessary. Wood was at a premium out on the plains. The lamps in the overhead chandelier had not been lit either, though the day was waning—but I didn't care. I hadn't come here to work, but to brood alone while Tess and Sarah slept in our room far above.

I leaned my head against the window frame and looked out over the dimming landscape. The clouds had gathered, and a soft rain had begun to fall, glistening on the blades of green pushing up through last winter's browns and tans. The prairie looked vast and empty. I knew we were some three miles from the little town of Springwood, but all I could see was the bare horizon beyond a straggling row of young trees that marked the perimeter of the seminary's land.

It was a new beginning, but not the one I'd imagined. I had pictured our emigration to Kansas as a momentous escape into a new life of possibilities, perhaps of great success. At the very least, I had thought Sarah would be safe from the gossip and contempt she would encounter back home as she grew. Here, nobody would look into her jade-green eyes and think of my cousin Jack's visit. Mrs. Lombardi could perhaps introduce me to ladies who would appreciate my dressmaking skills, and we could make friends in the surrounding community—

Except that there was no Mrs. Lombardi nearby and apparently no surrounding community either. I would be far more isolated than I had been at the Poor Farm. I would be infinitely more friendless than I'd been in Victory. There, the love people had had for my mother led them to accept my invention of a hasty marriage and unfortunate widowhood. On the surface, at least.

And in Victory, I'd had Martin's steady affection, which had more value to me now than ever before.

2
MORAL WELFARE

April 15, 1872

Dear Nell,

My dear girl, what are you about? Gone for more than a month already—your grand adventure well begun—and I've had precisely fifteen words from you on a third-sheet of paper to announce your arrival. I know you to be a dilatory correspondent, but if I don't hear more soon, I shall begin to worry. Are you, Tess, and Sarah all well? What are you doing?

I'm sending you a package with some trinkets that, I trust, are more than you can find in Springwood's mercantile. The fine weather in Chicago means that my men spend all their time building my store, so I have plenty of time to meet with my suppliers. Ships have started arriving in New York and San Francisco now that the winter is over, and I have to work hard to secure the best of the best for Rutherford & Co. I've begun hiring clerks and have rented temporary premises to house them. We spend all day producing reams of correspondence and rivers of calculations. Soon it'll be time to begin hiring managers, who will in their turn engage the staff.

You'll be glad to hear it's not all work though, thanks to Fass-

binder. Whoever would have thought that the refugee I housed after the fire would turn out to be such a business asset as well as a friend? He has secured me introductions, so I've received quite a few invitations to dine and have met some of the other merchants and their families. I'll tell you more about them when you've written to me—is that sufficient inducement to correspond?

Ah, I'm merely teasing you. I'm sure you're kept busy. But do write, Nell. I like to hear that my little friend is well and happy.

Martin

"WHO IS THIS MAN WHO WRITES TO YOU?" MRS. Calderwood's shrill voice echoed in the cavernous hallway. "Mrs. Drummond tells me this is the second letter you have received since you arrived—from the same man."

She waved Martin's letter under my nose. "And there's a parcel full of dress trimmings of the most impractical kind and some copies of Godey's Lady's Book. And a dreadful French publication of an even more frivolous nature than Godey's. Quite unsuitable."

"You opened my package?" My question came out as an incredulous squeak.

"Naturally." Mrs. Calderwood folded her short arms and stuck out her chin. "As your employer, I am responsible for your moral welfare. Who, I ask again, is this man?"

"A friend." I was aware I sounded defensive.

"A Mr. Martin Rutherford of Chicago. A single man? He mentions no wife."

"So you did read my letter. I thought as much." I fought to keep the anger out of my voice.

"I could hardly let it pass without scrutiny. And my husband must see it."

I had learned that Dr. Calderwood was in charge of the

day-to-day administration of the seminary as Dr. Adema's assistant. I'd seen him read out the notices before our daily chapel service. He was a massive man with a mane of tawny hair and huge white teeth, which showed frequently in an uncertain smile as his ever-darting gaze sought out his small, round wife in the front pew.

"Dr. Calderwood will find nothing wrong in Mr. Rutherford's letter," I said. "Mr. Rutherford is an old friend of the family who has known me since I was a small child. I entrusted him with the keeping and increase of what capital I have. He's much older than me."

Eleven years older, to be precise, which made Martin the grand old age of thirty. Still, I was ready to make him sound as old as Dr. Adema if that would allow me to receive his letters.

"And those ribbons? Those lengths of lace? Those hat trimmings?"

"Samples," I said. "Mr. Rutherford is a draper. He's building a store in Chicago."

"Building a store? That must be costing him a mint of money." Mrs. Calderwood smoothed out the thin sheets of paper, which had the words "Rutherford & Co." emblazoned across the top, and looked at them again with greater interest. "Is he rich?"

"I suppose he must be." I saw my way forward in the avid glint in the little woman's eyes. "I've never thought to inquire, but he is building a large store in a prime position. He's no doubt likely to become one of the richest men in Chicago."

"Which is a most prosperous city by all accounts." The voice that cut across Mrs. Calderwood's was musical and wholly unexpected.

I turned to look at the man standing behind me. It was a young man I'd seen in Dr. Calderwood's company—a handsome young man. A head of glossy black curls framed high cheekbones; he had a beautifully shaped mouth and eyes of that peculiar shade of blue that's sometimes called violet, slanted upward at the corners and adorned by long black lashes.

Mrs. Calderwood bestowed a gracious smile upon the newcomer. She must have seen him approaching, even though I hadn't heard his footfalls on the black-and-white marble tiles.

"Mr. Poulton is well informed in business matters," she said before clearly realizing she had just put herself in a position where an introduction—to a man!—would be necessary unless she were to be blatantly rude to me. I saw the latter possibility flicker over her face for the merest fraction of a second, and then she nodded at me.

"Mrs. Lillington, this is Mr. Poulton, our Old Testament teacher." She cleared her throat. "Mrs. Lillington has taken up the position of seamstress."

We shook hands, Mr. Poulton's eyes sparkling with evident awareness of Mrs. Calderwood's reluctance to introduce me. "I've seen you in chapel. With your baby and companion."

I felt my eyebrows rise. Mr. Poulton must have good eyesight. He was always seated at the front of the chapel while Tess, Sarah, and I occupied a half pew near the back. Our view was partially obscured by a pillar, on the other side of which sat Mrs. Drummond and the handful of white servants. The other servants, former slaves, sat behind us. A wide aisle and waist-high screen separated us from the curious glances of the students.

"So you're friends with a rich Chicago merchant?" Mr. Poulton glanced at the letter Mrs. Calderwood held.

"A rising one," I said. "He's an old family friend and kind enough to write to us and send us a few little trinkets. Mrs.

Calderwood doubts the propriety of the communication." I stared at the little woman, whose expression was less malicious than it had been a few minutes before.

"May I see?"

Mr. Poulton took the letter from Mrs. Calderwood's unprotesting hands and scanned it while I tried not to look as indignant as I felt. I needed allies, even nosy ones.

"It's quite brotherly," he said, handing it back.

"Mr. Rutherford's the nearest thing to a brother that I have," I said. "I have no male relatives—no relatives at all except some cousins in Connecticut. And I haven't kept in touch with them," I hastened to add. I would be on dangerous ground if induced to talk about my cousins in the East. "Please, Mrs. Calderwood—I give you my word there's nothing improper going on."

Mrs. Calderwood looked at me and then at Mr. Poulton.

"She *has* given you her word," said that gentleman, smiling. His smile was as appealing as the rest of his person, and Mrs. Calderwood visibly melted.

"Well, if you say so, Mr. Poulton." She handed the letter to me. "You may collect your package before supper, Mrs. Lillington."

"And may I write to him also?"

"I'm sure Mrs. Lillington will sing your praises for your kindness," added Mr. Poulton smoothly. There was something in his tone that put my senses on the alert. A conscious look crossed Mrs. Calderwood's face, and I wondered—did she open outgoing letters too? I would have to make sure no word of complaint made it onto the pages of my letter.

Once more, I reflected, I had sought freedom only to render myself powerless. As a married woman, I would have been in bondage to one man; as an unmarried one, I was apparently in bondage to everyone else.

"You may. Doubtless you have work to do, Mrs. Lillington."

Mrs. Calderwood moved off in the direction of the wide, steep staircase, bathed in multi-colored pools of light from the row of stained-glass windows above its first landing. She glanced back at us, her face a vivid green as she passed through one of the filtered splashes of illumination.

"I must go back to my workroom," I said, turning away from Mr. Poulton. "I'm under an obligation to you, sir."

He said nothing but bowed and smiled as he moved away, his face raised to Mrs. Calderwood, who was still looking at us. He raised a hand in a salute to her. She dipped her head in acknowledgment and continued on her way, her pattering footsteps echoing in the silent hall.

3

NEW FRIENDS

I tried hard to stay out of the corridors between classes, but when you have a baby in your care, things don't always go as you intend. Like a salmon swimming against the current, I soon found myself trying to ascend the staircase in the face of a rushing torrent of male humanity. The boys parted around us, to be sure, but impeded my progress more than I liked.

Sarah's eyes were wide with excitement at the noise. The boys' voices, ranging from bass to falsetto, bounced off the wooden paneling and surged around us as we climbed higher. My efforts to keep the soiled portion of my baby's nether regions away from my own clothing complicated my progress.

Some of the students weren't much younger than me. In the way of boys, some of the older ones looked more like full-grown men while others still had the smooth faces and high voices of childhood. Many, I noticed, had inches of flesh peeping from the wrists of their jackets and the ankles of their pantaloons. I had better ask Mrs. Drummond how to go about ensuring that I let out or replaced their clothing as needed.

"And whom do we have here?"

A hand on my arm arrested my climb as a short, balding, older man passed me. From the step above him, I had an excellent view of the pink patch in his black wavy hair as he took off his academic cap to scratch his head. He then remembered his manners and tipped the cap in my direction.

Bright, curious black eyes took in the sight of Sarah, who wasn't the least bit discomfited by her damp condition. She returned his interest by stretching out avid little hands toward the buttons on his rather dandified waistcoat. From his academic gown, I concluded he was a teacher of some kind. Mr. Poulton had not worn one, and I thought the custom had gone out during the war, but the gown suited this man.

"The new seamstress." The little man answered his own question. "And her bonny baby." He chucked Sarah under the chin, and she squealed. "You're a widow, I hear, ma'am?"

"I am." I nodded, too busy shifting Sarah into a better position to feel the usual pangs of a guilty conscience.

"Well, we're fortunate to have you, and I'm delighted to make your acquaintance. What do you think of the theories of Mr. Darwin? For or against?"

I was dumbstruck by the peculiar question. Darwin? I knew about him, of course, and had read one or two diatribes against his theories in the papers. But an opinion?

"I have no opinion whatsoever," I confessed, wishing I could find a way to end the conversation and tend to Sarah. "I manage to go through my day's work without giving Mr. Darwin's theories the least consideration."

But I couldn't help smiling. The professor's eyes shone brighter as his weather-beaten face wrinkled into an answering grin, showing heavily stained teeth.

"Come, come, you are in a place of learning." He watched as Sarah, fascinated by the play of light on his gaudy waistcoat, leaned toward it with a crooning sound. "A place, moreover, which exists for the 'bold and fervent defense of orthodoxy through the enlightened pursuit of knowledge.'"

I nodded. I had heard that phrase from Dr. Adema, who explained that his mission was to produce thinkers with a sound faith rather than dull conformists. Looking at the ragtag of noisy students heading to their classes, I wondered if there were any real thinkers among them.

Except for the one who stopped next to the professor and smiled at both of us. He looked a little more smartly dressed and sophisticated than the majority of the young men. Indeed, he exuded confidence and wealth. His suit was plain but well cut, showing no spare inches of flesh but fitting him in every particular. His boots shone, and his corn-blond hair was neatly trimmed and carefully oiled. Perhaps he was a teacher too, I thought, although he looked much the same age as me.

"Every man should have an opinion," the professor pronounced, reaching out to smooth back Sarah's frizzy curls. "And every woman too." He seemed to recollect himself and bowed to me. "I beg your pardon for not introducing myself. I am Gervaise Wale—W-A-L-E—no relation to the denizens of the deep. I teach Hebrew and Greek."

"And I'm Reiner Lehmann," the young man said, also bowing, "and I learn Hebrew and Greek. And you're going to be late for class, Professor Wale."

His blue eyes lit up as he watched the professor try to capture one of Sarah's little hands as she made a grab for his waistcoat buttons. She retreated from his gesture and grabbed my hair, dislodging a hairpin.

Professor Wale looked at the splendid gold watch Mr.

Lehmann had pulled from his pocket and flipped open, grimaced, and replaced his cap on his head.

"Class. Of course. Good day, Mrs.—?" He looked puzzled, as if trying to recollect my name, which I hadn't given him.

"Lillington. Eleanor Lillington." I held out my hand for the hairpin Mr. Lehmann had retrieved for me and poked it randomly back into my curls. "Thank you."

We both watched Professor Wale descending the staircase at a fast trot, his gown billowing out behind him like a ship at sail.

"I must go," I said. Sarah was becoming difficult to handle and smellier by the second.

"And so must I." But the young man remained in place, and I could feel his gaze fixed on me as I climbed the staircase. Reiner Lehmann, I mused. A student—a wealthy one. And from the look in his eyes, I had gained an admirer.

My impression that something about me had struck a chord of admiration in Mr. Reiner Lehmann received affirmation later that month.

Tess and I had gone outside for a little fresh air before the seminary's early supper. Sarah was already asleep under the watchful eye of a servant called Dorcas, who was busying herself with sorting sheets in the linen room. The servants had taken a shine to Sarah, and I encountered frequent offers to "watch the chile for a spell." They'd whisk her off to the kitchen and ply her with pieces of cornbread and her favorite treat, tiny crumbles of crisp bacon. I was still nursing her, but she was fast learning to eat and drink on her own, and I didn't think it would be long before I weaned her.

The weather had turned pleasant with the arrival of May. The constant breeze that stirred the prairie was now warm, soughing over the green grasses and setting them tossing like waves. The air had a freshness that caused windows to be flung open all over the seminary building. It was a time when being in such an isolated position didn't seem like hardship.

"She was such a pretty lady." Tess rested her hand on my shoulder, the better to peer at the face I was sketching.

"She was like—like a dainty porcelain doll, Tess. To look at, in any case. I exceeded her height by the time I was twelve and a half."

I tilted my head to one side, contemplating the drawing of Mama. I added a few more touches to suggest the shine on her beautiful pale blond hair, which I had drawn coiled and twisted into her habitual smooth, elegant style.

Grief was an odd process, I found. Mama had been gone for eight months—the best part of a year—and there were days when I didn't consciously think of her much. And then sadness and longing would hit me like a wave, catching me unawares. Tess and I had spent the day in concentrated activity, but in the quiet hour before the dinner bell, my pencil moved almost by itself, striving to delineate my mother's gentle face. At times like this, I missed her terribly.

"You're dainty too, Nell. No—that's the wrong word—you're *elegant*."

Tess lowered her head so her chin rested on my shoulder. I felt the tickle of her fine, wispy hair against my cheek and the movement of her jaw as she stifled a small yawn.

I leaned my head sideways a little so that my cheek touched Tess's. "And you're dearer to me than any sister could have been, Tess. What would I do without you?"

Tess considered this for a moment. "You'd have to do more sewing," was her conclusion. "Like the basting. I always do that."

I chuckled—Tess was always literal—but my eyes were on my sketch of Mama. We'd been such a tiny family, Grandmama, Mama, and I. What would they think if they could see me now, a seamstress on the remote frontier, rejecting their dreams of a fine marriage for me?

"You're quite the artist, Mrs. Lillington. May I sit down?" Mr. Lehmann nodded at Tess as he bent over my drawing.

"Of course, although—" I looked toward the seminary. It was a huge edifice of yellow stone, crenellated and turreted at the corners, surmounted by an odd tiered tower finished with a cupola of weathered copper. Its rows of windows were dark holes in the light stone. We were at the front, eastern side of the building, and the setting sun was behind it; the ornate outline stood stark against the soft yellows and oranges of the late afternoon sky.

"Although what?"

Mr. Lehmann folded his body into a kneeling position on one corner of the rug we'd brought outside. He wasn't handsome by any means; his features were a little irregular, and he had the kind of sturdy muscularity that might run to fat later. Yet there was something appealing about his broad, open face, and his smile showed teeth that were even, white, and strong. Not handsome, but likable. And quite out of bounds to me in Mrs. Calderwood's mind.

"I'm not supposed to talk to the students."

"Why not? Our last seamstress married one—at least, he came back for her after he'd been out in the world for a couple of years. And she wasn't nearly as pretty as you."

"Perhaps that's why." I couldn't help laughing at the expression on his face. "And I don't have any intention of marrying. I'm here to work."

"Mrs. Drummond doesn't want the students to have any distractions," Tess declared. I was constantly surprised by how well Tess got on with the housekeeper—and I wondered just how much Mrs. Drummond had told her.

"But we need distractions. It's so dull out here." Mr.

Lehmann extended a hand in Tess's direction. "My name is Reiner Lehmann, by the way. Mighty nice to make your acquaintance."

"I am Theresa O'Dugan." Tess's dignified reply was somewhat spoiled by a huge yawn that she half hid behind her left hand as she shook Mr. Lehmann's with her right.

A group of boys sauntered by, staring at us with open curiosity, some nodding to Mr. Lehmann. He returned their greetings with the lazy, careless air of a prince acknowledging the existence of his subjects. One of them must have made a joke—the others erupted in gales of laughter and a tussle began, with one of the smaller boys getting the worst of it.

"Silly oafs." Mr. Lehmann shifted his position so his back was to the group of shouting boys, gazing at me with what, unfortunately, was starting to look like slavish adoration. I was going to have to put a stop to that, I decided.

"It's not just Mrs. Drummond who disapproves of me talking to the students," I said, trying to sound as reproving as I could. "Mrs. Calderwood—"

I stopped short, wondering what, exactly, I could tell this young man without revealing too much of my past.

"Oh, the Mouse likes me," said Mr. Lehmann. "She won't bother us if I choose to talk to you."

"What makes you so sure?" I asked, amused. The Mouse? Well, I supposed she did look a little mouse-like with those beady black eyes and small, grasping hands. I suppressed a giggle.

"My pop's a generous—exceedingly generous—supporter of the cause of spreading the light of orthodoxy over the plains." Mr. Lehmann extracted his gold watch from his pocket and flipped open the case. A diamond set into a ring on his little finger caught the fire of the setting sun, winking like a tiny orange flame.

"Are you telling me you're allowed to do as you please just because your father gives money to the seminary? I can't imagine Dr. Adema abandoning his principles for money."

"Oh no, Dr. Adema's as straight as an arrow. But he's more concerned with the spiritual welfare of the students than anything else. The Calderwoods handle the money side of things—it's the Lion's job in name, but he's ruled by his Mouse. Haven't you noticed?" Mr. Lehmann opened his eyes wide and stared at me, his expression mischievous. "When the Mouse squeaks, the Lion obeys. That's why I, and a few other select students, have such pleasant sets of rooms on the first floor. The ostensible reason is seniority, but we all know we're the sons of the seminary's most faithful supporters."

"Hmph," I said. It was disappointing to think of the Calderwoods' greed undermining Dr. Adema's lofty ideals behind his back.

The sound of the bell housed inside the seminary's crowning turret brought us all to our feet, Tess and I brushing stray bits of grass from our skirts. It was suppertime at last. Small groups of soberly clad young men solidified into larger black masses as they headed for the building's imposing entrance.

"Welcome to the frontier, Mrs. Lillington, where there may be a sight more land and fewer rules about how to dress and drink your coffee, but money still counts." Mr. Lehmann rolled up the rug and tucked it under his arm, crooking his other elbow in my direction. "So may I take you in to dinner?" He grinned at Tess. "I'd offer my other arm to your charming companion if I didn't have this rug to carry."

Tess giggled and put both hands over her mouth. "I don't mind. I'll hold Nell's other arm."

I placed a hand lightly on Mr. Lehmann's free arm, feeling the strong muscle under the fine black wool of his sack coat. Tess grabbed my other arm, and we proceeded thus into the seminary, stopping to stow the rug and my drawing materials in the cloakroom for collection later.

By the time Mr. Lehmann handed us to our seats—we sat at the back of the large refectory, away from the students and at the same table as Mrs. Drummond—we were all laughing. I sobered when I saw Mrs. Drummond's gaze fix on me, cool and evaluating, with more than a hint of disapproval. I saw her glance toward Mrs. Calderwood, who sat with her husband, Dr. Adema, and several of the teachers on a raised dais below the windows.

I slipped into my seat with a warning glance at Tess and bowed my head demurely for the prayers—but not before I realized that Mr. Poulton, seated at the head table, was also looking in our direction.

4
OLD FRIENDS

April 26, 1872

Dear Martin,

I have some news to tell you at last—in a small way, you understand. Nothing as grand as your tales of building and stocking your store. Tess says your stories are as good as a novel, but I think they're much better. You know I have no love for fiction.

My news is that the Lombardis have come to the seminary for a visit. Mr. and Mrs. Lombardi, Teddy, and Thea are well—Teddy is almost as tall as his mother now. Lucy is thin and pale and has a cough, which is worrying.

As for your news, are you sure it was wise to lure one of the best people away from another store to be your general manager? This Mr. Salazar sounds ideal, but I'm sure the owners of Gambarelli's will bear a grudge against you for stealing away such a talented employee.

Oh, here I am trying to tell you how to run your business when I'm a mere seamstress. You'll laugh at me, I'm sure. I suppose I'm envious—I would give much to have a small business of my own. But what chance do I have of that out here on the plains?

And talking of the plains, here is Mrs. Lombardi come to walk with me to Springwood. I wish you could see that funny little place —I expect Victory looked just like it thirty or forty years ago. I will end this letter now and hope I can post it in Springwood so I don't have to endure Mrs. Drummond's looks when I place it on the table in the seminary's hallway. It has been raining, and I have no doubt that the track leading to Springwood will be muddy—but we have stout boots, and I need to get away from this place.

I send you much affection, as always, and a hug from Tess. Sarah sends you some babbles that sound more like words every day.

Nell

"I CAN'T IMAGINE WHAT IT MUST BE LIKE INSIDE THOSE soddies." I lowered my voice as we neared the outskirts of the town of Springwood.

Calling it a town was a feat of the imagination—especially at this end of it. The dwellings by the creek seemed nothing more than stacked heaps of muddy grass, limp yellow stalks dripping rainwater that formed channels as it sought its way downward. An astonishing variety of ramshackle pieces of tin or wood overlaid parts of the walls and roofs. Here and there, a larger piece formed a lean-to that sheltered a few logs or implements.

"They're better than you'd think inside." Catherine Lombardi was as neat and elegant as she'd been at the Poor Farm, but her dress was beginning to look a little dated and faded, as if she couldn't afford to renew or replace it. Her life as a missionary's wife had its hardships if the new lines in her face were any indication, and I had felt calluses on her hands when she grasped mine in greeting.

"You've been inside them?" I hitched my skirts a little higher as we came to a low part of the track where the puddles were worse than usual. "I suppose you would—you try to visit all the women for miles around, wasn't that what you said? Do you know these?" I nodded toward two women who were garrulously involved in washing something in a large wooden barrel. One of them drew water from a huge kettle hung over a smoking fire.

"I do."

"They're wearing bloomers," I breathed in her ear. "I've never seen such a thing in my life, although Mama said some women tried wearing them before the war."

I tried hard not to stare, but you could see their *legs*, just as if they were men or children. One of the women wore wooden pattens to keep her feet out of the sea of mud that surrounded them. The other wore a man's thick, ungainly boots and a cowman's hat.

"You'd soon grow impatient with skirts if you did the work they did," Mrs. Lombardi said under her breath and then raised her voice. "It's Mrs. Gordey, isn't it? And Sukey? Do you remember me?"

I hung back a little as Mrs. Lombardi spoke to the two women. The ever-present wind rustled the broken branches and greening twigs of a straggling line of cottonwoods that grew along the creek. I had imagined somehow that Kansas would be dry, but I was wrong. In this spring season, the muddy, rushing water in the channel came almost up to the rough wooden bridge that led to the main part of Springwood.

"She lost three children to the ague," Mrs. Lombardi informed me as we continued on our way. "This is a hard country, Nell, especially for the poorer settlers. Those soddies are all they can manage until they can scrape together enough to build a proper house. Don't forget how scarce lumber is out here, and building in stone takes time and expertise."

And yet the seminary building wouldn't be out of place in a city, I mused. And some citizens of Springwood could afford to build well. Beyond the creek were piles of lumber and stone and markers designating plots of land. Knots of roughly dressed men congregated around half-built houses.

Another ten minutes' walk brought us to the completed part of the little community. There were perhaps fifteen houses of respectable appearance, with a small church taking pride of place in an attractive spot framed by hickories and oaks. Two short rows of commercial buildings suggested the beginning of what might one day be a thriving town.

"My word," I said.

It wasn't the houses that had caught my eye, nor the gracious attentions of several well-dressed women of matronly aspect who nodded at us as we approached. Before the largest commercial building, Hayward's Mercantile, strutted a horse. Even to my untrained eye, it looked to be a fine, high-spirited animal of the sort favored by wealthy young gentlemen. Its gleaming coat and great height set it apart from the sturdy, mud-splashed workhorses tied to hitching posts along the street, like a prince among paupers.

Atop this magnificent beast sat a man incongruously dressed in a neat black suit and soft felt hat, putting the animal through its paces with the cool confidence of someone who dealt with expensive horseflesh every day.

"That's Mr. Poulton, isn't it?" asked Mrs. Lombardi, her eyebrows raised. "Doesn't he ride well?"

"He seems to do everything well," I replied. For it was indeed the seminary's Old Testament teacher. His lithe figure showed to advantage as he guided the horse through a complex series of movements seemingly designed to test every aspect of its gait. As he made the last turn, Mr. Poulton saw us and turned his mount in our direction, bringing it to a stop with the lightest touch on the reins and dismounting gracefully. He doffed his hat, smiling at us while the wind ruffled his black curls and a gleam of sunlight made them shine like ebony. It was hard not to smile back.

"Are you thinking of buying this horse, Mr. Poulton?" Mrs. Lombardi—or Catherine, as she was insisting I call her now—spoke cordially. "He's much too fine for the plains, to my way of thinking."

"His price is quite out of my reach, I'm afraid," was the answer, with another smile that brought a sparkle to his violet-blue eyes. I gave my hat a surreptitious tug, hoping he wouldn't notice the state of my boots and skirt.

"Fairland had him brought from Kentucky for his son." Mr. Poulton indicated a portly man with expansive whiskers and a red-veined nose.

"Give some tone to the place," proclaimed Mr. Fairland, tipping his hat in our direction. "He looks mighty fine next to your nags, don't he?" he called over his shoulder to the other men standing nearby. I knew from the signs on one of the commercial buildings that Mr. Fairland was, among other things, a Wells Fargo agent. From the look of the horse, business was booming.

"He'll look the same as the others when he's covered in mud," called one of the watching men, who spat a brown stream of tobacco juice into a puddle.

During this exchange, the matronly ladies made a beeline toward our group, keeping a careful distance from the horse. They greeted Catherine, whom they seemed to know, bestowed fond smiles on Mr. Poulton, and nodded politely at me.

"Ladies," said Catherine, "this is Mrs. Eleanor Lillington of Illinois. From near Chicago. She's taken up the post of seamstress at the seminary—and she's a special friend of mine."

Puzzlement flitted across the ladies' faces as they wrestled with how to treat me. As seamstress at the seminary, I was little better than a servant—but as Catherine Lombardi's friend, I deserved more consideration.

Mr. Poulton settled the matter by offering me his arm and bestowing a dazzling smile on me. The matrons seemed as one to decide I was an object of interest and charm. They made welcoming noises and remarks about how good it would be to have a new lady in their circle of acquaintance.

"Do you ride, Mrs. Lillington?" Mr. Poulton removed his hat to mop his brow.

"Unfortunately not." At that moment, I was exceedingly sorry I couldn't produce any evidence of knowledge about horses. Out of the corner of my eye, I saw one of the ladies, a fiercely corseted matriarch with an interesting, mobile face, sidle over to the man who'd spat tobacco juice. She gave him a look that made him instantly hook the wad of tobacco out of his mouth and wrap it in his handkerchief—from which I deduced they were married.

"Mrs. Lillington should learn to ride, shouldn't she?" Catherine had a mischievous gleam in her eye. "This country is most propitious for making horsewomen of us."

Amid the chorus of hilarity that followed, Mr. Poulton moved back to the horse and gave it a clap on the neck, whereupon it turned its huge head to bite his arm. Blue eyes fierce, he pushed its muzzle away with a barked shout of command and grasped the bridle again, pulling the bit back so that it made contact with the corners of the animal's mouth. The horse immediately quieted down, but not before I'd seen Mr. Poulton's arm tense as if he'd like to mete out further punishment. A faint flush appeared on his high cheekbones, but then he made a conscious effort to relax, and with a laugh, led the horse over to its owner.

"You've made a good purchase, Fairland." He handed the horse over to a shabbily dressed man standing a few paces behind the Wells Fargo agent. "You'll have to be firm with this one though. Don't let him think for a moment he's in charge of anything."

Mr. Poulton turned back to me, peeling off the sturdy leather gloves he had been wearing and brushing a few horsehairs off his black suit.

"The day's warming up," he remarked. "May I buy you ladies a glass of sassafras beer?"

I hesitated, mainly because the amused expression on Mrs. Lombardi's face told me she believed the invitation to be for my benefit. From the sly glances passing between the older ladies, they thought so too.

"The mercantile is quite respectable," Mr. Poulton said, misinterpreting my reluctance. "There's no whiskey barrel."

"And Mrs. Hayward washes the glasses after *every* customer," said the clever-looking matron, prompting laughter from her companions.

I gave in, of course. I'd been inside the mercantile before—it was, in point of fact, the only store worth visiting in the town.

An assortment of odors greeted us: the strong-smelling kerosene lamp that lit the crowded interior, coffee from the grinder that stood on the counter, molasses, leather, the spice of tobacco from the cigar boxes high on the shelves, the astringent smells of soap and patent medicines. One corner of the store overflowed with bolts of cloth, rough clothing of the sort the workingmen of the plains wore, ribbons, ladies' undergarments discreetly screened by a piece of linen, suspenders, hats, and a few pairs of shoes. Rifles, pistols, lamps, lanterns, cooking pots, and utensils hung from all available points, with boxes of ammunition stacked next to a tower of large round cheeses. A well-polished pine coffin stood in another corner with a sign announcing that other sizes and finishes were available—just ask.

The sassafras beer was cool, strongly flavored, and not too sweet, and I began to enjoy myself. I was back in the world I understood. Our polite conversation didn't go any deeper than remarks on the fierceness of the prairie wind, the types of horse best suited to the terrain, the selection of goods in the store, and the relative sophistication of Wichita.

"But the seminary," I said after a few minutes. "It never fails to astonish me, especially when I see how raw and new Springwood is. How on earth could anyone think of raising such a grand building in the middle of nowhere?"

"Dr. Adema is a visionary," Catherine said. "He looks forward to a time when—who knows?—Springwood may be as large as Chicago. Don't forget that great city was just a collection of wood huts only forty years ago."

"Professor Adema is a dreamer." Mr. Poulton's tone was light, but his musical voice had an edge to it. "An impractical man, at bottom. He imagines the brotherhood of all men and the expansion of knowledge to every African, Indian, and poor son of the prairie. He's fortunate he was able to rely on the generosity of the Calderwoods, who have steadier heads and a more realistic outlook on life."

I opened my mouth to protest that I preferred Dr. Adema's generous openheartedness to the Calderwoods' narrow conventionality, but then I shut it again. I was in no position to bite the hand that fed me, Sarah, and Tess—and I was sure Mr. Poulton was in the Calderwoods' complete confidence. And besides, Mr. Poulton was most decorative to look at, and I was in no mood to introduce a sour note into the pleasant hour.

"How is it you ride so well, Mr. Poulton?" Catherine asked. "Not that I have any reason to think a man shouldn't ride, but you seem—"

"More of a scholar?" Mr. Poulton's eyes slanted upward when he was amused, and I found myself waiting for those moments. "When I was a lad in Baltimore, I had plenty of opportunities to ride. When I was in England, I rode to hounds—fox-hunting, you know—and hunted pheasant and partridge. I had a generous patron when I was at Cambridge."

His smile turned a little wistful. "Alas, to be a poor teacher, Mrs. Lillington. I can't enjoy such luxuries now."

"I can enjoy them even less," I laughed. "I'm a poor seamstress."

"And I'm an even poorer missionary's wife," said Catherine, and we all laughed uproariously at our poverty.

"But you've seen England." I sighed when the laughter ended. "I've always wanted to go there. My grandmother was English. But I don't suppose I'll ever have the money."

"Nonsense." Catherine's tone was brisk and cheerful. "Both of you have the blessings of good looks, cultivation, and youth. Rejoice in those assets, which may take you far."

"I will," said Mr. Poulton, holding out his hand to me. "Mrs. Lillington, let us shake hands as allies in the search for better prospects. Who knows? We may each of us find a wealthy spouse."

5

TRAGEDY

May 20, 1872

Dear Martin,

I put pen to paper with a heavy heart. This time I have real news, and it's terrible.

Dr. Adema, the president of this seminary, has died in a fall. He was a poor sleeper, in the way of the elderly, I suppose, and was in the habit of walking around the place late at night. A servant found him at the foot of the grand staircase. His neck had broken—he must have slipped on the stairs and tumbled down them. They think he died before he reached the bottom—I hope so.

The memorial service will take place tomorrow, and I find myself in awfully low spirits. All the more so because the rumor is Dr. Calderwood will now be president, which means Mrs. Calderwood will rule the roost more than ever. And you know how she disapproves of me.

Dr. Adema was my ally, and I felt that in time, he would become my friend. I know I should be mourning him and not thinking of myself, but the future looks bleak to me.

Yours in sadness,

Nell

"Is somebody there?"

I shifted in my seat, looking around at the room behind me. The light of the small lamp I had carried into the remotest bay of the library did not shine far, and the shadows—combined with my low mood—made me nervous. The clock that usually provided a comforting tick in the large room had been stopped to mark Dr. Adema's death. This late at night, the silence was so deep it was almost a presence in itself. The click of the heavy door, made of solid oak with beveled panes of glass, had been quite distinct.

"Mrs. Lillington? I'm so sorry to disturb you." Professor Wale held a thick book in his hand, his index finger between the pages to keep his place. His thick, springy hair stood up around his bald spot, chalk dust mingling with the black and gray where he had run his fingers through it while teaching.

I breathed a sigh of relief. "You don't disturb me. I'm glad of the company."

I was learning to like the small, irascible man. He didn't tolerate fools—I'd seen him berating an older student for stupidity with acidic eloquence—but he was fair-minded. I'd found him, not long before, tweaking the earlobe of a boy who'd taunted another over his clothes. The lecture on pride and arrogance he'd delivered on that occasion was at a volume to make the windows rattle. Later, he'd sent the badly dressed boy to me to have his wardrobe supplemented —at the professor's expense.

"I thought one of the students left a lamp burning in the corner," the professor said. "They're careless little beasts, and an unattended lamp is a hazard in a library."

He put his open book down on a nearby table and slipped something that looked suspiciously like a pipe into his pocket. Seeing my eyes follow the movement, he grinned, revealing yellow-stained teeth.

"You didn't see that, Mrs. Lillington. This august institution frowns on the use of tobacco. But it's a comforting habit in troubled times."

"I don't blame you." I rubbed my eyes. "These past two days have been dreadful. I think the servants have taken Dr. Adema's death the hardest."

"He took many of them in after the war, you know, when the country was full of former slaves without employment. He worked through the churches to find the most deserving, those who still wished for a domestic place. They love him. Loved him."

He sat down heavily in a chair near me.

"Didn't you?" I asked.

Professor Wale nodded, leaning his chin on his hand. "Hendrik Adema had his priorities right. It galls me to think of that fatuous imp Calderwood presuming to take his place."

I looked down at the book in which I'd been writing. "It bodes ill for me, this change. Mrs. Calderwood takes a dim view of my moral character."

"Why?" The professor cocked his head to one side, looking like a curious, crested parrot.

I swallowed hard, realizing the trap I'd walked into. But I wasn't in the mood to concoct a story, and besides—I trusted him.

"I—I made a mistake, once." I hung my head. "My daughter is the result."

I could feel my cheeks burning, but I looked up when the professor let out a low whistle.

"O-o-o-h," he said. "Well, I made a few mistakes myself as

a youth. But as the great Johnson said, I cannot conceive, and my follies did me no lasting harm. The harm I did to myself happened later, and my sins are no doubt far more grievous than yours, my dear."

He leaned forward and patted my hand in a fatherly way. "Thank you for confiding in me. Is it anxiety about Mrs. Calderwood that keeps you awake so late at night?"

"In a way." I felt my shoulders slump. "When I came to Kansas, I thought I was setting out on a great adventure—that I'd be on my way to a new life, one I'd chosen for myself." I looked at him. "But I brought my problems with me, didn't I? And I thought I could bring Sarah up far from gossip if I moved away from my home, but the gossip has already started."

I gestured at my book, where columns of figures led to a depressingly small total. "And the worst circumstance of all is that I've trapped myself here. I don't see how I'm even going to afford the fare back to Chicago or have any possibility of escaping from this place without throwing myself on the charity of my friends."

"You were calculating your wealth?" Professor Wale's dark eyes, often so weary looking, sparkled with the sort of inquisitiveness that aims at helping rather than just enjoying another person's misery. "Of course, you were trying to work out how much you can save. What do you earn?"

"Sixty cents a day." Somehow I didn't mind confessing the smallness of the sum to this man. "With full board for all three of us—a generous amount considering the cost of food and lodging. I split my earnings with Tess—I could do little without her help—and we pool our resources to buy the things we need."

"Sixty cents a day." Professor Wale looked at the ceiling, where the lamp threw a golden pool of light from its chimney.

"I don't think I'd do as well in Chicago if I did plain needlework," I hastened to assure him. "Dressmaking work is getting harder to find now that the dry goods stores stock so many ladies' garments. In any case, by my calculations it will take nearly a year just to save the fare back to Chicago."

"But you're not friendless there, I presume." They were kind, those eyes, infinitely kind in their sadness.

"I have a friend I trust—an old friend of the family, who takes care of the tiny capital left after my mother and stepfather died." Because my stepfather, Hiram Jackson, had spent my mother's money as well as his own—but there was no point in telling *that* story.

"Yet you wish to remain independent of this person."

I frowned. "I'd like to be independent of everyone, I suppose."

"Ah, now we are getting to the essence of the matter."

Professor Wale crossed one leg across his knee and curled his hands around his ankle. "Forgive me, my young friend, if I seem overly curious. But I tire easily of small talk, and I would like to look into your heart a little, if you'll indulge a man old enough to be your father. So tell me, what are your priorities?"

The answer came with an ease that surprised me. "To provide well for my daughter and for Miss O'Dugan, who is like a sister to me. To make it possible for us to direct our own lives, even if we're only women."

"Aren't you directing your life now?"

"Hardly. I can't even write to my friend—I suppose you should know he's a man and unmarried—without Mrs. Calderwood reading my letters."

One of the reasons I was still awake was a nagging worry that either Mrs. Calderwood or Mrs. Drummond would read the letter I'd written to Martin that morning. Well, if my goose was going to be cooked, it might as well happen sooner than later.

The professor's thick black eyebrows rose, deepening the wrinkles on his forehead. "I would have difficulty tolerating such interference indeed." He fingered the pipe in his coat pocket as if he'd truly like to light it.

"I have little choice as things stand," I admitted. "Right now, to provide for my family I must submit to my employers."

"Hmmm. I suppose finding a husband is out of the question. Then you could tell the busybodies to go—well, let us say, to the door."

"Oh, a husband would interfere more than anyone." But I was laughing now, amused by the professor's puckish expression.

"Some do not." He waved a hand toward the ceiling. "They are in the minority, of course. So now that we've dealt with your immediate priority, what is the true desire of your heart? Your most selfish, most human craving?"

To my surprise, a new answer presented itself entire and complete in my head, bringing with it a wave of emotion that threatened to make my voice unsteady. I cleared my throat.

"I would like," I said, "to become someone greater than I am. To use my talents to the full, to stretch my capacities to the utmost. If I were selfish, I would spend my days doing what I always did when I had no obligation to earn a living. I would invent beautiful dresses on the page and turn them into reality. But it would be more than that—I would create beauty for other women. And I would direct other women to excel in the same field."

A few seconds passed in silence while I considered what I had just said. I twisted round to look at the pages behind me, covered with figures in my sprawling hand. I felt as if I were groping for some concept that was barely within my reach, like a child learning its letters and starting to comprehend the connection between A-B-C and the words in its picture book.

"You know," I said in a half whisper, not knowing if I was talking to the professor or myself, "until this moment, I thought I was content with my little ambition of bringing Sarah up away from gossip and providing for us all. I thought it was going to be enough."

I looked up, puzzled, into the silent professor's face. "I've fought for us, you know—to keep Sarah, to have Tess near me." Indeed, I'd fought for Sarah's very survival. I knew if I closed my eyes, I would see Hiram throwing my child into the river, so I kept them open. "And if I have to fight for both of them again, I'll do it—to my last breath. But it's not enough."

"Why not?" There was something strangely alert about the way the little man was sitting now, as if he expected something.

"Because Sarah will grow away from me, won't she? From the moment she was born, she was on a separate path from mine. And even Tess—there's nobody more loyal, but if she develops ambitions of her own—ones that conflict with mine —I won't hold her back." I picked at a tiny pull in the fabric of my skirt. "She likes it here a lot more than I do, you know. The whole business of being a housekeeper fascinates her. When she's finished the work I allot to her, she often leaves to go watch Mrs. Drummond, and they get on fine."

I realized I would make the pull in my skirt much worse if I continued and tucked my hands under my armpits, my fingers curled into fists of frustration. "None of this is in my figures, is it? No wonder this task seems so hopeless."

"When our sums refuse to come out right, it's often wise to ask if we've left out a step." Professor Wale beamed, his hair seeming to bristle with energy as he leaned forward.

"I've seen self-realization dawn on your face, Mrs. Lillington. This is why I teach; this is why I struggle to make my students look at all sides of a question. There's surface, and then there's depth. My passion is the depths. I would dive to the absolute core of the earth and bring mankind's most taxing questions into the open, for therein is the very mind of God."

"I wasn't aware I had any depths," I admitted. "But you're right, I suppose. I think you're trying to make me see that I have to overcome my immediate dislike of—of, well, certain people and circumstances—and spend a little more time thinking about what I'm doing here. Otherwise, I risk simply carrying my problems with me from place to place."

For some reason, I found myself thinking of Martin, who had needed to wait a long time indeed for the opportunity he was now pursuing. He had turned the years of waiting to his advantage, hadn't he?

"My friend—his name is Mr. Rutherford—wanted badly to join the Union Army when war broke out," I found myself saying. "But there were circumstances—they needed him at home. When the Enrollment Act came into force, he paid the three hundred dollars to buy his way out of conscription."

I shook my head. Was the lateness of the hour affecting my brain? "I'm not even sure why I told you that," I confessed. "Only that it distressed him greatly—to walk into the trap of a course of action he found almost unbearable."

"You think of him because you too feel trapped," Professor Wale suggested. "What did he do?"

"He buried his feelings and did his job." Now I was starting to see the analogy. "He learned his business inside out, and incidentally became skilled at handling money." I shrugged. "Which, I suppose, will redound to my benefit as well as his."

I rubbed my eyes, realizing how exhausted I was. "But he

lived half a life, Professor, for years. I'm not sure I could bear that."

"No." The professor rose to his feet, wincing as his knee joints cracked. "Yet wait awhile, Mrs. Lillington. Consider your options. Half a life for a year or two is preferable to living with regret for a lifetime."

6

AMBITION

June 16, 1872

My very dear Nell,

Great news! The fine emporium of Rutherford & Co. has opened its doors, with resounding success. Even I am surprised by the takings of the first few days.

They're comparing me to Marshall Field, although our strategies differ. Where Field seeks to be vast and comprehensive, my emphasis is on the well-dressed woman. I don't worry about her carpets or her writing desks, just her clothing, from the skin out (if I may mention such a thing without bringing a blush to your cheek). But like Field, I aim to give my customers exactly what they want.

Joseph Salazar is turning out to be an excellent general manager. He has religious objections to working on Saturdays but spends Sundays—with no customers to inconvenience him—clearing off the paperwork instead, so we're both happy.

And talking of Salazar, I can put your mind at rest about the Gambarelli family bearing a grudge against me. Their only course of action was to send along their heiress to congratulate me on my store and ask, in the mildest of terms, whether I had plans to poach—that was her word—any more of her father's people. Since Miss

Gambarelli's father is a notoriously sly old fox, I deduce he has sent his daughter along to charm me (since I'm a bachelor) and find out everything she can about me. Well, two can play at that game.

Look out for a parcel—I'm sending you something rather special to celebrate my success. You may as well know that I wrote to Dr. Calderwood, impressing upon him that I stand in loco parentis *(or at least in a fraternal relationship—I'm not* that *old) to you and can send you respectable gifts from time to time. Accept them and rejoice with me. There'll be something for Tess and Sarah in there too. Hug Tess for me, and tell her she looks pretty in pink.*

Yours, as always,
Martin

TESS'S FACE TURNED CRIMSON WITH PLEASURE AS I READ Martin's closing words to her. "A parcel! Nell, what do you think Martin's sending me?"

"I hope it'll be a nice dress cloth for the summer. It would be a mercy to have new clothes at little expense. I'm going to have to buy Sarah some new boots, and mine are wearing out, so I can't possibly afford fabric as well. Everything's so expensive out here."

I bent my head to the duck trousers onto which I was sewing buttons. Mrs. Calderwood's reservations about my unworthy self sewing nether garments for the students had given way to economic necessity. The cost of sending to Wichita for the boys' pantaloons exceeded the allowance the seminary charged for new clothing. I might be a fallen woman, but I was cheap.

"Momma, see!" Sarah toddled to my knee, holding out a wooden block that one of the servants had made for her. "Esssssssss." She screwed up her eyes as she pronounced the letter.

"You're very clever, precious girl. *S* for Sarah."

She was losing her baby fat now that she could walk with confidence. Sometimes we ventured out onto the open prairie so she could chase the little birds and rabbits that flitted among the waving grasses.

"Dat." Sarah pointed at the buttons I was sewing.

"It's a button." I reached for my scissors—stowed well away from Sarah's acquisitive hands—and cut the thread.

"Buddon. Sary wanta buddon."

"You can play with buttons once you stop putting everything in your mouth."

I sighed and looked out of the window. Sewing buttons on trousers was tedious, and the task always fell to me since Tess had never mastered it.

"You will be damned to hell!"

We all jumped, and Sarah lunged forward to clutch at my skirts. The declaration had been made at full volume in a tone that suggested damnation was not only certain, but imminent—and it was right outside our door.

I bundled my work onto the table, picked up Sarah, and went to see what the fuss was about.

The door jerked inward so suddenly it almost caught me on the nose, and Mr. Poulton stepped on my foot. I let out an involuntary yelp of pain. Sarah screamed in fear and buried her face in my neck.

"Where are you, you coward?" The second voice was Professor Wale's, followed by the man himself. He brought a whiff of the outdoors and more than a fragrance of pipe tobacco with him, from which I deduced he'd been breaking the rule against smoking again. He was bright red in the face.

"A blowhard, that's what you are." He addressed Mr. Poulton, apparently unaware of our presence in his rage. "Start a fight and then run for the hills. We had a name for men like you in the war—and your pretty face never saw a skirmish,

I'll be bound." He ran out of breath and coughed violently, bending forward with his face turning an alarming purple color.

"Of course I never saw a skirmish, you buffoon." In contrast to Professor Wale, it appeared that the angrier Mr. Poulton got, the icier his demeanor. "I was twelve years old when the war started—and you are frightening the child."

"Oh. I beg your pardon, Mrs. Lillington. But if you don't mind me saying so, it's typical of Poulton here that he'd come and hide behind the women and children to avoid losing an argument." The professor snorted derisively.

"I have the strongest objections to both of you being here." I stroked Sarah's hair, making a shushing noise to calm her. "Do you have to carry on your political arguments in my workroom?" My foot was smarting.

"This isn't mere politics we're discussing, it's salvation." Mr. Poulton turned his violet-blue glare on me for a moment, then returned his attention to the professor. "You're spreading poison that will hide God from every man, woman, and child who's foolish enough to believe this scientific claptrap. When you see them turn away from the Bible, won't you feel the weight of it on your own dirty conscience?"

He thundered like a pulpit preacher in full flow, pointing an accusing finger at Professor Wale, who clapped his hand to his forehead, still coughing.

"God save us from the irrational and emotional argument," he wailed. "The moment I begin discussing the How, you accuse me of disputing the Who—" His voice rose to a hoarse squeak, and he stopped to draw breath.

"I accuse you," said Mr. Poulton in a tone of righteous wrath, "of attempting to put ideas into the minds of innocent boys—boys with the noble aim of spreading God's kingdom in this whiskey-sodden, heathen-ridden country—that will cause them to doubt everything they're taught."

Professor Wale took a deep breath and spoke more calmly yet failed to keep an edge of sarcastic humor out of his voice. "If they doubt so easily, you can hardly claim to have taught them well. My own faith rests on more solid ground—on the very rock of Christ Himself. These boys," he gestured upward to the classrooms above, "will be tested soon enough, when they're out in the world. It's imperative to teach them to use their God-given intelligence to think—to *think*, Poulton—and by thinking, to affirm their faith so that it's unshakeable. Because they *will* meet challenges, small and large. We're called to form *men*, not mere mouthers of platitudes."

Mr. Poulton opened his mouth to reply, but I got there first.

"What on earth are the two of you arguing about?" I realized Tess had come to hover near my elbow and passed Sarah to her. "Dat," said my daughter, pointing at the two men.

"Yes, they're being naughty." I straightened my shoulders.

"Naughty," echoed behind me as I swept between the Professor and Mr. Poulton, indicating with a jerk of the head that they should step out into the corridor.

"Supposing the students saw this?" I fixed both of them with what I hoped was a gimlet stare. "Do the two of you have so much leisure on a weekday that you can roam the seminary fighting like a couple of schoolboys? Because I, for one, have work to do, and you have interrupted it. And, incidentally, upset my daughter."

"I have no classes at the moment," Professor Wale retorted.

Mr. Poulton, however, turned to me with a contrite

expression on his face, mingled with a warmth that sent a strange stabbing sensation into my limbs.

"I really am sorry," he said. "I was trying to defend this school's mission and forgot myself. We were discussing Professor Wale's eternal insistence that he be allowed to introduce the pernicious teachings of Darwin—and others of his atheist ilk—into our seminary. I can't agree with his position, and Dr. Calderwood is of the same mind."

"And yet Dr. Adema, God rest his soul, was of *my* mind, and you know it well." Professor Wale turned to me. "And I apologize also for my ungentlemanly behavior, Mrs. Lillington. But you must have heard Hendrik Adema say it: 'The bold and fervent defense of orthodoxy through the enlightened pursuit of knowledge.'" He laid heavy emphasis on these last words, stabbing the finger of one hand into the palm of the other as if to underscore them. "But he has most conveniently gone to his well-deserved rest, leaving his seminary in the hands of those determined to pursue the most narrow definition of Christianity that is possible."

Mr. Poulton went chalk white, his high cheekbones standing out under eyes that were narrow slits. "Your dirty insinuations hold no water here," he hissed. "Get thee behind me, Satan."

While talking, we'd been moving toward the large double doors of the chapel, and Mr. Poulton was close enough to reach them in four long strides and wrench them open. He stalked inside, and as the doors slowly closed, I could see him proceeding in the direction of the door that led to the president's office, which was part of a suite of rooms tucked between the chapel and the front of the building.

The doors settled back into their position, and all the air seemed to go out of Professor Wale in one long exhalation. He leaned against the wall and pinched the bridge of his nose, looking suddenly old and tired.

"What did you mean by that?" I asked. "That Dr. Adema's death was convenient? You can't possibly—"

"Oh, I have no proof. And I shouldn't have said that in front of you, although you don't seem the sort to gossip. It—well, call it an intuition, if you like. I refuse to believe Hendrik Adema simply slipped and fell. I'd like to believe it, for the sake of my peace of mind, but something inside me won't let go of a certain suspicion."

The hallway was silent except for the faint wail of the ever-present wind as it struck the corner of the building. I shivered despite the day's warmth as I watched Professor Wale cross the black-and-white marble tiles to the bottom of the ornately carved staircase and look up, his face lit blue and gold by the stained glass above him.

"He was a good man." He stared up at the figures in the glass. "He truly believed that faith could move mountains. He began planning this school when the frontier was still Indian Territory and we were fighting over whether Kansas would be a slave state or free. He wished to offer education to those who could not pay for it—the poor sons of the plains, be they white or colored, even Indians if they showed true evidence of faith."

He ran his hands over the riot of carving on the stair-post's finial. "But he made the mistake of throwing in his lot with the Calderwoods. Her money built the school, but it also gave her the power to insist on a majority of fee-paying students—to support the others, was the story. And they've thought up ways to bar all races but the white." He shrugged. "I sometimes wonder if we fought the war for nothing at all, Mrs. Lillington."

"Why do you stay here?" I asked, curious.

"Loyalty. Or it *was* loyalty, when Dr. Adema was alive. Now—how can I leave his work to those who would destroy it from within? I feel I must stay and fight, for his sake."

"With Darwin?"

The professor snorted. "You know, I don't really think Mr. Darwin has proved anything. I daresay that twenty years hence science will have forgotten all his theories. But I'll go to my death defending his right to postulate any idea he wishes. It is the right of all men to stare unafraid at any theory or piece of evidence that the years will throw in their path. The age of scientific inquiry is upon us, and if faith is to remain, it must grapple with these new ideas, not pretend they don't exist."

He glanced back at the closed chapel doors, and one corner of his mouth twitched.

"Beware that man Poulton," he said softly. "He is ambitious."

He turned his back on me and climbed the wide, polished treads of the staircase, his progress lit by the many-hued beams of light.

I turned to go back to the workroom, but the soft chunk of the chapel door opening arrested my steps. Mr. Poulton and Dr. Calderwood emerged, all smiles.

"Mrs. Lillington," Mr. Poulton called to me. "I must apologize again for inadvertently causing you to witness such an unseemly argument. I allowed myself to become heated in my efforts to make Professor Wale see sense."

Dr. Calderwood bowed, his huge white teeth bared in the uncertain grin I had so often seen during chapel services. Since Dr. Adema's death, of course, he presided over those services. His sermons were of the saccharine variety, full of little moral tales designed to make the hearer feel emotion, and I found them tiresome.

"We must sometimes endure a little unpleasantness in a community such as ours, must we not?" Dr. Calderwood bounced on the balls of his feet and rubbed his hands together. "But there are generally ways to reconcile our small differences to the satisfaction of all parties. For example, I have been telling my dear wife about the delightful letter I received from your friend Mr. Rutherford, who seems to be a most respectable merchant. He made a generous donation and put us quite right about the propriety of your correspondence. You may regard our little misunderstanding as entirely cleared up."

I stared at him, not knowing what to say. So Martin had bought off the Calderwoods? So much for my vaunted independence. Well, I supposed I would, as Martin had said, just have to accept the gifts he sent me—including my respectability. I rather wished Martin were close at hand so I could kick him.

"I must return to work," was all I came up with.

"My dear young lady, of course," intoned Dr. Calderwood, turning in the direction of my workroom and offering a massive arm to me. "Allow us to walk you to your door."

Mr. Poulton fell into step beside me, and I proceeded back to work in fine style. On the way there, we encountered Mr. Lehmann, who saluted us all cheerfully while standing aside to let us pass. A sardonic smile lit his face.

When we reached my door, Mr. Poulton took my hand and bowed over it, for all the world as if he were about to kiss my fingertips. An odd feeling ran through my entire body, something between excitement and danger—but the sensation was gone in a second and I was aware only of Dr. Calderwood's indulgent smile.

"We're most fortunate to have you in our establishment," said Dr. Calderwood unctuously. "Please do call on me—or Mr. Poulton, of course—if there is anything we can do to improve your comfort."

He held the door open, and I re-entered the monotony of my daily work bathed in the smiles of both gentlemen.

"Did they stop arguing?" asked Tess once the door closed behind me.

I nodded in the affirmative as I took Sarah into my arms, but my thoughts strayed far outside the room, chasing the slippery currents of all I'd just seen and heard. I had felt threads of meaning and purpose in the air all around me, drifts of deduction and intention that floated just out of my grasp. What was it about this place that felt so insubstantial and yet so charged with meaning? And were my problems with Mrs. Calderwood really over?

7
VIRTUE

"That's a pretty display."

Reiner Lehmann surveyed the yards of fabric spread across every available table. The summer vacation was upon us, and most of the students were gone, so Reiner, working on a translation for Dr. Calderwood and not returning home for the summer, had taken to haunting my workroom.

"What d'you call that?" He extended a hand toward the pool of shimmering pale green on the nearest table and then jerked it back in time to miss the swipe I made at him.

"Don't touch it. I don't mind if you take a closer look at the cottons, but not this silk. I barely dare approach it myself in case I get a drop of perspiration on it."

"Women. What are you going to do with it?"

"I've been trying to decide that for over a month." I grinned as I handed him the sketch I'd made. We had fallen into an easy, undemanding friendship that didn't seem to require much more than the occasional half hour together when his studies and my work permitted. Being so close in age, it didn't seem shocking that we'd progressed to calling each other by our Christian names when nobody else was near.

To be sure, Mrs. Drummond and Mrs. Calderwood kept a wary eye on us, but Reiner was a favorite with the Calderwoods. And I—well, I seemed to have overcome the bad impression I had made at first. I had achieved this change, I supposed, by diligent hard work and a great effort to remain demure and dignified when in the presence of any person in pantaloons. That, and whatever Martin had done to secure me in the Calderwoods' good graces.

Reiner studied the drawing, mopping his brow as I rolled up the silk. I worked with care, mindful of the hot breeze that wafted through the room from the open windows, bringing the sweet, honeyed smell of the prairie with it. I hadn't been able to resist unrolling my precious cloth and taking yet another peek before I began work on our everyday summer dresses. It was the palest green, shot through with a faint yet rich purple that only revealed itself when the light struck it exactly right. In the light of my night-time lamps, it was precisely the color of Sarah's eyes, the rich watered green of clear jade.

When Martin said he was sending us a parcel, I had never imagined his idea of a celebratory gift would be half a cartload of bolts and packages. As well as the green silk and practical gingham for summer dresses, he had sent yards of gauzy ivory silk for undergarments and ivory lace that made me gasp in astonishment at its fineness.

"To remind you that you will not be a seamstress in a seminary forever," the accompanying note read in Martin's neat, slanting script. And to emphasize the point, he had enclosed an accounting of my capital, which he had already increased by more than I could earn in six months at the seminary. The knowledge of that small increase in wealth rested inside me like a tiny, warm sun.

"I don't know when I'll have the occasion to wear it though," I said as I returned from putting the bolt of silk, wrapped in cotton, into my cupboard. "But I simply can't turn this wonderful fabric into anything other than an evening dress. Anything less grand would be a crime. Now all I need are some friends to invite me to dinner."

"So who are your friends?"

I rolled my eyes, smoothing out a length of pink cotton that had become a little creased. "Tess. And you, I suppose. Professor Wale, perhaps. And that's the sum total of my acquaintance in this part of the country—the Lombardis are too far away to count. If you're going to give a dinner, let me know."

Reiner snorted with laughter. "We'll have to work on that."

"I'd be obliged. But not for a few weeks. I'm minding the Lombardi girls while Mr. and Mrs. Lombardi—and young Teddy—attend a missionary meeting in Wichita. So I'll also be making both girls pretty dresses since I have enough to go round."

"What a ministering angel you are."

"Not in the least. I'm a dressmaker with a surfeit of gingham and some work to do that isn't, for once, sewing clothes for young men who grow too fast. Now make yourself useful and pass me that bundle of paper—carefully, don't crumple it!—so I can get on with Tess's dress. She's going to love this color."

"I mean, to take charge of two little girls. What are you going to do with them all day?"

"I'll find something." I picked up my box of pins. "I'm sure they'll be no trouble at all."

"Mrs. Lillington?"

I removed the last pin from between my lips and stabbed it into the layers of cotton. Thea was making painstaking basting stitches in the gingham dress that would be Lucy's. I was pinning up hers, which was a longer and most decidedly more grown-up version. It would have an overskirt swept to the back and sewn to fall into a pouf of fabric in imitation of a bustle, in place of Lucy's more childish bow. After all, Thea was nearly ten, and her skirts could now fall well below the knee.

"Yes, Thea?" Outside, I could hear Tess, Sarah, and Lucy, who were playing on a blanket in the shade cast by the building. The young trees on the seminary grounds rustled in the prairie's hot breath, which brought us the sweet smell of yellowing grasses and sunflowers.

"Why doesn't Sarah have a father?"

I looked at the child and encountered a candid gaze from splendid hazel eyes that were just like her mother's—but not nearly so benign. Thea was as prickly as Grandmama's favorite cactus and every bit as stubborn as I'd been at her age. Yet she was a hard worker and naturally attached herself to the busiest person in her vicinity—me, barring the servants—when she wasn't bossing the other children around.

I decided an indirect lie was the best response. "I am a widow, Thea."

"What was your husband's name? How did he die?" Thea's eyes were bright with interest and something else I wasn't quite sure about.

I racked my brains to see whether I'd ever given a cause for my imaginary husband's death. "He died of a fever." That was common enough and should cover all contingencies.

"And what was his name?"

"Jerome Govender." The name came too easily to my lips

after the months of practice I'd had in Victory, and I cursed inwardly. Thea would not miss the point—

She didn't. "But your name isn't Govender, it's Lillington." She looked at me from under her lashes.

"I resumed my maiden name after I became a widow."

"Why? Didn't you like your husband?"

I stopped pinning. "I just liked my maiden name better."

"Then why aren't you *Miss* Lillington?"

"People wouldn't want to call me 'Miss,' Thea. I have a child; I'm clearly not a maiden."

Too late, I sensed the abyss opening up under me.

"What's a maiden, Mrs. Lillington?" Thea's pretty mouth was sweetly curved, the picture of childish innocence.

"A woman who has not—who is not—"

I was going to have to resort to every adult's defense against juvenile curiosity.

"These are not matters a little girl should be asking about. Or at the least, you must wait to ask your mother."

"Oh, I did. Mamma says a maiden is a virtuous woman." Thea pronounced *Mamma* with a lilt, in the Italian fashion. "She says a married woman is no longer a maiden but is still virtuous because marriage is God's way of allowing a woman to remain virtuous while still enjoying the fruits of the flesh. But then she wouldn't tell me what the fruits of the flesh are. Do you know?"

"If your mother won't tell you, I certainly won't. Such things are a mother's province."

What on earth was Catherine Lombardi doing even mentioning the fruits of the flesh to this miniature inquisitor? Although I suspected Thea had simply worn her mother down to the point where she'd said more than she meant to.

"I asked Prudence, and she said the fruits of the flesh are fornication," Thea continued in a mild tone. "What's fornication?"

"Who's Prudence?" I asked sharply. The fine hairs on my forearms were standing straight up despite the heat of the day.

"She's a farmer's wife who helps out in the mission, to make the money go *furrader*." Thea said the last word with a strong Scots accent, in derisive imitation. "I heard her say to Marta once—she's Swedish; she cooks pies for us—that Mamma knows plenty about fornication because she consorts with wicked women who should be stoned for their sins."

I yelped, pulling out the pin I had driven deep into my thumb. Dropping the half-pinned piece, I sucked hard on the injured digit and scrabbled in my pocket for my handkerchief.

"I think Prudence was talking about the Poor Farm," Thea said. "There were inmates there who were in an interesting condition; that's what Poppa said when I asked about their bellies, and they didn't have any husbands either." She put her head to one side, smiling. "Were *you* at the Poor Farm? I don't remember."

I was not, categorically not, going to tell the truth to the small, neatly dressed entity who was narrowing its large hazel eyes at me like an embryo Mrs. Calderwood. An outright lie or a burst of outraged indignation appeared to be my only escape routes. The first was indisputably a breach of the ninth commandment; the second would be downright hypocritical. What was I to do? I sought for a middle way.

"I hope," I said in as even a tone as I could muster, "that your parents have taught you that gossip is wicked and that it's wrong to interrogate your elders and betters. I am your elder," I pointed out, trying to inject a note of menace into my voice.

A beatific smile spread across Thea's pretty face, and she batted her long eyelashes at me. "Of course you are," she cooed. "I didn't mean anything at all, Mrs. Lillington. I'm always so curious about everything, aren't I? Won't you come have a look at my basting and tell me about clipping curves again?"

Feeling as if a rattlesnake had just brought me a cup of tea, I whipped the handkerchief off my thumb, checked that the bleeding had stopped, and sucked the spot to clean it before inspecting Thea's handiwork.

"It's well done," I said, trying to push the last fifteen minutes into the back of my mind. "You're a most careful worker."

"You know what would be wonderful?" asked Thea. "My dress would look so much better trimmed with that dark gray fringe you have in your workbox, wouldn't it? It would make it look a lot more grown-up than Lucy's." She leveled her gaze at me. "A dress like that would make me want to keep all kinds of grown-up secrets."

"It would be rather ornate for a summer dress," I began, but Thea only smiled.

"Oh *please,* Mrs. Lillington. I would be so grateful."

I had been saving that fringe for my own dress. But faced with this budding blackmailer, a few yards of fringe more or less suddenly didn't seem all that important.

"Very well." I hardened my voice. "But no more questions, and no gossiping, you hear?"

"About what, Mrs. Lillington?"

Drat the child. "About anything."

"I never gossip, Mrs. Lillington. Mamma says it's wrong. Prudence and Marta gossip dreadfully—if I were to tell them one little thing, just *one little thing,* they'd spread it all over the county."

And with this final threat, Thea picked up her needle again.

"Could you finish my dress first?"

8

COMMISSIONS

December 5, 1872

Dear Martin,

After nine long months in Kansas, I finally feel as if the new life I so wanted is beginning to happen. And it's largely down to your generous gift of silk.

Let's see, I told you—way back in July—how interested Mrs. Calderwood was in the summer dresses I sewed with the cottons you sent me. Thea Lombardi's dress looked particularly fetching. She's a pretty girl, and since her parents brought back new boots, gloves, and hats for both young ladies, we were able to fit her out in a style that wouldn't look amiss in New York. All the more since she managed to cajole my good parasol out of me.

But that was nothing compared to the silk dress, which had its first airing in Springwood on Saturday. I received an invitation to the house of Mr. Joseph Lehmann, Attorney-at-Law, from a student who happens to be his nephew. It was a quiet family dinner, and in truth I felt rather too grandly dressed, but it was worth it to see Mrs. Calderwood's face when I swept into the seminary later that evening.

She certainly noticed my dress. The Calderwoods plan to give a grand dinner here at the seminary on December 15, and I am invited (perhaps ordered to attend would be more accurate).

I also have my very first real dressmaking commission from Mrs. Calderwood herself. Not that she has mentioned any payment for my services, you understand, and in truth I expect none. She's as tight as a clam when it comes to money. And yet someone's bound to ask her where she got the dress, and perhaps it'll lead to more work.

In any event, it's wonderful to create and sew something out of the ordinary. I'm running out of room to describe it to you, and with the cost of paper out here, I don't want to use another sheet. But prepare to receive a full description when it's done.

Yours always,

Nell

I LOOKED AROUND THE CALDERWOODS' ROOMS, CURIOUS. THEY were on the second floor, facing north, and like my workroom, they had large windows that gathered the light. But heavy velvet drapes, the color of blood, gave them a dark, brooding air.

Ponderous, highly polished furniture filled the rest of the available space. The Calderwoods were more fashionable than I'd expected. With its heavy red carpets and velvet upholstery, the parlor imparted an air of luxury and wealth. A strange contrast, and a stranger frame, to the winter sparseness of the prairie beyond the windows.

A second room, opening onto the parlor, boasted a grand piano. This was an object of true beauty and refinement, its gleaming wood inlaid with a pattern of tulips. I asked Mrs. Calderwood about it since it seemed much older than the rest of the furniture.

"It was Professor Adema's. A family piece, I believe."

She tutted over the skirt I was pinning, fussily rearranging the fall of the fine silk and making it quite impossible to proceed. "We didn't have the heart to dispose of it, and goodness knows he had little else in the way of furniture. And my dear husband plays."

I longed to snatch the fabric from her small, grasping hands, but instead sat back on my heels and looked up at her. "I could make the bodice a little longer at the front, if you like, but I think you'll find I can get the front to fall perfectly once it's sewn onto the lower piece of the skirt. All I'm doing now is getting a feel for where the upper piece should end. There'll be a fringe about here," I indicated a spot just above her knees, "and then the lower skirt will end in a matching fringe so that when you move, the light will catch the front charmingly."

And the horizontal swagging of the upper piece, combined with the cuirass bodice, would disguise Mrs. Calderwood's protuberant belly and make her short torso look longer. The velvet-striped silk of her train would end in a heavy velvet ruffle that would lend her dignity. Bustle, neckline, and sleeves were also designed to suit her age and position, being smart but not overly fashionable. A mouse still, but an elegantly dressed one.

Mrs. Calderwood quit fiddling with her dress and let me pin the skirt. She regarded her reflection in the cheval glass we'd brought from her bedroom and gazed at me as I worked.

"I suppose it was quite a coup for you, getting an invitation to dine at Mr. Lehmann's house."

"A coup?" I wrinkled my brow, then looked up as her meaning sank in. "I have no designs on young Mr. Lehmann, if that's what you think. We're on friendly terms, but—"

"He would be a catch. His father is extremely wealthy."

"I'm surprised you'd condone any interest you think I

might have, then. What would his father think if he fell into the clutches of a—what you think I am?"

Mrs. Calderwood's small black eyes gleamed. "Do you have another suitor in mind?"

"None at all."

My astonishment must have been evident in my voice since Mrs. Calderwood smiled a small, secretive smile.

"This dinner must be a great success, Mrs. Lillington. We're well on our way to achieving what Hendrik Adema never did—the expansion of our school to its full capacity." She looked over her shoulder into the glass, and I could almost see her nose twitch in anticipation. "We need more eligible students like Mr. Lehmann."

"THEY ARE SERVING LIQUOR."

Mrs. Drummond jerked her chair out of its place, sat down, and pulled the chair forward so fast its feet screeched on the floorboards. She looked with resentment at the far-off head table, where the Calderwoods presided over the usual collection of faculty members.

"They are?" I looked in my turn.

"Bread." Sarah leaned forward on her cushions, teetering as she made a grab for the bread plate.

"Bread, *please*," I corrected her, giving her a slice and pushing her back into her seat.

Sarah's sharp little teeth tore into the bread. "More, p'ease."

"Finish that slice first. What do you mean, serving liquor?" I asked Mrs. Drummond. "When?"

"At this blessed dinner." Mrs. Drummond glared at me.

"Well, don't look at me. I don't drink."

"She doesn't," Tess said, and Mrs. Drummond's wide

mouth decompressed a little. She had unbent toward me somewhat of late, but not for the same reason the Calderwoods had. It was her friendship with Tess that had led her to tolerate me and Sarah, just a little.

Sarah carefully picked up her cup with both hands and took a large swig of water, some of which went into her mouth. "Want milk, p'ease."

"There isn't any, darling. Miss Netta's sent for a goat for you, but you'll have to be patient."

Tess got up to remove Sarah's bib and help with the mopping operations. "I'm not invited," she informed Mrs. Drummond. "But Nell will look very pretty in her green dress."

I felt myself redden. "I'm needed to make up the numbers of women. Isn't the serving and consumption of alcohol against the rules?" I knew it was, but I wanted to distract Mrs. Drummond from my own failings.

"Dr. Adema must be spinning in his grave," the older woman said, grinding her teeth. "To think that this should come to pass."

"Won't it reflect badly on the seminary that they break their own rules?" I leaned forward and plucked a small, wrinkled apple from the bowl. It was December, and our diet was even more monotonous than usual, but the apples were sweet. "Wouldn't it make more sense to stick to their principles?"

"One of the guests is Augustus McGovern, a grain merchant with a large fortune. Dr. Calderwood anticipates a substantial donation." Mrs. Drummond relaxed so far as to bestow a tiny smile on Tess, who was nuzzling Sarah's neck and making her laugh. "Mr. McGovern has expressed the opinion that the Eternal Life Seminary is unnecessarily restrictive on what he calls minor matters. So they are throwing good sense and good rules to the wind."

"Papple." Sarah's giggles gave way to fascination as the apple peel slid over my fingers. "Want papple, p'ease."

"How we'll ever be able to enforce the rules with the students if the staff break them, I don't know," Mrs. Drummond went on. "There's that blamed Professor Wale and his pipe, and now this. And of course, the boys always find out about such things."

I shook my head. "I think it's ridiculous." This earned me an approving nod from Mrs. Drummond—one good thing to come out of the latest step in the seminary's march toward worldliness, I supposed. "Especially considering Springwood's a dry town."

I handed Sarah a piece of apple. "Take small bites, and chew it."

"Hmph. I wouldn't be too sure about that either. I've heard things," said Mrs. Drummond. "Dr. Calderwood says the atmosphere of the dinner should be relaxed and cordial and that he's already spoken to the Springwood guests."

I'll bet he has, I thought. No doubt Dr. Calderwood wanted his guests to be tipsy when the time came to ask them for money. I wished, for the thousandth time, that Professor Adema were still alive. There was something trustworthy about a man who had principles.

Sarah had stopped chewing her apple. An interested look came over her face, and she concentrated for a moment. "I did poo-poo."

"It's about time you started telling me beforehand so I can put you on the pot. You're almost two." I scooped up my sticky and now smelly child. "Would you excuse us, please, Mrs. Drummond?"

I left the housekeeper with Tess, who had thriftily commandeered my abandoned apple. Mrs. Drummond simmered, a look of concentrated fury on her face as she stared in the Calderwoods' direction.

"There's going to be an explosion," I murmured to Sarah as we left the room.

"'Splosion," she agreed.

"It's all right for you." I planted a kiss on the top of her head, the only clean part of her. "*You* don't have to be there."

9
MARY CELESTE

". . . Full of alcohol, you see."

Mr. Yomkins, the Springwood postmaster, put down his own glass and smirked at the assembled diners. "I'm downright convinced that the crew got liquored up and mutinied. Captured the captain and his family and set off to row them out to sea and drown 'em."

"Leaving no one aboard to steer the ship?"

Mr. Poulton's eyes were bright with amusement. Mr. Yomkins was in a state of mild inebriation, a condition that clearly provoked the ire of his lady wife.

"Whoever they left on board obviously drank to the point of insensibility and tumbled over the rail," growled Mr. McGovern, who held his liquor well. A lady he referred to as his fiancée sat next to him. She was a morose personage who had eaten her way through the soup, the fish, the turkey and oysters, and the ham and salad with silent application but never, apparently, with enjoyment.

"And if the mutineers did drown poor Captain Briggs—and his wife and child—why did they not then return to the

Mary Celeste?" This was from a pompous-looking elderly man whose name I did not know.

"Couldn't find it," sang out Mr. Yomkins. "Stands to reason. Big place, the Atlantic. Crossed it myself, y'know. With m'lady wife. Very big piece of water. Ever been to London, Mr. Polson?"

"As a matter of fact, I studied in Cambridge. Cambridge, England, that is."

Mr. Poulton was at his most charming despite Mr. Yomkins's failure to remember his name aright. He cut a distinguished figure in a tailcoat of English cut, with a frilled shirtfront and pale yellow gloves.

"The quality of your teaching staff does you credit, Dr. Calderwood," purred one of the other Springwood ladies. I stifled a smile as the president straightened his back and shook out his mane of hair in acknowledgment of the compliment.

"The point is," Mrs. Yomkins interjected, "the *Mary Celeste* was undoubtedly abandoned because the crew fell prey to the demon drink."

"You surely cannot assert that, with all due respect, dear Mrs. Yomkins," Dr. Calderwood said, showing his teeth in an uncertain smile. "They have probably arrived at a nearby port by now. And there is no evidence whatsoever as to what actually happened."

"I feel in my heart that the tragedy was due to drink, Dr. Calderwood," said Mrs. Yomkins. I liked her; she was horse-faced and long-nosed but for all that, there was beauty in the lively animation of her features and, above all, the intelligent twinkle in her deep blue eyes. "Drink makes a man foolish," she continued, rolling those eyes in the direction of her husband.

"Tarnation it don't," said Mr. Yomkins, making an attempt to pinch his wife's lean cheek. "I was sober enough when I married you, and I—"

"George!"

I picked up my napkin and placed it in front of my treacherous mouth, trying hard not to look at Reiner Lehmann. He was just as studiously not looking at me. Our eyes had met several times over the course of the dinner, each time with disastrous consequences. We were both trying to remain silent and politely attentive, as befitted the youngest members of the dinner party.

The conversation had worked its way through the re-election of President Grant without too many mishaps. Until Mr. O'Healey had gone off into a tirade against "Useless Grant"—he was clearly a Liberal Republican. He had gotten into an argument with Mr. McGovern that lasted through the turkey and baked oysters and had seriously endangered the vegetable platter. And now the *Mary Celeste* was steering us into yet more dangerous waters.

"Mrs. Lillington," said Mrs. Yomkins, turning away from her husband in a pointed manner, "I understand you made that splendid dress yourself."

I coughed and put my napkin down. Here was the opportunity I had been waiting for.

"I did." I reached for my water glass so that the silk caught the light and sat up straighter. "As you know, I'm employed as a seamstress here—but I have much experience in fine dressmaking."

Was I being too blatant? Or not blatant enough? It was hard to tell. I didn't want to sound like a shopgirl looking for a job; nor did I want to give the impression of a well-to-do lady with a dressmaking hobby.

"Do you—I don't want to imply—that is, Mrs. Calderwood suggested you may be open to a commission."

Mrs. Yomkins had a trim figure and wore a striped silk, possibly, I suspected, a reworking of last season's styles. That might suggest thrift or a shortage of ready cash; I hoped for the former. Of course, as a matron she should not wear such light colors as I was sporting, but—

"You would look wonderful in royal blue," I told her. "To match the color of your eyes. I have an idea for a blue bodice falling into deep, straight pleats at the front, with some kind of bold pattern—perhaps in black and white—in panels, do you see? And trimmed with a vivid contrast, perhaps even red if we could find the right shade."

I had hit on her tastes exactly; I could see it in her eyes. "Perhaps," I hesitated, "I could bring a sketch or two to your house? I am obliged," I lowered my eyes demurely, "to support myself by my own efforts. A little extra work would help me build my reserves."

"Of course, my dear." Mrs. Yomkins leaned diagonally across the table and patted my hand. "There are so many widows and spinsters around nowadays—the war, of course. Even now it seems to me that the pool of eligible young men is shrinking daily."

"So much the luckier you, my angel," said Mr. Yomkins, sipping his peach brandy.

The table was now laden with charlotte russe, blancmange, and cake, with bowls of nuts and oranges set out at intervals. Dorcas, one of the older servants, was pouring coffee, her eyes rolling at the extravagance when she thought no one was looking. I too was flabbergasted at the expense to which the Calderwoods had gone in their attempt to impress. Where on earth had the fruit come from? I had barely ever eaten oranges except as a Christmas treat.

"I am sure Mr. Yomkins is the favored one," said Mr. Poulton, with a sideways quirk of his mouth at me. I was glad that he too saw the humor in the situation.

"Any woman," said Mr. Yomkins, propping himself on one elbow, "is happiest when she gets herself a man. See, here's my better half fixing to get herself a brand-new dress, and am I complaining? Buy two, my darling. Three," and he sent a fatuous grimace in his wife's direction.

It felt to me as if the whole table came alive with the sensation that a stick of dynamite had landed among us with the fuse lit. Mrs. Yomkins maintained her dignity, but I could hear the faint sizzle of an oncoming explosion.

Reiner saw the danger at the same time, and we both jumped into the breach.

"But the *Mary Celeste*—"

"Some blancmange, Mrs. Yomkins?"

Our words collided and Mrs. Yomkins rolled smoothly over them. "I am glad you are such an expert on the happiness of women, George."

"I'm an expert on *your* happiness, Adelberta." Mr. Yomkins slid down a large spoonful of blancmange, made a face, and took a healthy gulp of peach brandy. He was, I was glad to see, the only one of the Springwood contingent similarly affected. The other ladies and gentlemen remained resolutely sober, most of them having left their wineglasses untouched.

Mrs. Yomkins accepted a slice of charlotte russe and took a few delicate forkfuls of the creamy stuff. Her gaze fixed itself on her husband with the alertness of a mountain cat intent on its prey. From where I sat, I could see that Mr. Poulton was watching her with fascination and something like gleeful anticipation, an equally alert expression in his violet eyes.

"And am I happy, George?"

Mr. Yomkins seemed to give this question careful consideration, holding up his glass and looking through the delicate amber liquid at his wife.

"I would count you," he said judiciously, "among the happiest women in Kansas. Yes, quite the happiest."

"Based upon your knowledge of what is going on inside my head and heart at any given moment?"

"Based upon," Mr. Yomkins looked around him and spread his hands wide, palms upward in an encompassing gesture, "why, based upon your happiness, of course. You *seem* happy." He appeared to think that this settled the matter, slapped his hands down on the table, and gestured to Dorcas for more brandy.

"Hmmmm." Mrs. Yomkins looked around her, catching the eye of the other matrons. Most of them had stopped talking, watching her with expressions of anticipation in their eyes. "And has it occurred to you, Mr. Yomkins, that the semblance of happiness can be manufactured? That in order not to appear scolds or malcontents, we often express ourselves in tones of greater delight than we actually feel?"

The other matrons said nothing, but I detected the faintest of nods and significant looks passing between them.

"No, no, no, no, no," Mr. Yomkins waggled his finger at his wife. "I would sher—certainly know if you were faking happiness. Other women may pull the wool over their husband's eyes, but not you. I would know."

"How would you know?"

"I would simply know." Mr. Yomkins assumed an air of dignity.

"Ah yes, I forgot. Because you are a man."

"And what is that supposed to imply, my treasure?"

"Simply that all men assume their wives are perfectly happy and that they would know if they weren't. And all women, at some time or the other, have expressed greater happiness than they feel in order to preserve the harmony of the domestic establishment."

"You don't think I could tell the difference?"

Reiner opened his mouth to say something, but I sent him

a quelling look. I most definitely wanted to hear what Mrs. Yomkins would say next.

"You would not have the faintest notion that I was dissembling."

Mr. Yomkins blew out his cheeks and muttered a vulgar term of derision under his breath. Mrs. Yomkins looked around the table—by now the eyes of all the women, and most of the men, were fixed on her—and, appearing to dismiss the subject, took a large bite of charlotte russe and addressed herself to me.

"Do you not think, Mrs. Lillington, that my husband is the most generous of men? *Three* dresses indeed. You must present yourself at my house at the earliest opportunity."

Relieved that Mrs. Yomkins had not forgotten dress-making in her eagerness to disabuse her husband of his illusions, I nodded with enthusiasm. *Three* dresses—I could double my month's earnings. Mr. Yomkins was going to pay dearly for his playfulness, not to mention his overconsumption of liquor.

"Where is your house, Mrs. Yomkins?"

"It is the third house along First Street; of course, our streets are not yet well marked, so I should inform you that my house is ochre yellow. A most thoughtful notion of Mr. Yomkins to have our home painted in such a distinctive hue, so well suited to the color of the dust that blows around us in the summer! And so clever of him to have chosen a home in such a location, in a town that will one day, I am sure, be quite as big as—well, really quite large."

She smiled, revealing good teeth. "I'm so fortunate to be among those blessed to show the way in making the plains our home. Don't you think, Mrs. Lillington, that we have the most healthy climate in America? And so spacious! Why, you can walk for miles without seeing another soul."

"You must be in a state of bliss, Mrs. Yomkins." Mr. Poulton spoke gravely, but his eyes were dancing.

"I am the happiest of women, Mr. Poulton, I do declare." Mrs. Yomkins cast her eyes to the ceiling in rapture. "I was so tired of the busyness of society in Saint Louis. The calls one had to make! And the endless shops! The constant round of idleness and chatter! Now I am woken at a most healthy hour by the sweet sounds of progress, the happy song of the workmen, and the gentle soughing of the prairie wind. I feel sorry for those women I left behind, I truly do."

Mr. Yomkins smoothed his whiskers and gave his wife an approving look. Across the table, Mr. Poulton had steepled his hands so that they hid his mouth. His shoulders vibrated, and his eyes slanted upward almost to slits. Farther down the table, Mr. McGovern's fiancée shouted out a sudden, explosive, "Ha!" then grinned hugely and covered her mouth with her hand.

Mrs. Shemmeld looked around for Dorcas. "Do serve me some of that charlotte russe," she said coolly. "It seems to have sweetened Mrs. Yomkins's temper. Perhaps it will do the same for me."

I might have broken down myself in a moment. Fortunately, Dr. Calderwood, completely oblivious to the currents of mirth swirling around the table, addressed a remark to the company at large about the Boston fire. News of that tragic event had just reached us and, along with the peculiar case of the *Mary Celeste*, was a great talking point in our little community. The discussion veered to the dangers of fire, and we were all saved from disgracing ourselves by laughing.

Mr. Poulton applied his napkin to his mouth, wiping away all traces of the smile that still lingered whenever he looked in the direction of Mrs. Yomkins.

"Did you not tell me, Mrs. Lillington, that you hail from Chicago? Were you at all affected by the Great Fire there? I understand that Boston was nothing to the Chicago conflagration."

"I didn't live in Chicago itself," I said, feeling a little shy with all eyes upon me. "But our little town housed several families dispossessed of all their goods in the fire." I hesitated. "And, of course, the Lombardis found themselves in the path of the blaze. It was a mercy they all escaped with their lives." I hoped I could avoid having to tell the story of the body that was mistakenly buried with Catherine's name on the grave marker. That would lead to the Poor Farm, and—

But I needn't have worried. Dr. Calderwood, happy to be the center of attention again, embarked upon a long story about the fate of the denominational office in Chicago, its rebuilding, and the number of souls who had turned back to the church after narrowly escaping a terrible fate in the flames. I peeled an orange, enjoying the fresh tang of the juice, and let his melodramatic account roll over me.

From time to time I encountered a glance from Reiner or Mr. Poulton, but I let my eyelids drop, concentrating on my task. I had learned my lesson about flirting with men at dinner. And besides—a thrill went through me—now I had my first real dressmaking commission, my initial step toward complete independence for myself, Sarah, and Tess. I could not wait to write Martin about this dinner.

I shifted in my chair, looking down the room to the door connecting with the kitchen in the hope that the servants would soon come to begin clearing away the dessert plates. Mrs. Drummond stood there, almost unnoticeable in her dark dress, watching the interplay of conversation around the table with a grim look on her face. I knew she had protested against the serving of liquor. I knew Mrs. Calderwood had told her, in no uncertain terms, that if she made trouble about the alcohol, the trouble would rebound on her.

I knew it because Reiner had heard their conversation and relayed it to me.

I gave Mrs. Drummond a look that I hoped expressed fellow feeling, but she returned it coolly. She did, I thought, understand that I was at the table under duress. And yet I had the distinct impression that seeing me in such company had brought back her impression of me as a sinner of the deepest dye.

"You look worried, Mrs. Lillington." Mr. Poulton spoke to me under cover of Dr. Calderwood's words. "Do you feel that making dresses for Mrs. Yomkins will be beneath you?"

"Not at all." I smiled at him, and in return received a smile of such dazzling beauty that I felt quite weak. "I'm delighted about the work."

"It's well deserved. That dress is quite the most modish thing I have seen since I left Baltimore, and you look wonderfully elegant in it. You could find no better model for your skills than your own face and figure."

I felt myself blushing and looked down, happy that Reiner was conversing with his uncle and couldn't hear us. He would definitely have something to say about that remark. It probably wouldn't be complimentary to Mr. Poulton, whom he disliked.

"If I were a man of fortune—but there, I'm in danger of saying too much." Mr. Poulton considered his wineglass, which was two-thirds full. "I have only drunk a few sips of this good vintage for politeness's sake, but I feel quite dizzy being in your company. I will have to find an opportunity to repeat the experiment, without the liquor next time."

Mrs. Calderwood had risen, so by the time Mr. Poulton finished his sentence, we were all getting to our feet. I took Reiner's arm—he had taken me in to dinner—and made a noncommittal reply to his remark that I looked rather warm.

In truth, I was aglow—and it had nothing to do with my

untouched glass of wine. Mr. Poulton was dangerously attractive, all the more so because he was so often aloof from me as befitted our different stations in this seminary. Reiner Lehmann's warm friendliness was pleasant, but I was starting to live for the little attentions I would get from Mr. Poulton from time to time—and the fact worried me.

PART II

1873

10

ACCIDENT

"I hope she won't be too disappointed." I cast a guilty look at the towering building to our rear, followed by a fearful one at the white expanse before us.

"You can build a snowman with your daughter later." Mr. Poulton—or Judah, as he had asked me to call him—put a hand under my arm to steer me toward the waiting sleigh. "Are you going to let the whims of a small child direct your life? I only have the sleigh for a few hours."

I looked up at the conveyance, drawn by a single horse. The animal, which looked as nervous as I felt, showed the whites of its eyes and put its ears back.

"Is that horse quite all right?" I asked.

"Perfectly. It's a young animal and a little unused to pulling a light cutter like this, but I drove him here from Springwood with no problems. I persuaded Shemmeld to buy a proper speeding sleigh instead of fitting up his buggy with bobs—pretty, isn't it? Perfect for a pleasure ride. He'll get his money's worth in the favors the young sparks will owe him."

"And all you need are a few young couples," I murmured as Judah handed me up into the conveyance.

"They'll come." He had excellent hearing. He hauled himself up into the sleigh and tucked the thick rug around our knees. I could feel his body close to mine, supple and slender. "The homesteads around here are full of young men and women who came here as children. Now that Springwood's starting to become a town, they're looking for some honest entertainment." He grinned and took the reins, every movement exuding confidence. "We're leading the way."

"We're not a couple."

I grabbed the side of the sleigh as we moved off. The lightweight conveyance skimmed over the icy snow with incredible smoothness. The sides of the sleigh were low, giving the impression that we were flying over the sheet of sparkling white.

"You'd be better off tucking your arm under mine. You won't affect my driving if you keep still. Why are you so afraid of the snow?" Judah looked at me from under his long black lashes. "You're from the Middle West, after all."

"Yes, but—" I shoved a hand up under Judah's elbow, feeling reassured by the hardness of bone and muscle. "My father froze to death in the snow when I was a little child. I used to have bad dreams about being lost and cold and seeing nothing but white all around me."

"Indeed?" Judah tilted his head and gave me the detached look of a natural philosopher examining a particularly interesting specimen. "I'm sorry to hear it."

"Aren't you afraid of anything?"

The smooth brow furrowed in evident perplexity. "Afraid? Of course not. It doesn't make any sense to be afraid."

"Oh. Is it your faith that makes you say that?"

He frowned again and then gave a short laugh. "My faith?

Oh, that—well, I suppose it helps. I just mean that emotion is an expenditure of energy I have little time for. It's for fools and weaklings."

I stiffened. "Which am I—a fool or a weakling?"

"You're a woman." I felt a tremor of laughter run through him. "And pleasing to look at, especially when you don't have a child and an imbecile clinging to your skirts. Beauty and sense and talent like yours should have a wider stage."

"Tess and Sarah are no burden to me." I went to draw my hand from under Judah's arm, only to cling tighter with a yelp as the sleigh went over a hummock.

"I saw you had a new letter this morning." Judah flicked the whip over the horse's withers, and the animal went faster. The sensation of speed was both alarming and exhilarating, and if it hadn't been for the snow, I would have been enjoying myself.

"Yes, my friend Mr. Rutherford wrote me." I spoke more to distract myself than anything else. "He's worried about the state of the banks. He wanted to reassure me that he's taken steps to secure my little capital."

"What does he say about the banks?"

"That there's trouble coming if the price of silver keeps dropping."

"Is he a Silverite then?"

"No-o-o." I held on tight as we embarked on a long, smooth curve. "He doesn't think increasing the money supply is a good idea, if that's what you mean."

"That's pretty much it. More money means more spending—a favorable climate for a merchant such as your friend."

"He doesn't think any system is worthwhile if it makes the majority of people less wealthy. And he says that if the banks start to fail, it's small investors like me who'll suffer. He says the railroad investors are likely to lose heavily." I breathed easier as we glided to a halt. My cheeks stung in the cold air. "He's awfully clever with money, so I'd do well to listen to him."

"And he has the power over your money, so you have no choice anyway."

"I don't need to choose. I trust Mr. Rutherford completely. Are we going back?" I looked longingly toward the speck on the horizon that represented my only point of reference and security in this snowy waste. We had headed west from the seminary, into emptiness. Although there were many farms and homesteads scattered around to the south and east, where Springwood lay, the open plains stretched endlessly to the west as if we were on the edge of civilization. I knew about California beyond the great Rocky Mountains and all the mining towns and miles of railroad track that were growing up to the west, but when faced with the great emptiness of the land before me, it was hard to believe they existed. I shivered.

"We're not going any farther, are we? The seminary's almost out of sight."

"Precisely, and I'm observing the proprieties, Nell. It wouldn't be proper to drive you so far that they could no longer see us. Do you think our little excursion is unobserved?"

"I know it isn't. Everything I do here is observed and judged."

It also disconcerted me that Judah knew I'd had a letter that morning, but I supposed it wasn't surprising. To think I'd imagined I'd be less noticeable on the frontier. Sometimes I longed for the anonymity of a large city like Chicago. And its absence of wilderness. There, Martin had told me, they shoveled the snow into large piles like the nuisance it was. Here, it dominated the landscape like a great white beast.

"Well, I hope they're watching as I bring you back. I'll

show them what this cutter can do. Hoy, get on!" He flicked the whip, and the horse almost jumped forward.

It was too fast, but at least the seminary was coming closer again. I began to relax, allowing my body to follow the movements of Judah's, making small shifts in my position as we rocked over hidden grasses and slight dips and rises in the prairie. Perhaps it wasn't so bad after all.

The sleigh lurched violently to the left. I wasn't sure how I got there, but the next moment I felt myself skidding along in icy powder, the dried grasses over which the snow had settled tearing at my face. I must have opened my mouth in astonishment and the cold snow filled it, momentarily choking me. I was blind and deaf, and the whole world appeared to be attacking me. Something hard struck my right hip a glancing blow, and I flung my arms over my head, feeling an onrushing force sweep past me.

And then I could hear and see again. I had rolled onto my back, and my first thought was how blue the sky was.

"Nell!"

The voice seemed so far off. Was it Martin? Was I hurt? My next coherent thought was for Sarah, and a chill that had nothing to do with the snow went through me. I coughed and spluttered, trying desperately to lever myself up out of the slippery mess of grass and icy snow. Had Sarah been with me?

"Sarah!" My attempt to scream ended in a cough, and I choked, feeling my insides heave as I fought for breath. Where was Sarah?

I couldn't see the horizon, I realized. I couldn't see anything—no buildings, no people, just snow, grass, and sky. For a heart-stopping moment, I believed myself all alone, lost in a frozen wilderness.

And then there was a flurry of powder beside me, and Judah was there.

"Where's Sarah?"

He looked puzzled, and I shouted my question again. Why didn't he understand?

"Sarah? She's back at the seminary, I suppose."

"No . . . no." My vision was filled with the sight of my daughter sailing through the air. "He threw her . . ."

I scrambled to my feet, my shoulder sending pain through my chest, my hip a dull ache. Suddenly, the world righted itself, and I realized I was standing in a hollow about three feet deep, with the white plains stretching beyond. I whirled round and then regretted the action as the world kept on whirling. I dropped to my knees and swallowed the bile that had suddenly filled my mouth.

"Nell. Nell." Judah knelt beside me, gently putting his hands under my armpits and pushing me upright. I yelled in pain, and he slackened off the pressure, but by then I was righting myself of my own accord.

"Nell, your daughter isn't here. I promise. You left her back at the seminary with Miss O'Dugan, don't you remember? We went out on a sleigh ride."

I turned and grasped the nearest object, which turned out to be Judah Poulton. The world came back into focus, and now I saw the seminary, its sandstone facade reflecting yellow light onto the snow beneath. Much closer to us, the sleigh stood at rest, the horse with its head lowered to the snow, seeking for grass.

I shucked off one mitten and drew my shaking hand over my mouth, tasting bile and coffee. My stomach cramped, but I took deep breaths, willing the world to remain steady. Pushing myself away from Judah, I scooped up a handful of clean snow, squeezing it into a ball I could nibble on for its fresh taste. Judah watched me with an expression more of alert attention than concern.

"Where are you hurt? Can you walk?"

I essayed two or three steps, motioning for Judah to come round on my right side so that I could grasp his arm with my good hand. Yes, I could walk. I stopped for a moment and put a hand gingerly to my hip, feeling for the ache. I located it on the salient part of my hip bone.

"Just a bruise here." I tried to lift my left arm up a little and winced. "My shoulder hurts." I felt it with my right hand, encountering a large, tender area that throbbed under my fingers.

"Can you bend your wrist and elbow?" Judah pulled off my left mitten and watched as I went through both of those motions. I discovered I could raise my arm up farther than before without anything more than a little discomfort. By now I was shivering with cold, my hands a raw red.

Judah moved close to me and, shedding his own gloves, enfolded both of my hands in his. My long, strong fingers were not so much enveloped by his own as mostly covered, but his warm flesh was a comfort. He gathered me to him and I went, pressing my face into his shoulder to get it out of the wind and for the comfort of the wool of his clothing against my sore skin.

We stayed like that for several minutes, and gradually I felt my shivering cease.

"We hit the edge of the hollow," Judah said into my hair. "With the back runner. The light was just right so that I didn't see it. You bounced out like an india rubber ball, and the runner nearly hit you. I thought for a moment the sleigh would fall on top of you."

"I think the runner did hit me," I said, massaging my hip as best I could while still enclosed in the circle of Judah's arms. "Thank heaven you didn't fall out too."

"We would have tipped over for sure," Judah agreed. "I took the logical course of action and threw myself over to the right. I gave the horse a sharp crack of the whip, and it jumped like a cricket; that pulled the sleigh clear." He delivered this economical and dispassionate account in an unemotional monotone and then took a step back.

"Are you warm? If you can walk now, we should return. I'm sure our accident has not escaped the attention of everyone in the seminary."

Sure enough, I could see several young men running in our direction. The sun shone off a blond head in the van of the group, and I thought I recognized Reiner's easy lope, fast despite the snow. I steeled myself against the aches in my body and took a few steps forward and then, walking more easily, a few more steps at a faster pace. By the time the students reached us—Reiner indeed at the front—we had reached the sleigh, which I regarded with fear. I wanted to get on it even less now.

"Nell—Mrs. Lillington—are you badly hurt?" Reiner was bareheaded and dressed in his indoor clothing, as were the other students. They were all flushed by the run and looked like a pack of healthy young puppies. His question prompted a chorus of remarks: "You flew through the air like an owl, honest to Pete!" "What a sight!" "Mr. Poulton's a better driver than any coachman I ever saw, and that's the truth."

Three of the students ran to the horse to check its condition. It was pawing at the buried grass in a determined fashion, so I had no worries on its score. One boy made a show of inspecting the sleigh, scrutinizing runners and gear as if he were about to charge for repairs.

"Hey!" A lanky, dark-haired boy called over to us, his voice switching registers alarmingly from gruff to squeaky as he spoke. "There's a cut in this nag's flank a half inch deep. I saw you give him a whack, Mr. Poulton; looks like you overdid it."

"We were in danger of going over." Judah's voice was

dispassionate. "The brute would have been in much worse case if the sleigh had toppled and dragged it down too."

There was a chorus of assent to this remark, but the tall boy looked at Judah with a doubtful air. The wind had picked up, and I began to shiver.

"We need to get back," said Reiner. "I'll help Mrs. Lillington back into the sleigh."

"I'd rather walk." The seminary was about a quarter of a mile distant, and the idea of riding turned my stomach. "It'll ease my hip if I walk a spell." My head had begun to pound, slow and heavy, like the beats of a distant drum.

Reiner, with a glance at Judah, took my arm, and I leaned on it, finding his solidity comforting. He did not seem to mind the cold at all. I could feel warmth radiating from his young body, his step firm and regular as he matched his pace to my slower one.

Judah nodded and pulled himself up into the sleigh in one smooth movement. One of the boys handed him the whip, which was lying in the snow, and without a word, he cracked it high in the air, well above the horse. The animal moved off without any apparent sign of discomfort, the sleigh running light over the snow, the rest of us trudging behind.

"I'd swear he hit the horse after the sleigh righted," the tall boy said.

"What if he did?" asked a tubby, greasy boy who was kicking his legs through the snow with great enjoyment, his hands in his pockets. "He was probably frightened out of his wits."

"Not him." The other lad pulled his jacket—I had made it for him back in May—around him as tight as he could. With a strangely detached business part of my mind, I noted he already needed another one with longer sleeves. His protuberant ears glowed crimson in the cold. "Never seen a cooler customer 'cept when I watched the cattle drive. You saw the way the sleigh tipped; it was going over for sure. Don't think one man in ten could've done what he did."

His tone of reverent admiration made the other boys laugh. A certain amount of good-natured teasing accompanied their brisk walk back in the direction of the seminary, not to mention the occasional snowball. Reiner and I walked more slowly to accommodate my injured hip.

"You gave me quite a scare." Reiner pitched his voice low so he wasn't heard by the others.

"Oh, you weren't nearly as scared as I was. I didn't like the sleigh even before I flew out of it."

"Then why did you go out in it?"

I shrugged and then winced as my left shoulder reminded me of its injury. "Mr. Poulton insisted."

Reiner narrowed his eyes at me. "And what Mr. Poulton says is law? Did you like it when he embraced you in full view of the seminary? We all saw it," he added needlessly, his grip on my arm tightening.

I sighed. "It wasn't an embrace. He was warming me up."

"Sure looked like spooning to me."

I looked sideways at Reiner, surprised by the bitterness in his tone. A flush had appeared on his cheeks that had nothing to do with the cold, and his pleasant homely face was twisted in derision.

"Reiner," I said gently, "there's nothing at all romantic about being thrown out of a sleigh into the snow, believe me. Judah Poulton isn't courting me, and I'm not encouraging him to do so. I'm not encouraging anyone to court me," I finished with emphasis. "Please don't say things like that."

"Shucks, I'm sorry." Reiner recovered from his bad temper with the easy grace of a child and looked abashed over his outburst. I said nothing but held tight to his arm as we completed the walk to the seminary in silence.

11
FISTICUFFS

March 28, 1873

Dear Nellie,

Has anyone congratulated you on surviving your first year at the Eternal Life Seminary? Sleigh rides notwithstanding. Still, I suppose after six weeks your shoulder is quite healed and I can stop worrying about you. I do, you know—I wish I could afford the time to come out and see my little friend.

Thank you for your sympathy on the passing of the peerless Tabitha Stone. Of course she hadn't been my housekeeper for a while. Despite her objections, I managed to persuade her to accept an honorable pension in the end. I visited her often and will miss her motherly affection and her dear old face, beautiful in its wrinkled softness and its halo of pure white hair.

I had the great pleasure of seeing your former housekeeper, Bet, at Tabby's visitation. I will whisper to you that she's stouter than ever but say out loud that she's in excellent health and delights in your letters with the stories about Sarah. I was also of some help to her after the funeral, moving her money out of the railroads into safer waters. Yes, I'm still worried about the railroads—there's far too much speculation.

Hearty congratulations on gaining more dressmaking clients. The ladies of Springwood are clearly thrilled that such a talented young lady has come among them. I'm impressed by your accounting and the money you've been sending to me adds well to your capital. The enclosed will show you just how much. Between your business acumen and my access to the markets, you're building a nice little nest egg that could one day represent the price of your very own house. You may be right about not needing a husband.

I object to your assumption that I never stop working—I do indeed. I spend a sufficient number of evenings in good society, some of it charming. I have purchased a new horse for riding in town, a splendid dappled gray called Gentleman. What's more, I've received a few invitations to hunt and fish at the country homes of some of the merchants. I have been told—by some—that my former air of a provincial draper has quite disappeared. I'm mortified to think I might have seemed provincial.

In the midst of my busy life, I often think of you, nestled in the peaceful prairie with Sarah and Tess. How quiet and calm your life must be.

Yours in haste,
Martin

THE HUBBUB OF STUDENT VOICES WAS SO LOUD I COULDN'T make out what any one individual was saying. I could barely squeeze into the hallway for the press of bodies; the whole school appeared to be there. What on earth had happened while Tess and I had been in Springwood?

Fearing another death on the stairs or—the thought washed over me like a cold shower—some accident that involved Sarah, I pushed as hard as I could at the boys in front of me. Not realizing who I was, they naturally pushed back. The general mood, I realized, was not that of tragedy but a feral excitement, diffuse and restless in nature. The pungent smell of a crowd of young men—sweat, dust, and the cheerful willingness to regard the impossibility of daily baths as an excuse to wash as little as possible—almost overwhelmed the scents of fresh bread, salt pork, and baked beans.

"What's going on?" I shouted into the ear of the nearest student, tugging hard at his arm to get his attention. "Is anyone hurt?"

"A fight," he proclaimed in awestruck tones. "A magnificent fight—didn't ya see it? It was bully." Seeming to realize of a sudden that I was not male, he straightened up and assumed a more respectful expression, then relaxed. "Oh," he said, "aren't you the seamstress?"

I narrowed my eyes and gave my best imitation of Mama when a tradesman, seeing a small, dainty widow, was less than prompt to give good service. "Young man," I poked him in the side, "where are your manners? Let me through at once." He was only about three years younger than me, but no matter.

The knot of pushing, shoving, male humanity parted like the Red Sea, and I barged through, not without a smug smile to myself. Perhaps I was becoming more forceful with age, I thought. But the smile dissipated like autumn mist as I regarded the scene that presented itself.

Blood spattered the black-and-white marble of the hallway. Judah Poulton sat at the bottom of the stairs, his lip split and puffy, his eyes almost black with rage. A small group of students were helping someone else to his feet; he moved with difficulty, as if his ribs hurt him.

It was Reiner. He had come off worse, even though he was taller and broader—not to mention younger—than the teacher. A gush of blood streamed from his nose and mouth, staining his shirt front and darkening the wool of his jacket. His nose was already swelling, and a cut above one eye gaped scarlet.

The Calderwoods stood in silence by the chapel door. Dr. Calderwood had a hangdog expression, but Mrs. Calderwood was in the throes of an anger so acute that she trembled up to the tip of her piled-up hair. Seeing Reiner on his feet, she took four steps forward, jabbing a small finger toward him and then toward herself. Seeing him interpret the gesture correctly and move forward, she gave a similar indication to Judah. He complied at a slower pace, carefully avoiding the gouts of blood.

Mrs. Calderwood tipped her head back, fixing the two men with a beady stare. She said nothing for at least three minutes, vibrating like a kettle building up a head of steam. Judah and Reiner pointedly looked everywhere but at each other.

When Mrs. Calderwood found speech, it expressed itself in the single word, "Disgraceful!" The boys, who had all gone silent as soon as she stepped forward, acknowledged the word with flicks of their eyes at each other but kept still.

Mrs. Calderwood vibrated again. "Disgraceful!" She glared at Reiner, who was smearing the blood sideways onto his face in an attempt to clear his nasal passages. "To—attack—a—teacher."

The words came out through clenched teeth, as though she was loath to bring them into contact with her lips. "And Mr. Poulton," her eyes took on a shade of incomprehension, "to hit a student? Harder, apparently, than he hit you?"

Reiner had gone a dull red color, a nasty contrast with the blood. Judah, if possible, went even paler, but he spoke first. "We had a disagreement. We—we should have settled it outside."

"And what, pray, was the subject of this disagreement?"

Mrs. Calderwood's nose wrinkled as if it had encountered a bad smell. Behind her, Dr. Calderwood stood helplessly, his huge hands dangling at his sides. He had a look on his face of a Great Dane who was sure it was about to get a scolding but wasn't at all certain why.

Judah, meanwhile, stared at Reiner with a look of intense dislike and something a little like triumph. Reiner looked at his shoes, and it was Judah who spoke.

"A private matter." His tone was even, reasonable, and he seemed to have recovered his composure. He gazed straight ahead, not avoiding Mrs. Calderwood's eyes but not exactly looking at them either.

I decided it was time to ask the logical question. "Who struck the first blow?"

My voice sounded high and clear in the echoing space, and I felt a hundred pairs of eyes turn toward me. I could feel —obviously, I could not see—Tess behind me, her distress radiating outward. I was sure this distress was for Reiner; she didn't like Judah.

The crowd behind me shifted. "Lehmann," came a cracked, adolescent voice from its midst.

"He threw a good 'un," agreed another voice.

"But Poulton fights like an Apache," was the soft remark behind and to my left. "Wouldn't no cowpuncher on the trail do better." That remark was not generally heard, but those who did catch it gave small grunts of accord. I wasn't sure whether the boys were expressing admiration or disapproval; being boys, probably the former.

The smells of cooking had grown strong, overwhelming even the concentrated essence of male. The servants had started arriving at the back of the crowd, hovering near Dr. Calderwood and giving him significant glances.

"My dear," said the doctor, "let us dismiss the young men into the refectory. There is no point in leaving them to go hungry." His own stomach gave an enormous growl at that point. His teeth showed in an abashed grin that faded instantly when his wife turned round.

"You heard the doctor," she told the nearest boys. "Dismissed on the double, and don't you dare gossip about this. Remember you are training to be the servants of the Lord, and gossip is sinful."

The students shuffled in the direction of the refectory, giving a wide berth to Judah, Reiner, and the various splotches of congealing blood. Paralyzed by curiosity and apprehension, I didn't follow them. Tess tugged at my arm.

"Sary," she said softly.

"I know," I replied, "but—"

"Do you think this has anything to do with you, Mrs. Lillington?" Mrs. Calderwood's voice cut across my hesitation.

It flashed into my mind that maybe it *did* have something to do with me—that maybe they had been fighting over me—and I felt my face grow hot. "Of course not." The outright lie was preferable to explaining why I might think I could be the subject of an altercation.

"Then why, pray, are you still here? Vulgar curiosity, or do you mean to tend to the injured?"

Out of the corner of my eye, I saw Mrs. Drummond approaching, followed by the servant called Andrew, who held a mop and bucket. I backed out of the way, bumping into Tess. I shot an apologetic glance at both Reiner and Judah, although I had no idea why it should be apologetic. Would either of them think I should bind up their wounds? Turning, I shot off in the direction of the refectory, Tess at my heels.

I had only been seated for a moment, having taken Sarah from the arms of Dorcas's daughter, Bella, when Professor Wale made his way toward us.

"Fisticuffs," he said with satisfaction. "Although I wish Poulton's pretty face had suffered a little more."

I gave him a look of censure, but a fresh wave of curiosity smothered my indignation. "Do you know *why* they were fighting? Has Reiner become an ardent defender of lessons on Darwin?"

Professor Wale's eyes crinkled in amusement. "Mr. Lehmann, with whom I see you are on first-name terms, cares not a whit for Darwin nor for any other principle, as far as I know. It astonishes me infinitely that he should become heated enough about any subject to have thrown a punch. I thought that maybe you . . ." He twirled a finger in my direction, his eyebrows raised in interrogation.

"Definitely not." I made myself sound more certain than I felt.

"Good. Although Lehmann's a good enough young fellow, if a little vague about his aspirations. Of course, with a wife and children to work for, he may do well enough."

He gave me a roguish smile, which I countered with what I hoped was a bland, unconcerned expression, but then his face darkened. "Poulton, though . . ." He shook his head, his brow creasing.

"I don't like him either," came a small voice from below me. Tess had seated herself and was munching cornbread, even though nobody had yet said grace. The Calderwoods were still absent from the refectory.

"Tess," I said in gentle reproof.

"Well, I don't. He looks at me like I smell bad, and he never pays any attention to Sary. And he tipped you right out of the sleigh—"

"—and is a conceited blatherskite to boot," finished Professor Wale with a grin. Tess nodded sagely, her mouth full.

"You're both being ridiculous." I settled Sarah into her

chair. "Professor Wale, hadn't you better go up to the front and say grace? The students are getting restless, and somebody needs to take the lead."

"I don't like him," Tess said stubbornly as the professor walked away. "I wish you didn't like him either. But I don't suppose you'll listen to me."

12

WORLDLY MATTERS

July 1, 1873

Dear Martin,

Your last letter perplexed me. First of all, how can my capital possibly have increased by so much in such a short time simply because I possess money while, for most people, it's running down rabbit holes and disappearing? And what on earth do the European markets have to do with it? I've tried looking at the Chicago Tribune*—it arrives here irregularly and always a few days late, but it does arrive—and I can find few clues to the mystery.*

I should tell you that despite my status as seamstress, I have of late received invitations to the library to spend an evening hour with some members of the faculty and some of the older students. They're terribly dull evenings, on the whole, but I don't feel I can refuse. People read the newspapers out in some detail and discuss them, by way of improving our knowledge of the world outside our little enclave. Such reading and discussion of worldly matters doesn't always meet with Mrs. Calderwood's approval, but it's a hallowed tradition begun in Professor Adema's time, and some faculty members still insist on it.

The other cause of perplexity is that you talk so little about yourself in your letters. What are you doing? How are you spending your evenings? I'm not at all bored with hearing about dinners and musical soirées and the like. Indeed, I wish you'd write down every detail, especially what the ladies wore.

I sometimes feel you're hiding half of your life from me, and I can't imagine why that should be. And—well, are you really so busy you can't find any time to travel to Kansas? It's been a year and a quarter since I last saw you, Martin, and I miss you.

I'll stop writing now because I'm out of temper and whining like a child. It's hot, and I'm feeling dull.

Your
Nell

"OH! THE BRIGHT, THE BLISSFUL FUTURE
In that realm beyond the skies!
Oh! the happy, blest reunion
With the loved we'll realize.
If we gently bow,—not murmur;
'Bear the cross and win the crown;'
Tread with footstep firm, unshrinking,
Every petty grievance down;
If we'll only love each other,
And temptation ever fly,
As it is for man appointed,
Once, and only once, to die.
Charity and truth but study;
Faults in others meekly chide;
Holy angels then will steer us
Safely to the other side."

The wooden paneling and coffered ceiling of the seminary's library absorbed rather than reflected Judah's voice as he read. Nevertheless, his musical tenor was pleasant to listen to, unlike his choice of reading matter. The long poem had conjured up many instances of death, including that of a young child, and I'd found it depressing despite its saccharine ending.

Not so Mrs. Calderwood, who applauded with delight.

"Such noble sentiments," she gushed. "So fitting to remind ourselves that death is close and that it is our Christian duty to stay reconciled to others in life lest God strike us down in a condition of sinfulness."

She looked with meaning at Professor Wale and Reiner, who sat near one another on the other side of the empty fireplace. Before it stood Judah, the latest copy of the *Chicago Tribune* in his hands.

"But does reconciliation preclude reasoned discussion? It seems to me that the human race will never progress if we spend all our time agreeing with each other," said Professor Wale.

"It doesn't say that. It says we can meekly chide," said Judah with a glare at Reiner. "The writer would not, of course, expect people to react to criticism with violence."

I bit my lip, not sure whether to laugh or groan. There had been no overt resumption of hostilities since Reiner and Judah had fought each other three months ago, but they weren't on friendly terms. I still had the nasty feeling I'd in some way been the cause of their disagreement, although neither of them had ever mentioned the fight in my presence.

"Would anybody else like to read?" Judah waved the newspaper over his head. "I cede the floor."

To my dismay, Reiner leapt out of his chair and took the newspaper from Judah's hands with an impish grin on his face. He had a nasty habit of seeking out the most inflammatory paragraphs he could find. Judah gave him a dirty look but sat down anyway, no doubt under the influence of the poet's rejoinder to stamp on petty grievances.

"I will read from the humor column," Reiner announced to a chorus of groans and catcalls. I mopped my brow.

"You will not, if you please, Mr. Lehmann. There are jests in that scandalous column that are quite unsuitable for young unmarried men." Mrs. Calderwood fixed Reiner with a gimlet eye. She had a point—the *Tribune*'s humorists were not known for being high-minded. Reiner turned a charming smile on her.

"If I exercise discretion, Mrs. Calderwood? I will not read out any jokes about newlyweds or—or religion. Although there's one here . . ." Reiner drew breath.

"Most definitely not about religion, Mr. Lehmann." But Mrs. Calderwood's tone of voice had the indulgent softness she invariably showed to Reiner, or rather to his father's fortune.

Reiner read out a half dozen of the most innocuous jokes, prompting some laughter and a certain amount of discussion. Of course, the writers directed some of them against women in general, but I didn't suppose the *Tribune* employed female humor writers, and I was used to such nonsense.

"And here's one about Darwin for Professor Wale." Reiner smiled round at his audience, now well warmed up. "In character, what's more." This elicited a smattering of applause since Reiner was a natural mimic and his character voices were much appreciated.

"The figurative party says—" Reiner launched into an Irish brogue, tucking his thumbs into his waistcoat—"So long as I am a man, sorr, what does it matter to me whether me great-grandfather was an anthropoid ape or not, sorr?"

I began to feel uneasy. I glanced at Professor Wale, who was leaning forward in his seat, his eyes like black stones and no trace of his usual sense of humor on his saturnine face.

Reiner circled his thumb and index finger and held them in front of his eye to mimic a monocle. He raised his upper lip so that his teeth stuck out and adopted an exaggerated English bray.

"And the literal party says: Haw, wather disagweeable for your gwate-gwandmother, wasn't it?"

There were a few snorts of amusement, but not many. All eyes were on Mrs. Calderwood, who turned beet-red.

"Disgusting." She rose and snatched the newspaper from Reiner's unresisting hands. "Disgustingly low, vulgar humor. That sort of thing belongs in a saloon, Mr. Lehmann, not a seminary. Henceforth, I will cut the humor column out of the *Tribune* before it is placed in the library." Her hair quivered, and she looked as if she would say more, but she turned away amid a hubbub of protests about her promise to excise humor from the Chicago paper.

Reiner stuck his hands in his pockets, looking unconcerned, but the evening was over. Young men began to rise from their seats and leave, making way for Mrs. Calderwood as she stalked from the room, the paper still clutched in her hand.

"Did you have to do that, Reiner?" I asked when the majority had left.

"It wasn't newlyweds or religion." Reiner shrugged his shoulders. "And I didn't invent the joke. It was there for all to see."

"And so appropriate for the setting." Professor Wale's voice dripped sarcasm, and the grooves that extended from his nose to the corners of his mouth were deep. "If I had not seen our revered presidentess's reaction with my own eyes, I might have thought she'd appreciate the joke. Such students as have remained for the summer will now pass it on to their younger counterparts and possibly even a male relative or two."

He turned to Reiner, and his eyes were cold. "Is there nothing you have respect for, young man?"

Reiner was silent, staring at the professor with an expression that bordered on insolence.

"I suppose it amuses you to make fun of me and all that I stand for," the professor continued. "You, of course, are young and one day will be wealthy while I am old—and will no doubt die a poor man. Unlike your father, I have spent my life in the service of the truth."

Reiner flushed a dull red, and his lips tightened. "Leave my father out of this."

"As he leaves you out of his counsel? He doesn't seem eager to have you at home."

"It's my own choice to remain here—and, as you well know, professor, I'm no longer a student. I may be young, but I'm now a junior member of the faculty." Reiner's eyes were watery with rage.

"A *very* junior member and retained primarily as a favor to your parent, I surmise. Your gift with languages is impressive, of course, but you lack application and the facility for hard work. And yet, no doubt, you'll get on well enough. It's easy to do so when the way has been made straight for you. Good evening, Mrs. Lillington." He bowed in my direction, turned on his heel, and walked out, leaving Reiner with clenched fists and me in a condition of some astonishment.

"What was that about? I've never known the professor not to appreciate a joke, even one made against him or in poor taste—and that *was* in poor taste. And what did he mean about your father?"

"Pop's been in some trouble." Reiner thrust his hands deeper into his pockets. "Nothing that anybody else doesn't do—buying a few votes here and there—but the Whale has decided to make an issue of it with me. If he weren't such a little runt, and an old man to boot, I'd bloody his nose." He flexed his broad shoulders.

"You won't do anything of the sort. Now for heaven's sake shake off your temper. You should know by now that punching people solves nothing."

"Don't *you* start." Reiner looked sulky.

I looked around the large room. "Dear me, we appear to be the last ones left. I'm going to retire, and if you'll take the advice of an elder—not necessarily a better," I grinned at him, "who's all of eleven months older than you, you'll not take your temper to bed."

A shamefaced half grin appeared on the young man's face. "I suppose I can bear your scolding. Especially—say!—especially if you promise to come on a picnic with me. You wouldn't miss this opportunity to cheer me up, would you?"

"A picnic? When?"

"Friday. Oh, do say you'll come. It's time you did something fun."

"But that's the Fourth of July."

"Precisely. Andrew has the day off and says I can borrow the cart as long as I have it back in time for the servants to load it for the dinner. It'll be our own celebration of freedom."

"And Sarah and Tess's." I was not about to let myself be spirited across the prairie without a chaperone. "I presume you mean to invite them too."

"Of course." Reiner's eyes were limpid blue pools of innocence. "I wouldn't dream of doing otherwise."

I thought for a moment. "I see no harm in it."

Reiner's face lit up as though the sun had come out. "You're the best girl in the world." And before I could stop him, he gave me a swift kiss on the cheek. "I'll look forward to this all week."

By the time he'd reached the door, Reiner was whistling.

Left alone, I yawned and wearily set about turning off the lamps. The servants wouldn't be by for a while, and it didn't do to leave an unguarded flame in a library. And naturally, it hadn't occurred to Reiner to perform such a menial task.

I yawned again. What a petty spat over a ridiculous subject. Truly, these gentlemen had far too much time on their hands.

13
PICNIC

"An excellent spot for a picnic." I stretched out my legs on the blanket, curling my toes in their light summer pumps. I had not needed boots since we hadn't walked.

"I found this place a while ago, when I was out here shooting jackrabbits," said Reiner. He watched Sarah, who was making ineffectual swipes at the nearby thicket of towering sunflowers with her stick. "The hollow and the sunflowers combined get you out of the wind, and it's close to the trail. I remember thinking at the time how nice it would be to bring a girl here."

I affected to ignore his smile, wondering exactly when I'd have to tell him he was presuming too much. If he thought to court me, he was far wide of the mark. I'd decided I liked Reiner a great deal—as a friend, and that was all.

"We can pick sunflowers, Momma?" Sarah ran back toward me, trailing her stick behind her. At nearly two and a half, she had almost completely lost her baby roundness and had strong, wiry legs, a straight back, and a sure step. "I want to take flowers home."

"I'll tell you what, Sary." Tess was breathing a little hard—running didn't suit her. "After we've eaten, we'll go for a nice walk all around the sunflowers and pick a bouquet for Momma."

"Or you can go for a walk right now, and we'll eat up all the food." Reiner held out his arms to Sarah, who flopped into them—she wasn't shy with him. "And you can have the crumbs we leave behind."

"No, me won't," Sarah said scornfully. "Reiner eat crumbs." She thumped his stomach. "Fat tum-tum."

Reiner looked down to where the tiniest suggestion of a future paunch pushed out his waistcoat. "You women are so hard on me. Very well, I suppose I'll give you some food. Netta packed chicken and eggs—which one should come first?"

"Eggs," replied Tess, and then, "Why are you both laughing?" But she started giggling too, just because we were. That started Sarah off, so in the end we were all giggling inanely at each other for no real reason at all. It felt wonderful.

I lowered myself onto my elbow—a corset is a great aid to sitting upright but difficult to lounge in—and watched Reiner unpack the meal. Like the sunflowers, the young man seemed to thrive in the summer's heat. The sun's rays picked out gleams of gold in his blond hair and had tanned his face to an agreeable, smooth, light brown that made the blue of his eyes stand out. Although not handsome, he was pleasing to look at and would make some—other—girl a fine husband.

THE MEAL EATEN, TESS AND SARAH SET OFF ON THEIR sunflower-cutting expedition. Of course, when you have a two-year-old in the party, an expedition proceeds slowly, with many diversions. I was thus able to enjoy the sight of them for a long while as Reiner, who refused all help, made a thorough job of cleaning up.

I was replete and rather sleepy, so Reiner arranged my parasol to give me some shade, and we both lay on our backs to rest. I heard the soft *thunk* of his Stetson as he settled it over his eyes, and his sigh of satisfaction mirrored my own contented mood.

We talked for a while of nothing in particular. I liked the way our conversation meandered, slow and quiet, through the day's peace. For once, my restlessness lay dormant, and I, who disliked being idle, was happy to rest in the undemanding company of the pleasant young man at my side.

I should have known it wouldn't last. As is the way of pleasant young men on a summer's day, Reiner began inserting little compliments into his conversation—how well I was looking, how pretty my dress, and so on. As my dress was one he'd seen a score of times, and I was sure the heat had reddened my face, I suspected Reiner of flattery, or worse, of—

My suspicions received confirmation when Reiner's hand lifted the parasol and his face appeared, earnest and intent.

"Nell—"

An awful foreboding stole over me and I pushed myself into a sitting position, narrowly missing Reiner's nose with the edge of my parasol. "Perhaps I should go help Sarah and Tess."

Reiner sat up too, capturing my hand in both of his.

"No, Nell—please stay. I have something to say to you."

"I wish you wouldn't." I tried to pull my hand away, but Reiner held on tight.

"I simply have to. My darling Nell—"

And Reiner launched into an impassioned, eloquent enumeration of my best qualities. He assured me of his complete enslavement to my charms and requested that I allow him to admire those charms all the days of his life.

I stared at him in dismay but decided not to pull away too roughly. I liked him too much to want to hurt his feelings, and besides, this was my first real proposal of marriage—since I was thirteen anyway. I should at least pay attention.

"It's nice of you to say all those things," I began weakly when he finally ran out of breath. "But, Reiner—"

"It's too sudden, I know." He let go of my waist, which he had gradually managed to encircle, and fondled my hand again, running his larger fingers over my own long, blunt digits. "But consarn it, it's not like I'm going to have many opportunities to let you know how I feel. And I need to get my word in before that ass Poulton does."

"What on earth do you mean?" I withdrew my hand with a suddenness that made Reiner pitch forward, throwing his arms around me for balance. "Stop it," I almost shouted as his arms tightened. "Let go, for heaven's sake."

He did—he really was a nice young man—and even seemed a little shocked that he had almost gone so far as to capture me in a full embrace.

"Mr. Poulton is not wooing me," I said once I regained my dignity.

"He's interested though. He looks at you." Reiner's eyes narrowed. "And now you're blushing."

"I'm embarrassed and quite rightly so. The very idea."

I was almost telling the truth. To distract Reiner, I decided to return to the main topic of conversation.

"You're a nice man, Reiner, but—" Good grief, I'd almost said a nice *young* man—and I wasn't even a year older than Reiner. Yet I felt ancient next to his youthful ardor.

"It's too soon for you, I know." All thoughts of Judah Poulton seemed to have vanished and the glow of puppyish adoration was back on his face. "You don't mind if I—if I renew my addresses at a later time?"

"As long as you don't mind if I say no again," I replied tartly. "And no getting ideas that I'm your girl or your sweetheart just because I haven't boxed your ears. We're friends, and that's that. I have Sarah and Tess to consider, and—"

"—and you won't countenance the idea of my suit because I'm too young and only a junior faculty member." Reiner raised his fair eyebrows.

"Whether being a junior faculty member comes into it depends on how seriously you take the job," I said. "Position and wealth don't matter to me—"

"—which is a pity, because Pop's provided for me pretty well."

"*Will* you stop interrupting me?" I was becoming exasperated, and somehow my exasperation seemed to have something to do with Judah and Martin, and that made me uncomfortable—and irritable. "Position and wealth don't matter to me, but industry and application do. I could never think of joining my life to that of a man who wasn't prepared to take his responsibilities seriously, whatever they are."

I put my head to one side, looking Reiner full in the face. "Do you truly think you could be a success as a teacher? I'll admit that from what I've seen your command of languages is impressive, but there's a lot more to the job than that, surely."

I didn't want to say it to Reiner, but I was certain Judah Poulton, even at the age of eighteen, must have possessed a far greater air of authority than Reiner carried. I had seen them often enough in the company of students to observe that Reiner seemed like a playmate of the boys while everyone looked up to and respected Judah—everyone, that is, except Professor Wale.

"I don't know." Reiner pulled at a stalk of grass that had

fallen over the edge of the rug. "I'm willing to give it a try though, and that's what matters, isn't it?" He lowered his head. "And Pop won't pay my fees any longer. I don't want to go back there and work in his railroad office and have a line of idiotic society girls paraded in front of me at every opportunity as possible wives. He's right that a good wife might be the making of me, but I don't see why it should be one of his cronies' daughters."

I sympathized, of course—the marriage parade had never appealed to me either. But—

"There's Tess," I said, waving in the direction of the sunflowers. "Perhaps we should think of packing up the cart. That horse must have eaten two bushels of grass by now."

As I hoped, this suggestion, combined with the arrival of Tess and Sarah bearing an enormous bouquet of sunflowers, was enough to ensure no more soft words or glances for the rest of the outing.

And yet I climbed into the cart prey to a strange mixture of elation and anxiety. Mrs. Calderwood's strict injunction notwithstanding, it appeared I had made a conquest.

14
EXHILARATION

August 3, 1873

Dear Nell,

You're right to upbraid me—maybe I'm getting rather dull. A lady of my acquaintance accused me, not long ago, of adhering to the narrowest type of bourgeois morality. She's wrong—I'm not a prig, for heaven's sake—but some of the things I see in the circles in which I now move shock me. Perhaps that's why I don't write to you of them, my child. If someone began opening my letters to you again, there would go both our reputations. At any rate, I'm being made to feel remarkably naïf and callow for a man of one-and-thirty.

Or perhaps I'm simply reacting to the air of feverish gaiety all around me. There's a bubble swelling around us of overheated wealth, driven by the idiotic speculation on the railroads and such-like grand schemes. The industrial magnates are the heroes of the day. Those who would, fifty years ago, have been mere merchants are now grandees of Chicago. At a cost—Potter Palmer looks nearer sixty-five than fifty, and Marshall Field's hair is turning white.

Extravagance is the rule in the grand social milieu I now frequent. Champagne wines flow freely, and the ladies' flounces, bows, and bustles are extreme. Entering a room full of women is quite as hazardous as in the old days of hoop skirts. I'm thankful to be thin enough not to take up much space.

Don't think I partake of the champagne—I have no taste for the sour, fizzy stuff, and no taste for drunkenness either. I accept a whiskey as being, at least, a man's drink, and make it last. I need a clear head for the currents of speculation, both financial and personal, that swirl around me, like the cigar smoke that billows around any place where the men gather alone. It's exhilarating, and yet there are days when I want to turn my back on it all and go back to my drapery counter in dear old Victory.

You needn't worry, by the way, that I'm speculating with your money. I am not, and not with my own either. I become more cautious every day, waiting for the fall. My wealth—and by extension, yours—is founded on solid ground.

I think of you often, Nell.

Martin

MARTIN HADN'T SAID A WORD ABOUT VISITING ME, NOR HAD HE really told me what he was doing. Was I such a child to him, to exclude me from the details of his life this way? His words rang in my brain in time to the cadence of my footsteps, which thumped hollowly on the rock-hard mud of the trail to Springwood. I was glad I'd come alone because it meant I could walk fast, my long stride accommodated by the extra vents I'd put in my walking dress. I barely saw the little town growing nearer, its trees promising shade from the sun and scorching wind.

It was impossible to use a parasol on the open plains. I'd had to resort to the most dreadful kind of old-fashioned bonnet to prevent my face from becoming burned. Its sides narrowed my field of vision like the blinkers on the bridle of a nervous carriage horse, and I was sure it was the cause of the tears that occasionally stung my eyes.

"Exhilarating, is it, Martin?" I spoke loudly into the open air. "Too much so to take me into your confidence, I suppose. If I ever had that privilege." Had he ever actually confided in me, told me his secrets as I'd always told him mine? At least, I had told him my secrets until Jack Venton had made a dishonest woman of me.

The only answer I got was the soughing of the hot, dry wind as it tossed the heads of the browning grasses and raised little puffs of dust where the trail was particularly worn.

"Do you often speak to yourself?"

I jumped and spun around. Judah Poulton was close behind me, smiling.

"I might, occasionally, when I think I'm completely alone." If it had been Reiner who had snuck up silently behind me, I might have been cross. But it was hard to be impertinent to Judah, and my words came out sounding more kindly than I intended.

"You shouldn't walk around unaccompanied," Judah said, offering me his arm, which I took. "The Indians may be gone as a general rule, but you still get a hunting party on occasion. And there are rough men around wandering from place to place, looking for work or goodness knows what."

"I feel quite safe, Mr. Poulton. I wished to run my errands quickly, and there's no quicker way than to be by myself."

"You promised to call me Judah." He pulled aside one of the flaps of my bonnet so that he could smile at me, and my heart fluttered a little at the attention. "Don't keep such a distance from me, Nell. I know I can be aloof, but it's hard to stay away from the only woman even close to my own age and class for miles around. And a remarkably beautiful one, at that. Even when wearing a ridiculous bonnet from my grandmother's time."

"I have a hat and a parasol for use in Springwood." Again I tried to inject a note of reprehension into my voice, and again I failed—I felt the corners of my mouth turn up at the word "beautiful." "I don't want to get freckled. And what are you doing here? If Mrs. Calderwood hears about this—"

"—I will tell her I saw you ahead of me on the path and hurried to give you the benefit of my protection."

Another man who interrupted me—but somehow I didn't mind it as much as when Reiner did it.

"Will she accept that explanation?"

"She accepts most things—coming from me."

We had almost arrived at the creek that ran a quarter of a mile from the center of Springwood. It was dry at that time of year, just a little damp mud remaining from its spring spate. The cottonwoods that bordered it were already dropping a few leaves, yellowish-brown and crackling dry at the edges. The soddies by the creek were bone-dry, the churned-up mud around them baked into an uneven surface riven by huge cracks.

Several new houses had arisen along the road leading to the town's center, but despite their fresh paint, the dry, weed-strewn dirt around them had a forlorn air. Yet they would soon be as respectable looking as their neighbors, bright with such flowers and lawn as grew under the hot sun.

I had donned my hat and parasol as soon as we'd crossed the creek, and I waved at the ladies enjoying their noonday rest on their front porches. Several of them were customers of mine now. They smiled affably, with just a tinge of curiosity at Judah's presence. He was so naturally dignified that I didn't think any of them would dare to entertain any adverse thoughts about our joint arrival in the town.

"What is your errand?" asked Judah.

"A paper of pins, a bag of taffy for Tess, any small thing I might find to amuse Sarah, and most important of all, a postal money order to put in my letter." I pulled the envelope out of my pocket and waved it at him.

I was sending it to Martin, of course. It wasn't a particularly friendly letter, although the "I think of you often, Nell" had the overall effect of softening my tone. It detailed my earnings of the last month, stated my understanding of what my total wealth now was, and asked him if that was correct.

Truth be told, my small capital had increased to such an extent that I was beginning to wonder if perhaps, in a few months, we could afford to return to Chicago. Perhaps we could buy a modest house somewhere, from which I could commence a dressmaking business. Whether Martin wanted to bother himself with me or not, I was becoming restless. While making dresses for the Springwood ladies was by far the most absorbing time of my day, they didn't keep me nearly busy enough. I wanted more. My skills had been tested and found more than sufficient, and I was ready to spread my wings a little. And yes, I too thought of Martin often.

"Ah, Mr. Rutherford of Chicago." Judah's perfectly white teeth showed again. "You've seen his name in the *Tribune* too, I imagine?"

"Yes." I kicked at a rock-hard rut that had tried to trip me up.

"In the company of Chicago's leading gentlemen. And ladies." Judah's smile grew wider.

"I'm sure he knows most of the elite by now. But look, Mr. Poulton—Judah. I think we must go our separate ways now. I've barely enough time to get back as it is."

"Could you perhaps entrust one of your errands to me?" He removed his hat and bowed. "I could purchase your pins and taffy and bring them back later, or get the money order and give it to Mr. Yomkins to send on."

I thought for a moment. "I don't think I trust you to distinguish one type of pin from another."

"The money order, then. I'll be sure to do it straightaway. I'm in no hurry. I promised to drop in on Mr. Fairland to commiserate with him over his nag. It developed the spavins after his son rode it too hard. I hope they won't have to sell it for glue."

I couldn't help smiling at that and impulsively fished out the folded paper that contained the money I had earned. "Very well." I handed the paper over, feeling the reassuring solidity of twenty dollars and thirty-five cents within its folds. There was something truly satisfying about knowing Tess and I were adding to our wealth by our own efforts—because, of course, part of it was hers.

Judah bowed again and headed in the direction of the Wells Fargo office while I turned my steps toward the mercantile. By the time I came out again, the street was deserted, and I saw no one on my way back to the seminary.

15
PANIC

October 10, 1873

Dear Martin,

Thank you for the reassurance about my money; it was good of you to write so soon, busy as you obviously are. Yes, even out here on the frontier we heard about the banks failing in New York and Chicago—bad news spreads fast, even beyond civilization.

I wasn't worried about myself—you told me you had invested my money wisely, and I trusted you. And so did Tess, of course, although money means little to her in the larger sense. Which is strange, isn't it, considering how much she likes adding up columns of figures in a ledger?

And yet when I heard the news, my blood ran cold. I wrote immediately to Catherine Lombardi because of something she'd written to me the week before, and my worst fears became reality. Martin, Pastor Lombardi invested almost all the money he kept by for a rainy day in the railroads. Their fortunes fell with the crash. Catherine was brave about it, of course, and thanked God for the home and employment they have left, but how are they going to send Teddy to school now? He was going to apply to the seminary, but even if he's not needed now to work at the mission, I doubt the Calderwoods will admit him for no fee.

My heart's too full of sorrow for them to write more. I must send another letter to Catherine immediately and offer her whatever help I can. Thank you for your letter.

Nell

I RAISED MY HEAD AT THE SOUND OF THE LIBRARY DOOR opening.

"Is there anything wrong, Professor Wale?"

I frowned, seeing the harsh lines drawn on the teacher's face. Defeat and fury were written there plain as a pikestaff.

The professor dropped into one of the large armchairs near the extinct fire and regarded me morosely. "What are we supposed to be?" he demanded, stabbing a yellow-stained finger at me. "A locus of rigorous intellectual inquiry or a—a —a nanny-school for rich imbeciles?"

"Another argument?" I asked. Professor Wale's animosity toward Judah and the Calderwoods had reached such a pitch that I was surprised the Calderwoods didn't give him notice. The other teachers had begun avoiding him.

"Cam Calderwood is a pompous windbag with no more faith in his black, rotten heart than a Mohammedan." The professor ran his fingers through his hair, dislodging a wisp of chalk dust.

"Isn't that unfair to the Mohammedans?" I countered, amused. I wiped my pen and laid it down. "I'm sure they're quite as sincere in their beliefs as any Christian, however mistaken the preachers tell us they are."

The professor looked sideways at me and barked a short laugh, the tension on his face easing. "A Mohammedan might sit down and hold a sensible discussion, come to that.

Calderwood—blast the man—just gives you his teeth and hair while that ass Poulton looks on with his pretty nose in the air. Dam—dang it all, that pair will bring this place to ruination."

"I thought we were prospering."

"In monetary terms, we are." Professor Wale fished his empty pipe out of his pocket and sucked on the end of it with a wet, smacking sound. The odor of stale tobacco mingled with the scents of dust and beeswax, old leather, and lavender. "Oh, we're doing very well indeed. Not one poor son of a plainsman has been found suitable to study here for over a year, d'you know that?" He laid a finger by his nose. "Not that you can spread that around, you understand. I had to resort to—well, underhanded means to ascertain the fact."

"What does the denomination have to say about that?" I asked. "Isn't it written into the charter, or whatever you call it, that the school support a certain number of poor boys?" I folded my letter to Martin, seeing the name "Teddy Lombardi" in my large, untidy writing. It looked as though my fears were well-founded; the boy would find no place at the school under the Calderwoods' rule.

A wet gust of screeching wind hit the library's French doors, and I jumped—and so did the professor. "Damned wind," he bellowed, twisting around in his chair and forgetting not to swear in a lady's presence. "Howling and screeching and moaning till you can't tell your grandfather from a jackass rabbit. I'm sick of this place."

"Why don't you leave?"

"Didn't I ask you the same thing eighteen months ago?"

"Not exactly," I laughed. "You interrogated me about what my priorities were, and then you counseled patience. Maybe you should take your own advice."

"I didn't need patience when Hendrik Adema was alive." The professor sighed heavily. "I was content to sit at the feet of a great and noble man. If we had differences of opinion, I knew we could resolve them. If he was blind to the faults of some of those around him, well, that was just part of the tolerance he preached and lived by. Or the pragmatism."

He shrugged. "The Calderwoods came with the land and the money to build the seminary, and I don't doubt that Dr. Adema thought he could keep them under control. And so he could, when he lived. But now the serpents are in charge of the Garden of Eden." His face darkened. "They should be rooted out. And they will be, by God. You ask if the denomination knows what they're up to—well, do they? I should not be idle in that regard."

"Don't be foolish either." I felt a sudden qualm, although I didn't know why.

"I'll be as wise as serpents and as harmless as doves." The professor smiled. "And what about you, Mrs. Lillington? No thoughts of leaving this place and returning to Chicago?"

I looked down at the letter in my hand. "I'm no longer sure of my welcome, should I return," I said. "And now I have my dressmaking."

"And your two swains."

I looked up, reddening, to find that the professor was gazing intently into my face. "Mr. Lehmann makes calf's eyes at you, and even the popinjay doesn't seem immune to your charms. Have they declared?"

I could feel the heat spreading through my body. "If you must know, Mr. Lehmann has proposed—and I have refused him. Mr. Poulton has been polite and friendly toward me—that is all."

"That is much, coming from him." The professor's face was suddenly grave and drawn, as if he had aged in a moment. "I'm glad you're not a rich woman," he said, so quietly that I almost didn't hear him.

16

UNEXPECTED

November 13, 1873
Dear Nell—

I FELT MY BREATH LEAVE MY BODY AS I ROSE TO MY FEET. THE disregarded enclosure to the letter in my hand tumbled down my skirt and landed with a soft hiss as it skidded along the polished floorboards. The room around me darkened at the edges of my vision, my whole consciousness focused on Martin's neat, slanted writing.

"Of course you did." I heard my own voice, high and strangled. Of course he had. How had I not guessed before this?

"Here, you're as white as the paper," said a voice in my ear. I felt a hand at my elbow, steadying me, and another at my waist, steering me back into my chair. "Sit down," the voice commanded.

I sat down mechanically.

"Have you received bad news? Should I fetch a glass of

water?"

Why didn't the importunate voice leave me alone? I'd been alone in the library just a minute ago, hadn't I?

"Nell, look at me." A hand cupped my chin and turned it. The disembodied voice resolved itself into Judah Poulton, bending over me with a puzzled look on his face. "Did someone you know die?"

I took a deep breath. "No, I'm all right. I had a surprise, that's all." I essayed a smile. "Surprising news. Very unexpected."

With a lithe, easy movement, Judah grabbed a chair from a nearby table and swung it round so he could sit near me. He gently pried the letter from my fingers—I was clutching it with the grip of a climber clinging to a cliff—set it on my lap, and took both of my hands in his, chafing them with his palms.

"It might be easier if you talked to someone." The pressure on my hands increased as he looked into my eyes. "It's a letter from Mr. Rutherford, isn't it? Has he done something alarming?"

"He got married." The words tumbled out before I knew I'd opened my mouth, and once I'd started, the rest was easy. "He got married to a woman named Lucetta Gambarelli—"

"Of the Gambarelli store, perchance? I see their advertisements in the Chicago papers."

"The same." My hands were starting to feel warm, and I pulled them out of Judah's unprotesting grasp. "She came to see him—my goodness, yes! He wrote to me about it—she came to see him when he opened the store because he'd enticed away one of their best men to be his general manager." No sudden *coup de foudre*, then—he'd known her for some time. Been courting her for a while, perhaps. And not a word to me.

Judah whistled, a soft, faint sound. "Quite a catch, the

Gambarelli heiress, from what I've read. She must have brought a stupendous dowry with her. Not in the first flush of youth, from the sketches I've seen of her in the papers, but reputed a great beauty. How old is your Mr. Rutherford?"

"Thirty-one."

"An excellent age for a man to marry, especially if he wishes to father heirs to his fortune. I've been reading about your Mr. Rutherford—he's making money like King Midas himself, and the financial panic has made him all the richer because he has the reserves to buy at a low price. If Chicago had its own stock exchange, he'd be richer still."

I stared at Judah. "I'm astonished you know so much about him."

"The great moneymakers of our age are a study of mine. After all, they're building this grand country of ours. Their shrewdness and application are good lessons to us all." Judah's face lit up with his dazzling smile. "Now, Nell, you must be happy for your friend. Did you find him such an old bachelor that the thought of his marriage shocks you? One-and-thirty really isn't so old, Nell. I'm twenty-eight myself."

"It's not his age." I felt my brow furrow as I tried to explain myself. "I just never thought he would marry—anyone." Except, perhaps, me. He'd offered that once, as an expedient to get me out of my stepfather's clutches.

Judah's brows rose. "Is he, perhaps, not the marrying kind?"

I knew what that euphemism meant—Martin had broken a man's jaw for suggesting it. "No, not that either. I would say he's extremely fond of women. But—well, I didn't think he'd go in for marriage," I finished lamely. I didn't want to explain to Judah about Martin's father, that dark, emaciated madman whose idea of a conjugal caress was a blow or tirade of abuse. And anyway, plenty of men hit their wives—not decent men, to be sure, but plenty of men nonetheless.

I folded the letter that lay in my lap. "I should return to work."

I was halfway to the door when Judah called me back.

"Nell?"

He was standing near the chair I had occupied, reading a piece of paper with a look of disbelief on his face. As I drew nearer, he looked up.

"I'm terribly sorry—I think this is yours, and I shouldn't have been reading it. I picked it up from the floor—"

"It *is* mine." Belatedly, I remembered the enclosure. I took the piece of paper from Judah's hand and folded it.

"But, Nell," Judah's tone was uncertain, but there was a gleam of what could have been suppressed excitement in his eyes. "I don't wish to pry, but—have you *read* this?"

Puzzled, I unfolded the paper. Martin had sent me many such enclosures, which I would copy into my ledger. They typically began with the total from the last one, proceeded to an explanation of the investments Martin had recently made for me, and ended with a tally showing increases and decreases. Usually increases—Martin had a real genius for investment.

I always tried to study what he'd done, feeling I should at least try to understand, but truth be told, I generally began by looking at the starting and ending figures. I did so now, and my jaw dropped.

"I don't understand." For some reason, I was having trouble thinking straight.

"It all makes perfect sense." Judah stood close to me, the mingled aromas of his hair, skin, and clothing in my nostrils. He gave off a faint scent of spun sugar, like a confectioner's shop. One long, finely shaped finger traced the numbers on the page.

"He's been quite cautious, hasn't he, about risking your money in his own business? Never too much or for too long, and he quickly turns the excess into bonds in the five percents. It's a wise man who knows to do that. And those private loans . . . Yes, I imagine quite a few Chicago businessmen have been a little overambitious about rebuilding since the fire. That name surprises me, in particular." He tapped the paper.

"He's tripled my capital." The import of the figures was finally making its way into my dull brain.

"More than tripled." Judah grinned. "It entertains me immensely that the seminary's seamstress is a wealthy woman." He looked around, as if fearing we'd be overheard. "I wouldn't show this to the Calderwoods, if I were you."

"I'm not in the habit of making the Calderwoods a party to my affairs." A line of Scripture, half-remembered, was threading its way through my consciousness as I stared across the room at the scudding clouds beyond the window.

"Nell?" Judah tilted his head to one side and regarded me quizzically.

"Oh, nothing," I replied, my mind still occupied with chasing the quotation. "Something about gaining the whole world."

"For what is a man profited, if he shall gain the whole world, and lose his own soul?" Judah quoted promptly. "Sixteenth Matthew. You don't feel you've lost your soul though, do you? You've done nothing wrong by acquiring this wealth, and Mr. Rutherford's dealings are honest—he could have charged a lot more for those loans."

"I've lost—" My eyes focused on Judah, some clarity returning to my thoughts. "I've lost a friend, I think. Or at least, a friendship as it was. How could it not change?"

"You'll never lack for friends, Nell." Judah's smile was warm. "When one fades away, another is ready to take his place."

PART III

1874

17

PHARISEE

"Preposterous!"

Professor Wale slammed the heavy chapel door so hard I could have sworn the row of stained-glass windows behind me shivered. A dull echo of the noise boomed around me where I stood at the top of the grand staircase's grandest sweep, my shawl clutched around my shoulders.

A dull December, whose leaden sky had matched my low mood, had given way to an icy January. Kansas was not as cold as northern Illinois, but the seminary's hallway was frigid, seeming to gather into itself the shreds of icy wind that made their way in under door and casement.

I descended slowly, my eyes on the professor. Was he about to suffer an apoplexy? His face was suffused with color, his fists clenched, his eyes dark pools of rage. He had clearly just left the Monday meeting, at which the faculty crowded into Dr. Calderwood's well-heated study to discuss I didn't know what.

"What's preposterous? Are you all right?"

I watched as the little man turned around several times,

like a dog seeking the right place to lie down. His head jerked up at the sound of my voice, and he made a beckoning motion, crossing to the front door without looking back or waiting to see if I would follow.

I sighed and pulled my shawl tighter. The door's huge iron ring froze my hands, yet that was nothing to the biting wind outside.

"It's too cold out here." I raised my voice against the gale, my teeth already chattering.

The professor whipped off his dusty academic gown and threw it over my shoulders, pulling it tight. The closely woven poplin was surprisingly effective against the wind. Nevertheless, I backed into the most sheltered corner I could find.

"For heaven's sake, tell me what's wrong be-before we both freeze."

The professor shouted his reply out to the prairie, the wind seizing his words and carrying them off in gusts toward the sodden, half-frozen wilderness before us. "That popinjay, that—that conceited ass, that indescribable bag of wind, that—" Professor Wale stamped hard on the flagstones of the porch and whirled to face me. "I should have known. I should have prevented this. I must act."

I shook my head, uncomprehending, and the professor took a step toward me. A wet snowflake landed on his circlet of wiry hair, melting into the springy gray-black mass.

"Your friend Poulton is made head of the faculty. It's—it's outrageous. It's unconscionable." He ran his fingers through his hair.

"I didn't know such a position existed. Who filled it before?" I didn't see where the problem lay either, but I wouldn't say so. Perhaps the little man was jealous, having coveted the post himself.

"Such a position has never existed before. But now it

does." He was beginning to shiver. "This is a tomfool notion of Calderwood's to advance his favorite. It effectively makes him the second in charge of the entire school."

"Do the other professors object?"

"No." Professor Wale shoved his hands under his armpits. "They're all congratulating the little—your friend on his excellent fortune. Don't forget, Mrs. Lillington, that most of them are new men, and the rest old dodderers grateful to still have a place."

That was true. The Calderwoods had hired a number of new teachers of late, and none of them seemed to have an opinion of his own.

"I must get inside." I tugged at the door. "We can't be found standing out here." They'd wonder at our sanity rather than at our propriety—but I wasn't taking the chance.

The hallway that seemed so cold a few minutes before was now a haven of warmth and calm. I shrugged off the professor's gown and returned it to him, listening with one ear to the murmur of voices in the chapel that told me the meeting was over. The men would be clustered in a group, no doubt discussing Professor Wale's abrupt departure.

"I shall, of course, contact our denominational office." Wale's voice was a low hiss in my ear. "And I have another string to my bow, one that Poulton doesn't know about. I have discovered that a friend of a correspondent of mine knew Poulton in Baltimore, and he has furnished me with some addresses. I am going to make inquiries about that—about him."

"You're chasing shadows," I said shortly. Not for the first time, I doubted the man's sanity. Was it possible that this whole Darwin nonsense had unbalanced him? I hadn't personally heard an argument for a while, but Reiner had told me they still went on. Most of the faculty were now against Professor Wale's position.

"You think I'm pursuing a chimera, eh?" His smile was strange. "You would, of course. I cannot blame a woman for wishing to leave well alone, especially when her own future may be involved. But the game is worth the candle, my dear."

He grasped my arm, squeezing it hard so that I opened my mouth in a squeak of protest. "You will thank me, one day. I, and I alone, am left to defend our rational, God-given senses against Phariseeism and ignorance. And with the Almighty's help, I will prevail."

"AND WILL YOU WEAR A PRETTY DRESS, MOMMA?" SARAH smoothed the hair of her rag doll, made of an improbably red yarn we had found in Hayward's.

At three, Sarah had begun to take an interest in what I, and she, wore—not that she showed any sign of being fascinated by the dressmaking process. My earliest memories included hovering at Grandmama's elbow, watching her cut or sew, but to Sarah, clothes were of value only in that they were pretty and involved as many flounces and bows as possible.

"I shall wear my sky-blue silk," I pronounced, folding Martin's latest letter and slipping it into my pocket. Our letters to each other were short these days—cordial but guarded. A married man with a fashionable wife and a business to run could hardly pour out his heart and mind to a seamstress in a Kansas seminary, although Martin did continue to send me the occasional package of trimmings. The pale gold lace that decorated the aforementioned sky-blue silk had come from Rutherford's and looked very well. I had cut the back of the dress into a deep V and trimmed it with a substantial border of lace, to shine against my pale skin and bring out the color of my hair.

I pulled my sketching paper toward me, smiling at the study I had done of Sarah earlier. The process of observing and tracing the lines of her face was a delight to me, especially now that the bone structure showed clearly under her skin. She was not, I was relieved to find, going to be one of those redheaded children who were covered with freckles—instead, such sun as was allowed to reach her skin turned it the light golden color of underdone biscuits. In the sunlight, her copper hair took on glints of gold fire—had my father's hair looked so?

"I want to go to fancy dinners too, Momma," Sarah pronounced. "An't I old enough now?"

"You won't be for a long time." I chucked her under the chin. "You'll have to content yourself with giving dinner parties for your dolls. Children are not to be present at an adult social occasion except if someone brings them down for five minutes to greet the company."

"But Tess is a grown-up," Sarah said. "Why isn't she invited?" Sarah was inordinately fond of asking "Why?" about everything.

"She didn't receive an invitation, I suppose, because she's not a particular acquaintance of Mrs. Shemmeld's. I am because I make dresses for her—and I'm invited to keep Mr. Poulton company."

"Why?" Sarah wrinkled her nose. "Does he have to have a lady with him? Why can't you sit with someone who talks about nice things like books? I never understand what Mr. Poulton says."

I sighed. Judah didn't have the knack of talking to children and generally spoke only to me when Sarah was present, ignoring her altogether. He ignored Tess too, and she was mute in his presence as a general rule. But children, even their own children, were not a man's province until they grew old enough to be worthy of attention, I supposed.

And boys would always get more of a man's attention than girls.

I turned the sheet of paper over and began sketching the lines of a walking dress I had in mind for Mrs. Froggatt, who would be at tonight's dinner. The ladies of Springwood were not exactly my friends, but I was on cordial terms with most of them—and there were more of them now since the town was growing fast. Sometimes one of them invited me to take tea in her parlor, amid a richness of décor that always seemed incongruous against the stark beauty of the land around us. How much had it cost their husbands to have these armchairs, these drapes, these antimacassars brought by rail and cart from far-off cities? Despite our newfound wealth, Tess and I were quite content with the plain, painted wood and simple decoration of our shared room. Our only problem was that our wardrobes were now sufficiently extensive that I'd had to move most of our clothing to a small boxroom I'd appropriated for the purpose. One day we would have to move—one day. But where would we go?

Tess bustled in, her short arms piled high with bedsheets, which she deposited on one of the tables with a grunt. I sighed.

"It's all right—I'll sort them. Sary can help me." Tess grinned at both of us. "Sary, Momma is going to have the vapors if she looks at another worn sheet. Can you help me find the holes?"

"Why do the sheets have holes?" Sarah dropped the doll onto a chair and stood on tiptoe to peer up at the pile of linen.

"Because the boys' heels and elbows are bony, I guess, just like yours." Tess poked a finger into Sarah's side, making her squeal and squirm away from her tormentor.

"I don't make holes. Look, there's one!" Sarah put her finger on the spot where the light from the window shone through the sheet Tess held. "Momma, it's like a game. Why don't you want to play?"

"Momma wants to draw pictures of dresses," said Tess. "She always gets that look on her face when she's making up a dress in her head and is itching to try it out on the paper."

I was quite sure I did no such thing as "get a look on my face," but my mind was on kick pleats, bundles of them spaced perhaps ten inches apart. This would be a pleasing dress and not too ornate—in fact, I could probably make a version for myself. My pencil flew over the page, making changes and additions as I also wrote little notes to myself around the edges. For my own dress, perhaps a bright navy blue—was there such a thing? Or would that be a dark royal blue? And where would I get it?

I listened with half an ear to Tess and Sarah's chatter, and their laughter as Tess pretended not to see the worn spots so that Sarah could discover them. Tess had far more patience with Sarah than I did and lacked my own tendency to correct my child, a legacy of having been corrected three dozen times a day myself. She was, in every way, Sarah's second mother.

"What comes between navy and royal blue?" I muttered under my breath, grabbing another sheet of paper to start a new drawing, this time for my own dress. "And would silk or wool be best?" I'd have to have a new dress before the year's end, that was certain—a dressmaker could not be shabby or behind the times.

Martin would know, of course. He had access to hundreds of bolts of cloth, thousands of samples, a million furbelows—while I sat on the prairie like a rooted clump of grass, endless miles from the nearest store of any worth.

My pencil, having sketched in the outline of my dress, hovered over the upper right corner of the paper. Should I write "navy walking dress" or "royal blue walking dress"? Did it, in point of fact, matter what I wrote? Perhaps I should ask Martin to send me a bolt of the right cloth. He would know. And I could pay for it too, out of my own funds. It wouldn't be a gift.

I realized I was sketching the outline of Martin's thin, rather beaky nose on the reverse side of the paper. If I were trying to flatter him—which I never did—I supposed I might call it aristocratic. A little like the engraving of the Duke of Wellington in Grandmama's book about Waterloo, only better shaped. Hmm. A squarish face—another book of Grandmama's sprang to mind, the one that had beautiful illustrations of Viking warriors protected by transparent sheets of paper. His lips—as a child I had always loved their shape, the hollow in the upper lip and the fullness of the lower. If it was late in the day and he needed to shave, my childish fingernails would rasp against the growth of pale stubble around them.

"What are you doing?" asked Tess, looking over my shoulder. "Oh! Martin! That's a very good likeness, Nell."

"Who's Martin?"

"You know, Sary, Momma's old friend who looks after our money." Tess folded up the last sheet with an air of triumph.

"Mr. Rutherford to you," I said reprovingly to my child.

"Why has he got a big nose?"

"You have a big nose." I picked up my progeny and plunked her on my lap, kissing the tiny proboscis that sported exactly three freckles. "You're very nosy about everything."

"You've got a bumpy nose," retorted my offspring. "What's elegant? I heard Mr. Poulton say it."

"That's enough of that." I rose to my feet, hoisting Sarah up so that she was resting on my hip. "Come and watch me put on my pretty dress for this evening."

"You'll be the most beautifullest lady at the dinner," Sarah declared. "And Mr. Poulton'll be the prettiest gentleman, I s'pose." She pouted. "But he's no fun."

"A gentleman in his position must be dignified, not fun. And men aren't pretty."

"He is," I heard Tess's voice on the breeze behind us as we left the room. "But he's not very nice."

I ignored her.

18

GOOSE

"This is a delicious bird, Mrs. Shemmeld." Judah took another bite of the tender meat and laid his knife and fork on the plate to reach for his water glass. Like me, he ate in the English fashion with both halves of the silverware involved. "Not a wild one, I think?"

"Certainly not." Mrs. Shemmeld, a tall, stout woman with the face of a governess, bristled a little. And then softened, as women tended to do when Judah smiled at them. "I had it delivered especially and slaughtered it myself this morning. It is quite, quite fresh."

The image of Mrs. Shemmeld with a cleaver in her hand, the goose's lifeblood dripping from its still-twitching neck and a surprised expression in its silly eyes, rose up before me. Still, one must eat. I cut myself another small bite of the savory flesh.

"Did you pluck it yourself, Mrs. Shemmeld?" Judah's face was angled toward me, and I could see his expression of polite interest, the limpid beauty of his violet-blue eyes as serene as the summer sky.

"No, my cook—oh, you're laughing at me, Mr. Poulton."

Mrs. Shemmeld's severe face wrinkled into a smile, and she raised her hand to hide her bad teeth. "You intellectual gentlemen have such a way of saying dreadful things with a straight face."

"Quite proper," said Mr. Lehmann, who sat on my right. He was Reiner's uncle; Reiner had not been invited to the dinner. I had seen that young man watching us as we left, an expression of wry discontent on his face. "A good housekeeper takes a personal interest in the preparation of the meat."

Well, Mama had never taken the slightest interest in preparing food. Whatever would I do if I found myself in charge of running a household? I didn't know how to boil an egg.

"Mrs. Shemmeld is a superb hostess."

Judah raised his glass in Mrs. Shemmeld's direction, its incised surface catching the colors of the magnificent prairie sunset. "I propose a toast of thanks for her hospitality."

Our glasses contained pure, fresh well water, so much better than Dr. Calderwood's wines. I drank heartily.

"Mrs. Lillington, do you not agree that Mrs. Shemmeld is the consummate hostess?" Judah turned the full force of his gaze upon me.

"It's a delicious meal," I told the older lady with perfect sincerity. "I'm enjoying myself tremendously."

Mrs. Shemmeld smiled, her lips closed. "I'm happy to provide an evening's diversion for the younger members of our little community. Of course, we in the town feel that the seminary, as it were, belongs to us—as if we were cousins." She gave a little giggle that was completely at odds with her forbidding countenance. "And you in particular, Mrs. Lillington, have brought delight and joy to the ladies of Springwood with your perfectly marvelous dresses."

"Indeed she has," interjected Mrs. Yomkins, bestowing a

warm smile on me. I returned it with interest. I was fond of this particular customer, whose sly wit and insight into everyone else's motives had often reduced me to fits of unladylike laughter. "Just think what a desert we'd be in otherwise. Why, we might all be obliged to force our husbands to take us to Paris just to augment our wardrobes!"

Mr. Yomkins visibly paled at the thought of the expense, and I made a pretense of wiping my mouth with my napkin to hide my smile.

"I can't imagine anything better than visiting a Parisian house of couture," I said. "I'd like to sit at the feet of Mr. Worth and worship. I've never seen one of his dresses, but I think I'd recognize one instantly, so carefully have I studied the descriptions in the journals."

"Oh, you should indeed go to Paris, Mrs. Lillington." That was Mrs. Froggatt, who was one of those women who never quite managed to be as stylish as she wished to be. "Then you could come back and make us more magnificent than ever."

A chorus of howls greeted this suggestion, all the ladies agreeing that once in Paris, I would never come back.

"You're too young to be a widow, Mrs. Lillington." This was from Mrs. McGilloway, who was fairly young herself—considerably younger than her husband. "Do you not think of marrying again? You'll never go to Paris by yourself, I fear."

I bit back the retort that I could perfectly well afford to go to Paris with my own money, then felt that strange pang that went through me every time I realized, as if for the first time, the extent of my wealth. I saw Judah's gaze flick briefly toward me and knew he was thinking the same thing.

"Not such an ordeal, I hope?" Judah asked as we watched Mrs. Shemmeld's buggy, which had brought us back to the seminary, bounce over the ruts on its way back to Springwood. The night was warm, but the breeze felt pleasant, and we lingered at the top of the steps, reluctant to exchange the fresh night air for the seminary's dusty atmosphere. The waxing moon hung in the sky, its light competing with the jeweled stars. I could see Judah almost as clearly as if it were daylight.

"Thanks to you, it wasn't. It's astonishing how often matron ladies return to the topic of marriage when there are spinsters and bachelors in the company, isn't it? But you steered the conversation onto other matters every time."

"I'm not fond of people interrogating me, and I don't suppose you are either." I could see Judah's white teeth as he smiled and the glint in his slanted eyes. "It's tiresome."

I laughed. "We'd better get inside." From our sheltered position under the porch, I couldn't see the window of Mrs. Drummond's room, but I knew it was there—and I was sure her curtain was twitching. "If we linger, tongues will wag."

"Will they?" Judah's voice was light. "The word is that it's young Mr. Lehmann who's courting you."

I dipped my head. "What am I supposed to say to that? I can't discuss a matter that's confidential to Mr. Lehmann." Especially to a man who had fought with him, possibly over me.

"I'm not asking you to discuss it."

Judah's voice had become caressing. He touched my chin with his gloved finger, lifting it, and then pulled off his fine evening gloves and stuffed them into a pocket. His face was in shadow now; mine must have been lit by the moonlight, transparent and open.

"I wish—I wish you to know, Nell, that Mr. Lehmann is not the only man here with an interest in your future."

Judah raised his hand again to brush a stray curl off my face. His fingers were cool on my warm skin, and a shiver ran over me, sending sparks of energy into my shoulders and wrists.

"Does—" My voice came out in a squeak, and I cleared my throat. "Has your interest in my future increased since you realized I have money, Judah?"

"Ah." He tipped his head, and I saw his eyes slant in amusement over his high cheekbones. "You're an astute young woman, and I suppose I deserved that."

He pushed his hands into the pockets of his jacket and turned to face the star-spattered night sky. "How am I going to answer that accusation?" he said into the empty air.

"With honesty." I folded my arms to still their trembling—it was strange, but whereas with Reiner I felt entirely in control of the situation, with Judah I felt—what? Danger?

"I think I've been honest with you all along, Nell. I made it clear from the outset that I couldn't afford to pursue a woman without money. Which doesn't mean I would pursue any woman simply because she has money. I'd have to feel an attraction toward her too." He paused for a long moment. "I have—always—felt such an attraction to you, Nell. The fact of your wealth allows me to express it."

He moved back toward me and caught one of my hands in his. Pushing back my lace glove, he kissed the pulse point on my wrist, and my knees turned to rubber.

"With you by my side, there's nothing I couldn't do," Judah continued, rubbing his thumb over the place he'd kissed. "And there's nothing you couldn't achieve with me behind you. If we joined forces," he lowered his lips to my wrist again so that I felt his warm breath caressing my skin as he spoke, "I could make you extremely happy." His head came up, and for a few seconds I felt his lips pressed to mine.

If I had drunk wine, I would know why my head was

spinning. If I'd been running, I'd know why I was breathless. I had been neither drinking nor running, and yet I felt dazed, mesmerized by the man whose beautiful dark curls were so close that I only had to sink the fingers of my free hand into them—

I took a step backward, freeing myself from his arms. "I don't know." I wanted to ask if he loved me, but I had no more idea of making such an appeal to Judah Poulton than I would have to the marble angel that stood guard over Springwood's small cemetery. Judah was just as beautiful as the statue and just as forbidding in his beauty.

"You don't have to say a thing; I know it's too sudden to contemplate." Judah straightened his shirt front. "We should go inside, in any case—I don't want to damage your reputation. I just wanted you to know, that's all."

He held the door open for me, and when I saw Mrs. Calderwood standing there, I felt a pang of guilt and shame. Did I look as bedazzled as I felt? But the little woman only smiled.

"A fine night, Mr. Poulton. And Mrs. Lillington, that is a truly beautiful gown. Allow me to see you safely to your room, my dear."

Her words and her benign expression confused me. Two years before, she had practically accused me of being a harlot, and now she saw me walk through the door with a man and was wreathed in smiles. I followed her dumbly up the stairs, answering her little questions about the dinner in monosyllables.

I undressed in the dark, laying my dress carefully over the table so I could inspect it for spots and snags in the morning. Tess's small snores and Sarah's gentle breathing competed with the fine hiss of the wind through the open window and the sounds of the night, muted this high above the ground.

I climbed into bed, but sleep didn't come. Instead, I stared through the open curtains at the stars, now partly obscured by long streaks of cloud.

Now what? I had, apparently, two men courting me, neither of whom liked the other. And neither of them knew that fact about my past life which I was duty bound to reveal to them. Perhaps telling them would repulse their attentions, even at the cost of bringing down opprobrium on my head and shame on Sarah's. Did I wish to repulse their attentions? I had no idea. But I'd have to tell them, wouldn't I? If I wanted honesty from them, I'd have to offer the same.

19
COURTSHIP

"They're beautiful, Reiner. Wherever did you find them? I've never seen such flowers growing anywhere near here."

Reiner's smile lit up his pleasant face. "Dandy, aren't they?" He touched the peach-colored roses with a fingertip. "Had them sent from Saint Louis, packed in ice."

"That's outrageously extravagant. Oh, they smell wonderful." I buried my nose in the cool, silken softness of the huge blooms. "But Reiner—"

"But me no buts." Reiner folded his arms across his broad chest. "Nothing is too good for the woman I—for the best girl in the world, particularly on the occasion of her twenty-first birthday. I'm just sorry they weren't here this morning, so I had to wait a whole day to see you smile like that."

I began to rise. "I'd better go find a vase. They'll make our room smell like an entire rose garden."

"No, you stay put." Reiner rose to his feet in a swift, easy movement and took the box from my hands. "I'll go to the kitchen and wheedle one of the good vases out of Netta. She has the key to the pantry, and it's in the little room off the pantry that Mrs. Drummond keeps her good crystal. I'll leave them by your door, and Mrs. D. won't know a thing about it. No plain jar for my lady."

I opened my mouth to protest that Mrs. Drummond surely would find out, and that I'd be the one to get the blame. My words were forestalled by the entrance of Professor Wale into the library, otherwise deserted on this fine Friday evening.

"A-wooing, Mr. Lehmann?"

Reiner's usually smiling mouth clamped into a tight line. "With all due respect, Professor Wale, it's none of your business. Many things aren't your business, and you'd do well to keep your nose out of them."

And to my astonishment, he stalked out, the box containing the roses clutched so tight that his knuckles showed white.

"What—Professor, what on earth have you done to him? He looks as if he'd like to cut your throat."

A small smile stole across Professor Wale's face.

"I? I have done nothing to the boy. I merely suggested, in a letter to a Saint Louis editor, that his father might do well to let some moral considerations enter into his business dealings. I would say the same about any of the railroad magnates who've been so ruinously speculating with other people's money. Although they haven't all been as quick to try to wriggle out of their responsibilities as Gerhardt Lehmann."

"A son is not necessarily like his father."

"The lad is weak." The professor sighed as he sat down in the nearest chair and motioned for me to sit near him. "He's indecisive about his future, and his father's shenanigans are not helping him. I would have almost respected him more if he had gone off to rob the investors alongside his father. At least that would have shown some ambition."

"I thought you didn't approve of ambition?" I could hear the acid in my voice. Professor Wale, I had decided, was a meddler. Perhaps his motives were good, but to write to the newspapers about Reiner's father when he must have known Reiner would find out—what was the point of it?

"There are different degrees of ambition." The professor rubbed a yellow-stained forefinger against the side of his nose, regarding me intently with his bright, dark eyes. "It is proper to be ambitious for a good cause, for example. It is not proper to aim at putting yourself at the top of the heap when such an ambition involves crushing everyone else on the way up."

Only the good manners instilled in me from childhood prevented me from rolling my eyes. By this last remark, he meant Judah. Clearly, neither of my suitors met Professor Wale's standards.

"You may very well stare at me in that manner, Mrs. Lillington. But believe me, I have your best interests at heart. I'm not sure, exactly, why Judah Poulton is showing interest in a seamstress—if you may forgive me for mentioning your station in life—but the fact that he is showing interest worries me. Especially considering this."

He withdrew a bundle of paper from the capacious pocket of his sack coat. The thin sheets crackled as he fingered them, and I could see that they were closely written over.

"What is that?" My curiosity overcame my better nature, and I leaned forward.

Professor Wale gave his little half smile again, leaning back into his chair and curling his hand around the papers. "It's a letter from England, Mrs. Lillington. About Poulton. And it doesn't make edifying reading."

A strange chill threaded its way through my veins. "Do you intend to show it to me?"

"For the moment, I simply intend to warn you. I've seen you in his thrall, like a rabbit kitten charmed by a snake. Perhaps my assurance that there are grounds for a warning will be enough, and I won't have to burden a woman's mind with the revelations contained therein. Not all subjects are suitable for someone so young and tender."

I felt my anger spark.

"Really, Professor? And you the great proponent of thorough inquiry and discussion? Are these discussions to exclude women?"

He opened his eyes wide. "Women are to be protected and sheltered, naturally. I'm surprised you should even consider the alternative." He shrugged. "Although I suppose that if I show this to Cameron Calderwood, his fair beloved must see it too. But she is a matron of mature years, and I imagine that after a decade or more of running a school of young men, these matters will not surprise her. Poulton will be out on his ear the day after I put these pages before her eyes."

My anger flared and crackled like a log catching aflame, and I rose to my feet.

"I think you should live up to your own principles, Professor. You've said that it's important to discuss matters openly, above all things—well, shouldn't you at least face Judah with whatever it is you have against him before you sneak behind his back to the Calderwoods?" My breath was coming fast. "So he did things in the past of which he may not be proud. Have not many of us done such things? Are they to follow us forever? Can we not begin life again?"

The professor's jaw went slack, the skin of his cheeks seeming to sag on his bones. He too stood up. "But—hang it all, Mrs. Lillington, you must trust me in this. There are things in this document—"

"Why should I trust you?" I was close to tears now, my own transgression in the forefront of my mind, and my voice sounded shrill to my ears. "People change—they do—and why should other people presume they'll repeat their former mistakes? Why is the past always to be shoved in their faces?"

I strode toward the long French windows and stared out over the prairie. The windows faced west into one of the glorious Kansas sunsets that were this lonesome country's most beautiful feature, but I derived no joy from it. I clenched my jaw hard, willing myself to get my emotions under control.

"I'm sorry." I felt the professor's hand on my elbow, turning me to face him. "I too have acts in my past of which I'm not proud. More, perhaps, than you can possibly imagine." He looked down at the letter. "Maybe you're right."

Up close, he cut a pathetic figure, his gaudy waistcoat a strange contrast to the drabness of his skin and the dust that seemed to cling around his hair and clothing. The red-gold sky cast the oddest shadows too, making him seem corpse-like, or perhaps a waxwork figure devoid of animation.

"Please talk with Mr. Poulton first." I made a huge effort to sound calm and reasonable. "Or at least accuse him to his face if you must go to the Calderwoods. Let him defend himself. Or in any event—to be honest, I'm not sure what the best course of action would be. But going hugger-mugger to the Calderwoods behind Judah's back isn't the right thing to do."

"Perhaps not." Professor Wale heaved a deep sigh, and to my surprise, held out his hand as if expecting me to shake it. I followed suit, and he grasped my fingers in a firm grip, shaking my hand as vigorously as if I'd been a man.

"You have my word, Mrs. Lillington, that I will take no further step without consulting you. In fact, I will give the matter considerable thought before I act—and when I do act, I will try to do so as a rational human being and as a Christian who has known forgiveness."

I let out a sigh. "You'll talk with him?"

"Y-e-e-e-s."

There was doubt in the professor's voice, and he stroked one yellowed finger over the sheets of paper he held in his hand. "But—would you understand if I prepared a little insurance for myself first?" He looked at me rather strangely. "No, I'm not sure if you would. You don't see what I see in Judah Poulton. And yet should anything—unfortunate happen to me, I would be misjudging if I didn't see you as the person most in need of protection. So I'll show you what I'm going to do."

I must have looked completely nonplussed. The professor laughed as he crossed to the bookshelves that held the Greek and Hebrew texts, row upon row of leather-bound tomes I couldn't read. He removed a row of books from the second shelf and placed them on a table.

"Now watch. You must press exactly here."

As he pushed against the paneling at the back of the shelf, a section of the wood came loose. He showed me how, by turning it sideways, the panel could be pulled out, revealing a small recess in the corner behind and to one side of it. Then he replaced the panel.

"Now you try."

It took me three attempts to make the panel move. It seemed quite solid until you pressed on exactly the right spot, and then a certain amount of dexterity was needed to extract the panel without damaging it. But in a few moments, I was triumphant.

"I discovered this little niche years ago," the professor said, fitting the wood back into its place. "There now." He replaced the books, ensuring they were lined up exactly with the place where fugitive beams of sunlight had taken a little color out of the wood.

"If I should tell Poulton about what's in this letter, I somehow don't wish to leave it in my room. I'll copy the most pertinent points onto a sheet of paper as an *aide-mémoire*, but I will, at some point in the very near future, conceal the letter itself in this hiding-hole. You have my permission to read, at any time, what is contained therein. If I'm no longer around to claim the letter, you may do what you wish with it. Throw it in the fire unread if you truly believe Judah Poulton is what he claims to be."

I looked at him doubtfully. "What, exactly, do you think might happen to you?"

He shrugged. "Poulton could cause the Calderwoods to send me away—particularly since I've now incurred Mr. Lehmann's enmity, and he is a favorite of the Mouse's." A rueful smile played across his lips. "I'm becoming a thorn in the flesh as far as the Calderwoods are concerned. I can't stop myself from speaking out—I can't sacrifice principle to self-interest or even tact. Perhaps I am a little mad." He tapped the side of his head.

"Where would you go if they made you leave?"

Suddenly, I hated myself for what I was doing, forcing the little man into an uneven fight. I didn't trust the Calderwoods to be impartial, whatever the professor had to reveal about Judah.

"Do you know, I don't really think it matters." A spark of amusement crept into the professor's eyes as he straightened his gown. The black fabric of his clothing absorbed the red light of the sunset, but his face and hands were lit as if with flame, and his gaudy waistcoat sparkled like the jeweled body of an insect. "I don't shy away from a fight because I fear the consequences, as I suspect you know. If Poulton attacks me, perhaps he'll end up digging his own grave instead."

20
TROUBLE

For weeks after my talk with the professor, I felt as if I were walking on the prairie under heavy black clouds, waiting for the storm to break. And yet it didn't, and as the heat of summer gradually gave way to the cooler air of fall, I felt myself relax again. I was too busy to be anxious, in any case. Tess and I had all the work for the seminary to do and, as Springwood grew, many new commissions from the ladies in the town.

And I was in the peculiar position of being openly courted by two men, yet that didn't touch off any fights either. Reiner and Judah were careful to wait until the other was not in the vicinity before suggesting a walk or a spell sitting outside or an hour spent reading a novel or journal in the library—respectable ways of getting to know each other better without offending the proprieties. Perhaps I should have felt relief that there were no stolen kisses either—well, in Reiner's case I did. I liked Reiner a great deal, but somehow I just didn't see—I couldn't imagine—

Judah was a different matter. Professor Wale had described me as a rabbit kitten in thrall to a snake—ridiculous, of course, but I had to admit Judah drew me like a magnet. Over the summer, he'd had his hair cut shorter, and with the advent of the cooler weather, he grew a small, neat beard and mustache. They gave him a mature and serious air, more in harmony with his new responsibilities as the head of the faculty. His authority within the seminary grew, and should we happen to be in Springwood together, our joint presence drew nods of approval and pleased smiles from the respectable townsfolk.

"Although, you know, I think they're laughing at me behind my back," I told Tess one day as we sat sewing shirt-sleeves into armholes. Sarah sat at her little table near the empty fireplace, laboriously copying letters from her alphabet primer onto her slate. She'd become obsessed with the notion of writing of late and would spend hours at a time doing "pretend writing" on her slate, row after row of squiggles and lines. I was sure I hadn't shown such an interest in scholarship at three and a half.

"Who are laughing, Nell? It's mean to laugh." Tess passed me another sleeve to baste—she couldn't work out how to fit a sleeve properly, but once I basted it in for her, she was able to sew it in with sufficient care for a schoolboy's shirt.

"I don't blame them," I mused, matching seam to seam. "I turn up in town with Judah one day, Reiner the next. I've tried to make it clear I'm not stringing them along. In fact, I've gone out of my way to inform my clients that I have no intention of marrying, and yet they never seem to believe me."

"Well," said Tess sagely, "if you really weren't interested in ever marrying again, then you should tell both of them to go away and walk to Springwood with me. Or wait till we can get a ride on a cart."

Tess hated having to walk the nearly three-mile distance to Springwood, not to mention coming back again. Sarah was both too small to walk the distance without complaining and too heavy to carry, so she never accompanied me either. I did sometimes wait until one of the servants headed for the town, but they seemed a little shy of me. Yet walking by myself was even more frowned upon now that there'd been reports of both Indian hunting parties and rough men in the vicinity in recent weeks.

"I don't see any harm in just walking with either of them," I said defensively. "They're both well known to be respectable men, and nobody at the seminary seems to mind."

"That's what you think," said Tess. "Eliza's very cross with you."

I counted to twenty in my head, reaching for Mama's tiny gold scissors to snip off a length of thread before I replied. My question still came out in a clipped, strained tone of voice.

"What, exactly, does Mrs. Drummond have against me now?" I thought we'd finished with all that nonsense. Eliza Drummond barely spoke to me, but she'd said nothing against me for months, to my knowledge.

"She's cross because you made Reiner and Mr. Poulton want to marry you."

"Made them?" I stamped one foot on the ground, my hands being busy. "Does she think I went about seducing them? No, don't bother to answer that—I'm sure she does. And how does she even know?"

I looked at my companion, who was sewing assiduously, her tongue thrust forward in concentration. "Tess, have you been gossiping?"

"Of course not." Tess raised her small nose in the air. "'Thou shalt not go up and down as a talebearer among thy people.' That's what the Bible says, and it means you shouldn't gossip. If Eliza asks me a question about you, I think very hard before I answer in case it's gossip. If you told me something in private and then I tell her about it, that would be gossip too, wouldn't it?"

"Yes, it would."

"So I never do that."

I smiled at Tess, but my mind was busy. Eliza Drummond could probably wheedle information out of Tess by clever questioning. Even Tess's loyalty was no match for a devious mind, and I was sure the housekeeper possessed one of those. Tess spent as much time as she could with Mrs. Drummond due to her passion for the details of housekeeping, particularly the careful compilation and adding-up of columns of figures. I had turned keeping our own daily accounts over to her—she did her sums slowly but with great care.

"Well, someone's been gossiping. Either that or Eliza Drummond's been spying on me and drawing conclusions. That's worse than gossiping."

"Oh, Mrs. Calderwood told her about Reiner and Mr. Poulton."

I jumped. "And how did *she* know?"

"Momma, will you write my name on my drawing?" Sarah ran to me, holding up her slate, which was covered with what looked like a cucumber crossed with a stick insect and covered in sheep's wool.

Relinquishing my sewing, I moved to one of my work tables, and Sarah clambered up into the chair beside me. I felt her warm breath on my cheek and the tickle of the wiry curls that had escaped from her braids as I wrote SARAH, saying the letters as I inscribed each one.

"Now write 'horse.'"

Well, at least I now knew what the picture was supposed to represent. I complied and handed the slate back to her.

"Try to copy the letters," I suggested. I looked at Tess, who had taken her cue from my own interruption of my work to head for the most comfortable chair in the room. Her expression clearly stated she was going nowhere for the next few minutes. "Show Tess when you've finished. I need to talk with Mrs. Drummond."

It was late September but still warm enough that my clothes felt heavy on me as I walked. At this time of day, the seminary building was almost silent. I could hear a far-off clatter of pans from the distant kitchens, but nothing else. The great staircase with its row of stained-glass windows brooded solemnly in the peace, the pools of colored light flickering as clouds passed before the sun.

I walked through the door to the left of the cloakroom, into the warren of rooms that surrounded the housekeeper's office. Dorcas was in the room that held the ledgers, complaining under her breath as she meticulously dusted each book and replaced it on the shelf.

"She bin makin' trouble," she whispered to me as I passed.

I stopped, feeling uncertain. "Trouble?"

"For you." Dorcas groaned and massaged her lower back. "Wit' Mist' Lehmann an' Mist' Poulton. It eat her up till she cain' help but talk, iffen you aks me. She had them gentlemans in here, one by one, this very morning."

"Dorcas?" Mrs. Drummond's voice, sharp and accusing, sounded from nearby. "What are you saying?"

Dorcas rolled her eyes at me. "Jus' them ledgers is heavy, Miz Drummond. I tell Miz Nell they makin' the misery in my back worse."

"Is Mrs. Lillington there? If she has something to say to me, she should come in, not stand gossiping with the servants."

"Yes'm." Dorcas made a meaningful face at me, and as I passed into the next room, I heard her say, "Lordy, Lordy," as quietly as she could manage.

I stiffened my spine. I had expected trouble to come from

Professor Wale, and it hadn't. But trouble had come indeed, so it would seem.

"Have you come about the sheets?" Mrs. Drummond did not bother to wish me a good morning.

"No, but since you ask, I'd like to order another bolt of cotton," I said. "I think we should pay the extra couple cents a yard for the long staple cotton—the cheaper stuff isn't nearly hardwearing enough."

Mrs. Drummond pulled one of her smaller ledgers from the pile on her table and flipped it open to the most recent page, running a long, strong finger down the column of figures. "Very well, we can manage that. Only Fruit of the Loom or Gem of the Spindle, mind you, none of those fancy New York cottons at seventeen cents a yard. I leave it to you to write the supplier."

I gazed at her glossy topknot of hair as she opened her small notebook and made a meticulous note of our agreement, her pen dipping, writing, and dipping again. Of course, all I had were my suspicions, but—what, exactly, had she said?

Mrs. Drummond closed her ledger and looked up at me. "And how is your study of Scripture proceeding, Mrs. Lillington?" she asked, a half smile on her face.

I seized the opportunity to pull out a chair and sit down. I was not going to suffer her to make me stay on my feet like a housemaid. I had struck a nerve—her lips tightened, but she said nothing.

"Tess and I study a passage every morning," I replied politely.

"And do you feel that your grasp of moral precepts is improving?" So might a cat smile, I thought, if it came across a mouse with its back turned.

Inspiration struck, and I looked Mrs. Drummond straight in the eye. "Tess taught me a valuable verse today," I said, making my eyes wide and innocent. "'Thou shalt not go up and down as a talebearer among thy people.' That means not to gossip, of course. You haven't been gossiping, have you, Mrs. Drummond?"

It gratified me to see a deep, dull red stain the housekeeper's cheeks. But the look in her eyes grew harder, her green-gray irises round balls of flint.

"Not all conversations where you impart something about someone are gossip. Sometimes, it may be necessary to warn another person of facts they do not know."

Well, that confirmed what I suspected. "I find it hard to distinguish the difference," I said as pleasantly as I could.

And there it was, that glimpse of triumph. "That is because you are deficient in moral sensibility," Mrs. Drummond said. "Read the Apostle, Mrs. Lillington, and strive to emulate his ceaseless efforts to better himself and everyone around him."

I ransacked my brain for an answer and found—nothing. Not all my wealth—of which, of course, Mrs. Drummond had no inkling—nor all my quickness of mind and boldness of spirit could answer the certainty in Mrs. Drummond's heart. I was the sinner, she was not. She had imparted my secret to both Reiner and Judah out of what she saw as the purest necessity, and nothing I could say or do would shake her conviction that she was right.

I walked back to my workroom through the smells of frying chicken and fresh cornbread, but it wasn't the scent of food that made my stomach roil. It was the horrible conviction that, somehow, Mrs. Drummond was in the right. If I was even contemplating, somewhere deep down inside, marrying Judah or Reiner, they had the right to know about my past. It was only fair.

I'd been so careless of the future in that May sunlight when I'd let Jack Venton have his way, as the saying goes, with me. The spoiled, bold girl I had been then thought only of her own pleasure and her desire to take the privileges owing to an adult without any of the consequences. And here were the consequences, unwanted and unsought, following me down the years—and, worse, they were also following Sarah and anyone else whose fate was, or might be, tied up with mine.

21
BARGAIN

The feelings I experienced over the next few days were odd. If anyone had asked me before that interview, I would have told them I entertained no specific hopes or anticipations as far as Reiner or Judah were concerned—and that had not changed.

Yet the knowledge that Mrs. Drummond had revealed my secret to them, stripped my pretense of respectability away, gave me the odd sensation that I'd lost a foot or a hand but couldn't quite work out which one. I felt raw, exposed—if I happened to be in the same room as either man, the back of my neck crawled as if covered with ants.

And yet the waiting stretched over ten agonizing days. If Mrs. Drummond had invented that particular torture expressly for me, I would have considered her a genius of exquisite refinement. As it was, I had to lay my long period of suspense at the door of the gentlemen themselves. Should I speak up? Or give them time to consider what they had learned? It was a fortunate thing that I had so much work to distract me, else I thought I might have run mad on the prairie.

And then Reiner spoke up. I suppose he had been biding his time for a chance to see me alone, which, naturally, was not easy. But Tess had taken a sleepy Sarah up to bed. I had a dress to finish for a new customer, and Tess had offered to return and help me once Sarah was asleep, but I didn't expect to see her. Tess tired far more easily than I did, and one of the reasons why she so frequently offered to take Sarah to bed was that she could lie on her own bed and half doze while Sarah fought sleep with chatter. This often led to Tess herself deciding she could not keep her eyes open, and that would be that.

I didn't mind. The walking dress I was making posed some interesting challenges. It was almost entirely in a pink plaid with a large check that had to be carefully matched, and I was enjoying myself. I was thinking so hard about the exact placement of my pattern pieces that I didn't even hear Reiner enter the room.

"Oh," was all I said when I looked up from my work and saw him standing before me. He started to smile, but somehow his smile failed, and an awkward silence descended between us. Reiner broke it by gesturing at the cloth spread across my cutting table.

"That's pretty. I like to see a woman in pink. Is it for you?"

I laughed at that. "You definitely do not want to see me in pink, not with my hair."

I was beginning to relax a little, but then I looked at Reiner's face again. His blue eyes, once so frank and ready to engage mine, looked as hard as pebbles.

"All right," I said, abandoning my work and leading the way to the pair of chairs that bracketed our empty fireplace. "I don't think the next few minutes will be easy for either of us, but we may as well be comfortable. You want to talk to me about what Mrs. Drummond told you, I presume."

Reiner politely handed me to a chair and seated himself,

looking as if he were heading for the gallows. "So it's true, is it?" was his opening salvo.

"Well, I'm not entirely sure what Mrs. Drummond has told you. If it's that I've never been married, that's true enough."

I watched his face darken at my admission but plowed ahead as best I could. "If she's been telling you that makes me some kind of scarlet woman, she's wrong. I was—foolish. Once." I felt my own cheeks redden. "I have not been similarly foolish since."

Reiner picked at a patch of dry skin on his thumb, scowling at it as if it were flaking on purpose to annoy him.

"And would you have told me?" he asked.

"If I'd settled in my mind that I would marry you, yes, I would have. In such circumstances, you would have a right to know. I don't see how you'd have such a right in any other situation." I knew I sounded arrogant, but the alternative was humble penitence, and somehow, with Reiner, I couldn't adopt that role.

Reiner's mouth tightened in a way that was becoming all too familiar. No longer being the carefree student was changing him, I realized, as was his growing antagonism toward Professor Wale.

"You let me court you under false pretenses, Nell," he said in the tone of a sulky boy who'd had his favorite toy taken away from him.

"I didn't ask you to court me. Do you think I can push away every man who shows interest in me with a declaration that I bore my child out of wedlock? It might be the nobler thing to do, but in practical terms, it simply doesn't work."

"You came here knowing men would court you. As you well know, unmarried women are rare on the frontier." Reiner had pulled so viciously at the tag of dry skin that he'd drawn blood, and he put his thumb to his lips with a muttered curse.

"I came here looking for a fresh beginning, where I could raise Sarah far from gossip. But the gossip followed me. Mrs. Drummond had no right to make trouble for me."

"She has a right to see that the truth comes out." Reiner rose to his feet, pushing back the chair. "Nell, I'd even written to Pop about you. He'll never accept a—a—fallen woman as a daughter-in-law, don't you see that? I couldn't marry you now even if I wanted to."

I tipped my head back to look at him, feeling my eyebrows practically meet my hairline. "Even if you wanted to?"

Reiner fished a somewhat grubby handkerchief from his pocket and wrapped it around his thumb. I almost laughed at the sight he made, standing there red-faced and angry with a wounded digit—but, truly, this was no laughing matter. Laughter had been a point of connection between us, but that was gone now.

"You must release me from any promise I may have made to you," Reiner said.

"I do." I stood up and went to put a hand on his arm, but he took a step back, sending his chair crashing to the ground. "And I'm sorry, Reiner. Perhaps I should have told you earlier. I suppose I thought—well, that if you loved me, one mistake would not make so very much of a difference."

"No difference?" Reiner's eyes were slits of blue, and his voice issued in a hiss. "It makes all the difference in the world, Nell. It's the difference between bringing a respectable bride home to my father and expecting him to sanction a marriage with—with a woman who won't be able to hold up her head in Saint Louis society. To expect him to accept a grandchild who's going to bear the taint of illegitimacy forever."

He looked down at his boots. "That poor child. There might well be men who'll accept what you have to offer, Nell, but it's beyond me."

And with that, he turned abruptly, picking his way over the fallen chair without bothering to set it upright. He slammed the door with such force that the pink taffeta on my table jumped in the breeze, and I darted over to prevent it from sliding sideways and undoing all my work.

"Drat it." I smoothed my hand over the cloth, feeling the sting of tears in my eyes. They weren't for the loss of Reiner —in many ways I thought I was better off sticking to my original plan to remain unwed, happy in my life with Tess and Sarah and free of a man who would wish to rule me and put his life before mine.

And yet it stung to think how right Reiner might be. If the knowledge of Sarah's birth became widespread in Springwood, could I hold up my head even in the society of that small town? Would people treat Sarah differently? And, dear God, would Reiner spread Mrs. Drummond's insidious gossip farther afield?

I didn't get any more work done that night but sat brooding by the empty fireplace for a full hour. Perhaps it was time to leave the Eternal Life Seminary—but where would I go?

"YOUNG MR. LEHMANN LOOKS AS IF HE'S BEEN CHEWING A lemon." Judah's thoughts uncannily echoed my own. He had appeared as if by magic when I went for a short walk before dinner. "Is it his obsessive hatred of Professor Wale that's the cause, I wonder, or dear Mrs. Drummond's startling revelations about your recent past?"

I glanced behind me at Reiner's retreating back. Judah's

description was accurate—the sour look on Reiner's face had not softened as he'd given me a grudging nod of greeting.

"It could be either, I suppose." I wrinkled my nose, feeling suddenly annoyed with both Reiner and Judah and not at all inclined to embark on the conversation Judah and I were about to have. Why was life so unfair to women?

"He was, I presume, entirely unaware of the nonexistence of the late Mr. Lillington?" Judah shot me a sideways look, challenging and perhaps even amused.

"Weren't *you*? And Lillington is my maiden name, by the way. I used the name Govender—before I came here."

Now Judah's expression was definitely one of amusement. "Govender." He rolled the name around his tongue, seeming to give it consideration.

"Did you know?" I asked again. "Or just suspect?" It was so hard to read Judah's face and just as hard to read my own emotions. In Judah's presence, I somehow always wanted to —how could I describe it? To impress, to look my best? There was something about Judah's sheer physical beauty and authority that made me feel he was above me—a mere mortal—in every way.

"I suspected. A husband who has left behind no mementos, no portrait of any kind, and no Christian name that is ever mentioned seems a trifle insubstantial."

"And do you mind?" Having begun, I was eager to get the business over with.

"Yes, of course I mind." Judah's face hardened. "A woman should be pure. Your sin will follow you all the days of your life and will follow your child too. Wherever you go, the truth will out, and respectable people will turn away from you and shun Sarah. They won't let their little ones play with her. You won't be received in society."

I nodded dumbly, my heart sinking. He was right, and I'd been foolish to think otherwise. In Victory, the love people bore my mother had sheltered me from shame, but nowhere else would I find such protection.

Judah watched me intently. He was hatless, and the prairie wind played in his dark curls—shorter than they had been but still abundant—as if it, too, were enamored of his beauty.

"Except, of course, if you marry a man who would claim Sarah as his own. She is very young—she could soon learn to call a man Papa. If we were to become one, Nell, I would forgive you. I would shelter you from the consequences of your past transgressions."

For a moment, relief and even gratitude washed over me. A solution—one that would give Sarah a name and make her respectable in the eyes of the world. And then common sense reasserted itself.

"My money, of course, has a great deal to do with your willingness to marry me."

Judah laughed, tossing back his head in apparent delight. "Thank heaven for a woman who knows a good bargain when she sees one. Yes, Nell, I've already told you I can't afford to marry a poor woman."

"So you don't love me." I said it with conviction.

Judah's brows drew together. "I'm not sure if I have the capacity to love, if by that word you mean the kind of romantic nonsense in novels. The emotions seem to have escaped me somehow. I'm guided by logic and rationality. Of course, if you'd like me to woo you, I could do that—rather effectively."

There was something in the way he looked at me that sent a shiver down my spine. "And I would never stray from the marriage bed, because other women would mean—do mean—nothing to me. A wife who was willing to put her future into my hands would be prized above rubies, Nell, especially a handsome and intelligent one. I admire you tremendously, you know." And for a moment, I felt the touch of a finger on the soft inner skin of my wrist below my glove.

"A bargain." I stared downward, watching my delicate boots—it was a dry day—appear and reappear from beneath my skirts.

"A marriage. One that would make us a force to be reckoned with. Cam Calderwood—" He stopped, as if he were unsure whether to proceed.

"What about Dr. Calderwood?"

Judah smiled again. "Dr. Cameron Calderwood thinks highly of me. I've been a great help to him in making a success of this place—making it more than poor, misguided Dr. Adema ever dreamed. And one day, Nell, that may mean our partnership will not be entirely unequal. Cam Calderwood has no children, you may recall. Nor brothers, nor sisters, nor sisters- or brothers-in-law, nor cousins of any degree. He and Mrs. C. are quite without heirs."

I frowned. "He'd give you—"

Judah lifted a hand. "Oh no, not *give*. Mrs. Calderwood never gives anything for nothing. The land and the seminary building are hers. The denomination has a substantial interest in the property, but that should not pose too great an obstacle. I've been of enough service," his lips pursed as if he were savoring a delightful memory, "that the price would be most favorable. A bagatelle to you, of course, given the extent of your wealth. But it would mean a great deal to me to own this place. I've worked hard for it."

I must have still looked puzzled because Judah placed a hand under my elbow, barely touching my sleeve.

"That might not happen for another five years, of course." He glanced briefly at the seminary building as he turned me to face him, and his voice became a caress. "But I wouldn't wait five years to marry you, Nell. I would be eager to wipe out your past mistakes for you. We would present a united front to the world, and nobody could touch us."

Over Judah's shoulder, I could see the windows of the seminary building reflecting the sky like blind mirrors, the row of stained-glass windows dark and blank by comparison. The great building glowed in the orange light of the afternoon sun, its gray slate roofs reflecting flame-like glints. Could I really make this place my permanent home? I wondered. And what would it be like with Judah in charge of it?

We walked on and talked no more of love or marriage. I didn't think we had reached an understanding—at least there was no understanding on my part—but Judah had the satisfied air of a man who had successfully overcome an important obstacle.

He handed me into the hallway with something of a show, bowing elaborately to Mrs. Drummond, who happened just at that moment to emerge from the passage that led to the housekeeper's rooms. She stared—hard—at the two of us, and then proceeded at a fast pace toward the kitchens, her back stiff as a board.

"I'll take my leave of you," Judah said, "and make myself presentable for dinner." And before I could reply, he was heading upstairs, his footsteps almost inaudible on the staircase.

I was going to climb the staircase myself, but something made me look round. There was Professor Wale, coming from the short row of classrooms that occupied the space alongside the stairs. Some of those classrooms, I knew, had windows that commanded a view of the area where Judah and I had been walking. The professor had no doubt seen us.

I hesitated at the sight of his pale scholar's face, half-hidden by the gloom lit here and there by a beam of light filled with chalky dust. He looked old and tired, the shadows accentuating the hollows under his eyes, the deep grooves that ran from nose to mouth, the shabbiness of his academic robe. I waited for him to speak to me, but he only shook his head slowly as he passed, the dust motes whirling in the air above his cap as he made his solemn way toward the refectory.

22

CURIOSITY

It was, in fact, two more days before Professor Wale spoke a word to me. I was idly reading the notices on the boards fastened to the paneled side of the great staircase—mostly examination results and notices of lost articles—when a voice spoke in my ear.

"I have talked with Poulton."

I jumped and turned, almost colliding with the professor. "You could have announced yourself a little less dramatically." I put a hand to my chest, feeling the rapid beat of my heart.

Professor Wale held up his hands in a gesture of apology and smiled at me for the first time in days.

"Pray forgive me. My mind was full of my news, and I forgot my manners."

I shook my head to indicate the matter was of little import. "What did he say?"

Professor Wale's brow wrinkled in a puzzled frown under his cap. "He denied nothing of what was in the letter. Admitted nothing either, come to think of it. He just sat there with that smug little smile on his face and listened, then told me that nothing in his past had to do with his present circumstances."

I felt a stab of curiosity but damped it down. If I were to hear the tale of Judah, it would not be from the professor.

"I told him I should inform the Calderwoods of what I had learned," the professor continued. "He said I was welcome to do so. He said that it would make no difference to his position whether the Calderwoods listened to gossip—he called it gossip—or not. I asked him if he'd repented and made amends; he assured me that the state of his soul was perfectly satisfactory. In short, he was damnably calm about the whole thing. He even put a hand on my shoulder," the professor twitched one shoulder in memory, "and told me I had better things to worry about than him."

"It doesn't sound as if—whatever it is could have been all that important."

"Hmph." Professor Wale tugged his cap down so that it settled more firmly on his head. "He's pulled my fangs, and no mistake. All that work to find that pompous English lawyer—and I still don't know whether I should speak to Cam Calderwood or chuck the infernal thing in the fire."

He glared at me in a theatrical manner, the shadows under his eyes deeper than ever. "And as for you—I wish you had more curiosity and fewer principles. But I can scarcely saddle you with a burden you refuse to carry."

"Oh, I'm not lacking in curiosity."

A group of students passed us; I smiled and wished them a good morning. They rewarded my greeting with a shower of "ma'ams" and tipped hats. They left a feral smell behind them to which I had, by now, become quite accustomed.

"Well," the professor continued, "should you wish to seek elucidation, the letter will remain in its hiding place, and you may remove it whenever you wish."

I nodded. "I think I'm rather hoping Ju—Mr. Poulton will

tell me about whatever it is, himself. When the time is right."

"Before you marry, I hope."

"We have no plans to marry at present. So I have plenty of time."

A rueful smile appeared on the professor's face. "So thinks every man until he looks up from his preoccupations one day and finds that time has slipped through his fingers. I swear to you, Mrs. Lillington, that they have been shortening every year of this last decade by two weeks without telling me, so quickly do the days seem to flash by." My laugh brought a light to his eyes now rarely seen.

"Here we are indeed, nearly at Thanksgiving," the professor continued. "And I understand you're not to spend it with us."

"No, we're not." I couldn't hide my smile of anticipation. "Tess, Sarah, and I are going across the plains to the Lombardi mission. Tess and I have decided that Sarah is old enough not to make the trip a misery, and we're all looking forward to the change. It'll do Sarah good to see some other children."

WE LEFT THE LOMBARDI MISSION TWO DAYS AFTER Thanksgiving, by which time I had revised my ideas about the benefits of introducing Sarah to other children. It was enlightening to watch my daughter attempt to fit the existence of the homesteaders' small children into a world that, by every evidence, had hitherto revolved around *her*. And she had immediately caught a cold, which meant we had to keep her away from Lucy, who suffered badly from wheezing and bronchitis.

It had not been a cheering visit despite all the efforts of Catherine and her husband. The loss of their capital during the financial panic had left them entirely dependent on the stipend paid to the pastor by his denomination and the gifts brought to the mission by grateful farmers and their wives. As the homesteads were spread around a vast area, the population was not large, and the Lombardis also fed a shifting crew of itinerant cowpokes and half-breeds—who seemed otherwise to exist on air—in return for a few hours' work at the mission.

They were all thin, and the shabbiness of their clothing made me bite my lip and wish I had loaded up the cart with bolts of cloth. In the end, I secured Catherine's promise to visit the seminary with the children for the express purpose of sewing them a new wardrobe. Persuading the woman who had once been my benefactor to accept my help had been a bitter struggle.

Sarah had antagonized Thea by her refusal to accept orders from a twelve-year-old. Since Thea assisted her mother with the mission's small school, such a loss of authority hit her hard. To make matters worse, Sarah decided to lavish her adoration on Teddy and clung to him like a limpet when we said our good-byes.

"When is Teddy coming to the seminary?" she asked as the pastor's wagon creaked and jolted along the dirt trail. "Why didn't he come back with us?"

"He's needed at the mission," I pointed out.

"Why doesn't he come and be a student? The other boys don't have to work."

I glanced toward the front of the wagon, where the pastor sat on the bench next to a stringy plainsman named Zeke, who smelled like a dead fish. "Teddy will attend the seminary later, perhaps."

The idea of trying to persuade Judah to make a non-paying place for Teddy flitted across my mind, but I had my doubts about the likelihood of success.

"When are we going to get there?" Sarah clambered to her feet and hung on to the back flap of the wagon. We had been heading east for a few hours, and the dying sunset's brilliant tones lit up the inside of our traveling conveyance and struck sparks of fire from Sarah's hair.

"It'll be dark by the time we do. Do you need to use the pot again?" Sarah was bouncing vigorously up and down on her toes.

"No."

"Then sit down, darling. You'll fall over."

"No, I won't."

I sighed and tried to make myself more comfortable. Our wagon was only covered as far forward as the bench, leaving the front hoop bare. As the eastern sky had grown quite dark, the pastor had lit his lamp, so I could see the shapes of the two men up front. An explosive sound with which I had, by now, become familiar informed me that Zeke had spat tobacco juice neatly under the horses' hooves again. Zeke had accompanied us because he needed to travel to Wichita, and this would "get him a fur piece" along the way.

Their conversation had ranged over wheat and rabbits, rattlesnakes, the grasshopper plague that had done so much damage to the crops in the summer, politics in Abilene and the Indian wars far to the west. Pastor Lombardi had been obliged to curb some of Zeke's more colorful stories at intervals by hissing "The women! The women!" For the moment though, both men were silent. We had been going since before dawn with occasional stops to rest the horses and provide for our own bodily comfort, and we were all exhausted—all, it seemed, except the jiggling child in my immediate vicinity. I groaned and looked with envy at Tess, who had long since rolled herself into a blanket and fallen asleep.

"Momma!"

"What is it, dear?" I had just started to drift off to sleep.

"I need the pot."

I groaned again and, after a few moments' undignified scrambling, located the necessary object and helped Sarah to ensconce herself on it. I held up the blanket I employed to protect my daughter's privacy and prepared for the onslaught on my ears.

It wasn't long in coming.

"Darewing young MAAAN onna tra-PEEEEZE . . . Gerrrr-atest of FEEEEEASE . . . Onna tra-PEEEEEEZE . . ."

I was beginning to wish that the daring young man had never thought to take to the flying trapeze. Sarah, who did not normally eat much, had consumed five whole biscuits, about a pound of leftover wild turkey, and most of our water. These evidences of the beneficial effects of fresh air and travel had led to many command performances of the daring young man, with occasional variations on the theme of "HooRAH! Hooooo-RAH! Jooooooooo-beeeee-leeeee." Zeke, a Union veteran, had taught Sarah "Marching Through Georgia" during our midday meal.

It had been Thea who suggested to Sarah that singing as she did her business would cover the noises inherent in using an enameled pot. Why had that been the one instruction Sarah had taken to heart?

It had become quite dark outside. "Are we close to the seminary, Pastor, do you think?" I had to raise my voice to make myself heard above the song.

"Kin see the seminary by its lights," Zeke answered laconically. "Fur way off though. Like seein' through the wrong end of a spyglass."

I sighed with relief, especially when I felt the wagon turn. We must have met the trail that led from Springwood to the seminary, having bypassed the town itself. Soon we'd be in our own beds, with an end to this interminable rocking and jolting.

The song came to an end, and I watched as Sarah dealt with the restoration of her clothing before dropping the blanket and picking up the pot. I would have to empty it off the back of the wagon—I wasn't going to ask the men to stop this late in the journey.

"I'm hungry, Momma."

"We've eaten all the food. But we'll be back at the seminary soon, and I'm sure we can find something."

I crawled over the boards, managing with difficulty to keep my balance while tugging at my skirts and petticoats with one hand and making sure not to tip the pot.

Sarah sighed and put her blanket down next to Tess, turning around and around like a dog to find a comfortable spot. I experienced the certainty that every mother of a young child knows—that after staying awake for the entire journey, Sarah would be fast asleep upon arrival, and I would have to carry her up flight after flight of stairs.

I at last managed to hang out of the back of the wagon, the canvas cover and its drawstring catching at my hair. The pastor had lit a second lamp, and the swaying light picked out strange shadows in the humps and hollows of dried grass along the trailside, illuminating—

I let out a shriek and dropped the pot, which hit the ground with a dull chinking sound. Sarah started up in fear, shouting, "Momma!"

I yelled again, scrambling toward the front of the wagon. Zeke was pulling on the reins, muttering, "Slow up, slow up now," as the pastor twisted around to face me. I grabbed the bench and hauled myself up, nearly tipping the two men backward until Zeke threw himself forward as a counterbalance.

"What is it?" The pastor's voice competed with Sarah's

shrill, tired whine and Tess's startled exclamations as she awoke.

I took several deep breaths, trying to control the trembling in my lower limbs. "I saw—it was—" I swallowed awry and coughed for a few seconds. "A man. A face. Lying in the grass."

Pastor Lombardi put one of his big hands over mine. Despite the cold air, he felt warm, solid, and comforting.

"A trick of the light, Nell. We didn't see anything."

"I was much closer to the ground than you are. And the light picked out the face perfectly." So perfectly that I had recognized it, but I didn't want to say. I wanted to be sure. "It's sort of half-hidden between two big clumps of grass."

"Very well." The wagon had stopped, and the pastor reached for the rifle that hung by its shoulder strap on a hook sunk into the bench. I felt Zeke shove the brake forward, and then the bench swayed on its springs as the two men clambered down, each to his side.

"Hold on to Sarah." I gave my daughter a brief hug and consigned her to Tess. "I think there's been an accident of some kind," I said in Tess's ear. "Don't let her look."

But I needn't have worried. Sarah was rubbing her eyes and burrowing her face into Tess's soft bosom, making small sounds of sleepy annoyance.

I pushed at the canvas at the back of the wagon, cursing my skirt and petticoats. How was I going to get down without help?

A shout from Zeke made me stick my head out farther, and the canvas caught at my hairpins, dragging some loose. I saw movement—had I been mistaken and he had only fainted?

The pastor's rifle barked, and Sarah gave a small yelp. In the combination of lamplight and starlight, I saw three or four pale shapes loping off through the grass—coyotes.

I curled my hands around the gate flap in frustration. The men had taken the lamps and I could see them swaying about forty yards off, silhouetting Zeke and the pastor as they stood deep in discussion.

I stamped my foot and marched to the front of the wagon, where the horses stood peacefully nosing into what grass they could find. I sat on the flare board, grabbed the uncovered hoop to help me balance, lowered myself until my foot encountered the gear, and launched myself forward. I landed in an ungainly sprawl on the lumpy grass, the memory of my fall from the sleigh vivid as the slender stems whipped at my bare wrists.

Righting myself, I headed toward the lights. I was suddenly aware of the vast emptiness all around us. I could see a faint glimmer that must be the seminary, but it seemed a great distance away. In the still night, my breath formed a thick cloud of moisture, and I shivered.

The men's voices drifted to me as I approached.

". . . with the rifle. We can't expect two women and a child to wait on the prairie."

"I kud light a fire, I s'pose. Got to find me a few stalks an' all, an' tear up a circle so's I don't burn up the blamed prairie and the corpus with it. If it's got to be me as waits." Zeke sounded sulky but resigned. "Lonely work standin' sentry over a corpus, Pastor. With wolves an' Injuns and haints an' all. Supposin' the redskins what shot him come back?"

"Now then, Zeke." The pastor's voice was firm. "A Christian man's got no business thinking about ghosts. And who says it was Indians who shot him?"

"Who says it ain't?"

My foot hit something with a dull clang, and Zeke, who had taken possession of the rifle, raised it to his shoulder.

"It's me," I said quickly.

"What the he—what the Sam Hill you doin' out the wagon, Miz Lillington?"

The object my foot had encountered turned out to be the pot. With a sigh of resignation, I hooked a fastidious finger into the handle and lifted it. We might be here for a while.

"It's Professor Wale, isn't it?" My voice wasn't steady.

"Ain't acquainted," Zeke replied. "Whoever it was, he's dead right enough. Clean shot, right through the back o' his noddle." He indicated a spot on the back of his skull, his dead-fish smell wafting over me as the breeze shifted. "Fresh, too. Them ki-yotes only got in a bite or two."

I walked past him.

"You ain't wantin' to look, ma'am. Tain't pretty."

"I've seen worse." I set my jaw and looked.

No, it wasn't pretty. His eyes were wide open as if in astonishment, filmed by death—and did there have to be insects? It was cold but there was no frost. Flies and ants, attracted by the blood, crawled over the professor's face and feasted on the sticky, black-looking mess of gore and brains that had gushed from an opening near the crown, running into the wiry black hair. One hand still clutched a silk hat. The professor was unusually well dressed, I realized, as if he had been dining. The other hand showed evidence of the coyotes' work, as did the tears in the well-cut pantaloons and spats.

There's a world of difference between seeing, up close, the body of a stranger and that of someone you have known, have laughed and talked with. I felt the hot tears well up in my eyes and slide down my cheek. The pastor drew me close, patting my head as if I were one of his children. He had set the lamp down to do so, and the light shone directly on the professor's face.

"Why?" was all I could say. But I was horribly afraid I knew.

23
ACCUSATION

We drove the rest of the way to the seminary in near silence, leaving Zeke to stand guard over the body until Pastor Lombardi could send for the sheriff. According to Tess, Sarah had cried and asked a thousand questions about why I had left the wagon, but by the time the pastor helped me climb back in, she had succumbed to exhaustion. In the end, it was the pastor who carried my profoundly asleep daughter up the wearisome flights of stairs to our room, but not before sending a servant to Springwood for the lawmen.

I hadn't expected to sleep, but I closed my eyes on the picture of the professor lying cold on the prairie and opened them to a dull, gray morning with gusts of drizzle falling from the lowering clouds.

I had slept so long that Tess was already awake and dressed, brushing out her fine, fair hair by the window as she sat with her legs folded up under her skirts to keep her feet off the cold boards.

"Where's Sarah?" I looked around the room, expecting to see the blaze of red hair.

"Bella came to fetch her earlier." Bella was Dorcas's daughter, a pleasant, thoughtful girl who frequently offered us little services as a way of breaking up the monotony of her day. "She said she'd give Sary a special breakfast in the kitchen and keep her out of our way while we recover from our journey."

"That's nice." I yawned, shivered as my feet touched the floor, then sat up straight as a thought struck me. "I hope Sarah won't be down there listening to the servants talk about the—the professor." For I knew the details of the poor man's grisly death would already be well known to the servants, who always seemed to know everything.

"Dorcas won't let them talk in front of Sary." Tess leaned forward to look out of the window. "There's men coming, look."

I crossed to the window and leaned over Tess. A straggling group of men—homesteaders and men from Springwood, to judge by their clothes—were approaching from the west, a few on horseback but most on foot. They hadn't come from the direction of Springwood—had they been scouring the prairie for Zeke's redskins? Most of them carried rifles.

"I wonder where they took Professor Wale?" I thought out loud.

"To the undertaker's house in Springwood, I expect," said Tess. "I asked Bella—I whispered, Nell, while Sary was getting dressed—if they brought the professor back here last night, and she said no. She said the professor dined at the house of Mr. Joseph Lehmann last night, and he must have been walking back since the weather was so fine yesterday."

I frowned. "Was Reiner there too? Did you ask?"

Tess's expression took on a look of concentrated excitement, and she hissed, "Nobody knows where Reiner was last night, Nell. He was in Springwood, but not at his uncle's—he said he walked around the town, but nobody saw him. He was in his room this morning."

Of course, because of Thanksgiving the students had a three-day holiday—there would have been no classes on Friday or Saturday. It was now Sunday, and—

"Heavens, chapel!" I exclaimed. "What time is it?"

Tess shook her head. "There's to be no morning chapel, but everyone has to attend in the afternoon. Dr. Calderwood has been to Springwood in the cart already, with Mr. Poulton. I don't know if they're back yet."

I slumped against the window frame. "I feel like I've missed half the day already. I'll hurry and dress, and then let's go see if we can find out what's happening."

UPON AWAKENING, MY MIND HAD BEEN CLEAR AND DETACHED, fastening, as it so often did, on the practicalities of the day rather than on the tragedy of the day before. But by the time I was pushing the last pins into my hair, my head seethed with questions and possibilities. The image of the professor's body was constantly before my eyes, so that on several occasions I quite forgot what I was doing.

Perhaps, as Zeke had suggested, it really had been a party of Indians. In our great building and its satellite town of Springwood, provided as they were with many of the luxuries and conveniences of civilization, it was easy to forget that battles were raging not so many days' ride from us. The Comanche and the Kiowa had attacked settlers and buffalo hunters a few days to the south and west of us in the summer, and all through the fall there had been rumors of groups of either hunters or warriors sighted on the plains around us. A lone man on the prairie, with no firearm—for the professor never carried a gun—would be an easy target.

We had intended to go straight down to the kitchen, but a hubbub coming from the second floor arrested our attention. With no more than a mutual glance, Tess and I darted in the direction from which the sounds were proceeding.

"Bastard! You bastard!"

The enraged howl came from the library, the door of which was open and which was crammed full of students and teachers. The air was a rank fug of male scents, a top note of tension and fear sharpening the atmosphere so that I could almost capture the tang of it on my tongue.

We pushed, barely noticed, through the crowd. At its center was, as I had expected from the voice, Reiner Lehmann, bright red with fury. The Springwood sheriff and two of his men stood to one side, their faces unreadable.

"You unspeakable bastard!" I realized Reiner was addressing Judah, who faced him squarely, no sign of emotion in his mien or posture. "You've set this up. I don't know why or how, but I know it's you."

"Of course it wasn't me." Judah's gaze flicked to me and then to a group of teachers who stood in front of a milling crowd of students. "I have nothing against you, Lehmann—nothing at all now."

And his glance strayed back in my direction. There were smirks from one or two of the older students, but they died under Judah's withering looks.

"Yes, we've had our disagreements," Judah continued, "but they've been minor ones—the sort of thing that must happen from time to time in a community such as this. And to accuse me of causing Professor Wale's death is ridiculous. You know very well, as does everyone else, that I spent the whole of yesterday afternoon writing in this library, in full view of several people—and that I didn't retire until ten o'clock, well after the professor's body was found. Another fact that any number of those present observed."

There were nods and murmurs of agreement from the assembled teachers and from some of the students. Well, at least that answered one of the questions that had been scratching at the surface of my mind. Did anyone else know that Professor Wale had been threatening to expose some kind of secret about Judah? I tried hard not to look at the row of Greek texts that concealed the letter's hiding place.

"And it was your rifle they found a quarter mile from the professor's body. The one your father sent you in the summer, that you were so fond of showing off," Judah continued in the ringing tones of an inquisitor. "Can you explain how it got there?"

"No, I damn well can't." Reiner looked as if he would strike Judah at any moment. "But I can only think of one slimy bastard who'd be likely to creep around and steal it from me for his own purposes."

Judah drew a deep breath and looked over at the sheriff, who nodded.

"First of all," Judah returned his attention to Reiner, "I beg you to modify your language. To speak such profanities in the presence of ladies is unpardonable."

I realized that Mrs. Calderwood was also there, clinging —most unusually—to her husband's arm.

"And second, throwing accusations at me will not dispel the force of the evidence against you. You can't prove where you were. I can."

"Could still have been Injuns," said one of the men from Springwood. "Bullet was just one of those like you get from the mercantile, and plenty of us have Winchesters—the braves too. His was just purtied up with some fancy scroll-work." A look passed between him and the other men that showed what they thought of Reiner's gun.

"So why'd I leave it on the prairie for everyone to find?" Reiner's voice was high and indignant. "What kind of numbskull would shoot a man and leave his gun lying around as evidence?"

I wriggled to the front of the crowd, as close to Reiner—and, because of our relative positions, to Judah—as possible.

"Nell." For the first time since Mrs. Drummond had told him about Sarah's birth, Reiner looked me directly in the eyes with his old, frank expression, his eyes showing a bright, guileless blue against the high color in his face. "You know I didn't do it, don't you? You know I wouldn't. I didn't like the old—the professor—but I wouldn't harm him."

I looked at him for a long moment, and then nodded. "I believe you, Reiner."

"So will you come quietly?" the sheriff asked, seeing a look of calm descend over Reiner's young face. "This isn't a lynching party, young man. We won't hang you without giving you a good chance to explain yourself."

I felt the blood drain from my head at the sudden realization that for Reiner, this could be a matter of life and death. But common sense told me that he could hardly fight or flee. He was trapped, and he would have to comply.

"Go with them, Reiner," I said. And turning to the sheriff, I asked, "Will you tell his uncle straightaway?"

"We already did." The sheriff was also the land surveyor, a steady man in his late thirties with a pleasant wife—for whom I'd made a day dress—and assorted small children. He gave me a reassuring nod. "Don't worry, ma'am, we're not about to be hasty. We'll give the lad his chance."

Students began to stream out of the library doors as Reiner was led forth between the two sheriff's men, neither of whom held on to him.

"You acted bravely, Nell," Judah said into my ear. "I find more qualities to admire in you every day."

"Do you think he actually did it?" Somehow I was not all that impressed by Judah's evaluation of my qualities.

Judah shrugged. "I don't know. I don't understand the business with the rifle, and I don't see what Lehmann was doing wandering around the prairie at night. Maybe it *was* Indians—and maybe we'll never know at all." He smiled. "All I know is, *I* didn't shoot the man."

"Did you see him?" Tess had waited to ask since my return from Springwood because Sarah was in the workroom with us, but the moment the door closed behind my daughter, she positively pounced on me. Sarah was so near to four years old that I now allowed her to make specific journeys around the building as long as she promised not to stray.

"I did not." I stretched my stockinged feet out toward our small fire. We were sparing with our scarce firewood, but the walk to Springwood and back over a waterlogged trail had made this small luxury necessary.

"I saw his uncle," I continued after a few moments, during which Tess fidgeted. "But Reiner is no longer in Springwood—they moved him to Abilene. Of course, his uncle asked me all sorts of questions since it was I who spotted the—the professor, but I couldn't help him a great deal."

"Why has he gone to Abilene? That's a bad place, isn't it?" Tess's brow furrowed in consternation.

"Because Springwood doesn't have a jail, Mr. Lehmann said. He didn't seem all that concerned about it. He told me he was sure there was enough doubt about Reiner's guilt that he could get him freed."

I moved my boots a little closer to the fire. "I wish I could feel so confident—but Reiner's uncle is a lawyer and understands these things."

Tess came over to me, draping her arm over my shoulders

and bestowing a light kiss on my forehead. "You look so worried, Nell. And tired. You look like you didn't sleep."

"I *am* worried and tired. And no, I didn't sleep well." Lacking the utter exhaustion that had ensured a night's sleep when we returned from the Lombardis', I had spent the previous night haunted by the memory of the professor's bloodied face and staring, insect-infested eyes. And what sleep I managed was beset by nightmares about Reiner standing with a rope around his neck, waiting for the drop into oblivion.

"I'll go to the kitchen," Tess said briskly. "Netta's sure to give me some nice, hot drink for you, and then tonight you must go to bed straight after supper."

I patted the small, plump hand that lay on my shoulder. "You're the most wonderful sister I could ever dream of," I said. "But I have to stay up late tonight. I have something to do."

24
RELEASE

Naturally, I'd had to wait until all the lamps in the library were extinguished, but I'd thought to bring the little shaded candleholder Tess and I used for nighttime contingencies.

The building was completely silent, and every creak of the stairs sounded as loud as a gunshot to my ears. My heart thumped so loudly I thought I'd wake the entire building. But now that the professor was dead, it seemed urgent that I retrieve his legacy to me, even if I didn't read the letter he'd kept hidden all these months.

Anyone who approached the library would see my light, of course. The glass-paned doors had no curtains I could close. But by the same token, I would see them by the light they held—and the distinctive click of the library doors would leave me in no uncertainty if someone entered the room.

I closed the doors with care, making sure they were tightly latched, and then proceeded to my work.

The candle wasn't bright in its pierced tin holder, so I had to feel my way through barely seen shadows of furniture, holding my breath in case I stumbled over a chair leg or caught my foot in a rug. The room had not been well aired, probably because of the pouring rain the day before. The taint of sweat still hung in its atmosphere, faintly acrid, a memory of the fraught scene of Reiner's arrest.

Only when I knew I was near the bookcase in which the professor had secreted the letter did I open the little door of my candleholder to its widest position. It took me a moment to realize I'd misjudged where I was—how easy to become lost in darkness! I was two bookcases over from my imagined position. I held the candle high, scanning for the right books, brushing my hand over the edge of the shelves to be sure of my path.

There they were, unmistakable. The indecipherable Greek lettering gleamed gold on the spines of the heavy, red-bound tomes. I set the candleholder on a nearby table and pulled out the first five volumes one by one, surprised by how heavy they were.

My hands shook as I fumbled for the loose piece of wood. For a moment, I thought I'd mistaken the location, so well did it fit into place, but finally my fingertips encountered a minute break in the smooth case. I pushed on the upper edge the way Professor Wale had shown me. Nothing happened; I pushed again, harder this time, and to my relief I felt the wood tilt back. I wiggled it until I was able to maneuver the wood out of its hole.

"You could have done this when you weren't so tired, you know," I grumbled to myself under my breath, angry at how ridiculously fast my heart was beating. I would probably not sleep this night either. Taking a deep breath, I thrust my fingers into the space—and found it empty.

A few minutes' frantic rummaging and close inspection, bringing the candle as near as I dared to the dry wood, convinced me that the letter was indeed gone. The professor might have taken it before he died, of course; had anyone searched his room? What exactly would they do with his belongings?

I replaced the piece of wood and the books and blew out the candle. I stood still for a few minutes in the dark, inhaling the scents of smoke and hot wax, allowing my eyes to become re-accustomed to the darkness—and thinking.

"I should have read the blasted letter while I had the chance," I said aloud to myself. But had I intended to read it or burn it? I didn't know.

I eased the muscles of my back as much as I could, feeling the pressure of a corset that I'd been wearing for too many hours. I should get some rest, I told myself, if not sleep. I willed my leaden limbs to move forward and fumbled my way to the door, guided by the faint light from the hall. I pulled it open and stepped out of the library.

"Can't you sleep?"

My heart contracted so violently that I felt pins and needles in my fingers, even though I knew the voice well.

"Judah, you scared the living daylights out of me. What are you doing here?"

"I think I should ask the same of you." Judah's voice was filled with amusement. "Why don't you use the candle you're holding?"

Could he see in the dark? Obviously, I couldn't tell him what I'd been doing.

"I figured I could find my way back upstairs without disturbing anyone. And no, I couldn't sleep. I've had a bad couple of nights."

"Are you worried about Reiner Lehmann? I know you went to Springwood, and I can guess you tried to visit him there. You're far kinder than the boy deserves, Nell."

By concentrating hard, I could see Judah's face as a pale blur in the darkness.

"They moved him to Abilene."

"I know."

"And what were you doing, wandering around the building in the dark?" I asked, unwilling to continue to talk about Reiner.

"In fact, I was wandering around *outside* the building. I was just beginning to wonder if I've left a trail of muddy footprints in the hallway—that will infuriate Mrs. Drummond. But with the professor murdered and all these reports of Indians and rough vagrants around the prairie, I felt restless and wanted to reassure myself that there was nobody on the grounds."

"Without a lamp?" Judah had taken my arm, and I felt a change in the air as he opened the door that led to the staircase. Now I could see him in the light of the lamp that always burned at the foot of the stairs, placed over a pan of water in case it tipped over.

"I see well in the dark, and a lamp only lights one small area. If you wish to see best outdoors, starlight and moonlight are sufficient companions, and I'm sure-footed enough not to fall."

Sure-footed he certainly was. And sure of himself, in every way—it was part of the attraction of the man, the air of assurance and authority he carried around with him. I shivered.

"Are you cold, Nell?" Judah's arms came around me, barely touching, and if anything, the shiver intensified.

"No." The word came out abruptly. "I'm frightened for Reiner. I wish I could have seen him."

"He'll be safe enough in Abilene's stone jail, safe from the lynching element of Springwood. Until he hangs."

I started violently at that, stepping backward out of Judah's arms. The movement brought me perilously close to the top of the stairs, and I teetered for a second until Judah recaptured me—tighter this time. I had never been so close to him, I realized. I could feel his heart beating, slow and steady, and smell the peppermint on his breath.

"Hangs?" I choked out when I could draw breath. "But Judah, they can't—he didn't—"

"The evidence is against him." I felt Judah's lips brush my forehead, and my treacherous body flooded with warmth despite my agitation. "And yet, I'm inclined to think he didn't do it either. I wonder what really happened?" Judah sounded merely curious, as if the affair were a newspaper item from far away.

"I must go to Abilene. I don't—I can't see what difference I'll make, but I must do something to help him. I can't stand idly by while a man is accused of something he didn't do."

"It's not seemly for a woman to meddle in such matters. Do you really think the Abilene sheriff will listen to a seamstress from a seminary?"

Judah brought his hands round to mine, running his fingertips over my back and waist as he did so, and imprisoned my hands in his, raising them to his lips. I felt the tickle of his beard, surprisingly wiry, and his mouth felt warm on my chilled palms.

"But I will go in your stead, if you wish." Judah's cool, slim fingers curled around mine. "After all, I entertain hopes of one day being in a position to guide and protect you. As I've already said. Would you consent to make me your protector, Nell?" He raised my hands to his lips again and then kissed me on the mouth, somewhat harder than he had done before.

I closed my eyes but soon opened them again and drew back—it was so strange, him wooing me on the seminary's staircase in the nighttime. Besides, my conscious brain had just caught up with what Judah had said.

"Did you just ask me to marry you, Judah?"

"I suppose I did." The amusement was back in Judah's

voice, or had it ever left? "Your promise would mean a great deal to me, Nell." He drew me closer to him again, and my skin warmed. I was so tired, and the night was so dark, and Judah's very presence seemed overwhelming, as if it would be wrong to be thinking of anything or anyone else. For an instant, I almost gave in to the temptation to let Judah take control of my life—

But no. "It's the wrong time to ask me, Judah," I said, making a feeble attempt to free myself from his arms—where, in truth, my physical self was perfectly content to remain. "So many dreadful things have happened—how can I think of marriage?"

"The dreadful things have nothing to do with us, Nell."

How I wished I could believe that. My mind was abuzz with emotions and sensations that seemed to be no longer under my control, but I still had an overriding sense that I dared not make a hasty decision.

"And there's so much more to talk about, Judah. Sarah and Tess—"

"Sarah and Tess will be guided by you as you are guided by me. They are children—they can have no say in their lot in life."

"Tess isn't a child." I felt a stab of annoyance.

"Tess is an imbecile and must therefore be treated as a child." Judah planted a final kiss on my lips and let me go. "But you're right; this is neither the time nor the place to talk of such things. You're tired, and you should go to bed. There's nothing to fear, Nell."

"There's everything to fear." I tried hard to focus on the essentials. "A man's life is at stake, Judah. If there's a possibility that Reiner might hang, I must do everything in my power to ensure that the truth prevails."

I climbed up a few steps and then turned round as a thought struck me. Judah's face was in shadow, the faint light of the distant lamp touching the edges of his hair with an orange glow. "After all, I have money. Why shouldn't I pay for a Pinkerton agent to investigate Reiner's case—to find out what his rifle was doing out on the prairie, for example? I'll go back to Springwood tomorrow and set matters in train."

"Nell." Judah's voice was soft, caressing. "You're too good. But would you let me talk to the Springwood sheriff first? I may not have your means, but I am a man. They will listen to me."

I nodded wearily, too tired to argue. "Very well, Judah. But I won't hesitate to take action if Reiner is still in danger by the end of the week."

JUDAH WAS AS GOOD AS HIS WORD. HE SET OFF INTO THE NEXT day's frost and ice—for a cold spell had swept in overnight to freeze the rain-soaked plains into crackling hardness—to talk with the Springwood sheriff.

The visit culminated in the departure of both men for Abilene. The study of the Old Testament was sadly neglected at the seminary for an entire week until Judah returned, triumphant. They had not exactly declared Reiner innocent, but they had released him. The Abilene newspapers spoke of the doubts raised by his uncle's legal skill, Reiner's protestations of innocence and general demeanor, and "information received."

And yet—Reiner had not returned to the seminary. Judah was silent on exactly what had transpired, informing me with a smile that it wasn't a woman's province to inquire into such things. Yet I did discover that Reiner had gone to his father in Saint Louis after a promise not to return to Eternal Life.

And that was that. I would have set off to talk to Reiner's uncle again if it were not for the early blizzard that swept in on the heels of Judah's return. It blanketed the prairie with snow that, over the next few days, thawed and refroze into a treacherous carapace of ice that made excursions well-nigh impossible.

Life at the seminary settled back into its routine, punctuated by increasingly unvaried meals as the servants drew on the winter food stores. The topic of Professor Wale's death was all too soon abandoned as a mere example of the dangers that roamed the frontier.

And I? I didn't have the letter the professor had so wanted me to read. I had no way of knowing whether it even still existed or whether somebody had thrown it in the fire. I had no contact with Martin, the snow making the sending and receiving of letters impossible. I settled down for winter with the strange impression that I had nothing left to me—nothing except Sarah, Tess, and Judah.

PART IV
1875

25
ANTICIPATION

"I'm not sure if you realize the amount of work involved in having a house built."

Judah leaned over my shoulder to look at the unfolded plat I'd spread across one of the tables in the library. It showed an area near the center of Springwood. "This seems like a hasty decision, Nell."

"I've been thinking of it all winter," I protested. "Mr. Shemmeld put the idea to me just after Christmas when I visited his wife."

And now it was March, and the notion of moving out of the seminary had begun to dominate my dreams. "Of course, he proposed a small house—he thought I merely had the money I've earned from dressmaking—but it does seem like a sound idea. And I don't have to build right away. I can buy the plot of land and build at my leisure. After all, prices are rising all the time, so the sooner the better."

"But if you married me, we'd live at the seminary." Judah's smooth eyebrows contracted. "As the Calderwoods do. I wouldn't wish to live off the premises. I would want to oversee the daily life of the seminary."

"I've never had a house of my own, Judah. I owned my mother's house for such a short time before I had to sell it." I refolded the plat. "Even if we get married, could I not pass the last months of my spinsterhood in my own house? My dressmaking business would be much easier to run if I were closer to my clients. And Sarah is four now, and Springwood has a little school she could attend—I'm a poor teacher, and she's so fond of learning."

"If you were my wife, you wouldn't be a dressmaker." Judah folded his arms with a frown but then gave me one of the dazzling smiles that always made me feel I should grant him any wish he might have. "Or at least you'd confine your sewing to dresses for yourself and clothing for our sons and daughters. You'd live the life of a lady, Nell, as you were born to do."

I had other notions about whether I should give up my business, but I remained silent on that point.

"And you're forgetting that Sarah's illegitimacy does not fit her for a life in society, even the society of Springwood. She'll be an unhappy outcast there if you're not married."

I felt my heart sink. Judah had a point—I'd given up on the hope that my unwed state could remain a secret forever. Indeed, I was pretty sure Mrs. Yomkins, that most intelligent of Springwood's matrons, already suspected or perhaps even knew for sure. Kind as she was, there was a certain coolness in her manner whenever our conversations turned toward Sarah.

"Your clients are gracious enough toward you now. You pose no threat to the proprieties in Springwood because you live here, and not there," Judah continued, his tone unemotional. "But if you live among them, a young, handsome, single woman with a doubtful past, they will begin to mistrust you."

I was obstinately silent, but there was truth in what Judah

was saying. My current life was beginning to chafe and irritate me like a badly fitting boot, but it was safe and predictable. Mrs. Drummond's hard stares were the only reminder of my plight. The boys and the teachers neither knew nor cared about their seamstress's life, and the Calderwoods' affability toward me in those days had to be seen to be believed.

Judah caught my hand—it was early in the morning, and the library was empty—and turned it over, inspecting my long, blunt-ended fingers. The gold ring with delicately incised flowers that I wore on my left hand gleamed in the soft light that filtered in through the French windows. It was Emmie's ring, the one that my late, unlamented stepfather Hiram had purchased for his first wife.

"Of course, you'd be safe enough if you had the protection of my name, and perhaps in time we could consider a house in Springwood. Sarah could certainly attend the school as my daughter—although she'd need a better school soon enough, in Saint Louis perhaps." Judah ran his thumb over my ring. "After all, if we married, Sarah would become a prominent member of Springwood society as she grew. We must raise her accordingly, with all the little accomplishments that adorn a young lady."

Sewing, painting, playing the piano, paying visits, and ordering the servants about, I thought. I tried to imagine Sarah as a society belle of the frontier. She would marry and live in idleness and have many children. And Springwood was growing into exactly the kind of town my own home, Victory, had been—staid, respectable, and prosperous.

"And the day is fast approaching when I may offer you marriage as a man with fine prospects, Nell." Judah smoothed the wiry hairs of his beard. "Mrs. Calderwood has about had enough, especially after the events of Thanksgiving." He nodded toward the black armband I still wore over my shirtwaist for Professor Wale. "Her thoughts have begun to turn to the delights of life in a large city."

I wondered, for a fleeting moment, how much encouragement Judah was giving to the turn in Mrs. Calderwood's thoughts. But my suitor was straightening his jacket, cuffs, and necktie in preparation to leave.

"I'm due to drum some understanding of First Chronicles into the younger boys. Will you accompany me downstairs?"

I tucked the plat under my arm and followed Judah out into the roar of young male voices. I nodded automatically as some of the young men heading to their first class of the day greeted me by name. It was well known by now that Judah was courting me. The boys seemed to accept the fact with no more than the occasional grin or whispered remark. Judah was too authoritative a figure to be the butt of jokes.

And this place would belong to me—to us—I thought, watching the throng of boys part before us as we made our way down the broad, ornate staircase. I would be a respectable woman with no need to worry about the future because the future would be fixed. I would belong—to Kansas, to the Eternal Life Seminary. To Judah.

GIVEN MY HESITATIONS OVER JUDAH, I WAS GLAD HE WAS NOT what you might call an ardent suitor. He was, as I was learning, a man who played a long game, waiting with the patience of a cat at a mousehole for the right moment to strike.

His remarks about the perils of moving to Springwood as a quasi-widow had been enough to cast a shadow of doubt across my mind. I let the weeks slip by without making the decision to move.

Judah's position in the seminary seemed unassailable.

Moreover, I noticed my own status among the faculty and staff growing more prominent in those weeks of early spring. The transition was almost imperceptible at first, and then came much clearer signals, which sat oddly with my position as seamstress. Change, it seemed, was in the air.

"An hour's notice really isn't enough time to dress for dinner," I grumbled as quietly as I could when I spotted Judah. Breathtaking in evening dress, he was waiting for me on the stairs. "Why am I invited?"

"Because I wanted you here." Judah held the door open as I maneuvered my way through, a dress with a train not being well adapted to doorways. "Mrs. Calderwood invited you at my express wish, although to look at you, no such intervention should be necessary. You belong in a drawing room, Nell, and in dresses like that."

I suppressed a grin. The one extravagance in which I could not help indulging, for Tess, Sarah, and myself, was new dresses, and I was particularly pleased with this one. I hadn't thought to find many occasions on which to wear it, but I had justified the expense to myself on the basis of its utility as a sample. Its base was pale gold silk faille of a glorious richness. I had trimmed it in a thin crimson cord of braided silk, with a squared bodice from which a ruffle of lace peeked. Martin had once complimented my neck and said it looked its best with a little lace, and I had to admit he had—as always—been right.

Several people recognized me as we entered the library, where the servants were distributing whiskey to the men and cordials to the ladies. They had transformed the room by the removal of several of the tables and desks. The extra space was necessary for the ladies' trains, as fashion dictated that evening wear perform the double duty of looking magnificent and sweeping the floor free of dust and debris. We ladies looked like splendid ships in full sail, and I noted with pleasure that I'd sewn several of the dresses myself.

Next to their wives, the gentlemen looked like plain hen birds. Most of them were stiff and uncomfortable in their winged collars and tailcoats and stepped carefully lest they tread on their wives' trains and incur their wrath. Judah looked as if he were born to wear good clothes and picked his way through the company with automatic precision.

"Mrs. Shemmeld, how nice to see you. Mrs. Mortimore, Mrs. Addis." I felt quite at ease now among Springwood's leading ladies. After all, I was intimately acquainted with the color of their money and the measurements of their waists.

There were about six couples I did not know. A round of introductions ensued, and not one person who knew me made any reference to my role as seamstress. That was due to Judah, of course. Yet I felt a stab of irritation that I, now a wealthy woman in my own right, needed a man to elevate my status. It also grated on me that Tess was never, and would never be, invited to such parties.

Bella, who'd brought round the cordials, gave a respectful murmur of greeting as she handed me the tiny glass. The sparkle in her dark eyes—that would have been a wink were she not so reserved in such company—was the only reminder of the help she'd given me during my frantic hour of preparation. We'd had a lighthearted argument about whether she should cut my front hair into modish bangs and frizz it up with the curling tongs. I had won, and my hair remained as I liked it.

"Good evening, good evening, my dear Mrs. Lillington." We had reached the Calderwoods, who were at the heart of the largest group of guests. Dr. Calderwood's shirtfront, teeth, and hair were all resplendent, and he was bowing and smiling with evident pleasure. In company, Mrs. Calderwood deferred to him with a wifely submissiveness that he clearly relished.

As for the Mouse, she was wearing the emerald satin I had just made. Her beady dark eyes gleamed with satisfaction as she gazed at the wealth on display. I gathered that all present were to be solicited either to make a donation to the seminary or to send their sons here.

"Thank you for inviting me, Dr. Calderwood. Mrs. Calderwood." I bowed and smiled in my turn, feeling as if I were an actor on a stage.

"You are always a charming addition to our little dinners, Mrs. Lillington. Charming indeed." Dr. Calderwood loomed over me in his friendliest fashion.

"Is she not?" Judah agreed with an air of pleased ownership that gave rise to significant looks and nods of approval between the matrons. In Springwood, I was generally considered to have made quite a catch. "Mrs. Lillington has been telling me she's so fond of Springwood that she would like to live there."

"Where do you reside now, Mrs. Lillington?" asked one of the newer guests innocently.

I looked to Judah for rescue, but his mouth twitched—in amusement or annoyance, I wasn't sure—and he stepped back, answering the summons of one of the nearby men. I would have to use my own wits to get out of the corner he'd painted me into.

Fortunately, Dr. Calderwood showed a more than usual astuteness. "Dear Mrs. Durkin," he purred, addressing the plump, fair young lady who had spoken, "your inquiry puts me in mind of a delightful surprise I have in store for Mrs. Lillington. She is, you must know, a close family friend of Mr. Martin Rutherford, the Chicago merchant."

Several people nodded with interest, as if they knew

Martin's name. All I felt was astonishment—what did Dr. Calderwood have to do with Martin?

I found out quickly enough. Dr. Calderwood, drawing himself up to his full, impressive height, turned to me and bowed to indicate the news he was about to impart was of great significance to me. "Mr. Rutherford has written to me asking the favor of a suite of rooms at this seminary for a few weeks in the fall."

He gazed at the assembled company, assessing their reactions, which were gratifyingly gushing.

His news certainly had an effect on me, if the swimming sensation in my head was anything to go by. I took a tiny sip of cordial to steady my nerves—instantly regretting it as the stuff tasted nasty—and turned to Dr. Calderwood to unburden myself of the question clawing at my mind.

"Why on earth should Mar—Mr. Rutherford want to come and stay here?"

To tell the truth, that wasn't really the question I wanted answered. "And why didn't Martin write to tell me he's coming?" was the real puzzle that had somehow given rise to a dull ache in my neck and my left temple.

Naturally, Dr. Calderwood answered the question I had actually asked. "Mr. Rutherford does not think his wife would be comfortable in a boardinghouse or such other lodging as might be available in the vicinity. Of course, when Mr. Addis has completed his hotel, Springwood will be amply supplied with the best of comforts. Alas, that happy day is not likely to occur before the spring."

"No more it isn't," interjected the tall, cadaverous gentleman who'd been standing by the fire hugging his whiskey glass and listening to Mr. Shemmeld's bombast. "What with the consarned weather and those blamed railroads—I'm telling you, they put the price of freight up every day. If I weren't a Christian man, I'd give that Cornelius

Vanderbilt a few choice words to chew on, so help me I would."

There were general nods of agreement from the men, but then Mrs. Addis piped up. "Mrs. Rutherford is a grand heiress, and she certainly doesn't belong in a boardinghouse. If only I'd known, I'd have offered her my best bedroom and the front parlor for her exclusive use."

She swept her long eyelashes down modestly, but not before I'd seen the gleam of ambition in her large hazel eyes. Mrs. Addis was a social climber if I ever saw one, and vain to boot. I knew at that moment that she would commission me to make a truly splendid evening gown before the Rutherfords' visit. And then I found it strange to realize I was envisioning Martin—the friend of my childhood—through the eyes of those around me, as a rich, powerful stranger.

"I'd still like to know the purpose of his visit," said one of the teachers—Gurney, Gurtley?—with the tenacity on which his reputation among the students was founded. "Is Springwood to have a department store?"

I noticed that Mr. and Mrs. Haywood, who owned the mercantile, looked alarmed at the prospect.

Mrs. Calderwood smiled the smile of one about to impart knowledge to an eager audience. "Mr. Rutherford informs us that his business partner has a firm interest in opening several small stores on the frontier. He wishes to see the region for himself before he makes any decision."

"And he brings his wife?" Mrs. Durkin's rounded, fair-skinned cheeks dimpled. "They must be a devoted couple."

"She's quite the society belle," one of the men said. "An heiress, with diamonds as big as goose eggs." He patted Mrs. Durkin's hand, from which I deduced that he was Mr. Durkin. "But we'll meet her right enough," he said reassuringly. "They'll never lack for a good dinner while they're here."

Naturally, this remark caused the ladies in the party to burst forth with reasons why they, rather than anyone else, should host such dinners. That left me rather out of the conversation. Judah had drifted away to talk to Mr. Shemmeld, so I had nothing to do but fret over Martin's visit.

I hadn't mentioned Judah in any of the letters I'd written to Martin. Partly because I was still not as entirely persuaded as Judah seemed to be that our futures lay together and partly, if I were to be honest, out of spite. If I did decide to wed, I wanted to spring the fact upon Martin in much the same way he'd sprung his marriage on me and see how he liked it.

I wanted to see him, of course. In fact, even so many months away from his visit, the notion sent a strange, buzzing sensation through my limbs of excitement mixed with apprehension. And yet I couldn't help feeling that Martin would try to interfere, somehow, in whatever plans I had elaborated by the fall. If he considered himself the closest thing I had to a brother, would he not want to have a say in my future? Add to this his role as the caretaker of my fortune and he would have a reason, if not a right, to try to dictate to me. And I didn't want anyone to dictate to me—especially not Martin Rutherford.

"Deep in thought?" A hand touched my elbow as Judah's musical tenor sounded in my ear.

I turned to him, smiling, not wishing to share those particular thoughts with him. "I was wondering how I should welcome Mr. and Mrs. Rutherford."

Judah shrugged. "Just be yourself. This is quite a coup for Mrs. Calderwood, isn't it?" He lowered his voice. "I'm sure she'll make the most of the opportunity."

I nodded, but the image Judah's words had conjured up troubled me. Would the Calderwoods pump Martin for a monetary gift or, worse, show him and his glittering wife off like a circus exhibit? I fervently hoped that they wouldn't be vulgar enough to do either, but I definitely had my qualms.

Heads turned as a small, silvery bell sounded, and Andrew, by far the seminary's best-looking servant, announced in a ringing voice that dinner was served.

I glanced at Judah from under my lashes and saw my thoughts reflected in his eyes. "Well," he said quietly, "at least they didn't dress him in livery like an English footman."

"Whatever will they come up with next?" I hissed as I took Judah's arm and ensured that my train hadn't snagged on anything. "If you become the head of the seminary, will you inaugurate an annual ball? Perhaps you could have the chapel cleared of its pews for the occasion; the floor is excellent."

I felt his body jerk in an effort to contain his mirth, and he pressed my arm tightly into his side with his elbow. The shared joke elated me, and for a moment I felt that Judah and I truly did belong together. Why should I worry about Martin?

26
PROPOSAL

"Hoorah for the Fourth of July!" Sarah ran ahead along the trail, her boots raising the dust.

"Hurry up, Momma," she called, turning back to me. "I'm so hungry I could eat a horse."

"Tess can't walk that fast," I called to her. "Come back and hold my hand."

Sarah groaned in frustration but complied, seizing my hand and Tess's so she could exert forward momentum on her sluggish elders. She'd be quite exhausted by sundown, and I fervently hoped we could find her a ride in a returning cart.

"I'm—so—hungry," Sarah moaned, letting go of my hand to clutch dramatically at her stomach.

"You should have eaten more at breakfast," I admonished in my best maternal tone. I nevertheless fished a small twist of paper out of my reticule. "Here—I'd been saving this for later, but I don't suppose it'll spoil your appetite."

Sarah whooped with joy and stuck the piece of rock candy in her mouth, once more running ahead of us in a half jig, half skip.

"You'll spoil her." Judah materialized at my side, as always giving the impression that he didn't walk like ordinary mortals but simply bethought himself from place to place.

"She's been running in circles all morning," I said defensively. "And I don't think she'll ever get fat."

I smiled at Sarah's tightly braided red curls—she was small, slim, and dainty like my mother, where I had been all arms and legs and knobby joints. Finely put together, she never slouched or slumped but held her head erect like a dancer and strode along straight-backed, her feet making a precise line of footprints in the dust.

"Even so, you must be careful not to overindulge her. I've noticed she speaks to you much too freely; children should be seen and not heard." Judah said this with his usual charming smile, but Tess shot him a reproachful glance.

"Sarah is a good little girl," she said. She thought for a moment and then added, "Most of the time."

Judah affected not to hear her. Not for the first time, I felt a pang of dismay that relations between my suitor and my best friend were so lacking in warmth. Judah tended to act as if Tess were not there; Tess responded with sullen, unhappy looks when Judah was present.

I shot Tess a glance to express my sympathy with her feelings and an apology for Judah's lack of warmth. She returned my look with a small smile, flicked her gaze at Judah—who evidently had no intention of leaving my side—and bustled ahead to catch up with Sarah. Judah slowed his pace a little, forcing me to follow suit.

Far behind us, I could hear the soft Southern drawl of the servants, interspersed with laughter. Up ahead, a dark mass indicated the main group of students and faculty who had stayed on over summer rather than undertake the journey home. It was a Sunday, and the Calderwoods were with them, so the students were in a relatively subdued mood.

I yawned, and Judah laughed.

"Is the exertion of walking too much for you, Nell?" He proffered his arm, and I took it; he felt cool and dry to the touch, as if the heat of the day did not affect him. I was conscious of the fact that I was perspiring freely, my chemise damp underneath my corset.

"I think it's the Sabbath rest that did me in," I admitted. "I have no gift for being idle on purpose, and there were two hours of Bible study besides."

"When we—well, soon enough we can study together. I look forward to directing your efforts." Judah gave me a sideways glance, his mouth twitching. "I hear you make little progress in memorizing verses; we'll have to change all that."

I kept my face as still as possible against the temptation to show how little I relished memorizing verses. I simply wasn't good at it, and even the prospect of Judah as my teacher didn't charm me.

But Judah seemed to have other things on his mind. "Once the meal is over, Nell, might we not take a little stroll? Just the two of us?"

I looked at him, torn between heart-skipping excitement and alarm. Since the dinner at which Dr. Calderwood had announced Martin's visit, Judah's attentions to me had redoubled. Had he chosen this evening to make sure of me? I had felt such a moment approaching, stealthily, as if it were a stalking lion and I were its prey. And I still wasn't sure what my answer would be.

WHEN I HAD LIVED IN ILLINOIS, I HAD THOUGHT THE SUNSETS beautiful. But they were mere daubs of color compared to the Kansas sky, and tonight's was especially striking. A deep fuchsia, haloed in gold, blazed behind the silhouettes of a sparse growth of trees. Above it, a strip of deep blue sky made a vivid contrast to the orange-lit ribbons of cloud that moved slowly across the firmament.

Mesmerized by the ever-changing vista of salmon, gold, and carnelian, I took a deep breath of the evening air, laden with the scents of dried grass and sunflowers. A few blocks away—Springfield was quite a town now—I could hear the band striking up the sentimental notes of "Beautiful Dreamer." Soon they would launch into livelier tunes, and there would be square dancing for the younger couples, at which point the seminary contingent would be obliged to return home. Dancing—particularly on the Sabbath—was still a point where seminary and town divided.

I could only half suppress my sigh, and Judah, of course, noticed—as he always did.

"What's wrong?"

"I was thinking how long it's been since I danced," I admitted. "Five years, at least."

I felt my face grow hot, remembering in whose arms I had so blithely skipped and hopped to the music. It had been at the start of my cousins' visit, and the flirtation between me and my cousin Jack had barely begun.

I had felt a sense of exhilaration that my handsome, grown-up cousin had been so willing to stand up with me. I had reveled in the envious glances of my friends and the crestfallen looks of two brothers from Libertyville who had been plaguing me with their gauche attentions.

I felt Judah's cool finger against my glowing cheek, and an interested look came into his eyes, as if he were storing away a valuable piece of information for later use. But all he said was, "Dancing is foolish."

We had reached a pretty spot on the southwestern edge of the town where the creek ran through a grove of tall cottonwoods. The brush had been cleared to give no encouragement to the mosquitoes, and a bench had been placed on a low rise that commanded a view of the water—when there was water. Behind us, the homes of Springwood's wealthier citizens looked far more solid and prosperous than they had three years before. Their yards were more carefully tended, and there were fewer unbuilt gaps between them.

Judah handed me to the bench, and I arranged my skirts, my palms damp. The band's music drifted by us in eddies, competing with the hum and buzz of the night's insects. The "Blue Danube," I thought. A waltz. I had always liked the waltz.

"A perfect night," Judah said softly. "And no better time for what I wish to ask you, Nell." He glanced back at the houses, and I looked over my shoulder too, seeing the blaze of red and orange reflected in their windowpanes. "All the town is waiting for news of our betrothal—shall we give it to them tonight?"

Judah had his back to the sunset so that his eyes were in shadow, the red-gold light limning his short, glossy curls and picking out the slope of his cheek under the high cheekbones. He had taken off his gloves, and his fingers grasped my lace-gloved hand with untroubled confidence.

"Do you hesitate to say yes, Nell?"

We retained the same position for several minutes before Judah spoke because I did, indeed, hesitate to say yes. That small word would give me an unassailable position in Springwood's society. It would give Sarah a name for which nobody could reproach her. It would fix my life in those rhythms to which I was already well accustomed and which I did not find oppressive.

To refuse Judah, on the other hand, would be to throw myself farther into uncertainty—would I not have to make plans to go elsewhere?

"Nell." Judah's voice was soft, insistent. "Will you not

honor me with your hand? You know we should be together." He leaned toward me and kissed me on the lips, his touch lingering just long enough to cause the heat to rise again to my face. Untouched by another man since my brief but ruinous flirtation with Jack, I yet understood the promise inherent in that kiss, and I couldn't hide from myself that I wanted what he promised me. And yet . . .

"I want to say yes." I was short of breath—it was hard to think with Judah so close to me. "But I'm not—not ready, I suppose."

The fears inside me suddenly released themselves in a torrent of words. "I never wanted to marry, Judah. That's why I wouldn't name Sarah's father after—after I made my mistake. And now I don't just have myself to consider; there's Sarah and Tess as well. I don't know if I'd just be marrying you to give Sarah a name, and how would it be fair to any of us if that were the case? That's not a good reason to marry."

"There are far worse reasons." Judah kissed me again, a little harder, but still allowing me to draw back if I wished. The problem was, I didn't know what I wished. I had the oddest feeling that the love I felt for Judah should be overwhelming, but the only overwhelming love I'd ever experienced was for Sarah. Why couldn't I see the right course I should tread, easy and clear as following a well-walked trail?

"I can't wait forever, Nell." Judah turned my left hand over and pulled up the edge of my lace glove, kissing the inside of my wrist. My arm tingled as my heartbeat increased, and a tiny smile came to the lips that touched my flesh, as if Judah felt it. Yet at the same time, I was conscious of the wedding band I wore, the one Hiram had given me, the one that, to me, symbolized my commitment to Sarah. I would have to take it off to accept Judah's ring.

"Six months." My wildly floundering senses threw out words that escaped my mouth before I could stop them.

"Give me six months; give me until New Year's Day, and I'll not fail to give you an answer, I promise. Give me time, Judah, please." The last sentence came out in a hoarse whisper; Judah was kissing my wrist again.

"Six months, then." Judah pushed the loop of lace back over the tiny pearl button that had slipped out of its fastening. "We will announce our engagement on New Year's Day."

He stood to assist me to rise, slipping my arm under his. "We'd better return to the celebrations before our absence is too much remarked upon. I'd hoped to bring them good news, but—" He smiled his beautiful smile. "Six months is not such a very long time. I know we're meant to be together."

27
BEDAZZLED

"So why, exactly, haven't you told Mr. Rutherford about Mr. Poulton?"

Catherine Lombardi's thin fingers plucked at a small tear on the bodice of her walking dress, trying to tuck a protruding piece of the lining back inside. I had almost finished its replacement; the entire Lombardi family had come on their long-awaited visit to the seminary a week ago. This had caused Mrs. Calderwood no little consternation since the length of their visit gave the pastor ample time to ask awkward questions about why the seminary was no longer taking in impoverished scholars—such as his own son.

And they were impoverished indeed. Catherine had lost a good fifteen pounds since I'd last seen her, and the children's clothes showed evidence of much mending. It was clear that the extra income from the capital the pastor had lost in '73 was sorely missed, and I'd wasted no time taking the measurements of Catherine and the children. I had ridden roughshod over Catherine's protests by proclaiming I had nowhere near enough to do, and it was true that the extra hours my new task involved were a merciful distraction from Martin's impending visit.

"I don't want to discuss Judah with Martin until we've settled things between us."

I straightened my hat and lengthened my stride; Catherine had become a good walker, despite the fact that my legs were longer. "And please don't say anything to him, either. It's none of Martin's business if I have a suitor."

"Why not? I'd think he'd have some good advice to offer, being an old married man himself." Dimples still showed in Catherine's cheeks when she smiled, even though she was so much thinner now.

"I really don't want to hear Martin's advice about my marriage prospects." I kicked viciously at a clod of dirt, watching as it skidded off into the dry grass. "He's bound to say something annoying. Besides, did he discuss his marriage with me? Not even a hint!"

Catherine laughed and returned her attention to her bodice. "Do you think the tear shows terribly? I'm almost ashamed to show my face at the mercantile."

I grasped her arm, wrapping mine around it so that we were walking in lockstep. "By tomorrow you'll be dressed like a lady of fashion. And it's just occurred to me—I can supply you with an extra dress with almost no more work. I have a maroon delaine, this year's cut, that I started in April, but my customer didn't like the color. I'd pieced in the arms, but I can take them out again in a snap, refit the bodice to you, and shorten the skirt. It'll suit your hair and skin admirably."

"How on earth are you finding the time?" Catherine asked. "Your work—"

"Tess can do nearly everything we have on hand for the seminary, and I'm waiting for Mrs. Howlett's merino to arrive, so I'm between commissions." I squeezed Catherine's arm to forestall her next words. "Let me do this for you, Catherine. The denominational office has provided the pastor with new clothes, and you must be smartly dressed to match."

Catherine said nothing, and I stared at the road ahead of us, pretending I didn't see her wipe away a tear. We were arriving at Springwood, which now extended across the creek in neat rows of small frame houses.

"Do you remember the soddies?" I asked her. "They won't allow them now. The poorer settlers have moved to a place called Fork Crossing, and the young men of Springwood made a party of leveling the sod houses. The Temperance Society is still trying to find out whether there really was a barrel of beer involved."

"I'll buy the children some candy." Catherine was counting the coins in her hand, not listening to my chatter.

"And I'll buy the girls some soap—would they like that? Hayward's has the nicest soaps. And Teddy—goodness, what on earth does one buy for a boy?"

Catherine laughed. "Food. Of any kind. But he'll be quite happy to have britches that actually come down to his ankles and a decent jacket. He won't stop talking about his new clothes."

I laughed too, but a corner of my mind remained somber. It was all very well to remedy the children's lack of new clothes, but there were some problems that had no remedy. Lucy, in particular—she was shockingly frail, with dark circles around her eyes and a bluish tinge to her lips. One dose of the ague that plagued many of the settlers would carry her off, I was sure.

"Good morning, Mrs. Addis." I smiled at my client, who was walking in the opposite direction. "Are you looking forward to the fall?"

"I'm certainly looking forward to putting on my new

wool dress." Mrs. Addis shook Catherine's hand in passing, then turned her shrewd round eyes on me. "But not nearly as much as you're looking forward to the New Year, I'll be bound."

I stared after her as she vanished in the direction of the Wells Fargo office, my jaw hanging in astonishment.

"How on earth—well if *she* knows, then everyone will know." A sensation of foreboding invaded me. "Who's been talking?"

"About what?"

"I promised Judah I'd give him my answer on the first of January."

"Ah."

Catherine bent and made a great show of retying a bootlace. When she straightened up, her expression was determined. "And I don't suppose you've told anyone—it wouldn't be like you. Which means—"

"—that Judah has let it slip."

"Insurance." Catherine's fine eyebrows rose nearly to her hairline. "He's making it harder for you to say no. If you do, your position in this town could become quite awkward."

She hesitated, then plowed on. "Is it so very possible you'll say no?" She looked at me with curiosity. "You seem quite bedazzled by the man."

"That's just it. When I'm with Judah, I find it hard to think straight. When he's not here, all the other questions crowd into my mind—Sarah, Tess, whether I should stay in Kansas at all. Whether I shouldn't use my money to set myself up as a proper couturière in a city. Being Judah's wife would permanently put an end to that dream. And, besides, there's some secret—"

I lowered my voice and stepped off the sidewalk, putting up my parasol to shield us from the sun and from any stray listeners.

"Before Professor Wale died, he showed me a letter he'd obtained from some English attorney. A letter about Judah's past, he said. I wouldn't read it, but after the professor's death, I thought I'd better. And when I went to where I knew he'd hidden it, there was nothing there. It was gone."

Catherine frowned. "Does Mr. Poulton know of the letter?"

"He did—but Professor Wale said he simply laughed it off. The professor was so odd that I can't help wondering if it was all nonsense anyway. He probably destroyed the letter himself in a fit of conscience." I turned to face my friend. "Catherine—wouldn't the denomination have made inquiries into Judah's past?"

She nodded. "I'd have to ask Roderick for more specific details, but I believe they require all teachers to supply several references, which are carefully checked."

"So Judah's unlikely to be hiding something scandalous."

She shrugged but grasped my arm, her large hazel eyes serious as she looked into mine. "You're probably right, but—would you spend Christmas with us? And bring Mr. Poulton also? And Tess and Sarah, of course."

"That might be possible, if there's no snow." We were almost at the mercantile, and I lowered my parasol. "But why?"

"Because I'm the closest thing you have to a mother, Nell." I felt Catherine's thin fingers curl around mine, much the way Mama's had, and resisted the prickle of tears. Nobody could take my mother's place in my heart—but this woman had welcomed me to the Poor Farm when I'd been alone, exiled from my home to give birth to my illegitimate child. And she'd been present at Sarah's birth, as a mother would be.

"I suppose I do need a mother's advice in some things," I said a little unsteadily.

"Then let me have Mr. Poulton under my eye—and Roderick's—for two or three weeks before you give him your answer," she said. "A man always reveals something more about himself when he's taken out of his environment."

I nodded, but Catherine was already brushing the dust from her sleeves and poking at the torn fabric of her dress, her eyes alight with anticipation. "I haven't been inside a store for months," she said with glee. "Don't expect me to leave until I've inspected every article."

"SARAH GOT MORE CANDY THAN I DID." THEA POUTED, HER shapely eyebrows drawing down in a frown.

"I don't think so," I said, my eyes on the sleeve I was setting. "Your mother was quite careful to be fair."

"Thea, you're way too old to be making a fuss about shares." Teddy, who had stuffed his own share into the pocket of his britches and grabbed his hat, making for the outdoors, spoke with the world-weariness of the oldest sibling. "Land sakes, young lady, you're thirteen now."

And she looked older, I thought. Like all the Lombardi children, Thea was thin, but there was an unmistakable womanliness about her figure that drew looks from the students. As I glanced up, her face darkened, and she stuck her tongue out at her brother's retreating back. My eyes met Tess's, and I could see we were both thinking the same thing. That young lady was trouble.

"You may have *two* of my pieces," Sarah said grandly. "I get plenty of treats. I just slip along to the kitchen, and I'm fixed, quick as molasses." Her imitation of Netta's speech made both Tess and me smile. It was accompanied by a careful flouncing of her pretty plaid dress as she sat daintily in her chair, setting her candy spoils on the table.

"You can have some of mine too," said Lucy in a placatory tone, a wary eye on her sister, whose eyes had narrowed dangerously at Sarah's speech. Being around Thea was a matter of constantly walking on eggshells. Her parents' kindness was no salve to her natural irritability and sense of grievance.

"Thank you, Lucy, dear." Thea's tone turned sugary sweet, and I saw Tess direct a sharp glance at her. "Why don't we go outside to enjoy our candy? The air in here is so—princessy."

She hooked Lucy's arm under hers and towed her toward the door. Lucy's face showed her feelings—ever the peacemaker, she rarely gainsaid her older sister, but it was plain she would have preferred to remain in the workroom with us. The wind, dust, and piercing sunlight of the prairie did not seem to be healthful to her as it was to most children. Rather, it seemed to sap all the energy she had left, leaving her pale and tired. I was desperately afraid she might have consumption.

"Why doesn't Thea like me, Momma?" Sarah asked through a mouthful of candy.

"Don't speak with your mouth full, darling. It's not ladylike," I said automatically before turning my mind to Sarah's question. "I think she's envious of you because you have so many nice dresses, you get treats, and you don't have to work hard like she does. And you live near a town and have pennies to spend at the mercantile."

Sarah considered that for a moment, chewing on her candy. "I don't care for Thea anyhow," she said once her mouth was empty. "She keeps calling me 'princess' or 'little precious' when there's no grown-ups around, and those aren't nice names when Thea says them. I like Teddy. Momma, can I have britches so's I can ride Teddy's horse? I don't want to tear my petticoats. Teddy says I will if he puts me up on Blaze in skirts."

I sighed. More work, but Sarah had a point.

"Well, I suppose I could make you some overalls, just for that." I was keen Sarah should learn to ride—I never had and was now afraid to try. Teddy's horse—not strictly Teddy's anymore since he had to share the gelding with Catherine, the other horses having been sold—was far too large for a small girl, but I trusted Teddy to keep a tight hold of her.

"Ladies ride sidesaddle," said Tess in a reproving tone.

"She can learn to ride like a lady when I can find her a suitable pony and instructor," I replied, wondering if I could find such things in Springwood. I would need to start sacrificing some of my quieter afternoons to ensure Sarah got some schooling and the company of other children. There was something far too grown-up about the way she spoke sometimes, and Thea was right, she had an air about her of royalty, of absolute certainty that others would obey her. Just like Mama, who had the most marvelous knack with servants and tradespeople, rarely raising her voice but exacting absolute and immediate obedience.

I rummaged in the large cupboard where I kept my smaller bolts of cloth and pulled out a folded piece of brown denim, of the sort used for farmers' overalls. "This should be enough."

Sarah pushed back her chair and came to inspect the fabric, rubbing it between finger and thumb and folding it up a little, the way I did when I was considering whether the weave was suitable for the job I had in mind. "It's quite heavy," she said judicially.

"It won't tear easily," I said. "And you're leaving sugary patches with your fingers—it's a good thing this isn't one of your dresses I'm making."

Sarah immediately took her hands off the fabric and inspected her sticky fingertips. "Oh."

I nodded in the direction of the washbasin that stood on a

small table by the stove. "I'll start on this later," I said. "When I'm done with Mrs. Lombardi's sleeves."

"May I go find the others?" Sarah scrubbed her face and hands with the washcloth, dripping water down her dress.

I hesitated, wondering if Thea would still be angry at Sarah.

"Pleeeeeeease, Momma." Sarah raised her eyes to me imploringly. Jack Venton's eyes, jade green with black flecks in the irises. Every time the light caught them the way it did now, I felt his gaze on me, confident, a little mocking.

The memory of Jack made a queer feeling curl somewhere under my ribs, denying my vehement inner assertion that Sarah was mine, all mine and no one else's. She was also, I had to concede, her own person, and that person wanted more freedom than her circumstances—that were not, after all, her fault—allowed.

I looked back at my work, gauging how much time we would lose if I or Tess had to accompany Sarah. "Very well."

"I won't get lost, Momma. I won't go any farther than the trees, I promise." Sarah was already halfway out the door, the pale green ribbon in her copper hair the last glimpse I got of her.

I turned resolutely back to my work. Tess, who had been steadily basting the long edges of the sleeves and body of a boy's shirt the whole time, gave me a cheerful grin, blinking behind her round spectacles.

"Isn't she a big girl? She can do all sorts of things by herself now."

"That, Tess, is what worries me."

28
RUNAWAY

"You look beautiful, Momma."

I smoothed down the front of the dress I had just put on and regarded myself in our small bedroom mirror, tucking an errant curl back into place. The day that Martin and his wife were due to arrive had finally dawned, and I was, as Mama would have said, making an effort.

My dress was an elegant shade somewhere between purple and maroon, trimmed with velvet of the same color. A pieced, stand-up collar framed the neck that Martin had once described as "swan-like." The only ornament I needed was the brooch he had given me, its single pearl luminescent against the dark velvet.

"I'm going to find these sleeves a nuisance while I'm working." I inspected the elaborate, low-cut cuffs with their swept-back decoration, pleased at how small and pale my hands looked emerging from the dark fabric. "Maybe Tess was right and I should change later—but then, supposing they're early?" I twisted round to look at the train of my dress; it too was going to be an awful nuisance all day, but I had cut it so well, and it did look elegant.

I laughed inwardly at the fuss I was making over my appearance and turned my attention to Sarah.

"Now do remember to remind Teddy you're to be back no later than three o'clock. Lucy has promised she'll take care of washing and dressing you, and you must let her brush your hair out thoroughly. And no yelling about the tangles."

I smoothed a hand over the tight braids I had begun high on Sarah's head to keep her hair as free of burrs and prairie dust as possible. Her pale green dress lay on my bed along with a new pair of stockings and her best satin slippers, brushed free of dust.

"I wish Lucy could come with us." Sarah hitched up one strap of her overalls, and I smiled at how pretty she still managed to look in clothing better suited to a boy.

"Lucy's too ill, darling. She's better off indoors, reading quietly in the library with her Mama. Thea and Teddy will look after you."

"Thea calls me Princess Nobody and gets cross with me if I don't do exactly as she says," Sarah pouted.

"She won't do it while Teddy's around. And for shame, a big girl being mean to someone much smaller."

I held out my hand to Sarah and felt her small, warm hand grasp my long fingers in total trust. I was a little nervous about allowing Sarah to go out on the prairie with Teddy and Thea, but the notion of having her underfoot all day when I—

I didn't know why I was so fretful about Martin's impending visit. I wanted to make a good impression, I supposed, to show him I had my new life well in hand and he needn't worry about me. And I didn't want to be introduced to Martin's resplendent wife wearing the plain skirt and shirtwaist of a superior servant. I was determined to appear as the lady I was in fact, if not in position.

We proceeded slowly down the stairs, Sarah's stout boots —boy's boots, purchased from the mercantile—making a clomping noise that almost drowned out the elegant swish of my dress. As we reached the first floor and headed toward the kitchen, Teddy's lanky form, made even taller by the Stetson clapped onto his head, loomed out of the dark corridor. He was carrying a saddlebag that bulged promisingly.

"Is that food?" I asked, eyeing the bountiful haul.

Teddy grinned. "Bread, chicken, cheese, new apples, and two big jars of lemonade." He hefted the bag to demonstrate its weight and then clapped a hand to his flat stomach. "It's making me hungry again just thinking 'bout it."

"How can you possibly be hungry?" His sister appeared behind him, her tone teasing rather than tinged with her usual irritability. "I've never seen anyone eat as much as you do. You should be in the circus." She saw me and Sarah and smiled, holding out something to my daughter.

"Look, Sarah. See this pretty hat? It was mine once, and then I gave it to Lucy; but she doesn't mind at all if I give it to you. We don't want you to get freckles, do we?" She bent and showed Sarah the hat, a wide-brimmed straw affair trimmed with blue ribbons and small white flowers.

Four-year-old girls don't bear a grudge for long. Sarah reached for the hat and placed it on her head, smiling with delight. Thea crouched so she could fasten the ribbons under my daughter's chin.

"And I made a batch of jam turnovers especially for you." Thea patted the saddlebag, a winning smile on her face. "Except maybe you might have to give one or two to Teddy. He eats like a panther, doesn't he?" She turned her smile on her brother, who regarded her warily.

"Why are you in such a good mood?" he asked.

Thea sighed. "I guess I'm looking forward to a holiday; working as hard as I do does give me a temper at times." She raised her eyes to me. "You look beautiful, Mrs. Lillington. Are you looking forward to seeing your old friend today?"

"I am."

My mind was racing to discover why the child was acting so pleasantly. This was a side of Thea I had never seen and didn't trust. "You look very pretty yourself."

She did—she wore a dress I had just made for her, a dark blue sprigged calico that was rugged enough for everyday wear but an elegant article for a young girl. It skimmed her ankles, a length perhaps more suited to a girl of fourteen or fifteen, but given the incipient womanliness of her figure, I didn't think she looked well in shorter dresses. The bodice fitted perfectly, showing off her small waist and the curves above and below. She had brushed her hair till it shone and put it half-up in a style that enhanced the effect of her large hazel eyes with their thick fringe of lashes.

"Thank you, ma'am." Thea bobbed a sort of mock curtsey in my direction. "You're very kind to a simple girl from the plains."

This was the first real sign she had given of insincerity, and I felt my eyes narrow, but Thea smiled at me again—she had small, even white teeth like her mother's—and put her arm around Sarah's shoulders.

"I'm such a tease, aren't I, Sarah?" She picked Sarah up, pretending to protest at my daughter's weight. "Oof, you're such a big girl now."

"You will take care, won't you?" I couldn't help myself asking. "Don't go too far, and don't let Sarah get too hot or tired."

"She'll be fine," Teddy said, slinging his bag over one shoulder. "She gets to ride Blaze all the way there and back."

"Aren't you lucky, Sarah?" Thea asked, her voice a soft coo

as she kissed my daughter on her cheek. "Don't worry, Mrs. Lillington," she said over her shoulder as they turned to go. "We'll take very good care of her."

"A QUARTER PAST THREE ALREADY." THE BALCONY OUTSIDE THE library was not long—six paces from side to side. And I knew this because I had paced across it some fifty times already, noting the same chip in the stonework each time I turned toward the south. When I stopped and looked west for a sign of the children, the sun, if not obscured by the fleeting drifts of cloud that raced across the sky, shone into my eyes, so I had to shade them with both hands and squint.

"Nell, stop." Tess put out a hand to restrain me as I set out to resume my pacing. "The students are laughing at you."

"Not anymore, they aren't." Judah stepped out onto the balcony and came to stand beside me. "I presume by your dress that you're expecting your friends from Chicago to arrive directly; but aren't you waiting on the wrong side of the building?"

"It's the children." Tess said, tipping up her head to peer at Judah, the sunlight reflecting off her spectacles. "They were supposed to be back by three, and Nell's fretting."

"Yes, I can see you're fretting." Judah spoke to me rather than to Tess, but then he glanced sideways at her. "And you, Miss O'Dugan, not yet in your finery?"

"That's why I came to find Nell," Tess said a little sullenly. "I need help to dress. I didn't want to get my pink dress all dirty by wearing it earlier."

"Well then, here's the solution." Judah touched my arm lightly. "Nell, you go help your friend dress, and I will take over your lookout duty. It will be good for you to have something to occupy your mind. You've been stalking around like a cat on a wall all day."

"AH, THERE YOU ARE." JUDAH GREETED ME ON THE STAIRS A half hour later as Tess and I—she now arrayed in fetching pink—descended from our room. "We have one of the miscreants safe, at least."

"One?" I felt as if a lump of ice had dropped down the back of my dress.

"Miss Lombardi. With some tale of your daughter taking it into her head to run off from the party."

"Where is she?" I was already running down the stairs, a difficult feat in my smart clothes.

Judah opened the door leading to the second floor, where the guest rooms were located. "With her parents. They're none too pleased with her, I think."

I barely gave Pastor Lombardi time to respond to my knock before bursting into the room. The whole family was crammed into one large bedroom, as the Calderwoods had reserved the better suite for the Rutherfords. The little parlor that adjoined it barely had space for its two heavy armchairs, a bookcase, and an inconsequential table that served to hold a lamp.

Pastor Lombardi sat in one of the armchairs, Catherine in another, and before them stood Thea, her back to me. She twisted around as I entered, and I could see her eyes were dry, if slightly red, her mouth set in a line of sullen obstinacy.

"Why didn't you stay with Sarah?" I asked her.

She gave a slight stamp with her foot. "Because Teddy took the horse to go after Sarah and left me all alone, so I had to walk all the way back by myself, and now *I'm* the one in trouble because of it. It isn't fair."

She darted a furious look at her mother, whose face was set in an expression I knew well from when she was the matron at the Poor Farm. The skeptical expression that said she was sure she was being lied to.

"But why did she run off?" My heart pounded in fear.

Thea's eyes hardened, and her mouth clamped shut even tighter.

"That's precisely the question," Catherine said. "It seems highly unlikely to me that such a small child would run away on a whim." She stared hard at her daughter, but Thea didn't move a muscle.

"We'll get no straight answers here." Pastor Lombardi rose to his feet, grabbing his flat-brimmed black hat from its resting place on the bookcase. "Best to waste no more time and to go after them; it'll be dark in two hours or so. I'll get the servants to put the horse to the cart."

I turned to see Judah shaking his head. He had stayed outside the parlor but had heard everything through the open door. "Andrew took the cart to Wichita this morning. He'll be staying overnight, I'd imagine."

"And my mule is at the farrier's in Springwood; an hour to walk there . . . No, it'll put us two hours behind, going in the wrong direction." The pastor's expression of calm imperturbability shifted into alarm.

"Teddy would look after Sarah though, wouldn't he?" Tess was also outside the door, her face creased in anxiety.

"If he could find her." I felt panic rising up inside me, a viscous bubble. "She's so small, and it's not all short grass around here. She could be in among some taller plants, and he wouldn't see her. She could have fallen into a swale or a gully—and there are wolves . . ." A trickle of sweat ran between my breasts, and my palms were damp.

"We'll need lanterns and matches. A blanket or two—tied up in a bundle so I can sling it over my shoulders. Some oats in case we see Blaze—that nag's all too inclined to spook at shadows once it starts getting dark." The pastor spoke to Judah, who nodded and set off in the direction of the stairs.

It was fully twenty minutes before the men were ready, and I waited for them in a fever of impatience by the outbuildings. I had not dared to go upstairs to change my dress, fearing they would start without me. The cloakroom yielded a hooked iron stick of the type used to handle snakes, with which I could hold up my train. I also found some overshoes belonging, no doubt, to one of the students. They would have to do.

As I waited, I scanned the horizon, but no small dots appeared that could be Teddy or his horse. I didn't think I would be able to see Sarah from any distance; whatever had possessed me to allow so small and fragile a being out in that vast wilderness?

29
WOLF

"A needle in a haystack."

Pastor Lombardi flexed his back, squinting toward the sun, which hung serenely above the horizon in a sky devoid of cloud. The seminary was out of sight. By my reckoning, we must have walked two or three miles, and still no sign of Sarah or Teddy.

"I'm slowing you down. I'm so sorry," I panted for the dozenth time, wiping sweat and dust off my forehead with the back of my hand. Despite my attempts to keep my dress clear of the grass, the lower portions of my skirt were constantly caught at by dried stalks, the burrs ripping off to attach themselves lovingly to the velvet panels. The ground beneath our feet was uneven—there were no proper paths in this direction, only the faint trails left by animals or Indians long ago—and I had turned my ankle in my overshoes more times than I could count.

"In truth, we would have been quicker by ourselves." Judah smiled as he helped me tug my skirt free of the embrace of a multi-stemmed plant. "But I can understand that you'd find staying at home unbearable."

"Since we've stopped," said the pastor, "perhaps you could call again, Nell?"

I cupped my hands around my mouth and called "Sarah!" as loud as I could several times. Then we listened for about two minutes, and when no answer was forthcoming, Pastor Lombardi shouted his son's name and Sarah's in his stentorian voice. This had been our practice since we set off; the answer was invariably the faint sighing of the prairie wind, gentle today but never flagging.

"I see something." Judah whipped round toward the south, shading his eyes with his hand. "Call again," he said over his shoulder to the pastor.

Pastor Lombardi complied, and the moving dot came closer. My heart leapt into my throat.

"It's the horse." Judah evidently had keener eyes than the rest of us. "No rider though." He dug into the cloth bag he was carrying for the small sack of oats.

And indeed, within five minutes the gelding Blaze ambled up to us with an expression of curiosity in its large brown eyes. It snuffled at Judah's coat as he ran his hands down its forelegs to check for injury. The horse was saddled and bridled and looked perfectly at ease with the world. It chewed its oats thoughtfully and flicked its soft-looking ears back and forth to catch the small noises of the prairie.

"If he spooked at something, it was some time ago." Judah checked the girth of the saddle and adjusted the stirrups as he spoke. "Let's hope he didn't throw one of the children off."

I felt sick. It must have shown in my face, as Pastor Lombardi put a firm hand on my shoulder.

"It's unlikely," he said with a swift glance at Judah. "He's a good enough horse for not rearing or bucking. Just a tendency to bolt when he's no rider on his back." He looked over the saddle and its equipment. "The saddlebags are missing—and look," he said, showing me a piece of rope that dangled from the bridle, "Teddy probably tied him instead of hobbling him—which would have been more sensible," he muttered under his breath. "No matter—we now have a horse, which is a great advantage."

Judah grasped the pommel and swung easily up into the saddle, settling down against the high back as if it were a comfortable chair. He spent a few moments putting the gelding through its paces, evidently checking for the uneven gait that would suggest an injury.

"All well." He looked down at me, smiling. The sun, now sinking fast to the horizon, haloed his hair with gold. "I'll begin by circling around the area from which the nag came. We'll have some kind of light for another hour, by my reckoning—time enough to travel quite a way if this animal's as fresh as it seems. Light the lanterns as soon as dusk falls," he added, looking at the pastor. "I'll take care not to lose you, as long as you keep heading directly west."

And with that he was gone, the gelding's hooves raising small clouds of dust as Judah urged it into a trot.

He circled around twice before we lit the lanterns. When he left us for the third time, the western horizon was a brilliant red shading into whiteness before it met the deepening blue of the sky, with the brightest stars beginning to emerge.

I was slowing down. The overshoes were horribly uncomfortable, but when I tried taking them off, I seemed to struggle even more with the uneven ground under the thin soles of my best shoes. I appeared to have developed a skill for finding every hidden hole and stone under the lush dry growth of summer and had fallen to my knees more than once, leaving large patches of dust on the front of my skirts. I cursed myself for not stopping to put on something more practical.

The approach of nightfall made the squeezing sensation in my chest increase. Once it was night, we'd never find them, and the chill of evening was already beginning to settle over us. Did they still have the blanket Teddy had brought with them for their picnic? Would Teddy have the sense to ensure Sarah was warm? If he had found her, a voice inside me said, and a chill that had nothing to do with the evening air raised gooseflesh on my arms. Sarah could be huddled in a hollow, chilled to the bone, that very moment.

My heart sank as I saw Judah ride back to us again, alone on the gelding. He had not found her, then, and surely he could not continue to search in the darkness. I braced myself to hear that we needed to return to the seminary, that the situation was hopeless, but to my surprise, Judah began shouting, "I've found them!" as soon as he was within earshot.

"Where? Why aren't they with you?" I grasped the bridle, straining to see Judah's face in the dim light.

"Sarah won't come. She says," Judah swallowed and licked his lips briefly, "that she never wants to see you again."

"WHAT THAT CHILD NEEDS," SAID JUDAH AS HE TIED THE bundle of blankets to the saddle, "is a good spanking with a wooden spoon. She bit young Lombardi, you know, on the arm. You'll be lacking in your moral duty if you don't punish her severely."

"Perhaps we should wait to see why Sarah has acted thus before you advocate punishment?" asked the pastor mildly.

We had decided to walk the distance—not much more than a quarter mile, Judah estimated, only we had been walking in quite the wrong direction—to rest the horse. It would be carrying at least Sarah on the way back to the seminary. It could not carry all three of us in any case.

Judah assured me that Teddy had a tight hold on Sarah,

but that didn't stop me from grinding my teeth in impatience as we set off. Before I had become a mother, I had never understood the meaning of the word "longing." Now I knew it well, that visceral urge to have Sarah by my side again, to hold and not let go.

"The child's motives are irrelevant," Judah said. He led the horse with one hand, a lantern in the other, and the rocking pool of golden light illuminated a rank growth of tangled grass, browned by the sun. "Children must learn to behave, that is all. A child who is not corrected will grow into an adult without a sense of moral responsibility."

I listened with only half an ear, straining to see into the darkness in front of us. I wished we hadn't lit the lanterns. The night was clear and starlit, and we probably could have seen farther ahead without them.

My attention was so drawn to what was ahead of us that I forgot to pick my way carefully across the uneven ground. I stumbled twice in quick succession, once tearing the hem of my dress so it dragged along the ground and had a tendency to get under my feet. I was holding the hook that supported my train with both hands now; it felt dreadfully heavy. Why had I been such a fool?

After what seemed a lifetime, I thought I heard Sarah's voice ahead of us. I quickened my pace—and caught my overshoes in the hem of my dress.

The sudden entanglement sent me flying forward so I landed with a thump that completely winded me. I slid along in the dirt, feeling a sharp stinging sensation in my nose, forehead and wrists, helpless to stop my forward momentum, conscious of popping and tearing sensations in the bodice of my dress as the ornamental bows caught and ripped.

"Are you all right?" It was the pastor's voice. Large hands

grasped my shoulders. I sat up, wheezing and spitting dirt and grit as I fought for breath.

"Momma? Teddy, let me go. I think Momma fell over." Sarah's voice, high and piercing, carried easily in the still night air. In just a moment, I felt her small hands on my neck and clutched her fiercely to me, still unable to speak.

Sarah pushed back a little and studied me in the lamp-light. "Your face looks terrible, Momma. You're bleeding."

"I thought you weren't going to talk to her ever again?" Teddy's voice sounded behind her, almost indignant.

"That was before she got hurt, silly. Momma, say something." Sarah sounded on the verge of tears, and I forced "I'm—all—right" out between gasps as I tried to get the air back into my lungs.

I looked at my child in the lamplight. Her face was smeared with dirt, the tracks of earlier tears cutting pink streaks through the grime. Her hair had completely escaped her braids and waved around her face in a tangle of copper curls. Her shirt was torn, showing one pale shoulder, but her overalls were, if filthy, at least intact.

Teddy ambled up to me, grimacing as he saw my face. "That's gotta sting. Anyone got any whiskey?" He coughed as he saw his father's expression. "Hank reckons it's good for cleaning a wound, Pa. Never tried it myself."

My breathing had finally returned to normal. "You scared the life out of me," I told Sarah. "You're much too young to run off by yourself, no matter why you did it." I kissed her soundly on one dirty cheek, shifting my position as I did so; I appeared to be sitting on a fist-sized piece of rock. "But are you going to tell me why?"

Sarah's mouth straightened into a line, and her expression grew thunderous.

"You're a bad woman," she muttered. "Thea told me. She said her Mamma worked in a place where bad women went to have their babies, and that I was born there. She said that they call the babies bastards, and that's a real bad word, and that I'm going to be a bastard all my life because of you."

She ended the sentence with a wail, shoving against me with all her might. "I don't want to be a bastard, Momma! Thea said you don't even pretend to have had a husband, and that you never had one, and that ladies who have children and never had a husband are bad, bad, and—and—" She was sobbing now, the tears cascading down her cheeks in a welter of grime.

I looked up hopelessly at Teddy, who hovered over me, rubbing at a welt on his arm that clearly showed the imprint of small teeth. "She only stopped screaming at me when I promised to run away with her," he said, anxiety creasing his bony face. "I tried to tell her you're a repentant sinner, and I tried to tell her about Jesus and the woman they wanted to stone—but she's too little to listen."

"That's the trouble," I said, my eyes on Pastor Lombardi. "She's too little to understand, even if I knew how to explain it to her. Even if I knew how to explain it to myself."

My voice broke and trembled on the last words, and an unbidden tear ran down my own cheek. "I'm sorry, Sarah, I really am." I hugged her to me, feeling her tears soak into my bodice as her small body shook, breathing in the scents of dirt and salt and the indefinable essence of a small child after a long day.

The pastor shook his head slowly. "Thea should not have told her this. The telling of it properly belonged to you, Nell, at a time when you judged her old enough to hear it." He blew air out through his nostrils, his eyes on Sarah. "I can't even begin to know how to punish Thea for this. Heaven knows we have little enough that can be taken away from her. I've never used a strap or a switch on her, but I'm tempted to begin."

"She's a little old for that now, isn't she, Pa?" There was a cynical edge to Teddy's voice I'd never heard before. "It'll just make her mad at you; she'll never admit she's in the wrong."

"True enough." I saw the pastor clap a hand on Teddy's shoulder, raising a small puff of dust that looked like smoke in the lamplight. "My son, at least, has behaved like a man today," he said to me, smiling.

I too smiled at Teddy, wincing at the sting on the bridge of my nose. "You have. Thank you for keeping her safe."

"I'd have been a sight smarter if I'd hobbled Blaze 'stead of tying him," Teddy said.

"Why did he run off?" Judah asked.

"A wolf came by; don't think it was looking for a meal 'cause it looked at us and just walked on real quiet, but Blaze went wild."

"It was a big wolf, Momma." Sarah had recovered herself and looked excited, her eyes glowing green in the lamplight.

"And supposing it had been looking for a meal?" I shook her very gently. "And you'd been on your own with nothing to defend yourself?"

As if in answer to my question, there was a sudden cacophony of wails and yelps like a pack of demons fighting, sounding as if it were just a few yards from us. We all jumped, and Sarah flung her arms around my neck. Out of the lamplight, I could hear the horse snorting and bucking, and Judah's muttered imprecations as he clung to the bridle.

"Coyotes." Teddy, at least, sounded calm. "A lot farther away than it sounds; noises really carry at night around here."

"Far away or not, we'd still be best advised to make a start for home before we lose this horse," Judah said through gritted teeth. "I'm hesitant to put the ladies up on this brute though." I heard a smack of leather; I thought he might have struck the horse with its reins but could not be sure.

"We'll both hold the bridle," Teddy suggested, a small frown on his face.

This proving agreeable to all parties, Sarah and I were hoisted unceremoniously into the saddle, and our long trek back to the seminary commenced.

From my vantage point, I could see two bright pools of light. The pastor went ahead of us, using his lantern to check for pitfalls that might trip the horse. Judah had the other lantern, the light from which illuminated his profile as he walked along, his other hand tight on the bridle, his feet making no sound. Above us, the stars were a carpet of jewels in the clear sky, showing the dark horizon as a distinct line, which seemed to dip and sway as the horse moved.

Once I had nothing to do but hold Sarah—who almost immediately fell asleep—I realized just how exhausted I was. My hips, elbows, and shoulders ached from my fall. The bridge of my nose and my forehead stung horribly, and I welcomed the flow of cool night air over my face. I began to experience the feeling of unreality that precedes dropping off to sleep, and several times had to pinch myself to stop from falling into a doze.

I had the impression that a wolf was running alongside us, staying out of the lamplight but always circling, always looking for a way in. The huge, gray shape was whisper-quiet, so silent that no one else saw it, not even the horse; yet it constantly slipped into my field of vision, looking at me, always at me. Or was it looking at Sarah? Where the lamplight caught its eyes, they glowed as red as rubies, as orange as fire; I saw the whisk of its tail, held low, and heard its hot breath as it circled.

It had a name, the wolf. It was Shame. It would always be circling around us, around Sarah and me, waiting for a chance to strike. It was the secret that few people knew but that everyone seemed to suspect when they saw us. It was the secret that, if known, would bar us from all good society and make our names a hissing and a scandal. It was circling . . .

"Nell!" A hand pushed me back into the saddle, and I came awake with a great jolt of alarm. Where was the wolf? I looked around wildly, but no gray shape whispered past this time.

"You fell asleep." Judah's voice was tinged with amusement. "Should we tie you to the saddle?"

I shook my head, confused. Sarah was a warm weight on my chest, her breath hot on my neck, and I shifted in the saddle to try to make myself more alert.

I realized we could see the seminary, pinpoints of light in the distance, and relief washed over me. I could stay awake for that long.

The next thought brought me wide awake, heart pounding. Had Martin arrived?

30
ENCOUNTER

We entered through the door that led to the kitchen. Sarah woke up when I handed her to the pastor so I could get off the horse, an undignified procedure since I'd been obliged to ride astride, my ruined skirts bunched up around my limbs. I'd been so exhausted I'd forgotten to be afraid, and on dismounting, I felt a momentary stab of pride—I had ridden a horse across the prairie!—before the consequences of that ride began to make themselves felt in my, well, in the bones I used for sitting.

"Nell!" Tess darted out of the kitchen, her eyes alight with joy. "And Sary! You're safe, just like Mrs. Lombardi said you would be. And guess what, Nell? Martin's here, and his wife, and a maid who's all freckles and who's sleeping in a boxroom on the floor because she says she won't share a room with a darkie servant. And Martin is very grand, and Mrs. Rutherford is very beautiful, and she wore a dress to dinner with a bustle this big," Tess opened her arms wide, "and sparkly jewels all over her. And Dr. Calderwood keeps kissing her hand."

"That's nice," I said, deciding that I absolutely, categorically did not want to see Martin and the very beautiful Mrs. Rutherford that evening.

The faint aromas of a good dinner still wafted around the corridor, making my stomach growl loudly and competing with the odors of horse attached to my person and Sarah's. I just wanted to get out of my dress, which by now was about fit for the ragman, wash the dirt out of the scrapes on my face and arms, and use the chamber pot.

Sarah was yawning repeatedly, and I was sure she would be asleep again before long. Better use the intervening time to wash her a little.

"Tess, let's go up to our room and put Sarah to bed," I suggested. "I need a wash and some food." I hitched Sarah up a little in my arms and headed toward the staircase, being very careful not to tread on my torn hem and wishing that the builders of the Eternal Life Seminary had thought to put in a back stair.

When you desperately wish to avoid someone, that is precisely the moment, I have observed, when you're most likely to encounter them. So it was with a sense of inevitability that, having reached the chapel doors, which I had to pass to attain the staircase, I heard them open, and the Rutherfords stepped out, accompanied by Dr. and Mrs. Calderwood. If my heart had been able to sink farther than my boots, I believed it would have kept on going until it reached the earth's core.

The first thing I noticed was the perfectly blank look on Martin's face, as if all emotion had been wiped from it. At first, I hoped he had not recognized me, and then the truth came flooding in. *He's horribly ashamed of you,* I told myself, *and trying to hide it.*

Then more details began to impinge on my consciousness. The elegant cut of Martin's evening coat made him look far more broad-shouldered than I remembered him to be—

or had he, in fact, gained muscle? His face was harder, somehow, in expression and feature than it had been three and a half years before. Its former smooth pallor was now a weatherworn tan that made his shock of white-blond hair stand out like a beacon against the shine of the oak doors.

The woman beside him stood as if turned to stone, magnificent in pale turquoise silk, glossy raven curls cascading over her shoulders from her beautifully dressed hair. Her eyes were large, black, and thickly fringed by long lashes, their expression of astonishment gradually pervaded by amusement as she realized who I was.

We seemed to freeze in place for an eternity, but in reality it must have been about two seconds. Then Martin spoke, his face relaxing.

"I'm glad you're safe, Nellie."

It was strange to hear his voice again after so long; but it was, I realized, the most familiar thing about him.

He took two quick steps toward me, reaching out a long-fingered hand to touch Sarah's hair. "And this little lady—do you know," he addressed Sarah directly, "the last time I saw you, you were an infant? And now, I believe, you're old enough to ride a horse—from what Mrs. Lombardi tells me. I like riding too."

His gaze flicked to my face, and I felt the heat rising in my cheeks. I hadn't seen myself in a mirror, but I was sure I looked dreadful, scraped and torn with my hair in a wild tangle, my once-smart dress ripped and dirty.

Sarah had been silent in my arms, but at the mention of riding, she spoke. "I'm four and three-quarters, and Momma is going to find a riding instructor for me soon. And make me a riding dress because ladies ride in a dress, but overalls are really very comfortable. I wish I were a boy."

"No, you don't." Tess held her arms out, and I gratefully lowered Sarah to stand beside her, feeling the strain in my aching shoulder muscles. "You love your dresses, don't you, Sary? If you were a boy, you couldn't wear them." She held out a hand to Sarah and began to lead her upstairs. Sarah, evidently tired enough not to protest, followed her without a word, leaving me alone with the Rutherfords and the Calderwoods.

"I'm forgetting my manners," said Martin. "May I introduce my wife? Lucetta, I'm happy that you are finally able to meet Mrs. Lillington."

I held out a hand, hesitated as I saw the state of my glove, and pulled it off so I could offer a cleaner article.

"How do you do? I'm terribly sorry about my appearance," I said. My hand felt large as it grasped hers, which was small and compact but very strong under its lace covering. She was about the same height as me but more rounded in figure, her tiny waist emphasizing the swell of her bosom, on which sparkled an impressive diamond necklace.

"My dear, think nothing of it," she said. Her voice was beautiful, a rich contralto that carried with it a sense of easy confidence born of a life spent in society. "I'm delighted to meet Martin's young friend, about whom I've heard so much."

"Mrs. Lillington is an ornament to our seminary," intoned Dr. Calderwood ponderously, and then he broke into a fit of coughing as he realized just how incongruous his intended compliment sounded, given my appearance. His wife banged him on the back, all the time shooting looks at me from her beady eyes that indicated her wish to have me removed immediately from the face of the earth.

"Mrs. Lillington has had a remarkably hard day." The voice was Judah's; he had appeared behind our little group and now moved to my side, placing a hand under my elbow. "She has suffered a high degree of alarm and distress, is injured, and has walked for miles."

He turned to Lucetta—somehow I found it hard to think of her as Mrs. Rutherford, that being the name I had connected most of my life with Martin's mother—and flashed his charming smile. "May I beg your indulgence, Mrs. Rutherford, to take Mrs. Lillington upstairs? She'll be quite recovered by tomorrow." He made a movement in Martin's direction that had the hint of a bow. "And I apologize for intruding without an introduction; my concern for Mrs. Lillington must be my excuse. My name is Poulton."

"Mr. Poulton is our head of faculty and our Old Testament instructor," Mrs. Calderwood broke in, her saccharine tones indicating that Judah was still very much in her favor. Judah's appearance had suffered little from our hours on the prairie; aside from a little creasing in his clothes, he looked as if he'd just come from an evening stroll. I could see Lucetta was regarding him with an expression that indicated her approval of his handsome face and lithe figure.

"I look forward to making your acquaintance properly at a more propitious moment." Judah's hand slid up my arm and tightened its grip a little. "Nell, won't you let me escort you to your door?" His voice was caressing. "You're quite done in, and I'm afraid you may faint."

I glanced at Martin, who was watching us, his expression unreadable, and then smiled at Judah, feeling a stinging sensation as the abraded skin on my nose moved. "I've only fainted once in my life," I said with the ghost of my usual energy. "But I would like to go to my room now."

I nodded apologetically at the small group in front of me and turned in the direction of the staircase, weary in every limb. Judah offered his arm, and I slipped my hand beneath it, feeling the eyes of the visitors on me as we walked upstairs, conscious that the most familiar presence in my life was one and the same as the tall, hard-faced man who didn't seem to know what to say to me.

31
FRIENDS

I awoke the next morning feeling as if the Lombardis' horse had rolled on me, paying particular attention to my backside and shoulders. The scraped skin on my nose and forehead didn't look as bad as I had feared, thanks to the iodine Tess had fetched from Mrs. Drummond the previous evening. The yellowish-brown patches that would not wash off completely weren't the most flattering of facial adornments, but they were better than the inflamed, angry-looking red of the night before.

I dressed in my workaday costume of skirt and shirtwaist, being sure to select the newest and cleanest articles. I cast a longing glance at the clothes press, in which I had several much more attractive dresses, and sighed. One look at the ruined maroon confection that lay bundled in a corner, its velvet panels scuffed and filthy, convinced me I would be tempting fate to try to impress my visitors this morning. I pinned the brooch Martin had given me to my collar, straightened my shoulders, and held my head high.

Sarah, whom Tess had bundled, exhausted, into bed with little more than a quick swipe with the washcloth, was now enjoying a bath in the small room near the kitchen where the tubs were kept. Tess had promised to help her put on the pretty green dress she had not had a chance to wear yesterday. They had both been giddy with excitement as they headed downstairs.

Thinking of their happiness put a smile on my face, and by the time I reached the second floor, my mood was buoyant, and I was almost able to ignore the aches in my shoulders and hips. Breakfast would not be for another twenty minutes, as we'd all risen early. I could spend ten minutes in the library perusing the periodicals table for new arrivals before heading off to find the Lombardis.

I clattered down the last few steps and yanked open the door, humming a tune as I did so but wincing a little at the tug on my sore shoulder. I had plenty of reasons to be cheerful, I reflected. Sarah was safe, and although I was still at a loss as to how to deal with her sudden knowledge of her illegitimate status, at least this morning she had smiled and chattered as usual. I'd cross that bridge when I came to it.

"Nell?" a voice called from somewhere in the row of small study rooms that ran along the wall of the library. "Is that you?" There was a movement from within, and then Martin's head appeared around the door of the second room, followed by the rest of him. The study rooms had no windows, and the corridor was consequently rather dark, but I could see Martin's hair and the flash of his teeth as he grinned.

"How did you know it was me?" I asked ungrammatically, hearing my mother correct me in my mind.

"You always hum tunes in the morning," he replied, coming toward me. "At least, you did when you stayed with me those few weeks. You have the gift of being both an early riser and a cheerful one."

"So have you," I grinned back.

"The habit of years spent running a store," Martin admitted. "I don't think I could stay abed if I wanted to."

He gestured to the room he had just left, and I followed him into it. It contained a desk—now covered with papers I supposed were Martin's—two hard chairs, and a low bookcase containing a miscellaneous collection of Bibles and hymn books. A truly dreadful portrait of Martin Luther, looking fat and discontented beneath a squashed-looking hat, adorned one wall.

Illuminated by a lamp, the desk had a workmanlike, purposeful air. As did Martin himself. His finery of the evening before had given way to a brown suit of good cut and material but otherwise quite ordinary, making him look far more like the man I had known.

Martin raised the lamp so he could inspect the scratches on my face. The light revealed lines around his eyes and mouth that had not been there when I had last seen him, and a delicate hint of blue in the fragile skin below his eyes. The hand that extended to—I thought—touch my face but then hesitated and dropped back was not as white and smooth as it had been. There were calluses on the palm and the fading scars of cuts and scratches on the back of it.

"You don't seem to have come to much harm." Replacing the lamp, Martin leaned against the desk and folded his arms.

"Now can you tell me why you took it into your head to wander all over the prairie yesterday?" he asked. "The Calderwoods didn't seem willing to divulge much. They're quite a pair, aren't they?" He cocked his head to one side, waiting for my reply.

"Thea Lombardi informed Sarah that she's illegitimate. And told her what that meant," I said baldly. "So Sarah refused to come home." I bit the inside of my lip, annoyed to feel the prick of tears at the back of my eyes, and just as annoyed at Martin for asking. "You could say you're pleased to see me before you begin interrogating me about my business," I shot at him.

"Ah." Martin's eyes, clear gray in the lamplight, widened. "That would account for the absence of young Thea at dinner. Mrs. Lombardi—she's dreadfully thin and worried looking, isn't she, Nell? What are they—or is asking about the Lombardis 'interrogating you about your business' too?" The ghost of a smile twitched at his lips but then faded and his face went still, his eyes on mine. "And I'm very glad to see you, Nellie."

For some reason, that remark gave me a queer feeling in the pit of my stomach. The sensation dissipated when Martin's brow creased and his expression became more focused, as if thinking back over my words. "Does Sarah—understand? What Thea meant?"

"I think so," I said, feeling myself redden a little. "She seems all right this morning, but I suppose at some point we'll have to talk about it. I'm not looking forward to that," I ended ruefully, running a finger over my scraped wrist.

"Will you tell her about Jack Venton?" Martin asked softly.

I jerked my head up, feeling the blood suffuse my cheeks. "How do you know it was Jack?" I blurted, knowing my face had given the game away in any case. The door of the room was open, and I glanced around it as a precaution, but the corridor was quite silent.

"My dear," Martin's eyes were serious, wide with sympathy, "I met your cousin often enough during that visit, and I saw how you flirted with him. It amused me at the time." His mouth twisted wryly. "I suspected even when Sarah was a baby, and now—the resemblance is plain, especially the eyes." He took a deep breath, hesitating, and then whispered, his voice a little hoarse, "Did he force you?"

My hands clenched into fists at my sides. "That," I said with hauteur, "is none of your business, Martin."

His fair lashes swept down to cover his eyes. "No, I don't suppose it is." And then in a different tone as a bell clanged on the floor below us, "We don't seem able to get off to a good start, do we, Nellie? I'm sorry I seem to do nothing but interrogate you, as you put it. I presume that's the breakfast bell—will you join me? I can't ask awkward questions if we're in company." He extinguished the lamp and moved out into the corridor, extending a hand toward me.

"They'll expect you at Dr. Calderwood's table, and I usually sit at the back of the room." I tried to sound cheerful, but my buoyant mood of half an hour ago had evaporated, and my words had a petulant edge to them. "I'm just the seamstress, if you remember."

"You will be my guest," Martin told me gravely. "And hang your status." He grasped my hand and all but pulled me through the door, letting go as he looked up at the stream of students hurrying down the stairs. "We'll talk like friends again if it kills me."

"Will you join me at Dr. Calderwood's table today, Nell?" Judah, most unusually, stood at the refectory door, waiting for me.

"I've already extended that invitation." Martin's tone was friendly, but his eyes were wary.

"Oh, good morning, Mr. Rutherford. I trust you slept well? And your charming wife—she does not join us?"

"She does not accept the existence of eight a.m."

Martin adjusted his cuffs with a gesture I remembered well and surveyed the room. Dr. Calderwood was beginning to call those present to attention with the slow sweep of the head that indicated he would like to start praying soon. Students slipped hastily into their places as the servants placed dishes on the tables. "Her maid will attend to her later —are the servants here the helpful sort?" He addressed this question to me, over his shoulder.

"They are," I said shortly, quickening my pace as I headed to the table so that both Judah and Martin were behind me. I hesitated as I saw Dr. Calderwood notice me; but he bowed toward me and bared his huge teeth in a genial smile. Murmuring, "Dear Mrs. Lillington," he gestured to a place near him. The Lombardis were already at the far end of the table—at least Teddy and Lucy were there with their parents. There was no sign of Thea.

Busy waving a greeting to the Lombardis and indicating in sign language that yes, I was quite all right, I barely noticed as the gentlemen most likely to disconcert me during the meal took their places. Dr. Calderwood interlaced his fingers, bowed his massive head so that his mane of hair fell forward—it had a few streaks of silver in it now, I noticed—and embarked on a long, rambling prayer of thanks.

When I could legitimately open my eyes again, I saw Martin seated on my left, opposite the Calderwoods, and Judah across the table from me. I twisted round to look at the room.

"Where are Tess and Sarah?" I looked across at Judah. "You did invite them too, didn't you?"

"I haven't seen them," said Judah coolly.

The places around us had filled up with faculty members who, now that prayers were over and the food was arriving, came forward to introduce themselves to Martin.

I frowned but then relaxed as a small figure in pale green, crowned with a flame of bright copper hair, strode into the far end of the room. Tess had brushed out Sarah's hair but left it loose—she could not braid hair—simply using a ribbon to keep it off her face. Left thus to its own devices, it formed crisp waves at the crown, very like Jack's hair, and fell into ringlets only at the ends. Martin was right, I thought, seeing Sarah's face light up as she spotted me at the high table. In the shape of her face and, above all, in her eyes, she was undeniably the daughter of John Harvey Venton. Of all the places in the world we might go to, Hartford, Connecticut, was the one I need most stringently avoid.

"May I sit next to Teddy?" was Sarah's first question when she reached me.

"You may." I smiled at Tess, who looked a little flustered; dressing Sarah by herself was quite an achievement. "But please say good morning first."

"Good morning, Doctor Calderwood. Good morning, Mrs. Calderwood." Sarah hesitated. "Good morning, Mr. Poulton." Then, fixing her attention on Martin, who had turned round in his chair to see her, she bobbed an elegant curtsey, carefully holding her dress, which came an inch below her knee and was stiff with petticoats. "I'm pleased to meet you, sir," she said, studying Martin's face. "At least, I know we met last night, but I wasn't really myself. I don't remember knowing you when I was an infant, so I feel like we're meeting for the first time."

A delighted smile spread across Martin's face at this long speech, delivered in a childish lisp with several hesitations. I realized with a pang that this was the first time I had seen him look genuinely relaxed and happy since he arrived. With me, he seemed somehow on edge, as if he couldn't quite feel comfortable in my company. He rose to his feet and held out a hand for Sarah to shake; she complied, and then an expression of joyous wonder spread over her face.

"Momma! I have a loose tooth!" Turning away from Martin, she tugged at my sleeve, indicating one of her front bottom teeth.

I groaned inwardly. Sarah's baby teeth were so pretty, small, white, and even, and it seemed a shame that she had to lose them. Outwardly, I smiled and murmured something appropriately maternal.

"I'm happy I was present at such a momentous discovery." Martin's eyes met mine for a second, full of amusement, and then he held out a hand for Sarah. "May I escort you to your chair?"

She slipped her hand into his without hesitation, and he turned toward Tess, offering his other arm. Tess's round face beamed with joy, and she practically grabbed Martin's arm. I was glad of his tact, as no place was left for her beside me.

"Mr. Rutherford is quite a favorite with the ladies," Judah remarked, watching Martin greet Catherine and Lucy Lombardi.

"His wife is quite—quite spectacular," ventured one of the professors. I couldn't quite recall his name—Bassford? Blackford?—like all the new men at the seminary, he was a colorless nonentity with few opinions of his own. "I have never seen a lady like her." Seeing I was looking his way, he coughed, blushed, and busied himself with his napkin.

I wondered for a fleeting moment if Mrs. Drummond made a point of informing each new faculty member of my status as a scarlet woman. The seminary's housekeeper kept very much to herself since Professor Wale's death, taking meals in her office and avoiding unnecessary contact with practically everyone. I hadn't seen her at the breakfast table for months. And besides, if she did gossip, what could I do?

I smiled at Professor Whatever-his-name-was, causing him to blush even deeper, and remarked that I had met Mrs. Rutherford the day before, and indeed she was most elegant.

Martin returned to his seat, and the conversation became more general. I applied myself to my cornbread, bacon, and fried apples with gusto since I had eaten very little the night before. I listened as Dr. Calderwood tried repeatedly to vaunt the qualities of the seminary to Martin. He was barking up the wrong tree, I thought, since Martin had no sons—or was he hoping to elicit another general donation?

"We broke our journey at Kansas City," Martin said in answer to a question from his left. "For the Exposition. A fine old mansion they have there on the fairground."

"Did you see the James boys?" Professor Hoggart's long face lit up in gleeful anticipation. He was a Southerner, a faculty member of long standing, and afflicted with severe halitosis.

"Ah yes, that was in the Wichita papers," Judah remarked. "They put detectives on the trail of two men who were behaving in a suspicious manner, but they let them get away—"

"And some people recognized them for certain as being Jesse and Frank James," Professor Hoggart interrupted—to Judah's evident annoyance—in a loud voice. "And the yellow cowards," he pronounced it "yalla," "let them get out of town without arresting them because they were too frightened to tackle the outlaws. Lily-livered sons of Jehoshaphat . . ." His speech degenerated into a wheezing laugh, and I saw Mrs. Calderwood wince at the blast of bad breath.

"Would *you* draw a gun on the James boys?" Judah shot a contemptuous look at the professor and turned his attention back to Martin. "They robbed the Exposition in '72," he continued. "I hope you and your good lady were well protected. Kansas City has a reputation for harboring the worst sort."

"And that, Mr. Rutherford, is precisely why our seminary is so necessary," said Dr. Calderwood unctuously, and I saw Judah nod in agreement. "We are a beacon of light in a dark land, a rock of Christ where the true word of God is preserved without question. We send out men to the wicked cities of the plains, to the Sodoms and Gomorrahs where outlaws thrive and immoralities of all kinds are rampant . . ."

He seemed to lose the thread of his thoughts, and Professor Hoggart jumped in.

"Did you see Jefferson Davis at the Exposition?"

At this point, the conversation became guardedly political. I listened with half an ear, knowing how circular such conversations tended to be. Even Professor Hoggart, who stood out as the only faculty member likely to venture a real opinion in the face of Dr. Calderwood's bland platitudes, was circumspect about mentioning events in the Southern states.

I was conscious of Martin beside me, fending off attempts to get him to speak his mind about President Grant with the laughing comment that he was only a merchant and must keep his opinions to himself for the sake of trade. It was strange to hear this group of men deferring to Martin. They all—including Judah—seemed to look upon him as a representative of commercial power, a force that would sweep into Kansas along with the tide of immigrants and make it—when economic circumstances improved—into a paradise of prosperity.

Mrs. Calderwood said little, but her beady black eyes darted glances around the table. She occasionally observed me with an expression of approval of my womanly silence in the presence of the debating men. Judah also smiled at me several times, clearly pleased that I was playing an ornamental role at the table rather than venturing to try for a speaking part.

In truth, I found most of the conversation ridiculous. I didn't think the men, with the exception of Martin and Judah, had any real knowledge of political affairs. Most of their so-called points were simply reiterations of what they had said a few minutes before.

"Are we boring you, Nell?" Judah spoke softly, but I felt

Martin shift beside me as if, perhaps, he were listening. He couldn't have failed to notice Judah's repeated use of my first name in public, a circumstance that I too found a little surprising. After all, we were not actually affianced.

"Not at all," I replied. "I'm waiting for the conversation to take a more practical turn. I prefer to reserve the expression of my opinions for moments when I actually have one."

"No, political blather isn't your domain, is it?" Judah turned the full force of his dazzling smile on me with a twinkle in his eyes that was, for him, almost flirtatious. "Shall we talk of summer days and sunsets instead?"

This reference to his proposal brought a faint blush to my cheeks—as Judah must have known it would—and his smile widened. We were now two and a half months into the six I had asked for, and I was no clearer in my mind as to which answer I would give him. Until now, he had made no allusion to our future together, and I had been grateful for his reticence.

"Have you taken any hurt from our adventures on the prairie?" Judah asked. "Other than—" He indicated the scratches on my face, extending his hand and then quickly withdrawing it, as if he had felt the urge to touch me and then remembered we were in company.

"None at all," I said, conscious that my heart was beating a little faster than usual. It was not, I thought, necessarily for Judah's sake, but because I knew Martin would be aware of the intimacy of Judah's tone.

I glanced sideways at Martin, but he had his head turned away from me. I had the impression that his easy, relaxed posture of a few minutes before had been replaced by a kind of frozen immobility.

"Do you find Mrs. Lillington in good looks, Mr. Rutherford? You have known her so much longer than I have."

Judah's direct question recalled Martin's attention, and he

shifted in his seat again. "And of course," Judah continued, "your letters are always a great comfort to her. You are, I think, the closest thing she has to a brother. It's fascinated me to hear about the musical soirées you have attended, the hunting parties and so on."

To hear him talk, you would have thought I had read all of Martin's letters out loud to him. Still, I supposed it was Judah's way of making friendly overtures toward Martin, and I could hardly blame him for wanting to be on cordial terms with someone I had known for so long.

"I find Mrs. Lillington to be in extremely good looks." Martin's tone was bland, his face unreadable under its mask of urbane courtesy.

His stated aim of having us talk as friends at breakfast had gone nowhere, I realized. The others had monopolized his time, and we had barely exchanged ten words.

"The prairie air agrees with her, I think," Martin continued, looking at me directly for the first time. "But I wish—"

But Mrs. Calderwood had risen to her feet, prompting several of the professors to do likewise. A wave of movement spread outward from the middle of the table and rippled across the room. The scraping of chairs and exchanging of final remarks swallowed up whatever Martin had been about to say. His attention was immediately engaged by Pastor Lombardi, who had moved with purpose toward him with a question about the rebuilding of Chicago. Martin answered with ease, and the two men stood talking together as the crowd thinned around them.

"Will you walk with me later, Nell? It promises to be a fine afternoon." Judah appeared at my side, silent and swift as a panther. I turned away from Martin to answer him.

"Well—" I hesitated, wondering whether I should ask Martin what he was doing that day. But of course his plans would have to include Lucetta, and she had not yet made an appearance.

"Or are you sick of seeing the prairie?" Judah offered his own interpretation of my hesitation.

"Of course not," I laughed. "My ankles are a little sore. Oh, I probably shouldn't mention those," I added, recollecting that Judah was, after all, a gentleman. One did not mention one's lower limbs to a gentleman, even if he had hoisted you astride a horse the day before.

Judah threw back his head in a rare burst of laughter, his glossy curls catching the light. "We won't walk far," he promised over his shoulder as he turned to hurry through the door. "Not today."

32
INTERROGATORY

"We have punished Thea," Catherine said quietly.

We were standing, arms linked, on the balcony leading from the library. Below us in the yard, the Lombardis' cart stood ready, their mule's long ears twitching as Teddy and his father finished loading the last few parcels.

I looked at Catherine, but her expression was closed. Evidently, she didn't wish to tell me what Thea's punishment had been. I decided not to ask her.

"In any event, Sarah seems to have recovered from the shock," I said. "Perhaps it's better this way. I would have had to tell her sooner or later, I suppose."

"Perhaps." Catherine let go of my arm and turned to face me. "If you were already married to Mr. Poulton, for example, you'd have no need to tell her. She's very small; she may forget what Thea told her. Better to let her think she has a father and spare her the shame."

I bit my lip. Catherine looked much smarter than she had on arrival, being dressed in one of the gowns I had sewn for her; but her responsibilities seemed to be settling back over her as the time of departure neared. Her tone was more severe than was quite comfortable for me.

"And yet you want me to think twice before I say yes to Judah," I said, a little reproachfully.

"I do." Catherine gazed out into the yard. Martin had joined the Lombardi men while we had been speaking, and the three of them were engaged in a conversation that occasioned much hilarity.

"It's a pity it could not have been Mr. Rutherford," she said. "He's a good man, and like you in many ways—hardworking and kind, ambitious without being ruthless. And his affection for you runs deep. But it's too late for that." She sighed, responding with a wave to Teddy's shout that they were all ready. Martin turned, saw me, and tipped his hat with a hesitant smile, then turned back to Pastor Lombardi.

"Martin was ready to marry me, once." I resolutely turned my back on the sight of Martin. "To save me from my stepfather. But I wouldn't countenance such an arrangement; and, as you say, it's too late now."

Dismissing the thought, I felt my brow furrow as I wrestled with the implications of Catherine's words. "Is it your opinion that I *must* marry? That if it's not Judah, I must go husband-hunting for Sarah's sake?"

"As I've told you, I can't express an opinion on Mr. Poulton until I know him better." Catherine's voice had taken on a more acid edge than usual. "And he's a hard one to get to know. But yes, if you want my completely honest opinion, the options in front of you—if you have Sarah's well-being in mind—are to marry him, marry someone else, or move away to where nobody knows you and construct a more convincing web of lies about your dead husband. And I supply that last solution as a practical, not a moral, one. You're an eminently practical woman, Nell."

Once again, her tone made me uncomfortable, and my

expression no doubt reflected my unease. Catherine hugged me fiercely and kissed me on the cheek.

"Forgive me," she said. "Thea's behavior has put me out of sorts, and I can't seem to find my Christian charity this morning." A ghost of a smile flickered on her lips. "I hope you know that whatever your choices, I love you as a daughter. Come to us at Christmas."

"I will."

I hugged her back, but my limbs felt strange and heavy as I watched her cross the library with rapid steps, hurrying to find the younger children so they could leave for the long journey home. I had refused to reveal Jack's name to my mother and stepfather because I didn't wish to sacrifice myself to a loveless marriage. Would I have to make that sacrifice after all?

"THAT CHILD," SAID MARTIN AS WE WATCHED THE LOMBARDIS' cart jolt over the ruts on the trail, "is trouble."

"Sarah?" I asked.

I was distracted, focused on the small bright spot that was my daughter's hair bobbing along the trail in the wake of the cart. She had promised faithfully she would come straight back, and Tess was in hot pursuit, but the sight of her running away from me still made me feel cold inside.

Martin's soft chuckle recalled me to his presence. "Thea," he answered. "I gather she received some kind of punishment."

I glanced up at him, noting the small changes in his face that were more apparent in the strong morning light. Faint lines at the corner of his eyes and mouth suggested that his sense of humor had not abandoned him, and indeed those laughter lines gathered now as his smile broadened. But a small, straight line between his brows was evidence of worry and the burden of responsibilities. The tired look I had noticed earlier didn't leave him even when he smiled.

"Teddy was right though," I said and saw Martin's brow contract in puzzlement. I seemed to be aware of every line of his features, and that disconcerted me. Would this fascination fade as I became more accustomed to him again? I drew a deep breath, determined to resume my normal, workaday frame of mind, and crossed my arms against the faint chill of the morning wind.

"Teddy said punishing Thea would only anger her, and she wouldn't admit she had done anything wrong. I'm afraid he's right. Did you see how she looked at me? As if I'd taken a switch to her myself." I hugged my arms tighter to my body, remembering the chill I had felt under Thea's steady glare.

"What she did was wrong," Martin said, and I could see his eyes had darkened to the storm-gray color that betrayed his anger.

It appeared that Tess had finally caught up with Sarah. They were turning back from pursuing the cart, which was now only a speck in the distance.

"They'll be all right," Martin said. My face was averted from him as I scanned the prairie, my hands shading my eyes, but I had the unnerving impression he was staring at me. Quite possibly, I had changed too. Was he noticing the signs of age on me? I was twenty-two now after all—well out of my first youth.

"I must do some work," I said, trying to shake myself out of my inactivity. Tess and Sarah were definitely heading back toward the seminary, but knowing the two of them, the journey would be a long one, interspersed with romps in the dry grass and the picking of interesting seed heads and such flowers as might remain at this time of year. "I didn't do a thing yesterday, and for the last three weeks I've been sewing clothes for the Lombardis. I'm worried about them, Martin."

I turned toward the small door that led to the area by the kitchen, threading my way past two of the women servants carrying clanking buckets. They greeted me cheerily and looked curiously at Martin, who followed close behind me. He raised his hat to them and spoke a genial greeting, which earned him broad smiles and nods of approval.

We emerged opposite the row of stout oak-paneled doors that denoted the rooms of the wealthier students. I thought, as I often did, of Reiner, now somewhere in Saint Louis. I felt a pang of sadness for the pleasant young man who had, for a while at least, been genuinely attached to me. I wished I had been able to return that attachment.

"You're very quiet." Martin's voice echoed in the corridor. Wednesday morning's classes were in session, the public areas of the building deserted.

"I was thinking of a friend," I admitted, pushing open my workroom door. "One who's no longer here."

"A friend you were fond of?" Martin's tone was light.

"Yes, to a certain degree," I admitted, opening a window to let in the morning air. The northern exposure of my workroom allowed no beams of sunlight in to fade my fabrics, but on a fine day like today, the high windows let in a bright, even light. It winked in my scissors, left carelessly on a chair, and brightened the dull yellow of the nankeen spread out on my cutting table. Fretting about Sarah the day before, I hadn't tidied up as I usually did.

"Was he fond of you?"

I felt myself redden. "He was. He asked me to marry him. But I wasn't sufficiently attached to him for that."

"And not a hint in your letters? Merciful heavens, Mrs. Lillington, you are quite the dark horse." Martin's tone was light and the maiden-auntish "Merciful heavens" was a definite invitation to playfulness, but there was a note of cynicism that was new to him.

I picked up one end of the nankeen and snapped it to shake off a few loose threads, then smoothed the cloth back over the table and reached for my basket of pattern pieces.

"You didn't inform me about your own wedding until it had already happened," I pointed out. "Besides, I didn't want to marry him, so what was there to tell?"

"I'm sure the corridors of the seminary are littered with rejected swains." Martin laughed, but it wasn't a pleasant laugh. "Mr. Poulton, perhaps?"

I affected not to hear him and went in search of my pincushion, which had ended up on the sewing machine. "I really do have a lot of work, Martin."

Martin pulled up a chair and sat down, stretching his long legs out before him.

"So Mr. Poulton is not rejected, then? I thought he was trying to get that point across to me at breakfast. Conceited sort of fellow, isn't he?"

There was nothing I could say to that remark, so I said nothing, concentrating on pinning the pattern pieces at the correct angle. Through the open window, the sound of faraway laughter reached me in tiny spurts, borne by the west wind that occasionally rattled the frame as it pushed against the glass. Behind me, I could hear the soft creak of the chair as Martin shifted position, the gentle rasping sound of his hands sliding into his pockets. A fly buzzed around my head, and I swatted it away, watching it zigzag toward the window, bouncing off a pane of glass as it made good its escape outdoors.

I breathed in the warm hay scent of the prairie in autumn, trying to enjoy what normally would have been a peaceful morning's work. But my peace was being torn down, minute by minute, by the silence gathering between me and Martin like the calm that precedes the onrushing storm.

We both ran out of patience at the same moment. My hand faltered, its normal easy dexterity replaced by a heaviness that seemed to start at my shoulders. I turned to see that Martin had straightened up in his chair, all pretense at relaxation abandoned.

"Good," he said, but his eyes were hard. "I rather hoped I wouldn't have to conduct this conversation with the back of your head. I'll ask you straight—has Poulton asked you to marry him, and have you said yes?"

I slammed down the scissors, which I had unaccountably picked up, and moved to the window. The north side of the building had little to commend it, offering only a view of a particularly flat and uninteresting piece of prairie and the young trees that marked the seminary's boundary. I leaned against the window frame and crossed my arms, glaring at Martin.

"Since you're evidently not going to let me work until you've *interrogated* me, then yes, Judah has asked me to marry him, and no, I haven't yet said yes. But I haven't said no either. He's going to ask me again around the New Year, and by that time I intend to have an answer for him."

"Do you love him?" Martin asked and then shook his head so that a lock of white-blond hair fell over his forehead. He pushed it back impatiently. "No, forget I said that. If you loved him—passionately—you would have married him long ago. You have a deep well of devoted love in you, Nellie. Once it fastens itself to a person, I don't imagine either an ocean or a century would be sufficient to part you from them."

"You might be right," I said, wishing we were not having this conversation. "But there's more to marriage than just love—isn't there?"

"Indeed." Martin rose and came to join me at the window, his face bleak as he stared out at the undulating line of trees, from which a few parched brown leaves would occasionally fall. His profile, with its high, beaky nose and slightly full lower lip, was as familiar to me as my own face, and yet unfamiliar.

"I don't like him." Martin shoved his hands back into his pockets and turned his head toward me, his expression serious. "I don't think he loves you at all. I don't think he even wants you, not as a man wants a woman. I would understand him better if he did. Oh, I know he's all smiles and pretty gestures," he continued as I opened my mouth to retort, "and I'll bet he's not above kisses and caresses too, when you're alone."

I reddened, and he laughed, a short, cynical sound that twisted one side of his mouth upward. "It's easy to offer such —compliments—to a lovely young woman." The arm nearest me jerked convulsively, as if his hand were trying to lift upward, but he only shoved the hand deeper into his pocket, his face hardening. "But that's not love, Nellie, that's seduction. And it's usually a means to an end."

"That's ridiculous." Anger rose up through me, hot and acid. "You barely know him—"

"I've seen enough." Martin's mouth tightened, reflecting my fury. "And I understand the power of seduction too, Nell, better than you realize."

He moved a couple of inches closer to me, staring into my face. "You're vulnerable, and without a protector for all intents and purposes. The Lombardis are too far away, and they have their own problems. What's more, you're rich. He knows that, doesn't he?" His lips twitched as another thought plainly crossed his mind. "But the Calderwoods don't—now *that's* interesting."

I pushed at Martin's chest with the flat of my hands,

trying to shove him away. My shoulder was up against the window frame, and I couldn't step backward. To my surprise, I couldn't budge him. He was far more solid than I remembered, and it was like pushing against a large animal that was looming over me.

He *was* looming over me, and I wasn't sure what I thought about that. For a moment, I considered kicking him in the shins, but I wasn't sure what I thought about that either. So I did nothing, my hands resting on the rough silk of his waistcoat, aware of the warmth of his body and the strong thump of his heartbeat.

"You're letting your imagination get the better of you," I said, realizing as I did so how like Mama I sounded. "Really, Martin, you sound like a dime novel. Why should Judah have any motive for wanting to marry me except—wanting to marry me? Perhaps he's simply reached the age and position in life when a man wishes to marry, and I—I'm not entirely devoid of charms, am I?"

I bit my lip, wishing I had not let that last question out. It negated the brisk, no-nonsense tone of the first part of my speech and sounded childish and desperate. I felt a flush heat my cheekbones but refused to lower my eyes, looking steadily into Martin's face.

The silence that stretched between us was broken by a giggle from somewhere to my right. Martin's face changed, and he stepped back, breaking the contact between us. I moved so I could see out of the window and waved at Sarah and Tess, who were heading toward us, clutching the anticipated bundles of grass and flowers.

"We're going round the back to find a vase," Tess called, a little breathless.

"Hurry up—we have a lot of work to do."

I shut the window and glared at Martin, who had the

expression of a man just waking from a dream. “Hadn’t you better go find out what’s happened to your wife?”

“Yes.” Martin turned on his heel, buttoning his jacket as he did so. He moved around the table to retrieve his hat and turned back to me. “But I haven’t said my last word on this subject.”

“I have.” I could feel my face assuming its most stubborn expression. “Shall we meet up again later, at a more suitable time for Lucetta? I’d like to get to know her better.”

My shoulders slumped, and I put as much sincerity into my voice as I could summon. “Martin, this visit isn’t going to be much fun if we keep arguing. I really have looked forward to seeing you, you know.”

“I know.” Martin opened the door, his hat in the other hand, and turned again. “You’re not entirely devoid of charms,” he said brusquely, and with that, he was gone.

33
SOCIETY

"What are you going to find to do here for three whole weeks?"

Judah passed the plate of tiny sandwiches to Lucetta with his usual charming smile. She didn't exactly smile back, but there was something flirtatious about the twinkle in her eyes.

I should know, I thought. I'd been a most irrepressible flirt some six or seven years ago—heavens, was it really that long?—and was well acquainted with the uses to which a pair of fine eyes could be put. Lucetta's were lovely—large, and that deep brown that looks black in some lights but soft velvet brown in others. They were thickly fringed with black lashes, and the few lines around them did not detract from their beauty.

She wore an afternoon dress in jade-green silk, trimmed with gold fringing, and with a bodice and train in navy overlaid with gold guipure lace. It shimmered as she moved, catching the light from the chandelier above us.

I had changed my dress, of course, as soon as Judah had informed me of our invitation to take tea in the Calderwoods' parlor. My pretty gold faille was high fashion in

Springwood, but next to Lucetta's magnificence, I felt like a dove keeping company with a peacock.

Opposite us, Martin sat next to Dr. Calderwood with an impenetrable expression of polite interest on his face that could have disguised anything from boredom to outright hilarity.

"I could practice my music, I suppose." Lucetta's glance strayed to the room adjoining the Calderwoods' parlor, where we were sitting. We could see Dr. Adema's piano, its inlaid woods catching the golden glow of the afternoon light.

Dr. Calderwood saw where Lucetta was looking and responded immediately, baring his huge teeth in a gallant smile and bowing obsequiously. "If you wish to make use of my piano, my dear lady, you are most welcome, most welcome. It will be a pleasure to hear you play."

"I'm more of a singer than a pianist, although of course I can acquit myself reasonably well at the instrument," Lucetta replied. She looked at Martin, seemingly waiting for him to say something.

"My wife has a voice worthy to compete with Patti's, although in my opinion it is even richer," Martin drawled obediently.

"You've seen Adelina Patti?" Mrs. Calderwood was breathless with excitement.

"At the Academy of Music in New York," Martin replied, and for a moment his glance flicked in my direction, the same unreadable expression in his eyes. I wondered whether he wanted to see if I was impressed with the Academy of Music in New York—I wasn't—or whether he was sharing the joke that he, Martin Rutherford, the draper from the small town of Victory, could now sit talking about Patti with his heiress wife.

"Dr. Calderwood plays the pianoforte extremely well," Judah obligingly supplied the next round of compliments.

"Perhaps he could accompany you while you sing, Mrs. Rutherford?"

This remark set off a small fireworks display of protestations of too little talent from Dr. Calderwood, interjections to the contrary from his wife, and polite noises of assent from Martin, who was playing the part of the city sophisticate well. He was definitely amused now, I realized, watching the alert lift of his eyelids and the delicate flaring of his nostrils as he suppressed a grin.

Lucetta, on the other hand, seemed to take the offer seriously. She peppered Dr. Calderwood with questions about his musical experience and preferences. It surprised me to find the man really did know music. For a moment, he seemed quite sincere, the constant darting of his eyes ceasing as he fixed them on Lucetta.

Before another quarter of an hour had passed, the three of them—Dr. Calderwood, as always, deferred to his wife's brisk management of his schedule—had arranged a trial hour or two of practice together the next day.

"We've quite left Mrs. Lillington out of the conversation," Judah remarked. He took my teacup from me and handed it to Mrs. Calderwood, who raised inquiring eyebrows and asked if I would like more tea. I declined. My English Grandmama had raised me to appreciate a well-brewed pot of tea, and the Calderwoods' potion left much to be desired.

"I'm not musical," I admitted. "My talents lie more with my needle and my pencil. My grandmother encouraged me to play the piano, but somehow I never found the joy in it that I've observed other people do."

"Martin is the same," sighed Lucetta. "At least he was until I undertook to give him a musical education. Did you never hold musical soirées in that little town of yours?"

"I worked too hard in that little town of ours to have the energy to attend soirées," Martin said. His tone was equable but held just a hint of annoyance. I had the impression that a well-worn marital discussion of his faults lay behind Lucetta's remark. "Idleness and extravagance weren't traits that my parents encouraged. Musical fripperies came under both categories, I believe."

His eyes darkened, and I shot him a sympathetic look. From what Mama had told me, Martin's childhood hadn't been particularly cheerful even before his father's mind had begun to falter.

"I'm quite enraptured by the idea of hearing you sing," Judah said to Lucetta, diverting the conversation away from the dangerous path it had decided to take. "Perhaps it would be possible to arrange a small concert or two for the benefit of the better folk of Springwood? We have so few interesting entertainments out here on the frontier. Patti herself would barely create less excitement than you would."

The Calderwoods exclaimed in unison over this notion, the doctor's bass rumble a heavy counterpoint to Mrs. Calderwood's excited squeaks. The ensuing conversation prompted a general move to the piano to rummage through the sheet music stored inside the footstool. Martin and I, as the nonmusical members of the party, stayed behind.

"Pray tell, Mr. Rutherford—what are *you* going to do for three weeks?" I put four of the small sandwiches and a soft, dainty little cake onto my plate; the tea was foul enough, but Netta's cooking never failed.

Martin's eyes were on the party gathered round the piano. His expression was strange, a mixture of wariness and derision that puzzled me. But as soon as I spoke, he turned back toward me, grinning when he saw my loaded plate. He reached over to the platter and disposed of one of the tiny sandwiches in a single bite before settling back into his chair.

"I'm here to see the frontier and to spend time with old friends. That's a pretty dress, Nellie."

I looked down, brushing a crumb of cake off the gleaming faille silk. "Not as grand as Lucetta's. I would swear hers was from the House of Worth in Paris."

"It is. So are several of her gowns. I could see you looking at it out of the corner of your eye. I wish I could show you our workshop. We have a client—whose name I'll never divulge—who gets gowns from Worth's. She wears them only once and then sells them to us so my couturières can see exactly what Paris is doing and use them for inspiration. We don't copy, of course—we're above that." Martin leaned forward a little to see the details of my dress more clearly. "But what you've done, with only the fashion journals and your own imagination to guide you, is quite remarkable. You know how to cut for the best drape as well as any of my own ladies, and several of them hail from Europe and have a high opinion of themselves."

"I so wish I could meet them."

I meant it. The sight of Lucetta's gowns had awakened a longing in me to see a city again—to see Chicago, with its newly built shops and thoroughfares . . .

A thought struck me, and I looked up at Martin. "Martin—you haven't actually *been* to Paris, have you?"

"Well, yes, as a matter of fact." Martin looked abashed. "In May. I didn't tell you because—well, I felt you were in such a tranquil and healthy spot, and I didn't want to make you feel restless. Now I've seen this place though," his gaze roved around the ornate parlor in its shades of red and brown, "I don't feel nearly so sanguine about leaving you here. There's something odd about this institution, something secretive. It's like when you're certain there's a worm in your apple, but you can't for the life of you see a hole where it got in, and it makes you uneasy about taking a bite."

And yet, I thought, Martin was happy keeping secrets from me. It hurt me more than I cared to admit that he had been to Paris—sailed across the ocean—without telling me about it. What else had he kept from me?

My face must have fallen because a look of deep concern spread over Martin's.

"I've made you unhappy," he said softly. "I'm sorry."

I was trying to formulate a reply when Judah emerged from the adjoining room. Martin saw the direction of my gaze, and his anxious look changed back to the polite, indifferent one he'd worn earlier. "I intend to ride out to the Lombardi mission—what do you think of that, Nell? And I'll have to make a trip to Wichita to meet Fassbinder there. I wanted him to accompany us, but he planned another route. He's prospering mightily in the leather and dry goods trade and tells me he can make a much higher profit by extending his chain of stores as close to the frontier as possible. I have a stake in his business, as you know, so his profits are my profits—I must go about with him a little and hear his ideas."

"Mr. Fassbinder is a longtime business associate of Mr. Rutherford's," I explained to Judah, who had seated himself beside me.

"I read about Mr. Fassbinder occasionally in the papers," Judah replied, looking interested. "He has some powerful political connections among the German interests, I believe."

"He lived with Martin for a while after the Great Fire," I said. "But he moved to Saint Louis—he has two daughters who have settled there. And their husbands are successful in their own right, so Martin tells me."

"You have an exalted circle of acquaintance, Nell." Judah's voice was soft, intimate, almost possessive. "We'll have to make sure you don't remain a seamstress for much longer."

"I agree with that in principle," Martin said, "although our methods may differ."

He looked hard at Judah, and I felt like a bone lying between two large dogs. I sat up straighter, feeling indignant.

What did Martin—what did either of them—think they were doing, presuming to arrange my life for me?

"I think it's for me to determine at what point I cease to be a seamstress," I said. Again I heard Mama's—or was it Grandmama's?—patrician English accent ringing in my own voice.

I rose to my feet, smoothing down the bodice of my dress. "After all, the power of decision is entirely mine, is it not?"

I gave both of them what I hoped was a quelling look and made my way toward the Calderwoods to make my excuses and get back to my workroom. I had had quite enough of society for one day.

34

REVELATION

"When's Martin coming back?"

Sarah carefully copied the *r* in "October" on her slate, making a good job of it.

It was the first day of that month. Martin had been gone for five days, visiting the Lombardis' mission. He intended to ride around with the pastor to see the "real frontier" of homesteaders and prospectors.

I'd wondered how Martin would get on with so much rough riding until I saw him dressed in well-worn denim britches and scuffed chaps, looking for all the world as if he'd spent his whole life on horseback. He had laughed at my evident astonishment, reminding me that he now often went hunting with his business acquaintances.

"You should call him Mr. Rutherford," I admonished Sarah, but I knew she wouldn't. She had taken to Martin, behaving with him much as she did with Teddy—demanding piggyback rides and chatting to him about her real and imaginary worlds. She'd climb into his lap to smooth her small hands over his freshly shaven cheeks when he visited our workshop in the morning, just as I'd done as a small child—except then his cheeks had barely needed shaving.

"Pinch and a punch for the first of the month, Momma!"

Sarah ran to me and administered a vigorous pinch on my hand, followed by a punch to the arm that would not have disgraced a prize boxer. I yelped and rubbed the sore spot. Sarah laughed and ran to Tess, who threw her hands in the air, shouting, "White rabbits!" to ward off the attack.

A great deal of foolishness ensued, culminating in a mad chase around the workroom. Sarah had the distinct advantage of being able to duck under the tables. She was successfully eluding capture when she suddenly squealed, "Martin!" and launched herself at the tall figure who had appeared in the doorway.

"Good heavens, did you ride all night?" I collapsed breathlessly into a chair and squinted at the watch pinned to my shirtwaist. "It's only a quarter past ten."

"I left well before dawn; Lombardi thinks we'll have rain, and there's nothing worse than the chafing you get from riding in wet clothes."

Martin dropped into a chair in his turn, removing his Stetson, which was much newer than the rest of his outfit. He placed it well out of the way of the length of black cashmere spread across my cutting table. He smoothed a hand over his hair, which had a dent in it from his hat, and winced as Sarah vaulted onto his knees. The bridge of his nose was sunburned, and dust had settled into every crease of his clothing and much of his skin.

"Oooooh, your face is all prickly." Sarah rubbed a hand over the pale stubble on Martin's chin, making a faint rasping sound. She held up her palm to assess the resulting dirt, then wiped her hand on Martin's sleeve.

"And you smell of horse." Tess, her round face rosy with joy, came to drop a light kiss on Martin's cheek, wrinkling her nose. "But I missed you, Martin, and I'm glad you're back."

"I suppose I do smell somewhat." Martin squinted down his long length of leg, eying the dust on his boots critically. "I'll have to wash up before I face Lucetta; she can't abide me when I stink. But I thought the circus was in town—I had to see what all the ruckus was about." He poked Sarah in the side, causing her to shriek with laughter as she doubled up.

"What are you working on?" he asked me, gesturing to the spread of black on my table. "Looks funereal."

"It is." I ran a finger over the cashmere, enjoying its dull sheen and delicate softness. "Mrs. Addis's mother passed yesterday—she lived with them. After Mrs. Addis had finished talking to Dr. Calderwood about a funeral service, she came straight to me to order her mourning. It's as well I've caught up with my work for the seminary."

"And we won't be going out this afternoon." Tess stood on tiptoe to shut the window. The pastor had been right about the rain, which was already splattering on the panes of glass and bringing a smell of wet dust to our nostrils. "So we can get lots done, Nell. Mrs. Addis said again and again and again how black would look terrible on her," she added to Martin, "but Nell made such a pretty drawing—see?" She held up a piece of paper on which I had sketched a design that would flatter Mrs. Addis's well-kept figure. "So she stopped crying about wearing black and cried about her mother instead. Then she made Andrew drive all the way to Wichita and back for the cashmere and some silk and some black fringe. I don't know how she can do that because he's not her servant, but he didn't mind because she gave him two dollars."

Tess ran out of breath and leaned on the edge of the table, pink with pleasure at being the deliverer of the latest news.

"So I do have rather a lot of work." I stood up and moved around to the end of the table where I had started arranging the pattern pieces. "But you can stay there as long as you like, Martin; Tess was going to read to me."

"Out of the Bible?" Martin was beginning to look sleepy. Sarah had laid her head on his chest and curled up on his lap, her skinny little legs in their practical black stockings half-hidden under her petticoats.

"We're reading a novel." Tess held up a volume bound in lilac and gold with a lavishly illustrated cover. "It's called *Around the World in Eighty Days,* and it's full of adventures."

"A man jumped out of the fire," Sarah said lazily, patting Martin's vest. Then, a little more alert, she asked, "What's this?"

Martin fished a lumpy shape out of his vest pocket and gave it to Sarah. "I found it in a gully when I stopped to rest the horse," he said. "It's a shell that's turned all to stone—it's called a fossil."

"I know what a fossil is." Sarah turned the petrified shape over in her hands. "God made them to make the world look old, that's what Dr. Calderwood says in his sermons. They're very long, his sermons." She yawned, gazing at the shell. Then she straightened up, fetching Martin such a punch on the arm—fortunately not with the hand that held the fossil—that he grunted and swung her down out of his lap, frowning. "What was that for?" he asked.

"Pinch and a punch for the first of the month."

Sarah, with a cheeky grin, tried to pinch his thigh—he moved his leg in time—and then skipped backward a few paces. "Can—may I have this?" she corrected herself with one eye on me, holding up the fossil.

Martin groaned and rubbed his arm in an exaggerated fashion. "You may," he replied, "especially if you behave yourself for a while." He settled back into his chair again, watching as Sarah sat at her table and cleaned her slate in preparation for some drawing.

I busied myself with the placement of the remaining pattern pieces while Tess found her spot in the book and commenced reading. We had discovered that when she read out loud she did not stutter much, as long as she concentrated fiercely on the page. I was grateful for her newfound enthusiasm, as Sarah, who loved stories, would play quietly as Tess read and thus leave me free to work.

I didn't find Mr. Verne's story all that fascinating, to tell the truth, and listened with half an ear, letting my mind wander over the task ahead of me. I had designed the dress with a diagonally cut overskirt over a tiered underskirt. It had close-fitting sleeves and a high neckline since Mrs. Addis's neck gave away her age much more than her figure did. How best could I use the silk she had bought, which was surprisingly delicate? And I didn't have time to add overmuch detail. Martin would know . . .

But Martin's eyes had closed. His head rested against the high chair back, showing his beaky nose in profile. His arms were folded over his body, his long legs stretched out in front of him. He did not, for a mercy, snore or sleep gape-mouthed, but dozed quietly, his hair falling forward over a forehead which showed a faint line of grime where his hat had been.

My hands faltered at my work, and I found I was regarding Martin with an almost avid concentration, as if I were a painter setting out to paint his portrait. His hands, large and long-jointed but sensitive-looking, had relaxed in sleep, a fresh, shallow gash marring the knuckles of the left hand with a stripe of brownish-red. The skin on his hands and face was faintly bronzed, his eyebrows wirier and darker than I remembered them. The eyelashes that lay on his cheek were as I had known them, light—almost white—at the ends but shading to brown near the eye. This made them look short, but I knew that up close they would be longer than they appeared.

I had a sudden memory of being perhaps nine years old and deeply repentant about something I had done or said. It was during the war—around the time of Shiloh, I realized, the name of the battle leaping out of my memory as if significant. Martin had been sitting in a high-backed wooden chair, much like the one he was in now, but in a state far from relaxation. Every line of his young man's body, his long, thin limbs, was expressive of impatience and fury, his mouth clamped shut in a tight line and his eyes storm-dark with anger. He was so easily angered in those days. He was a man of twenty, forced to cling to his mother's side to protect her from his father's violence while his friends were away at the war, living the life he would have chosen. I had lit the fuse somehow with my careless teasing and felt sick inside, desperately searching for a way to bring a smile to Martin's face.

I had climbed on his lap—something I had not done for some time, and my longer skirts caught under my knees and infuriated me. I kissed his face repeatedly: the high bridge of his nose, his cheekbones, his forehead, his closed eyes . . . I remembered the strange feel of his eyes under the delicate, soft skin of the lids, the tickle of his lashes on my lower lip, his warm breath on my neck as he finally, reluctantly, began to laugh. I tasted in memory the tiny salt tang of a tear he had been unable to suppress and knew again the sorrow and relief I had felt as I understood I had made him feel better, but only for a moment.

My workroom seemed to tilt around me as I stood there, my hands useless at my sides. An odd buzzing in my ears muted the soft drone of Tess's voice, the scratch of Sarah's chalk on her slate, and the light tapping of the rain at the window. Heat spread through my body from my core, invading my limbs and sending a tingling warmth into the tips of my fingers. I was perhaps five feet from where Martin sat, but I could *feel* him, a strange intimacy of the mind that yearned to become intimacy of the flesh, the memory of the innocent love of my childhood transmuted into a love that was anything but childlike—

And then, as if summoned, he opened his eyes, his expression serious and alert, as though sleep had not claimed him only seconds before. He looked straight at me, and I had to rest the fingertips of both hands on the table to steady myself because I knew—finally admitted to myself—that my love for Martin Rutherford was as overwhelming and inescapable as the fierce possessiveness I felt for Sarah. The difference was a visceral longing I had never experienced anywhere, not even during those heady days of flirtation with Jack. It was also, of course, completely impossible.

"I need some air." My voice sounded faint, tremulous. I was aware of Tess and Sarah pausing, their heads turning toward me as I pushed a chair out of the way to gain the door. I fumbled with the doorknob—my hand felt cold and numb and incapable of grasping aright—and yanked the door open, feeling the dry dust of the corridor envelop me as I ran.

I had no idea where I was going. I had just enough presence of mind left to be grateful that classes were in session and there was nobody to see me, to stop me and ask what I was about, running through the building like an insane woman.

I passed the staircase, the colors of the stained-glass windows dull under the cloudy sky. I reached the front doors and pushed hard, breathing in great gulps of air as I came to a halt on the small porch.

Below me, the rain slanted onto the yellowed tussocks of grass, creating small rivulets of mud that pooled here and there into opaque puddles. The wind was a sullen growl that bent the tops of the young trees, tearing off their dry, tan leaves and flinging them toward the prairie in an endless shower of destruction. I huddled miserably into the corner of the porch, heedless of my clean shirtwaist, wishing I had somewhere to run to. But Kansas was a great blank canvas, an unfinished patchwork of green, brown, and tan under an oppressive, leaden bank of shifting cloud.

I'd left the door ajar. I was so intent on flight that I didn't hear Martin step through the gap at first, only turning my head as the door shut with a soft *thunk,* and he pivoted toward me.

"Go away." I folded my arms tighter, hugging them against my chest until my back ached. "Leave me alone."

"I won't ask you what's wrong." There was desolation in Martin eyes but also something like joy in their depths. "I saw it in your face—you're not very good at hiding your emotions." He took a step toward me and raised a hand as if to touch my cheek, dropping his arm as I recoiled from his reach. "If it's any comfort to you, it's the same thing that's been wrong with me since I arrived here."

He spread a hand on the yellow sandstone of the archway, leaning against the rain-splattered stone and staring out at the silver shafts of the downpour. Judah and I had kissed in this place, I thought, and waited for the memory to stir some sense of guilt. But all I felt was dull indifference, as if Judah and I were a story in a book.

"When you came in from the prairie the day we arrived, you looked as if something had dragged you in the dust." Martin settled himself more comfortably against the stone, wiping rain off his forehead with the back of his hand. "Your hair had bits of grass sticking out of it, your dress was all torn and your poor face—dirt and blood and tear tracks like a three-year-old who's been out in the yard too long. And I couldn't speak—I didn't think I was going to be able to speak. I was already pretty sure I loved you, but that—that was like having the fact trampled into me by a team of horses." The laughter lines gathered at the corners of his eyes. "You certainly know how to make an entrance, Nellie."

I wasn't laughing. I clung to my anger like the lifeline it was, my only defense against my desire to close the gap between us and ruin both of our lives at one blow.

"You were sure that you loved me?" I spat, trying to keep my voice low—there were classrooms immediately to our right. "Did you love me the day you married Lucetta?"

"Yes."

I aimed a blow at Martin's cheek that would have raised quite a welt if it hadn't gone wide and bounced harmlessly off the side of his skull. He grabbed both my wrists, pulling my hands onto his chest and holding them captive against the rough material of his vest. I struggled against the imprisonment, staggering forward so I could shove at him harder. I found the attempt just as useless as it had been the first time he had held me like that, in my workroom.

"Let me go."

"Only if you promise not to hit me again." Martin's breath was coming fast. Under my fingers, I felt his heart thumping rapidly, the quick rise and fall of his chest slowing as he regained control over his breathing.

I nodded, and he released my wrists. I realized I hadn't wanted him to let go after all and hated myself for it.

"Why?" I wailed, stepping back a pace.

He didn't have to ask what I meant. He became still, staring at me for a long time as if he were making up his mind about something. Then he spoke.

"She told me she was with child." His mouth twisted as if in pain, and he looked around him, clearly wishing he could punch something. I felt as if a lump of ice had dropped down my back.

"She wasn't?"

"She never will be. Never can be. She told me that in Paris, after she'd had one glass of champagne too many. I dreamed of a son, Nellie." Martin pressed his palms against his forehead, burying his fingers in his thick hair. "I wanted that child. We haven't even been married two years and every dream she sold to me, she's destroyed." He slammed a hand against the thick, ornate door, causing it to resonate with a dull vibration. "I don't think there's been one minute in our marriage when she's been faithful to me—she has barely bothered to hide it."

Pity and horror were robbing me of my anger. I searched desperately for some small shred of it, however unreasonable, to sustain me.

"And at what point before all of this happened did you intend to tell me you loved me? You didn't seem to be in love with me in Victory. You let me go—"

Martin dragged his hands out of his hair and shoved them in his pockets so hard that I heard some stitches break. "Oh, for heaven's sake, Nell, would you have listened? And besides—" His face hardened, and he looked away.

"You may as well say it." My voice sounded cool in my ears, but I wasn't calm. I knew what was coming. I linked my fingers behind my back to hide the trembling in my hands.

"You were a foolish girl who had let a man seduce her, the mother of his by-blow." The words fell between us like stones. "And I was taught to think myself above such things. *He* had plenty to say about loose women and about how I should keep myself pure."

He. Martin's father.

"And one morning I woke up in Lucetta's bed," Martin went on in a rush, the words sounding strangled, "and realized it didn't matter. That we were no different, you and I—and you, at least, succumbed to temptation only once. That I only had to disentangle myself from a liaison that was already becoming stale, set myself on a better path, and confess it all to you. Then perhaps you would forgive me, and we could start again."

I was pressing myself so hard against the stone that my hands, still linked, throbbed with pain. It was hard to believe I could be so angry with someone and yet so eager to forgive him. I eased up on my hands, feeling pins and needles spark as the blood flowed back through my wrists.

"It's too late now, in any event." I was surprised at how even my voice sounded given the turmoil in my heart. "You're married, and I—I think I'd better accept Judah's proposal. He'll take me even if I don't love him, and I think I'm too much of a prize for him not to treat me well."

I moved to the door and twisted the huge handle, feeling the ornately carved wood move smoothly on its oiled hinges.

Martin was behind me immediately, his hands curling around my shoulders, fingers digging into my flesh. "Not him." His breath was hot on my cheek just above my ear, and I shivered convulsively. "Not him," Martin said again, turning me to face him.

I thought he would say something else, but then his mouth was on mine, and all rational thought fled from my mind. I hated myself for kissing him back, and yet I didn't seem able to get close enough to him, tasting the sweat and dust on his skin as if it were ambrosia. My fingers dug into the close-cropped hair at the nape of his neck in an effort to bring him nearer to me. How had I ever thought I welcomed Judah's kisses?

Martin broke the contact after just a few seconds and pushed me gently away, opening the door and steering me through it. For a moment, I was blind, seeing nothing of the cloud-darkened hall but a vast empty chasm.

As shapes began to resolve themselves in the gloom, I realized that Martin had moved away from me and was heading for the stairs. He turned with his foot on the first step and spoke in a low, urgent voice.

"I don't know what to do. I really don't. But please—"

"Wait for you?" The anger was back again, made worse by the sheer frustration of that all-too-short kiss. "Do you presume to direct my life from afar?" I strode in the direction of my workshop, pausing to speak over my shoulder to Martin as I did so. "You had better return to your *wife*, Martin, and leave me to order my own affairs."

35
BUBBLE

I barely saw Martin in the days that followed. At least—I tried not to. I realized I had developed an acute sensitivity to the change in the air that meant he was in my vicinity, and I tried hard not to turn in his direction like a compass needle seeking north—but it wasn't easy.

I barricaded myself in my workroom and had Mrs. Addis's mourning dress done in no time, concentrating furiously on every tiny detail of ornament, every pin tuck, every stitch. Anything to distract myself from the terrible lurch my insides gave every time I thought of that dizzying moment when everything changed for me, of our conversation on the porch, of the fact that Martin Rutherford loved me. Had kissed me. And was married.

I was angry. At precisely whom I was angry, I couldn't say. Martin? He had acted honorably enough, as far as I could see, by marrying Lucetta. He had said nothing to me indicative of love until I had given myself away completely, and since that day he had not tried to see me alone. Perhaps I was angry at myself for having such a disastrous talent for choosing the wrong man at the wrong time.

But Martin shouldn't have kissed me. "That was wrong, and completely unfair to boot," I muttered under my breath as I folded Mrs. Addis's black dress. It wasn't a simple operation given the yards of slippery cashmere and silk involved.

Tess, who was unraveling string for the parcel, looked at me curiously.

"What is wrong with you, Nell? You're sort of bad-tempered. Have you quarreled with Martin? He looks sad too."

I let out a hiss of annoyance as the bodice of the dress slid sideways. Pulling it back into position, I inserted pins to secure the bundle.

"We haven't exactly quarreled," I said. "But sometimes when you haven't seen someone for a while, things are different between you, and that's not always easy."

Well, that was the truth, although I wished I could take Tess into my confidence. But I didn't know where to start. Maybe, just maybe, I would wake up tomorrow morning and find the whole thing had been due to an overabundance of nerves or suchlike. Martin and I would be old friends again and nothing more.

Tess was silent for a few moments as I folded the stiff brown paper around the bundled dress and indicated where she should place her hands to hold the whole thing together while I wrapped it in string.

"Martin's wife is very pretty," she said judiciously, watching how I twined the string around itself for extra security. "But, do you know, Nell? I'm not sure if she's nice."

I felt my eyebrows lift in surprise. I'd thought Tess admired Lucetta. "What do you mean, Tess?"

"Well," Tess pulled herself up onto a chair and indicated that I should do the same, "for one thing, when I say 'good morning' or 'good afternoon' to her, she doesn't answer me. She just walks on by like I'm not there. That's not polite, is it?

And I don't think she's hard of hearing because she says 'good morning' back when other people speak to her."

"Maybe she's shy of you, Tess."

"I don't think so." Tess swung her legs, which were too short to reach the floor. "She's not at all shy with *other people*."

She put so much emphasis on the last two words that I looked at her sharply.

"Is this going to turn into gossip? Tess, where were you this morning? With Mrs. Drummond, I'll be bound. I'm not sure if she's quite right in the head since Professor Wale died. You shouldn't listen to her."

"I don't think it's gossip when we're concerned about putting a stop to things that are happening." Tess looked at me sideways, her almond eyes gleaming with significance. "Bad things. Eliza thinks because you're Martin's friend, you should be the one to tell him."

"Wait." I was puzzled but thought I grasped the sense of Tess's hints. "You're telling me I should pass gossip on to Martin about his *wife*?" I stood and paced the floor, pushing chairs out of my way. "No. Oh no. Tess, I'm the last person to entrust with that particular task, believe me." I stopped dead, my shoulders slumping as I gave in to curiosity. "Very well. What bad things?"

Tess squared her shoulders and looked important. "Well, Mrs. Rutherford and Dr. Calderwood play music a lot together."

"I know. They're rehearsing for a concert. What of it?"

"And while they play music, they drink wine."

"Hmm. Well, that's against the seminary's rules. But Dr. Calderwood has made a practice of relaxing the rules for guests. I know it makes Mrs. Drummond angry, but I don't think—"

"And sometimes they don't play any music at all. For a long time." Tess stared hard at me.

"Oh, now that *is* ridiculous." I resumed my pacing. "Nobody would be that indiscreet. In a place like this? And —*Doctor Calderwood?*" To be honest, it was the notion that Lucetta Rutherford saw anything at all in the pompous, preening man that shocked me the most.

"She likes Mr. Poulton too." Tess was watching me carefully. "But he doesn't go in a room with her. He keeps Mrs. Calderwood busy—"

"No!" I put my hands over my ears. "This is Eliza Drummond's deranged mind speaking, not reality. Judah in cahoots with Mrs. Rutherford to—oh no, it's just too preposterous for words."

"You haven't seen much of Mr. Poulton in the last week or so, have you, Nell?"

"Well, no, now that you mention it. But I've been occupied, and it's a busy time of year for Judah." And it hadn't bothered me in the least that Judah hadn't been assiduous in his attentions, I realized. But did I expect the man—any man —to dance attendance on me day and night? It was proper for men to have other things to do.

I snatched up the parcel, dismayed at its weight. "Are you going to put your hat on?" I asked Tess. "I need to deliver this to Mrs. Addis."

Tess stuck out her lower lip ever so slightly. "Eliza was going to teach me about dealing with tradesmen," she said. "And you can't leave Sary with Netta too much longer, or she'll be underfoot when they're cooking, and Netta won't like that."

I sighed. Tess was right, and besides, I wanted to walk fast and she hated that. "I'll have to go on my own then."

"Without a chaperone?"

"I'm not going to waste my time looking for one." I glanced out of the window. The rain had ceased the day before, and the trail wouldn't be too muddy.

I put the parcel down again so I could look at my watch. An hour to walk to Springwood. Say twenty minutes to listen to Mrs. Addis chatter while she rummaged in her pin-money drawer for the rest of my fee. I needed to stop at the mercantile for soap and bootlaces—two and a half hours, then. I would just be back in time for our noonday dinner if I hurried.

I pinned my hat to my hair and shrugged into my jacket, buttoning it quickly. "Don't let Sarah eat too many of the tarts she's making," I instructed Tess. "I'll be back as soon as I can."

IT FELT GOOD TO BE ALONE. DESPITE THE RULE—IN PLACE since Professor Wale's murder—that we were not to walk to Springwood alone, and despite my own memories of the silent, bloody corpse flung like a discarded suit of clothes on the ground, I did not fear for my own safety. As long as it was not exceptionally cold or snowing, I liked being outdoors. And breaking the rule lent a certain spice to the outing, a conduit for the nervous energy that had fizzed in my limbs and invaded my sleep for days.

Tess had given me even more to think about. Perhaps a little solitude would help me regain some mastery over my unruly thoughts.

I had walked perhaps a quarter of a mile with the wind full in my face, and my thoughts had settled down into two overriding notions. First, that fashionable hats were too small to shade one's face from the bright sunlight, and I should have brought that old bonnet. Second, the parcel was dreadfully heavy, and my arms were aching already. And in and out of these two nagging realities wove Tess's tale of Lucetta, Dr. Calderwood, and Judah. Their faces played tag in my mind, dodging in and out of view as I stomped along as fast as I could.

"Nell!"

The shout was so close behind me that I nearly dropped the parcel. I whirled round and took a step backward, tripping over a clump of grass and saving myself from falling only by performing a sort of Saint Vitus' dance on one foot.

"I thought you weren't supposed to wander around alone." Martin had evidently been running but was not particularly out of breath. One hand was clutching his hat, his hair blown wild by the wind.

My heart gave its now-familiar lurch at his appearance. Yet in truth I was becoming so used to its antics that I was able to face Martin with as much equanimity as is possible when you think you're quite alone and then discover you're not. Was this what being in love was like? I wondered, and then shut that thought firmly in a box and sat on it.

"I have Mrs. Addis's dress to deliver, and Tess wasn't inclined to accompany me," I said with as much dignity as I could muster. "And what are you about, sneaking up on me like that?"

"I was *not* sneaking up on you," Martin said with emphasis. "I must have shouted your name twenty times—I thought you were ignoring me on purpose."

"I didn't hear a thing," I admitted. "I was thinking—and the wind—"

"And the person who, I understand, shot one of the seminary's faculty on the prairie could have been upon you and plugged you with a bullet in a second."

Martin dragged his free hand through his hair and stuck his hat back onto it, whereupon the wind promptly tugged it off and sent it bowling into a clump of sunflowers, their stiff stalks still green against the waving grasses. He retrieved it and ran back to me, glaring in a way that cheered me immensely because it felt so normal, as if the world were slowly righting itself around the correct axis.

"Who told you about Professor Wale?" I asked as Martin took the parcel from me and tucked it under one long arm, where it fitted much better than in mine.

"The servants." Martin frowned. "It perturbs me that I've neither heard of it from you nor from anyone else. Would you mind telling me your version of the story?"

The next mile passed quickly as I obliged Martin with the detailed story of how I'd spotted Professor Wale's body on the prairie. He was particularly interested in the dramatic scene in the library when Reiner had been accused. He asked so many questions that I ended up relating what had happened almost verbatim.

"His father is Gerhardt Lehmann, then? I believe Fassbinder is a friend of his," he said.

"Yes. I do hope he's doing well—do you know, Martin, I rather miss him. He gave up on the idea of marrying me, but I thought of him—and Professor Wale—as friends of mine. Reiner would have offered me his protection to cross the prairie today, I'm sure."

"You'll have to make do with me."

Martin offered me his arm and I took it, feeling somewhat self-conscious but glad of his solid warmth under my hand.

"I'd rather walk with you than with Reiner anyway," I sighed. "Only—"

I felt myself redden and looked away across the prairie, suddenly awkward again in Martin's company and all too aware of the buzzing warmth inside me.

"Don't worry—I'm not going to make a nuisance of myself," Martin said. "We need to remain friends, above all things—putting all other feelings aside. I'm not going to drag you into any wrongdoing, but I can't go around behaving as if you don't exist. Whatever happens, Nellie, you've been part of my life—the *best* part of my life—for twenty years. I can't bear to think I might destroy that through wanting more than I can have."

I nodded, wanting to say something but finding it difficult to shape the words. So I walked on in silence, my steps easily matching Martin's long stride. The wind shifted and quieted a little, and I opened my parasol to shade my face, angling it so it blocked much of my view of the prairie. With Martin beside me, I felt as if we were in a small world of our own, a moment of calm between storms, a fragile soap bubble of contentment and longing that would burst if one of us made the slightest move in the wrong direction.

"I'll take you to Mrs. Addis's door," Martin said as we crossed the bridge over the creek. "Then there's a fellow called Fairland I'm told I should look up—do you know him?"

"Vaguely," I replied. "He's the Wells Fargo agent. He'll probably be in his office near the mercantile. You can't miss it."

"Promise me you'll look for me there when you're done. Don't think of walking back alone." His arm pressed my hand tight into his side for a second.

I pointed my parasol in the direction of Mrs. Addis's street. "That way. As long as you don't make me late for dinner—what are you talking to Mr. Fairland about anyway? Business?"

"Horses. It seems he's quite the horse fancier. I'm hoping for a letter of introduction to a certain breeder in Kentucky."

The wind had died down now that we were in the shelter of the houses. Martin handed the package back to me so he could rake back his hair with his fingers and put his hat back on. He smiled down at me as he regained possession of the parcel.

"You have a curl coming loose." He indicated a spot on the back of my head. "I'd fix it for you, but—" His glance at the surrounding houses was eloquent.

I located the errant curl and pushed it back into the mass of hair. "I'll be making some purchases at the mercantile in twenty minutes' time," I said. "Don't let Mr. Fairland talk your ear off."

EXACTLY TWENTY-FIVE MINUTES LATER, I EXITED THE mercantile with a brown paper parcel—containing three cakes of Rose Soap, two pairs of seven-eighths-yard laces, and a dozen hooks and eyes—dangling from its loop of string around my wrist.

I spotted Martin immediately. His height and his pale hair made him easy to pick out from a distance, even if he had not suddenly become the lodestone of my existence. He was deep in conversation with Mr. Fairland, whose whiskers and girth had both expanded since I had last seen him. They were standing outside the Wells Fargo office, poring over what looked like a closely printed and illustrated catalogue. Next to Martin stood Judah Poulton, shorter than Martin by half a head. His sleek, lithe build somehow contrived to make Martin look even more like a Viking warrior by comparison.

Martin saw me first, his head lifting as though by instinct, but Judah was quick to follow his gaze, and it was he who greeted me.

"Nell!" He came toward me and drew my arm through his, relieving me of my small parcel and adjusting my parasol to shade me from the morning sun. "Are you on your way back to the seminary? I must also return—I have a class to teach." He turned to the other gentlemen, laughing. "A poor man must sing for his supper, unfortunately. Speaking of singing, Rutherford," he said to Martin, "your lady wife has the most spectacular voice—our good doctor is quite enchanted with her. Are you coming to the grand dinner, Fairland? You'll have a treat."

Not waiting for a reply, Judah drew his watch from his vest pocket and flipped open the case, still keeping my arm tucked firmly under his. "We must leave, Nell—oh! If I may." He ducked his head under my parasol and, leaning in close to me, touched my hair. "You have a loose curl." He poked at my woven tresses, an intimate, possessive gesture, his eyes intensely blue in the diffused light cast over his face by my shade.

"There. Shall we go?"

I looked over at Martin, whose face had assumed the unreadable expression I had thought was disdain but now realized to be a mask for some powerful emotion. "Are you not coming with us, Mr. Rutherford?"

The corners of Martin's mouth turned upward in what might have been a smile. "Mr. Fairland has suggested we eat a morsel together at his house. I'm confident I may relinquish you to Mr. Poulton's care."

Judah stepped an inch closer to me, hitched my hand a little more securely into the crook of his elbow, and regarded me with a confident smirk. "Oh yes. She's quite safe with me."

36
POSSESSION

"I want *this* one." Sarah smoothed her hand over the pages of her children's magazine. She flattened it out so that the gruesome illustration of a little girl with her hair and clothing in flames was more clearly visible.

"But it's a horrible story," I protested. "And you'll be going to bed soon. You'll have nightmares."

"No, I won't." Sarah scooted her small, bony posterior along my lap and settled her skirts neatly. "Tess says I won't get burnded up because I'm a good girl, and good girls don't get burnded."

"Burned," I corrected, my eyes on the nasty drawing. I loved the times when Sarah and I were alone and could sit in the glow of a single lamp and talk or read together, but I preferred to choose the subject matter of our reading. Sarah had a taste for the most severe of moral tales, and even though I had been raised on them myself, I still found them chilling. The one about the little boy who had his nose bitten off by an escaped tiger because he refused to use his handkerchief had ensured I couldn't sleep without checking behind all the curtains and under the bed for wild animals. I still hated Little Goody Two-Shoes for her role as a comparison with my own wretched self.

I sighed and drew a deep breath. "How Margaret Died, or Some Instructions For The Child Regarding Fire," I read. "Fire is a pretty thing, is it not, little one? Its flickering flame gives us light, its warmth renders the winter's chill bearable . . ." The image of my own child bursting into flame crept into my mind and made itself comfortable there, leering at me as I wound my way through the tedious description of fire's benefits.

I had just reached "Now take heed, O tender Reader!" when a loud knock heralded the arrival of Mrs. Drummond.

Now there was a sight to scare a child, I mused. The housekeeper, once a handsome woman, had in the last year become gaunt to the point of emaciation. The skin of her face stretched tight over the broad cheekbones and rounded chin. Her once-glossy hair had lost its sheen and acquired silver streaks and white patches over the temples. Her hands were nervous, plucking at her skirts obsessively as she spoke. And her eyes—those gray-green irises that had assessed me so coolly upon my arrival at the Eternal Life Seminary—now positively burned in their sockets. It gave me the grues just to look at her.

"Ah, you are not alone, Mrs. Lillington," was her opening salvo. She moved nearer to us so she could see what we were reading and nodded her head approvingly. "You do well to instruct your daughter in the ways of righteousness. Child, remember it is better to burn in the fires of this world than to spend eternity in the flames of hell," she remarked conversationally to Sarah, who slipped her little hand around my neck and held tight.

I mentally cursed the woman but kept a polite smile on my face as I stood, hoisting Sarah into my arms. "I think Mrs. Drummond wants to have a talk with me," I told her. "Why don't we go to the stairs, and then I'll listen while you run all the way up to our room? Tess is there; you can call down to let me know when she opens the door."

"All right," said Sarah stoutly. "I'm not afraid of the stairs." In fact, the stairs made her nervous at night, with their dim shadows rendered somehow darker by the lamp in the hallway and their echoing emptiness. We had been making a game of letting her run up ahead of me, as it was in Sarah's nature to try to conquer her fears.

It was a full five minutes before Tess's voice reassured me that she was not yet asleep. Sarah had taken her magazine with her. I hoped Tess would refuse to read "How Margaret Died" to her, as Tess would certainly have nightmares if she went to bed thinking of that story.

Mrs. Drummond still stood where I had left her, staring at the flame of the lamp as if sleepwalking. I turned up the flame so the lamp burned brighter and resumed my seat, gesturing for her to sit down.

"If you'll forgive my saying so, you don't look very well, Mrs. Drummond," I said. "Have you been ill?"

"A touch of ague, nothing more." The woman nodded, brushing at an imaginary speck on her black skirt.

"Nothing more? You're wasting away." I decided to confront the matter square on.

Mrs. Drummond linked her bony hands in her lap and gazed at me, the whites of her eyes showing. "It is this place, Mrs. Lillington, that is eating away at me." She glanced over her shoulder, but my door was shut, and I had heard no footsteps in the corridor. "This place, and the people in it. I once thought this building a Garden of Eden, a city upon a hill, a light shining in the darkness. But the Serpent dwells here now, and he is spawning others like him."

A chill rippled over my skin, although I was uncertain

why. She was surely insane; but she sounded rational enough as long as I didn't look too hard at her eyes.

"Why did you wish to talk with me, Mrs. Drummond?" I asked, my voice sounding high and faint in my ears.

A strange, wary look came into her eyes, as if she didn't quite trust me. "I wish to know if you will marry Mr. Poulton," she said. "Tess thinks you might."

A ghastly grin stretched her mouth, and I moved back slightly in my chair. "She would prefer you to marry Mr. Rutherford, but he has a wife already. She asked me if it would be possible for him to take a second wife in the manner of the patriarchs of the Old Testament." She giggled, a horribly girlish ripple of high-pitched mirth that froze the blood in my veins.

"I—I doubt I will marry anyone at present," I said. "And with respect, Mrs. Drummond, I don't see the purport of your question. Do you really expect me to lay open the state of my heart to you? And precisely why do you wish to know?"

"You have behaved with more discretion and sense than I expected of you," Mrs. Drummond continued, not heeding my question. "When you came here—well, I will admit I anticipated trouble. And I concede I was wrong about you. I believe now that you have never sought attention from any of the gentlemen. You cannot help it, I suppose, if Mr. Poulton's eye should fix itself on you."

"No, I can't," I said bluntly. "But please don't think for a moment that I would follow any dishonorable course of action. Mr. Poulton's—virtue is quite safe with me."

How absurd this conversation was, I thought. I wished the woman would get to the point and leave me be.

"Oh, I am not at all concerned for Mr. Poulton," was her surprising rejoinder. Her eyes opened wide, and she stared at me. "It is your well-being that preoccupies me."

"Mine?"

"If I tell you something in the strictest confidence, will you swear before God you will not breathe a word of it to anyone, most of all Judah Poulton?"

"Yes, of course. I swear."

"Before God?"

"Before God."

"I am to leave this place on the twelfth of December." Mrs. Drummond drew herself up, and for a moment she sounded like her old self, confident and in command. "I am engaged as an under-housekeeper in a large establishment in Boston."

"An under-housekeeper? But you've been in sole charge of this place for years. Isn't that a step down?"

"It is no matter." Mrs. Drummond smiled grimly. "I do not feel—secure in this place anymore. It is fear that has changed me, Mrs. Lillington. Fear has made me reluctant to leave my rooms and made my food repellent to me. If I seem a little—unbalanced, that is to be expected. I have lived with the anticipation of sudden harm these last six months, and I live with it still."

"From Judah?" I breathed the words out in an incredulous whisper. "But that's ridiculous—and won't he already know that you're leaving? He's in the Calderwoods' confidence."

"Nobody knows I am leaving." Mrs. Drummond hissed the words at me, leaning forward in her chair. "Except you."

A soft knock on the door made me almost jump out of my skin. "Who's there?"

"It is Dorcas." Mrs. Drummond smiled. "She is to accompany me to my bedroom." And indeed the door opened a crack, and Dorcas's dark face appeared. She nodded once and then closed the door again gently.

"But you can't just leave," I protested. "Not without making some arrangement for a replacement, surely."

"I have trained the servants well." There was a note of pride in Mrs. Drummond's voice. "They know what is expected of them, and Mrs. Calderwood is also thoroughly acquainted with everything I do. I will ensure that the provisions store is full before I go. You know your job to the utmost degree; and Tess understands my bookkeeping methods better than anyone." Her face softened. "I'll miss Tess. You won't desert her, will you, even if *he* wants it?"

I shook my head vehemently. "No man will ever come between us. Nor between me and my daughter."

Mrs. Drummond rose to her feet. I did likewise, and she placed a bony hand on my arm. "That is what I wanted to hear." Her emaciated face seemed to glow with a strange fervor. In her eyes, I saw the flame of the lamp reflected as twin sparks of light.

"Now, listen carefully to me. The twelfth of December is a Sunday. I will depart while everyone is at chapel. And just before I do, I will hide—something—in a place you know about. Do you understand? I know you know about it because I saw you search for it after Professor Wale's death. You must go there straight after chapel while everyone is still talking. Do not delay—and do not forget."

The penny dropped. She meant the hiding place in the library shelves.

"It was *you*—" I began, but Mrs. Drummond made a chopping motion with her hand to cut off my words. Yet I was certain I was right—it was she who had taken the letter Professor Wale had shown me. And now she wanted me to have it back.

"But why not give it to me now?" I asked.

Mrs. Drummond shook her head. "It keeps me safe." She raised a finger to her lips, tapping my arm several times with the other hand. "My room has been searched."

Before I could speak, she spun on her heel and reached

the door with astonishing speed. The air around me shifted as the door closed, the flame of the lamp flickering for the merest fraction of a second.

I extinguished the lamp as quickly as I could and almost ran out of the door, following the receding footsteps as they headed toward the stairs. Suddenly, I was not at all keen on wandering about the seminary at night either.

But as I reached the second floor, my footsteps faltered. A light came from the study rooms that lined the long wall of the library, a golden glow pooled on the polished wood of the corridor like liquid fire. Moving as quietly as I could, I approached the open doorway.

Martin sat surrounded by closely written papers, running one hand over his tired eyes as he leafed through several pages containing columns of figures. His jacket hung on the back of his chair. The sleeves of his shirt were folded back, a pair of onyx cufflinks abandoned on the desk in front of him. His hair was disheveled, as if he had been pushing his hand through it, something he often did when he was thinking.

It was a familiar scene. I had frequently seen him work of an evening, those weeks I had spent at his home in Victory after my escape from the Poor Farm. I leaned against the doorjamb, comforted by the thought that here, at least, was someone I could trust.

He looked up and saw me standing there, and his lips curved into a smile. "Have you been working late too, Nellie?"

"Not exactly," I answered. I hesitated, wishing I could tell him about Mrs. Drummond. But she had sworn me to the strictest secrecy about her departure, and I didn't think I could begin to unravel the tale of the poor woman's fears and accusations without inadvertently stumbling onto that part of the conversation.

"I'm going to bed," I said instead, pushing myself away from the jamb. "Good night, Martin."

"Good night, my dear."

An old friend could have said it thus; but my heart lightened, and the darkness seemed less threatening as I climbed the last few flights to the safety of my own room.

37
DANIEL

And then Martin was gone to Wichita, and the last days of the Rutherfords' visit were sliding toward us with the inevitability of a rising river. Lucetta remained behind, and we all heard the muted sound of her voice ringing out from behind the Calderwoods' closed doors as she rehearsed.

As the day of the grand dinner and concert approached, a kind of febrile excitement settled over the seminary. It infected even the students, who, with the exception of the very wealthiest, whose parents were coming, were not invited. Deliveries arrived of a young pig, a brace of turkeys, a half dozen prairie chickens, and a pail containing a dozen live trout. That was the count reported to me by Sarah before an increasingly irritable Netta banished her from the kitchen.

"And liquor too, I suppose?" I said to Judah, who found me in the library after he had spent hours closeted with Mrs. Calderwood, going over endless lists and table seating plans.

"French wines." Judah looked pleased with himself. "I

procured a dozen cases from a merchant in New York, and Dr. Calderwood has tasted them and found they've traveled well."

And when I first came to the seminary, they didn't permit a drop of alcohol—but I said nothing.

"You'll sit with me, quite in the thick of things." Judah brushed his fingers surreptitiously over the back of my hand. We were not alone in the large room, although we were well away from the others.

The touch did not produce the same sensation in me as it would have done a few weeks before, and I felt a now-familiar pang of anxiety. Had I committed myself so far with Judah that refusing his proposal would cause awkwardness, at the very least, and perhaps even accusations of trifling with his affections? I pretended to cough, removing my hand from his reach, and sought for a way to divert his attention. But another thought struck him.

"You must be well dressed, of course," he said, his gaze roaming over my practical shirtwaist and skirt, "but not so well as to outshine the other ladies. You already have the advantage over many of them in terms of youth and beauty."

"I won't be able to outshine Mrs. Rutherford, whatever I do," I noted, ignoring his compliments.

"That is to be expected. But the other ladies will make an effort, do you see? And you must—"

"Not make too much of an effort?"

"Make it look as if you have made a great deal of effort but with a limited palette. Keep it—well, simple I suppose." Judah threw out his hands in a gesture of male helplessness in the face of all feminine matters. "Don't draw undue attention to yourself."

I nodded. I understood what he meant. Perhaps this was the inspiration I needed for the half-finished dress I had been working on in the evenings. The silk was an interesting color, a muted reddish-brown that so far had rebuffed all my attempts to find a contrasting trim. Perhaps the answer was not to try to contrast with it, but to keep it plain and let the color speak for itself. And I would keep the bustle a reasonable size rather than the huge confections that were now in fashion. Some of the fashion plates in the magazines showed bustles that looked as if you could sit on them.

"I know I can trust your taste and common sense," Judah said. "This occasion is as important to me as it is to the Calderwoods—as important to us, to our future."

My heart sank at that—but in truth, what could I say? I could hardly tell Judah—or even hint—that my affections had transferred themselves elsewhere when the object of those affections was a married man. A married man who, moreover, was clearly determined to remain faithful to his wife in the strict sense of the word. I was glad of that, for I wouldn't have wanted Martin to be anything less than honorable, but it did render my own future uncertain in the extreme.

The anger that had calmed somewhat in recent days revived for a second, a flickering flame that had little to feed on. For whom should I blame for the situation I was now in, other than myself?

"I'm sorry Tess and Sarah will be excluded from the concert," I said by way of changing the subject. In fact, I resented Tess's exclusion most strongly. I could understand it wasn't suitable to have a child at a grand dinner, but Tess was a grown woman and my friend. Even if no obvious dinner partner for her was readily identifiable, it must be possible to find someone.

In truth, I was chafing at my subordinate position in the seminary more than ever. I had as much wealth—more, probably—than most of the other guests and was their social equal, but I had only been invited on Judah's behalf. It really was time I made some decisions about my future.

But then Martin—I jerked into a more upright position, gritting my teeth to disguise my restlessness. This line of thinking got me precisely nowhere every time.

"I'm sorry too." And for a moment, Judah looked genuinely sympathetic. "But it'll be a tremendous crush as it is—the Calderwoods' rooms are not suited to a crowd."

"Well, why not use the chapel? Or even the library? Why try to cram us into two rooms?"

"We have considered both locations," Judah answered. "But Mrs. Rutherford says her voice does not sound at all well in the chapel, and that the paneling in the library deadens its resonance. She says the lieder and operetta pieces she has chosen will work better in a more intimate setting."

For a fleeting moment, remembering what Tess had told me, I wondered just how intimate that setting had been. And that instantly led my thoughts down yet another path they most definitely did not want to follow.

I rose to my feet, and Judah politely followed suit, looking surprised.

"Leaving so soon?"

"I promised Sarah I'd only be gone an hour," I lied. In fact, I knew Sarah would already be asleep and so, probably, would Tess. But every aspect of this conversation was like a pin sticking into my side, and I could feel my temper beginning to fray. I'd been avoiding heading upstairs to bed because the oblivion of sleep was proving hard to achieve lately—but I didn't want to remain in Judah's company either. Encouraging him to think of me as his intended was unwise given my increasing qualms on his account.

But as I pushed open one of the double doors leading out

of the library, a thought hit me like a thunderbolt, and I almost gasped aloud.

Supposing—just supposing—Mrs. Drummond's fears about Judah were not simply the product of a mind deranged by grief? If he were dangerous in any way, I could still presume myself safe while he was waiting for an answer to his proposal of marriage. But the moment I refused him—I felt the hairs on my arms stand up and my fingers prickled as a jolt of alarm shot through me.

Above me, the stairwell faded into darkness. Below, the lamp threw strange shadows suggestive of lurking assassins. As I began to climb, one thought dominated all others. If I planned to refuse Judah, I might need to put many miles between myself and the seminary first.

"YOU'RE SO BEAUTIFUL, MOMMA." SARAH DANCED AROUND ME, careful not to step on my dress, dangling her doll in one hand. "You'll be the most beautiful lady of all the ladies."

I stared at my reflection in the cheval glass I kept in the corner of my workroom for my Springwood clients. In the waning light of a brilliant sunset, not visible from my northerly windows but evident in the pink-gold hue it was casting over the pale walls of the room, the silk of my dress glowed a deep reddish-bronze, almost the same color as my hair. I had arranged that hair in a style that was barely more elaborate than my everyday coiffure. My only ornament was the jet brooch, its twined silver and single large pearl catching sparks of crimson fire from the light.

It was strange, I thought as I twisted around to view the dress from the back, but the absence of fashionable tiers, frills, pleats, and bows really did suit me. For one thing, you could see the cut of the dress clearly, and cutting was a skill on which I particularly prided myself. Nobody, not the House of Worth itself, could have faulted the drape of the silk that cascaded down from the tightly fitted bodice and gathered into a small, elegant bustle at the back. I had set out with the express purpose of not outshining the other ladies and yet, I realized, I had outdone myself.

Sarah's stomach gave a loud gurgle, and we both laughed.

"I'm hungry, I'm hungry," Sarah chanted and grinned impishly at me, showing the gap where she had lost both of her lower teeth.

"You certainly are." I reached for her hand, using my free hand to lift my train clear of obstacles. "Let's go upstairs and see if Tess has your special supper ready."

It still rankled that Tess couldn't even attend the concert. But I supposed I couldn't leave Sarah alone anyway, and no servant would be free to watch her. If Sarah had lived in a conventional household, I mused as we climbed the stairs, she would no doubt have some kind of governess or nursemaid to look after her. And I still hadn't done anything about enrolling her in a school. This whole business with Judah—and then Martin—and men and marriage in general was proving a ridiculous hindrance to decision making.

Tess and I had decided to treat Sarah to a supper in our room, with sugar-plums and little cakes begged from Netta. They were the inducement for Sarah not to fret after seeing the ladies and gentlemen in their finery. A new box of marbles and another of jackstraws would provide a novel diversion until it was time for bed.

I hugged both of them hard, feeling unaccountably guilty that I would enjoy some elegant society while they hid far above.

"Don't worry, Nell," was Tess's rejoinder when she saw my face. "I wouldn't want them all staring at me anyhow."

"They wouldn't stare at you if they knew you."

"But they don't want to know me." Tess smiled, but there was a tremor in her voice. We were speaking in undertones while Sarah lay on her bed, inspecting the beautiful colors of the new marbles. "They want to know *you* because you're pretty and talk like a lady."

"We're going to have to change this," I sighed. "When we were all hidden away together, I didn't mind so much. But I don't want to spend my time in the light while you skulk in the shadows."

"If you marry Mr. Poulton, that's just where I'll be." Tess's lower lip stuck out. "He thinks children should be seen and not heard, and I'll bet he thinks *imbeciles* shouldn't be seen at all."

I gave Tess a level look, trying to convey my earnestness to her. "I don't think I'm going to marry him, Tess. But listen—don't even hint as much to him or anyone else before I've given my answer, will you? I've gotten myself into an awkward situation with him, and I have to think hard about how to get out of it. I don't want any unpleasantness."

Tess's face brightened, and she hugged me again. "I've been praying you'll say no," she said. "I want you to marry, but not him. I wish Martin were free."

And what should I say to that? I wished Martin were free too. I simply shook my head and smiled as brightly as I could. "I'd better go," I said. "I feel like Daniel marching into the lions' den."

Sarah heard that last remark and made a loud growling noise. Tess joined in, and they were both snarling and growling at me as I backed, laughing, through the door onto the landing.

And now all I had to do was to listen to a concert sung by a woman whose existence was, well, inconvenient to me, after sitting at a grand dinner next to a man who thought he was going to marry me but wasn't, in the presence of a man who—

"Just stop that right now, Eleanor Lillington," I muttered to myself as I walked downstairs, the silken train of my dress rustling behind me. "It's just a dinner. Nobody's going to pay much attention to you, and nothing is going to happen."

38
GILDED CAGE

"Can I not tempt you to another morsel?" Dr. Calderwood smiled ingratiatingly as he waved his hand toward the platter Bella was holding.

"I eat very little when I'm about to sing," Lucetta replied.

She was a bejeweled vision in deep blue silk trimmed in silver, with sapphires and diamonds sparkling at her ears, neck, and wrists. Beside her, Martin, immaculately turned out in a beautifully cut dress coat with a pearl-gray waistcoat, was a suitable foil to her magnificence.

Martin was deep in conversation with Mr. McGovern, the grain merchant, but I saw his gaze flick in my direction from time to time. I tried not to look at him too often, of course. Judah was making a point of referring to me frequently as the conversation wandered around the news of the day and local concerns, so he kept me busy answering questions and volunteering opinions. Talking nonsense, Bet would have said, and she would have been right.

With forty guests, the gathering was both noisy and warm. The servants had arranged the refectory tables in a U-shape, with the Calderwoods at the center of the main table. The room was a bustle of servants arriving and departing with dishes and the occasional guest seeking the retiring rooms.

Several of my clients were there. Mr. and Mrs. Shemmeld and the Addises were at the main table, and the Durkins, Mortimores, Fairlands, and Haywards were on the flanking arms. It was amusing to see so many of my dresses in one place, although I couldn't see them all that well because my back was to the room. I vowed to make the most of the opportunity offered by the concert to observe the dresses of all the ladies, especially those from farther afield.

I had let my thoughts wander as Lucetta talked about her music with the couple opposite her. A direct reference to me by Dr. Calderwood pulled me out of my woolgathering.

"Mrs. Lillington, of course, has been content to fulfill the role of seamstress in our establishment, which is most gracious of her." He bowed in my direction. "But a little bird tells me she is destined for a much more prominent role in society in the future. I, for one, will rejoice at her elevation."

Coupled with my position next to Judah, this was tantamount to telling the assembled company we were engaged to be married.

I felt the color rise to my cheeks, and saw Martin's mouth tighten. He had definitely heard the remark, but he continued talking commodity prices with Mr. McGovern and the latter's morose wife, who seemed to know a great deal about her husband's business.

"Mrs. Lillington could take on any role in society with ease," gushed Mrs. Addis, who was several seats away but had been craning her neck to hear the conversation at the center of the table. I noticed she wore a deep purple gown and not the black I had made for her. Evidently, she was willing to cast aside her full mourning when it suited her.

"Indeed, indeed." Dr. Calderwood turned the full force of his teeth on Mrs. Addis and myself in turn. "Mrs. Calderwood and I believe the time has come to begin thinking about an expansion of the Eternal Life Seminary. Indeed, we are running short on the kind of accommodation we would like to offer to our young gentlemen, and our facilities are sadly old-fashioned, I fear. Gas lighting, indoor, ahem, plumbing—if I may mention such a thing in the presence of the ladies—and a properly leveled road to Springwood, such things as these are improvements that we must, nay, *will* make in the near future."

He had the attention of several of the diners by now and shook out his mane of hair as he continued. "After all, the frontier is moving westward. The wretched Indians are gone —although I hear they're causing considerable trouble elsewhere. Civilization is spreading its bounteous joys even to the plains of Kansas. We must rise to the challenge—although, when I say 'we,' Mrs. Calderwood and I feel that maybe a younger man should shoulder the task. A younger man—or perhaps a younger couple."

I stared at my plate, feeling myself go hot and cold at once as the table reacted in a babble of sound. So Judah had done it. I didn't know how he'd done it without securing my hand first, but Dr. Calderwood's words were a broad—and public —hint that Judah was in line to take over the seminary.

And begin an expansion. That was the first time I had heard of those plans. This would involve a great deal of money, I realized. My money, possibly. Had Judah told the Calderwoods about my wealth, then?

"I'm surprised, Dr. Calderwood, that you speak of expansion when you have still not solved the question of the danger that seems to lurk around this place. I understand one of your faculty members was murdered on the path to Springwood last year?"

Martin's drawl cut across the other diners' remarks with the nasty clarity of a trumpet call. "I'm not sure it behooves Mrs. Lillington to stay in a place where a woman's safety cannot be guaranteed."

A shocked silence descended as each of the diners absorbed what Martin had just said. From under my lowered lids, I could see faces turning to Dr. Calderwood for an answer.

I couldn't speak. I was furious at Martin for acting as if he could order whether I would stay at the seminary or not. I was equally furious at Judah for assuming he could use my money as he wished. I crushed my napkin between my hands under the table, waiting for the doctor to reply. But it was Judah who spoke.

"We're now quite certain that the perpetrator of the tragedy was one or more of the inhabitants of Fork Crossing —a degenerate spot, quite like Abilene used to be."

His melodious tenor voice carried well. He directed his remarks to Martin, but it was certain the other diners heard them.

"It's impossible to carry on any kind of investigation," he continued. "They won't answer questions and present a united front. There's been some bad feeling among certain undesirable characters after the young men of Springwood became a little overenthusiastic about helping some people remove to that settlement. Mr. Shemmeld here is taking a leading role in strengthening the number of deputies in Springwood. We are making it clear to the inhabitants of Fork Crossing that if they direct any more violence against the town or the seminary, there will be reprisals." He nodded at Mr. Shemmeld.

"You must forgive my husband." Lucetta laid a hand on Martin's arm, the tips of her fingers making creases in his immaculate sleeve. "He's worried about his young friend, whom he loves quite as a sister. He has perhaps spoken a little more forcefully than he meant to. The frontier is daunting to us city folk."

By this point, I fervently wished that the floor beneath me would open up and consign the entire dinner party to oblivion. I was almost grateful when Judah spoke again.

"We're a little rough around the edges, to be sure." I couldn't see his smile, but its effect was apparent from the sparkle in Lucetta's large eyes. "But as Dr. Calderwood so astutely noted, we're becoming civilized."

"So you can guarantee Mrs. Lillington's safety?" Martin's tone was neutral, but there was a hardness in his eyes that alarmed me.

"Yes, I can." Judah also sounded friendly, but I felt him tense a little beside me.

"You'd better prepare to answer to me if you don't make good on that promise." There was no mistaking the threat this time.

"Martin, my dear, you're being a boor." Lucetta laughed, a musical sound that seemed to offer some relief to the diners, who were watching the scene avidly. "Don't spoil such a delightful little gathering, not when I'm about to sing. Drink some more of this excellent wine."

But Martin had barely touched his glass. Like me, he disliked the taste of alcohol. I waited with bated breath to see if he would continue in the same vein. But he turned back to Mr. McGovern and made a remark about President Grant's overseas policies that made the big man guffaw and slap him on the back.

The posture of the other diners softened into relaxation. The aroma of coffee had begun to fill the air, and the servants were walking around with trays of sweet morsels that met with sighs of appreciation from the ladies. Mrs. Shemmeld, her stern governess's face flushed with wine and too much food, made a remark about my dress, and the other ladies took up the cry. Thus my own face was able to resume its normal color, and I turned it resolutely in her direction, ignoring both Martin and Judah. I would have to speak to both of them later.

THEY HAD EXTINGUISHED THE LAMPS IN THE LIBRARY, AND A faint sweetness hung in the air from the flowers left there from the pre-dinner gathering.

The servants had set all the tables and chairs back in their customary positions. I could easily find my way through them thanks to the gibbous moon hanging in the clear sky. Moon and stars combined cast long strips of cool blue light over the polished woods and ornate carvings, here and there picking out a gilded bee or a painted flower.

I unlocked the French doors and pushed them open, grateful for the cool air that enveloped me as I stepped out onto the balcony. My head rang with the chatter of people; my eyes ached from a surfeit of lights and the dazzle of jewels and silk. Lucetta's superb voice and Dr. Calderwood's surprisingly fine playing resonated still in my mind, the notes twisting and turning around each other in a tangle of liquid sound.

The company was still dispersing. I could hear bursts of female chatter and the booming voices of the men as they made their way to the staircase. Carriages would be waiting for them on the other side of the building. Just about anyone in Springwood who had a conveyance of greater standing than a farm cart had lent it for the occasion.

I heard the latch of the library door click and tensed,

wondering if it were either Judah or Martin. If it were, I would need to have matters out with them on the spot, not an attractive prospect given my weariness and the ringing in my head.

Squinting into the darkness, I was surprised to hear the rustle of silk and catch the glint of moonlight on diamonds. It was Lucetta, her raven curls gathering the starlight as she moved toward me.

"All alone in the dark, Mrs. Lillington?" There was a note of amusement in Lucetta's rich, musical voice, and her lips curved as she stepped out onto the balcony to stand beside me. Below us, a glow of light and a burst of chatter suggested the servants were resting for an interval.

"It's not so dark." I motioned at the starlit sky and the glowing moon. "And I needed some fresh air after all that chatter and bustle."

"So did I." Lucetta chuckled, a low, soft, somehow secretive sound. "It occurred to me that if I absented myself, the guests might make their way downstairs a little faster. That little plump woman and that dreadful Southerner with the bad breath must have made me the same compliments twenty times over."

"Don't blame them, Mrs. Rutherford." It was odd to hear Martin's name thus on my lips. "You and Martin are the most exciting things that have ever happened to this patch of the Great Plains. And your voice is magnificent—it deserves compliments."

I had plenty of reasons to wish Lucetta Rutherford had never been born, but I was not going to begrudge her praise for her talent.

Lucetta's smile turned wistful as she nodded in acknowledgement of my words, staring out beyond the outbuildings to the dark wilderness beyond. "I would have liked to train for the opera," she said. "I had teachers, of course, very great ones. But Papa didn't deem it suitable for his daughter to perform on a stage. My career will forever be confined to drawing rooms and little assemblies like this one."

I caught the rich scent of her perfume—gardenia?—as she raised a smooth, jewel-bedecked arm to push back a lock of hair. "I envy you," she continued.

"Envy me?" I couldn't imagine why. She had everything any woman of taste and talent could desire—beauty, wealth, and connections, and the world as a stage on which to display those assets at her will. And she had Martin. At least, I thought, hoping that the rising color in my cheeks would not show in the moonlight, she had the bond of marriage to Martin, which he couldn't break without abandoning his honor.

"You have so many possibilities before you." Lucetta indicated the dark prairie with a graceful sweep of her gloved hand. "You've forged a profession for yourself, and even should you marry, Martin will ensure that the wealth he's built up for you remains in your control. I never had that. Until I married, my father, my brothers, even my cousins determined my life for me. I live in a cage, albeit a gilded one."

"Martin would let you do anything you wished, I'm sure." My voice sounded hoarse, and I cleared my throat. "He's not the kind of man to keep any woman in a cage."

"Martin?" Lucetta sounded surprised. "No, my dear. My cage was built for me long before Martin came. I simply opened the door and invited him in."

A cold finger ran down my spine at her words. In my mind, I saw the two of them together behind gilded bars—trapped, perhaps, but together, with the world outside. With me outside.

Lucetta had seen me shiver. "Are you cold, Mrs. Lillington? You must preserve your health. After all, you have that delightful little girl to live for."

"A goose walked over my grave," I replied automatically and then swallowed hard. For a split second, I could have sworn I heard my mother's voice, speaking in tandem with my own. I blinked, realizing with astonishment that tears were threatening to come to my eyes, and shook my head to dispel the emotion.

"That was one of my mother's favorite expressions," I said under my breath. "And she's been in her own grave for four years now." I shook my head again, smiling at Lucetta. "I'm sorry. It's silly—grief still catches me unawares sometimes. I suppose I'm tired."

For a long moment, we listened to the faint howl of a lone wolf far off, a desolate sound drifting across the plains like the cry of a lost soul. It was strange to be standing here dressed in the fine raiment of civilization with the wilderness so near.

"My Mama died when I was not quite five years old," she said suddenly. "Of a fever. There was no warning. She'd been quite well, and we were all so happy together, Papa and my brothers and I, with Mama at the center, merry and laughing and always singing. And then I woke up one morning and they told me she was ill . . . They wouldn't let me see her lest I catch the infection. That same day—that very same day, Mrs. Lillington—they told me my Mama was in heaven. She was snatched away from me without a last kiss or a farewell of any kind. The loss is with me still."

She gathered up her skirts, a rich rustle of perfumed silk, and the diamond and sapphire bracelets on her smooth arms winked like a constellation. "When I love someone, my instinct is to hold them fast so they too do not disappear in the night." She turned to leave but then looked back over her shoulder at me. "Good night, Mrs. Lillington. I hope you'll take full advantage of your freedom."

I stared after her, my limbs chilled and stiff. I didn't think for a moment that her words had been mere conversation. She meant to remind me that Martin and I were on opposite sides of a bridge to which she held the key. She wasn't going to let Martin go, ever.

39
LOSS

I awoke next morning with a headache and dyspepsia. Neither was helped by sitting in the chapel for two hours listening to Dr. Calderwood's sermon on generosity.

We only just made it to the chapel before the service started, so I was able to slip into our usual pew in the back—a great relief. Now that my status had been so publicly elevated, I had been afraid that Judah would require me to sit with him in the front pew. That would incur a great deal of awkwardness all around.

Between the pangs of intestinal discomfort and mental anguish, I didn't attend much to the sermon. I watched the row of heads in the front pew—Martin's bright blond next to his wife's raven locks, and beside her, Judah's black curls, cropped close to his head.

Some of last night's guests were there too. I could see the bulk of Mr. McGovern next to his wife's narrow-shouldered rigidity, Mr. and Mrs. Addis—she in the black I had made for her—and the soft, plump outline of Mrs. Durkin with her head of baby-fine hair, sheltered by her husband's stout, prosperous form.

Dr. Calderwood's sermon was shorter than usual. He looked a little jaded himself and had his hands firmly planted on the pulpit as if he needed to lean on it for support. Serves him right, I thought. I was no temperance fiend, not even a teetotaler like Tess, but the excessive consumption of alcohol by the faculty of a seminary that taught abstention to its young men was hypocritical at the very least.

I suppressed a belch as the service finally dragged to its conclusion and we rose to our feet. Sarah, who had been swinging her legs in a most irritating fashion for the last half hour, hopped cheerfully down from our pew. She dodged under it and made a dash for the door before I could say a word to her.

"Netta said she could have some cakes from last night." Tess grinned at me.

"Ah. And she's old enough to know that if she asked me, I'd tell her to wait until after luncheon." I sighed and shifted uncomfortably from one foot to the other. "I'll go to the kitchen and negotiate terms with Netta."

"Don't be silly." Tess gave me a gentle shove in the direction of the chapel door, through which a crowd of students was milling. "Go lie down and take something for your stomach. There's some Soothing Syrup in the top of the clothes press, where Sary can't see it. If Netta sees you complaining of stomachache, she'll think you don't like her food."

"I think it was the combination rather than the individual items of food." We squeezed through the press of students, and I headed gratefully to the staircase. "A rest and no lunch will set me up. I'm not so sure about your Soothing Syrup though. It makes me feel dizzy."

I put my foot on the first stair and looked over my shoulder. The ladies and gentlemen from the front rows of pews had just emerged from the chapel. Martin had been captured by Mrs. Addis, who was trying to tow her prize toward her husband. Judah had his back to me, his elegant head cocked in the direction of Mrs. McGovern, who was haranguing him about something or the other.

"If Judah asks after me," I instructed Tess, "please be sure to say I'm unwell and don't wish anyone to disturb me."

"Of course," Tess replied. "But you'll be at supper, won't you? Don't forget that Martin and his wife are leaving tomorrow morning. You'll want to visit with them some more before they go."

"I haven't forgotten." I smiled at Tess, but my smile felt forced and unnatural. I turned to climb the stairs, wincing as my eyes encountered the brilliant magentas, golds, and turquoises of the stained-glass windows, made glaringly bright by the noonday sun.

No, I certainly hadn't forgotten that Martin was leaving the next day.

It was mid-afternoon before I re-emerged from my room. My indigestion had mercifully passed away, but my head throbbed with a dull ache that reclining seemed to make worse. I was never at my best after sleeping during the day, and I had dozed—fitfully, to be sure. My restless sleep teemed with whirling dreams of an endless dinner, during which people constantly asked me impertinent questions about my money and my nonexistent late husband.

When I finally dragged myself back to consciousness, I realized I was horribly thirsty, and there wasn't a drop of water to drink in the room. The creak of the pump in the yard outside brought me to my feet in a fever of longing for the taste of cool well water. I hastily did what I could to make my hair look tidy and headed for the stairs.

My heart gave a somersault as I got halfway down the first flight of steps and realized there was someone sitting on the next flight, just around the turn. It only took me a fraction of a second to identify Martin, but that didn't make me feel any better.

"Are you all right?" he asked, rising to his feet.

"Tolerable," I replied. "What on earth are you doing, sitting on the stairs? What will people think if they see you here?"

"I don't particularly care." I could see by the set of his jaw that his mood was no better than mine. "I want to talk to you."

"Not here." I lowered my voice, wishing my head didn't hurt quite so much. Why did Martin insist on talking to me now, when all I wanted was to slake my thirst and get some peace and quiet? "People can hear—"

"To the devil with them—they shouldn't be listening."

But Martin seized my arm just above the elbow and steered me back upstairs. He hesitated outside my door but then thought better of it and pulled me along the corridor, well away from the staircase.

"What is *wrong* with you?" I yanked my arm out of Martin's grasp and backed away from him, toward our room. "You behaved like—like a complete fool at dinner last night, implying you could decide whether or not I stay at this seminary. As if you only need snap your fingers and I'd climb into your carriage. Or would you like me to sit by the driver, like the maid? Because the seats inside are already occupied."

A dull flush outlined Martin's cheekbones, making his hair look startlingly pale. "And you—you sat there allowing that bombastic imbecile Calderwood to practically announce your engagement to Poulton and said nothing. What am I supposed to do, smile and congratulate you?"

I drew myself up as tall as I could, annoyed that I still had to tip my head back to face Martin. "I think it's up to me to decide when I speak and what I say. It's certainly not up to you to speak for me."

My head was pounding, and somewhere in the back of my mind, I knew I was being unreasonable. All I had to do was to explain to Martin that I was afraid to show Judah my hand too soon. But he was being unreasonable too, and I didn't see why I should let him get away with it.

"Quite apart from the fact that you've made your wife suspicious about your feelings for me."

"I have?" Martin's eyebrows shot up to his hairline. "And what makes you think that?"

"She talked to me last night. She reminded me—not in so many words, but I took her meaning well enough—that you're hers. That you'll never be mine, no matter how many fine speeches you make to me about how I have to wait to see what you'll do. You see, there's the problem, Martin." I was trembling, my hands pressed against the smooth paint of the wall to steady myself. "I'm free to make my own decisions. You have ties—"

"Yes, I have ties." Martin's hands, long-fingered and strong, closed around my upper arms. "I'm tied to you, heart and soul, and you don't seem to give a damn about that."

I pushed hard against his chest. To my satisfaction, just this once I caught him off guard, and he took a step backward, releasing my arms.

"You're tied to Lucetta." My voice sounded cold and hard. "There are three of us in this situation, Martin—five, in point of fact, because whatever I do affects Sarah and Tess."

"You think they'll be better off if you marry Poulton? He'll send Sarah away to school and Tess to a home for defectives, you see if he doesn't." Martin raked his hands through his hair and then let them drop to his sides in a gesture of hopelessness. "He'll isolate you and control you. You love me—you know you do—you can't do this. I won't let you."

All the rage inside of me seemed to catch fire at once, an uncontrollable blaze that made it hard to speak coherently.

"You won't let me?" I shouted, heedless of who might hear us. "You have—you have *nothing*—no control—you cannot presume to tell me what to do. Yes, you made me rich"—a pang of guilt assailed me with that recollection, but I pushed it firmly to the back of my mind—"and it was generous of you to work so hard on my behalf, I'll grant you that. But it gives you no rights over me. You're not my father or my brother or my husband—you're someone else's husband—and just because you act toward me as if you love me so that you can kiss me and—and—you never said you loved me after all—I'm—I'm *sick* of men thinking they can tell me what to do."

I pushed the heels of my hands into my forehead, trying to still the sickening pounding in my head so I could think. There didn't seem to be any point in saying any more, since what was coming out of my mouth was so disorganized that it was worse than useless. A small voice inside me said I should simply explain to Martin that I no longer had any intention of marrying Judah, but I ignored it.

"Go *away*, Martin," I wailed. "Leave me alone. Go back to your wife."

The silence that fell between us seemed to stretch on and on, and I closed my eyes so I didn't have to see the bleakness in Martin's. He took two or three steps in the direction of the stairs and then turned back to face me.

"I do love you," he said. "I've always loved you—I just wish I'd realized it sooner. And working to increase your wealth was part of that love, I suppose. I wanted you to have the freedom you've always craved. And now you have it."

He spoke the last words in a whisper, but then his voice hardened. "And you're going to throw it away on a man who doesn't love you—for what? Respectability? Because despite your grand pronouncements about not wishing to marry, you don't have the courage to live up to your convictions. You're scared to take your life in both hands and do what your head and your heart tell you to do."

"Which is what?" I swallowed painfully, my throat dry. "To follow you to Chicago? To become your mistress? To live in the demimonde while you strut around in society enjoying all the respectability you say I want? And what happens to Sarah then?"

"That's not what I want."

"What *do* you want, Martin?"

"You." The word dropped into the space between us like a stone, and suddenly I wanted to cry. I wanted to fling myself into Martin's arms.

I did neither. I let the anger and indignation I had been stoking for days sustain me, bolstering me up so I could give the only possible answer.

"You can't have me."

My treacherous voice broke on these words, and I turned away, fumbling blindly along the wall until I found the doorknob to our room. I slipped inside before I could say or do anything that would betray how much I wanted Martin in return, shut the door with a bang, and turned the key in the lock.

"Nell!" Martin was outside the door in an instant, his voice muffled by the wood. "Don't be ridiculous."

"I'm being perfectly reasonable," I said unsteadily. "One of us has to be. Go away, Martin."

And, much to my chagrin, he did. I heard the sound of

his retreating footsteps, and then the corridor outside my room shook with a resounding bang. He must have taken his temper out on a door, or a banister, perhaps. For a fleeting second, I hoped he hadn't hurt himself, and then the sobs I had been withholding forced their way to the surface, and I flung myself on my bed, my fist pressed to my mouth to stifle any sound. I cried until my head felt ready to explode; and then at last I undressed and crawled under the bedcovers, pulling them up over me to shut out the world.

I AWOKE EARLY THE NEXT MORNING, LIGHTHEADED AND ACHING in every limb. Tess and Sarah, who must have thought I spent the entire afternoon in bed, slept peacefully. Tess was deep under the covers while Sarah lay sprawled on her back, her breath whistling through the gap in her teeth.

I dressed quickly and quietly, grateful that someone had filled our washing jug and the large stoppered bottle that held our drinking water. I drank half the bottle, filling my glass again and again and sighing with relief as the cool water soothed my parched throat.

After bathing my eyes to remove some of the puffiness from crying, I made my way to the kitchen, too impatient for coffee and food to wait for breakfast.

The kitchen was in more of a bustle than would be usual that early in the morning. The Rutherfords' maid, whose name was Trudy, I thought, was there supervising the loading of a tray with breakfast items. She clearly regarded our servants as beneath her because of their race, and her manner of speech to them was disdainful.

"The Rutherfords are leaving early, then?" I asked as I settled myself at one corner of the table with a cup of coffee and a freshly made biscuit liberally smeared with butter and honey.

"They are, to be sure." She had a faint Irish accent—no doubt her parents had been immigrants. "And not before time neither," she added under her breath.

She looked hard at me, evidently trying to judge whether I was servant or mistress. Yet she must have seen me dining at the head table during her stay, and her gaze didn't linger for long on my practical shirtwaist and plain gray skirt.

She placed the sugar bowl on the tray and bobbed a tiny curtsey. "Begging your pardon, ma'am—this being where you live and all. But I find it a terrible dull place, being used to Chicago." Her small freckled face screwed up in a frown as she stared at the tray, one finger upraised in an apparent attempt to remember if she had included everything. "And idleness and dullness lead to wickedness, as my Gran always said."

"I'm never idle." I smiled at her, although a strange qualm made my heart beat a little faster. "And neither are you, I'll warrant."

"Oh, I didn't mean you, miss—ma'am." The maid sounded shocked. "To be sure, I haven't had enough to do, seeing as how mistress don't have society visits as usual. I've never written so many letters in my life, having all that time on my hands. No, I meant—well, in general, you know, as a rule of things." She hefted the tray, making sure it was balanced right, and then hesitated as if she wished to say more.

"You're an old friend of the master's, I hear?" she asked tentatively.

"I am." I took a sip of my coffee, bitter and strong against my tongue, and waited with what I hoped was an encouraging expression on my face.

"Perhaps you could tell him—in a general way, if you take my meaning—that it doesn't do to leave the mistress alone so much. I don't want to speak ill, ma'am. But I'm a respectable girl, and I think them as is married should cleave to each other, like the priest says. Not leave the way open for the Evil One to come calling—it ain't right. I don't mind telling you I'll be looking for a new place once we're back in Chicago." She dropped her voice even lower. "And those as serves here shouldn't give themselves airs about who they're working for neither. There's been wickedness done this last fortnight."

I watched her retreating back as she maneuvered the tray through the doorway, suddenly far less keen on the food in front of me. Was she making trouble? Tess had hinted that she had already spoken to Mrs. Drummond, so why did she find it necessary to direct her veiled allusions at me?

I forced myself to take a few bites of the biscuit. I had gone a full day without eating, and it would be no good if I fainted from hunger. I knew from the conversations around me that the hired carriage was already at the door, and that they were loading Martin and Lucetta's trunks. I would have to make an appearance at their departure, if only to forestall Martin from seeking me out to say his good-byes in private. But I now had several reasons for wishing I didn't have to look him in the face.

Tess and Sarah made an appearance by seven-thirty, the time set for the Rutherfords' departure. Sarah clung to me a little more than usual. I wondered if she was able to sense the misery and confusion I hid behind a painted-on smile as I watched Martin check the trunks and boxes loaded onto the old-fashioned carryall. He had greeted me with a cautious "good morning" and a tentative smile, which I had returned. So we were not parting on a note of ill-feeling, but I could feel the tension between us, as brittle as a glass bridge.

I shook Lucetta's hand and made a few conventional remarks of farewell, then watched as Martin handed her into the carriage. She leaned out of the window, talking to both of the Calderwoods, who wore their Sunday best, all smiles. What, I wondered, was the extent of Mrs. Calderwood's complicity in the "wickedness" Lucetta's maid had referred to? Was she really ignorant of the dalliance that had, I could only assume, been going on under her nose between Lucetta and her husband? Or—a cold sweat bedewed my brow at the thought—had she encouraged it, thinking to turn the situation to her own advantage? Blackmail, my own inner demon whispered in my ear, and I shuddered, my eyes on Martin as he took his leave of the Calderwoods and turned toward Tess, Sarah, and me.

"Well, Nellie." Martin straightened up from hugging Tess and replaced his hat. "Look after yourself until I come back." His face was inscrutable, but the shadows under his eyes told me he hadn't slept well.

"You're coming back soon, aren't you?" Sarah, who was holding tight to my hand, tugged at Martin's jacket to get his attention. He lifted her into his arms and held her so that their eyes were on a level.

"I do have a business to run," he said almost apologetically. "I have to spend most of my time in Chicago. But if you want me to, I'll come back and visit the very next time I head west." He smiled at her, fingering her bright copper hair. "I don't want to wait another four years to see how you grow—you'll forget me entirely in all that time."

"I won't forget." Sarah's eyes glowed green in the sunlight as she smoothed a hand over Martin's freshly shaven cheek. "You're nice. And I wish I could go to Chicago and see your horse."

"I'd like that." Martin kissed Sarah, his lips lingering for a split second. He really would like a child of his own, I realized, and the feeling of desolation that gave me was nearly unbearable. "Be good to your mother, Sarah."

He put her down and turned in my direction, kissing my cheek just as gently as he'd kissed Sarah's. "Good-bye, Nell." He did not wait for me to answer but stepped back, turning toward the carriage and pulling open the door.

I closed my eyes for a split second, feeling the warmth of his mouth on my skin and the sense of loss that followed immediately after. "Good-bye, Martin," I said under my breath as the driver shook the reins, setting the carryall in motion.

For once, Sarah didn't run after the carriage, but turned to me and held up her arms, a gesture she had not made for some time. I picked her up, and she wound her arms around my neck.

"I'm sad he's going away," she whispered. "Why am I so sad about that, Momma?"

"I don't know, darling." I tried to laugh, but the attempt didn't succeed. "I guess I'm sad about it too."

"I hope he comes back soon." Sarah rested her head on my shoulder, fiddling with the jet brooch pinned to the collar of my shirtwaist. "But he doesn't have to bring the pretty lady back. Her dresses are beautiful, but I don't like the way she laughs. And she doesn't like Tess. Is it breakfast time now?"

"I suppose it is," I said, torn out of my reverie. "We'd better go inside." I turned my head to catch one last glimpse of the carriage, a moving speck in the bright sunlight, and then I followed the Calderwoods indoors. I wished with all my heart I could ravel back the last two days and start them all over again.

40
DROWNING

November 10, 1875
Nell,

I barely know what to write to you. Within the confines of my own mind, I talk to you constantly, asking for your forgiveness, your patience, your—yes, your love, although I believe I already have that. Yet as soon as I'm confronted with this blank sheet of paper, almost every topic becomes a dangerous terrain beset with pitfalls and prickling with mines that will explode at the slightest movement.

I fear I've touched off one of those mines already, angered you by talking of love. You're perfectly correct; I have no right to make any demands on you. I have no right even to advise you, save the right of an old friend who wants only to see you safe and well and happy. You, and the child and sister—for Tess is your sister of the heart, is she not?—whom you hold dearer to you than your own self.

I'm afraid for you. There, I've written it. I sit here at my desk, late in the evening, with the day's correspondence to hand—which I must be ready to discuss with Salazar in the morning, as there's always more to follow. I, who am not given to worry, as you know, find myself fretting like a mother hen over a single chick, and as a result, falling behind on my work.

I was too preoccupied with my jealousies and simply with your presence to talk to you sensibly, so you may not realize that my trip to the frontier was fruitful in the business sense. I'm in daily correspondence with Fassbinder, whose ideas for making a fresh fortune out of the frontier trade now strike me as worthy of immediate investment—by both of us, if you'll allow me to continue to act on your behalf until such a day as—

And now I've wandered into the dangerous terrain again, haven't I? You know what my fears for you are, my dear. You know what my hopes are too, perhaps—that I can find a way out of the mess I've put myself in and offer myself to you honorably. I know that there's no other way.

Yours ever,
Martin

I COULD FEEL MARTIN'S LETTER, FOLDED IN QUARTERS, IN MY skirt pocket as I bent over my task. Its words whispered in my head as a counterpoint to the dull thudding of the wind against the panes of the workroom windows.

His letter, the longest I'd had from him in over a year, both elated and dismayed me. What could I possibly write in return?

The answer came more easily than I expected: the truth. I could at least give Martin a truthful account of my intentions and feelings with regard to Judah. It would help, of course, if I could decide exactly how I intended to go about freeing myself from Judah and how far I would have to run to do so. I would hand the letter to the postmaster myself—and remind Martin to write less freely of his feelings. Dangerous terrain indeed.

I returned my attention to the fabric spread across my cutting table. Another dress for Mrs. Addis. It was a deep lilac color, opulent and yet muted in the light of a November day, with sky the color of pewter, flashed with an occasional patch of silver or white as the great mass of clouds shifted and roiled.

I would have to light the lamps in the chandelier soon, I realized. Then the fabric would change hue in the yellow light, becoming the dark, sullen purple of a bruise. I needed to trim the dress—in the conventional black—to avoid that purple color coming into direct contact with Mrs. Addis's skin, which was a touch sallow.

"Are you ever going to do anything with that stuff besides look at it, Nell?" Tess took her feet off the paddle of the sewing machine with a sigh of relief. She was a little too short to sit comfortably at it for a long time.

In the sudden quiet, I heard Sarah chanting, "Man-hen-mop-pig-pan-ten-top-gig," as she conscientiously worked her way through her primer. She loved to learn and was so absorbed in analyzing the magic by which the marks on the page became words that she had read the simple book ten times already. She'd barely looked up from her page the last hour.

"I'll begin pinning soon." I hoped I didn't look as sheepish as I felt—I knew my thoughts had been straying. I slipped my hand in my pocket, feeling the paper's edges against the ball of my thumb. "But I want to get this right, and this won't be easy stuff to work with. It's so new to me and so very expensive."

"I think Mr. Addis will have to make lots of money with his hotel," said Tess. "Is this really silk?" She crossed the room to stand beside me, fingering the warm yet wonderfully light silk crêpe de chine.

"Yes. But it's a new kind of fabric, and I want to be sure I think through all of its possibilities before I cut."

"You're a true artist," said a soft voice behind us. I swung round to find Judah leaning against the door jamb.

"May I beg a moment of your time?" Judah asked formally, uncoiling himself in one fluid movement. He gestured toward the open doorway, indicating that he wanted to see me in private. I hesitated, but I hardly had any reason to refuse him. With a last look at the deep lilac silk and a regretful sigh for the work I hadn't done, I followed him out of the room.

He led the way to the chapel, tugging open the large ornate doors and ushering me in. The great, echoing room was chilly and dim, the gray November light barely penetrating to it through its row of stained-glass windows.

Judah waited till I sat in one of the back pews, then curled himself into the bench in front so that he faced me.

"I feel you've been avoiding me, Nell."

He was right, but I didn't want to admit that. I felt the shape of Martin's letter in my pocket and realized once again that I had a fine line to walk. I dared not commit myself in any direction, but neither was I in a position to burn bridges. I strove for a neutral, friendly tone of voice.

"I've been very busy, Judah. So have you—you seem to spend an extraordinary amount of time in Dr. Calderwood's study."

"Great plans are afoot." Judah's words came out with a little puff of breath that indicated amusement or derision—it was hard to tell in the deep shadow.

He took my hand, rubbing his thumb over my palm. I did not pull it away, noting with interest that a small shiver ran through me at his touch. Yet it was so different from the yearning I had experienced when Martin held me that I wondered why I ever thought it might be love.

I neither wanted to cross Judah nor encourage him, of that much I was certain. So I let my hand lie limp in his, hoping our interview would be short.

"Is that what you wanted to see me for?" I prompted, trying to sound lighthearted. "So you could berate me for my absence?"

"Well, I've also been wondering about something." Judah turned my hand palm up and affected to study it, although unless he had eyes like a cat's, he would barely be able to see it. But he did have eyes like a cat's, I thought, remembering how he had boasted about seeing well in the dark.

"I think," Judah continued, his eyes on my hand, "that you're rather more fond of Mr. Rutherford than you should be."

This time I did try to snatch my hand back, but his fingers closed firmly around my wrist, and I thought better of struggling. My stomach had begun to tie itself into knots, and I was sweating despite the chill.

"And I think he's much more fond of you than befits a married man." Judah's fingers tightened, cool and hard. "Don't deny it, Nell. Wasn't it George Herbert who said that love and a cough cannot be hid? It would have been touching to see how well the two of you suit each other—had Mr. Rutherford been free to marry."

"We've done nothing wrong." I could hear the tremor in my voice. "Nothing improper." Except a kiss. "Martin is an honorable man."

"But you're in great *danger* of doing wrong." Judah's voice sounded earnest, sincere. "Even the most honorable man can suffer moments of weakness, Nell. And a woman—well, women are naturally weak creatures, are they not? We cannot blame you overmuch for acting according to your nature. And you have a passionate nature, Nell. You crave warmth as a butterfly does—you can't live for long without it. Sooner or later, the state of celibacy will become unbearable to you."

I felt a shock of recognition at his words and could not suppress the shudder that ran through me. My physical reactions to Judah, I realized, and the fact that I had been in a state of celibacy for some time, were not entirely unrelated.

"He won't be able to divorce his wife. The law isn't easily persuaded to permit such things. Has he asked you to wait for him?" The jerk of my head as I tried—in vain—to see his face gave Judah his answer, and he chuckled. "That course of action can only end one way, Nell. And you, of all people, can't afford another mistake. That would put you beyond the pale of good society forever and condemn your daughter to the shadows."

"What do you propose I do?" My throat was dry, and I swallowed hard to relieve it.

"I've already offered you the protection of my name," Judah said. "I don't require love from you, and my affections are not—and will never be—engaged elsewhere. You would have a young, ambitious, and vigorous husband—I think, in fact, that in my arms you would begin to forget your hopeless infatuation." I could see a flash of white teeth as he grinned at me. "And in return, I would make very few demands on you."

"Except for my money," I said drily.

"What is wealth?" Judah shrugged. "You're no miser, I believe. Money has little hold on you—you've been quite content to live in a simple manner. And the advantages on your side are great. I'm rescuing you from past shame and future seduction. I'm giving you and your daughter an irreproachable name and ensuring that your children will henceforth be born in wedlock. Isn't that worth a little gold?"

I pulled my hand back again, and this time he let it go. "We have, what, six weeks or so before the agreed time elapses, do we not? Let me put it this way, Nell—your choice is clear before you, and there's only one possible outcome. I expect you to yield to me."

"Or?" I whispered hoarsely.

"Or you will be outcast." Judah's voice now had an edge to it I had never heard before. "You can't expect to continue to live here—or in any decent society—in a state of moral turpitude. I am offering you a raft to cling to, Nell. You're already drowning."

"A LITTLE MORE OF THIS EXCELLENT BACON, DEAR MRS. Lillington?" Dr. Calderwood, who had disposed of more rashers than I ever imagined a person could manage in one sitting, held out the greasy plate with what, I believed, he thought was a winning smile. I shook my head.

"I've eaten quite enough, thank you." I took another sip of my coffee and cast a longing glance over my shoulder at the far end of the room where Tess and Sarah sat, happily conversing over their breakfast.

In the two weeks since Judah and I had spoken in the chapel, he had summoned me to the head table for every meal. He didn't invite Tess and Sarah, but the omission didn't bother them since neither of them—as Tess had pointed out—wished to be under the Calderwoods' scrutiny while they ate.

"He'll isolate you and control you." Martin's words had come back to me often in the last few days. With Judah—who always sat at Dr. Calderwood's right hand now—and the doctor and his wife opposite me, I was starting to feel like a plump turkey in the presence of a pride of lions. The impression grew stronger whenever Dr. Calderwood licked his lips or shook out his mane of silver-streaked hair.

I had the nasty feeling that Judah had at least hinted about my wealth to Mrs. Calderwood. The little woman's manner toward me had become decidedly deferential. She directed the choicest cuts of meat to my plate, asked after my health with a proprietary gleam in her small black eyes, and refilled my coffee cup with her own hand.

She did so now, her hair trembling in its piled-high coiffure as she leaned forward.

"I have given much thought to your request to spend Christmas at the Lombardi mission," she said to me as she returned my cup and saucer to their place. "I've arranged with one of the farmers to borrow his pair of Percherons and his covered wagon. Mr. Poulton will accompany you, of course."

I looked at Judah in alarm. "But not just Mr. Poulton, surely—we'll need a chaperone too, won't we?" I didn't want to cross the plains with just Tess and Sarah as protection against Judah. "I thought Andrew could drive us," I began again.

"Andrew may take you and bring the wagon back here. I doubt the Lombardis have sufficient hay to feed such large horses over Christmas." Mrs. Calderwood's face folded into a fatuous smile. "As for a chaperone, I consider that the presence of Miss O'Dugan and your daughter will be sufficient. After all, you and Mr. Poulton are practically betrothed. Now, as for the date—"

"I've written the Lombardis that I'll set off on the thirteenth," I said hurriedly. I hadn't forgotten that Mrs. Drummond intended to depart on the twelfth. My plan was to secure the letter, be on my way to the Lombardis' before anyone thought of asking me if I had known anything about the housekeeper's flight, and peruse the letter in the presence of Pastor Lombardi and Catherine.

"Oh no, that won't do at all." Mrs. Calderwood clasped

her small hands under her chin and cocked her head to one side. "You must leave on the sixth. That way you'll have three full weeks before your return, which should be on the twenty-seventh—I would say the twenty-sixth, but that is the Sabbath. After all, a little bird tells me that there will be an announcement on New Year's Day, and we must have you back in good time to celebrate it. We must host a dinner with our dear friends from Springwood, do you not think, Doctor?"

"Certainly," mumbled Dr. Calderwood, who had surreptitiously taken another piece of bacon from the plate and was chewing industriously.

"You have time to inform the Lombardis that your plans have changed if you write this morning," remarked Mrs. Calderwood briskly. "Mr. Poulton will walk you to Springwood in time for the mail collection." She rose to her feet, occasioning a general scraping of chairs as the gentlemen rose with her. Dr. Calderwood hastily swiped his napkin over his greasy mouth and hands and smiled vaguely at no one in particular.

"But the sixth is less than a fortnight away. What about my work?" I was also on my feet, grateful for the movement to disguise the dismay I felt. "To leave that early in December —before the students, even—would make it difficult for me to catch up upon my return."

"Ah yes—about that, Mrs. Lillington." Mrs. Calderwood had scurried around the table to cut off my retreat to the refectory door. She laid a confidential hand on my arm, its tiny sharp nails shining like glass.

"I instructed Mrs. Drummond to place advertisements in the *Dickinson County Chronicle* and whatever suitable Wichita paper she could find. She's already receiving replies. Our intention is to bring in a young person within the next fortnight to receive a little training from you before you go. If she proves suitable during your absence, you'll be quite free of your responsibilities and ready to assume new ones by January. We will have much to talk about when you return."

She patted my hand and trotted after her husband, who was, as usual, delaying the start of the day's work by chit-chatting with faculty members who did not have a class immediately.

I glanced at Judah, who favored me with a nod and a smile. He evidently knew the gist of what Mrs. Calderwood had said to me.

They had been colluding, I was sure of it. They wanted to make certain I was under Judah's eye for practically the whole of December, giving me no opportunity to turn elsewhere for advice or help. Also, I'd be back at the seminary before the appointed date for giving Judah his answer, so that the Lombardis couldn't interfere. Judah intended to make certain of his prize.

41
KEY

The sickroom had a sweet, fetid smell that made some instinctive part of me shrink away in horror, even though I knew Mrs. Drummond's ague wasn't contagious. It was more than the normal taint of illness—the room reeked of death.

Perspiration bedewed Mrs. Drummond's brow, but when I touched her hand, skeletal and claw-like as it lay on the counterpane, it was clammy and cold. The skin of her face had a stretched, yellowed look, like old parchment. The faint breaths that issued from her mouth were sour, unwholesome.

"Will she live?" I kept my voice low in case the sick woman could hear.

"My heart tellin' me otherwise." Dorcas's voice was also low. "She done starved herself to a skellington, and now the ague come for her again, she don't have anythin' to fight it with."

"It looks worse than just an ague," I remarked. "What does the doctor say?"

"That we wait and see."

Dorcas dipped a cloth into the basin of water that she kept on the floor near her chair and gently swabbed Mrs. Drummond's forehead. The housekeeper's eyelids flickered, and she moaned, a faint, faraway keening that faded into silence.

Wait and see. But I couldn't. While I'd been breakfasting with the Calderwoods, Mrs. Drummond had taken to her bed with the first chills of malarial fever. Like a fool, I'd suppressed my initial urge to tell her about my early departure and press her to deliver up the letter immediately. I'd been reluctant to disturb her on her first day of illness. She would recover, I had thought, and I'd have time to ask her before she went.

Yet she had gotten worse instead of better, and now I might never come into possession of the only weapon I might ever have against Judah.

I was running short of options . . . and of allies. It was not in my nature to gather a wide circle of friends around me, as I saw some people do. My attachments were few, and all the more passionate for being rare. As a result, I had kept my clients—women who might have become my friends—at arm's length. With Reiner and Professor Wale gone, I had only the Lombardis to flee to as a possible haven from a situation that was becoming unbearable.

But getting to the Lombardis meant bringing Judah along with me, an undertaking akin to hitching up a tiger to the cart that would carry me across the prairie. Who would stand between me and this beautiful, dangerous man?

I HAD WISHED FOR A STRONG SHIELD. INSTEAD, I FOUND A strength more akin to a root that does its work in the dark, unacknowledged until it cracks the stone.

I visited Mrs. Drummond early in the morning, unable to sleep for worrying. I returned now to our room to find Tess mostly dressed and helping Sarah with her buttons. Tess's soft, fine hair was in a state of flyaway disorder, and my daughter's was worse. She had undone her braids in the night, finding them uncomfortable. Her springy curls had twisted themselves into a Gordian knot of interwoven copper.

"You'll never untangle her hair that way," scolded Tess after Sarah yelped for the twentieth time. "You keep forgetting where you started, and you're pulling much too hard." She dampened her brush and smoothed her own hair into submission, then took Sarah's brush away from me and began to tease her hair with short, brisk strokes.

"What's wrong with you, Nell?" she asked, looking sideways at me. "You're scatterbrained. You've been scatterbrained for days."

"It's nothing," I replied, gazing out of the window at the scudding clouds that sailed over the prairie in sullen procession.

Tess pursed her lips but didn't say another word until she had untangled Sarah's hair and watched me braid it into two tight pigtails.

"Now, Sary, why don't you read your book for a while?" she suggested, handing Sarah our latest purchase, a copy of *The Water-Babies*. Sarah could not yet read properly, but she found it amusing to pretend she could, pronouncing those words she understood and skipping over the others. "Momma and I are going to have a little talk."

She grabbed me by the forearm and tugged me in the direction of the door.

"It *is* something," Tess said in her version of a whisper—which was more like a loud hiss—when she had shut the door. "I know very well that you keep things from me,

Eleanor Lillington, because you think you're being nice by not worrying me, but I'm not a child to be told to go play. And I'm not a parcel to go sit in the corner till I'm called for neither. I'll thank you to be honest with me and tell me what's bothering you."

I blinked, taken aback by the sight of Tess's jutting chin and furrowed brow as she tried her best to look forbidding.

"I didn't mean to keep things from you," I said, but I knew I sounded unconvincing. Since the day I'd realized what Martin really meant to me, I had kept my most important thoughts and feelings locked inside me—and I knew I suffered as a result. Perhaps it was time to come clean.

"Then tell."

"Not here."

I led the way along the corridor till we reached the linen room and fumbled in my pocket for the key that unlocked it.

The fresh smell of starch, the underlying metallic note of the heat from the flat-iron, and the fading sweetness of old lavender greeted us as we stepped into the room. Its shaded windows cast a dim glow over the stacked ranks of immaculate linens, free of dust and insects. Another reminder of how well Mrs. Drummond had done her work. I had never particularly liked the housekeeper—after all, she had been quick to pass judgment on me. Yet now I realized I would miss her efficiency and the sense of peace and order she brought to everything she touched.

I sank down onto the swept boards, wishing my corset didn't prevent me from curling up into a ball of misery and hopelessness. Tess, who wore a soft corset without a single steel spring, sat too—much more comfortably. She folded her legs up under her skirt in the complicated way that Sarah often tried, unsuccessfully, to imitate.

"I'm worried about two things," I began. "Judah, first of all. I'm sure now that I don't want to marry him, Tess."

"That's the best news I've heard in a long time." Tess's smile was almost a gloat, but then her expression turned to puzzlement. "Why don't you tell him, then? You haven't told him, have you?"

"No. For a variety of reasons, no. I want to tell him when we're at the Lombardis'."

Tess made a face. "I'd rather not have to go on a long journey with him first."

"Neither would I." I twisted my hands together, feeling Hiram's ring dig into my fingers.

"Don't worry, Nell. I'll be with you." Tess leaned forward and patted my knee. "I don't like it when gentlemen get cross, but I'll stand beside you when you tell him you don't like him anymore. I won't be afraid. I'll remember that the Lord is my strength and my shield, like the Psalms say."

I let my head drop into my hands, suddenly afraid I would either laugh hysterically or cry like a child. I always underestimated Tess. My instinct was to protect her from my own worries in the same way I protected Sarah—but Tess wasn't a child. And she had a faith I found hard to emulate. Her unquestioning, absolute assurance of divine love had nothing to do with my view of the world as a place filled with problems I had to solve by practical means.

"Well, if you're not afraid, I guess I'd better not be," I said when I regained control of my emotions. "But there's another thing—something that would perhaps help me with Judah. Mrs. Drummond was going to give me a letter—something about Judah that Professor Wale thought I should know, but it disappeared after he died. I don't think it's in her room, and I doubt somehow that she hid it in her office either." I wiped my nose with the handkerchief I held balled up in my palm. "And—I'm very afraid she may never be able to tell me where it is now."

Tess nodded, her mouth turning down at the corners.

"Eliza is very sick," she agreed. "Dorcas said her ague will probably carry her off this time. I think so too because I don't think Eliza wants to be here anymore. I think she wants to be with Jesus and not be unhappy all the time."

Well, she certainly wanted to leave the seminary. Knowing she had planned to leave for employment elsewhere, I wasn't so sure dying had been her planned course of action.

Tess brightened for a moment. "Maybe your letter's in the hiding place in the library," she said. "You take out some of the big books, and there's a panel—"

"It's not there," I interrupted. "I looked this morning before I went to see Mrs. Drummond. Tess, you *knew* about it?"

"Of course." Tess looked pleased at my astonishment. "Eliza showed me."

"What other secrets of hers do you know?" I felt an unexpected surge of hope. "Are there more hiding places?" In such a big building, there could be many. Perhaps even some that Judah had not ferreted out.

Tess screwed up her face, concentrating.

"Not good ones," she said finally. "Not really, really safe. Those boys get into everything, you know. And if I were hiding something, I wouldn't put it in any place I regularly work in, would you? You expect people to hide things in places they know well."

"And Mrs. Drummond was—is—very cautious by nature. You're probably right, Tess. I've always thought it odd that she has so few personal possessions considering the amount of time she's lived here. What on earth did she even do with the money she earned? Give it away?"

"No, she took it—"

Tess stopped short. Her eyes widened, her mouth formed itself into a perfect *O*, and she scrambled to her feet. "Nell," she breathed. "I think I know. And I think I have—" She did not finish the sentence, but jumped up and down in excitement, squealing as quietly as she could manage.

I pushed myself up from the floor—an ungainly operation when one's midriff is encased in steel—and grabbed Tess's shoulders to quiet her.

"Well for goodness' sake don't let the whole building know," I said. My heart thumped. Tess was trembling with excitement, and my own legs began to shake a little in response.

Tess took a few deep breaths and then reached into her pocket. She withdrew her set of keys. Like me, she had a key to the workroom, to our bedroom, and to the linen room we were now in. Mrs. Drummond had also given her keys to her own office and to the room where the ledgers were stored. Tess loved to study her methods and would pore over the ledgers for hours given a chance.

But the key Tess was holding up to me was one I had never noticed—and why should I? A bunch of keys was a commonplace thing. It was an ordinary iron key, small and slender, of a plain, old-fashioned design.

"Eliza gives me copies of some of her keys," Tess explained in her loud, hoarse whisper. "But this one is not a copy. It's the only one. Eliza said, 'They don't watch you, Tess.' And she's right. They look through me or over me, never at me. They think, 'Tess is an imbecile; she's not smart like Nell or Eliza.' But if Eliza gives me something to keep safe, I don't lose it or tell anyone about it. Except I have now." Her mouth pursed in consternation, but then she brightened. "But I only told you for the letter Eliza wanted you to have, Nell. Not for the other things."

"It's for a strongbox of some kind? Where she keeps her money? But such things can be easily broken into, can't they?"

Tess grinned. "Not if nobody knows they're there. Nobody in the seminary, anyhow. Mr. Yomkins knows because it's in his big safe. He says a postmaster shouldn't have such a thing in his keeping, but it's been there ever so long. It holds Eliza's bank book and the bit of money she keeps by for emergencies and a pretty necklace with pink pearls and some papers. Eliza used to go to Springwood most Saturdays, don't you remember, Nell? That's when she sent her money to the bank, just like we do. But she stopped going months and months ago. She gave the key to me, and one day she had me put some money in there for her—'Be very careful no one sees you, Tess,' she said. And I was."

I felt a swell of indignation that Mrs. Drummond had been using Tess—had exposed her to danger—but I let it pass.

"Did you see a letter in there when you put the money in?"

"I didn't really look," Tess replied. "I was real quick—Mr. Yomkins stands outside the door, but he doesn't like me to spend long at his safe. But wouldn't you put a secret letter there instead of in a hiding place near you? I would."

"I might," I mused. "But if you're right, what are we to do? I don't like the thought of you—or I—carrying a letter around that Professor Wale may have been killed for and that Mrs. Drummond was so afraid about. And if she—does not recover, we run the risk of the box being surrendered to—someone, I don't know whom. Either way, the Calderwoods and Judah have their eye on me, and anything I do out of the ordinary will arouse their suspicions."

"So let's be ordinary, Nell." Tess's round face was rosy with anticipation. "Let's do exactly what we always do—and if *I* do it, nobody will think we're being clever."

42
JOURNEY

November 27, 1875

Dear Martin,

I write this in great haste. We're sending you something that may be of interest. I don't know what it says because Tess is sending it on before I can see it, but I trust you to take the appropriate course of action when you've read it.

Of course it may be nothing at all. Didn't you tell me about a novel in which the heroine is greatly agitated to find a hidden paper, only to discover it's a laundry list?

Tess, Sarah and I are traveling to the Lombardi mission in the company of Mr. Poulton on December the sixth. Please don't worry too much. I hope you are well.

Yours,

Nell

"HOW LONG DO YOU THINK IT TAKES A LETTER TO REACH Chicago?"

Tess's loud whisper was fortunately masked by the sound

of the sewing machine. Jane Holdcroft, the young woman Mrs. Calderwood had hired to replace me once I rose to the status of Judah's fiancée, was working industriously on yet another set of new pillowcases. From the number of torn ones the servants had found lately, I suspected the students weren't using them for their intended purpose.

It was five days after I had watched Tess's small figure recede into the distance, accompanying Bella to Springwood on her usual Saturday errands. Dorcas, who generally accompanied her daughter, had been busy in the sickroom.

Tess had returned elated at her success in locating a letter very much like the one I had described to her. She'd enclosed it with the note I had written in a wrapper addressed to Martin. This she had put into our customary mailing to Chicago. We still sent money to the banker Martin had found for us and still felt a sense of achievement in doing so, even though the wealth Martin had garnered for us had eclipsed our small earnings.

Tess had been able to accomplish this feat of derring-do in time to join Bella at the mercantile. She had purchased eau de cologne for the two of us and a penny whistle made of persimmon wood for Sarah into the bargain. She had been right—nobody had paid any attention to her.

"How long for a letter to get to Chicago? I'm not at all sure," I said. "At least four days, I'd imagine—quite possibly a week. And then it must reach Martin—he may be traveling again, for all we know. Why? Do you imagine he'll come charging up to the door on a white horse and rescue us?"

"That would be so exciting," Tess sighed.

"I suppose it would."

The last time I had needed Martin to rescue me, he hadn't turned up until I'd hauled myself and Sarah out of the river into which Hiram Jackson had thrown my daughter. True, he had been of invaluable comfort and assistance in the aftermath of that dramatic scene, but hardly the knight in shining armor Tess was hoping for.

I hadn't yet told Tess that our friendship had, as the novelists say, ripened into something deeper. And I never might since my most sensible course of action—once I left the seminary—was to start life anew as far away from Martin as possible.

I stretched my cramped fingers and looked at the list I had been making. I was attempting to itemize our tasks by season. Tess had thought of several things I'd forgotten, and I would have to write the whole thing out clean later, but I was fairly satisfied.

In our nearly four years at the Eternal Life Seminary, we had made many improvements to our role. Tess's mania for list-making and her admiration of Mrs. Drummond's methods had allowed us to anticipate the demands of the seasons. I had negotiated favorable terms with some of the newer suppliers in Wichita, Saint Louis, and even Chicago. I had put systems into place to keep the boys well supplied with basic linens.

And at the same time, I had built up a successful business as a dressmaker. I'd learned much in the process about the difficulties of dealing with women who decidedly had too much time on their hands. I'd faced the challenges of interpreting catalogues and sales circulars to find the best-quality fabrics at the lowest cost. I'd learned to harness my drawing skills to interpret my clients' wishes. I'd taught myself to follow through by producing dresses that did not deviate too far from my original designs and yet incorporated the ideas that swarmed into my mind as I considered the drape of a fabric and the properties of the trimmings.

When we arrived at the seminary, I was a callow girl with an illegitimate baby. I was grieving my mother and unable to look much farther forward than the end of my nose. Now, I saw the future as an endless vista of possibilities.

If I could only escape the trap I had unwittingly walked into.

DAWN HAD NOT YET BROKEN WHEN WE LOADED OUR WAGON and took our leave of the seminary. Yet by the time we turned west, the sun had risen, and its first low rays struck sparks from the frost that clung to each stalk of grass or wizened seed pod.

Tess and Sarah were fast asleep, shaded by the wagon's canvas cover. The only sounds I could hear were the steady plodding of the horses' hooves, the soft rasp-*hunk* of their breathing that sent puffs of steam toward the crisp sky, and the creak-rumble-creak of the wagon.

We'd watched the farmer liberally grease the gear and wheels from the barrel hanging off one side of the wagon. He had proudly demonstrated the new rifle concealed in a compartment near the driver's bench. Tess and Sarah squealed and put their fingers in their ears as he worked the lever and fired out into the empty prairie a couple of times before reloading.

Judah held the reins. Andrew, assigned to drive us, was even now in his bed, suffering agonies from having eaten tainted pork at a certain establishment in Fork Crossing. I was fairly certain Judah could not have had a hand in that turn of events. My alarm at realizing we were not, after all, to have someone else with us quickly turned to anger against the hapless Andrew.

This would never have happened if Mrs. Drummond had been her old self. She had been particular about knowing exactly where the servants were at all times. But Mrs. Drummond had not awakened for days. She lay motionless, her skin a waxy yellow and her eyes sunken, a picture of death in life. Tess had been very upset about leaving her thus and had sobbed over her as if over a corpse—which she almost was. I didn't think we would see her again in this life, and I had taken my own leave with a murmured word of blessing and forgiveness. She had, after all, only ever done what she thought was right.

Judah was silent beside me, other than speaking occasionally to the horses. I had plenty of time to think.

I should perhaps have been afraid, I reflected, but I was not. It was exhilarating to be free of the seminary building and out on the plains with the great vista of tan and gold grasses before us, waving in the crisp, cold breeze that swept over us in gusts and eddies.

I wasn't cold—the farmer had supplied two huge buffalo hides, and Judah had draped one over my shoulders. The thick, coarse fur on the inside formed a surprisingly warm cocoon so that only my nose and cheeks stung from the frosty air. Inside the wagon, Tess and Sarah huddled under a collection of fairly clean Indian blankets and the other hide.

Idleness freed my mind to roam around its memories. Unfortunately, the image that consistently invaded my thoughts was that of Professor Wale, wide-eyed in death, a bloody hole in his head.

It was strange how easy it had been for people to accept that the mysteries surrounding his death—and Dr. Adema's, come to that—would likely never be solved. Of course, Dr. Adema's death could have been an accident—but Professor Wale's definitely wasn't. The frontier attracted the rough sort of man who would kill for nothing; that was what the people of Springwood said. Commit murder because a man looked at him sideways. Or Indians—some kind of retaliation for a land lost to the cause of manifest destiny. Theories abounded —and none of them made sense to me.

I shivered under the buffalo hide, and Judah sensed it. "Are you cold?" He turned his head in my direction, and his breath misted the fur collar of his greatcoat. He managed not to look cold at all. He was well dressed for the journey in high fur-lined boots and a hat such as I imagined a fur trapper wearing, fur-lined leather gloves encasing his slender hands.

His clothing always looked new, I realized, remembering how worn Martin's riding clothes had been. I'd always thought of Martin as a well-dressed man, but Judah's sartorial elegance seemed to go a step further. It was studied, somehow, as if he put great thought into dressing with precision for every occasion.

"I'm all right." My voice sounded loud after the silence between us, and I felt oddly embarrassed. To cover my confusion, I twisted round on the "lazy seat"—although how one could be lazy on a bouncing wooden bench some ten feet off the ground was a mystery—and peered into the wagon's dim interior, noting the motionless lumps in the bedding.

"We'll stop when they wake up," Judah said. "You may remember that the trail descends into a gully. There's a spring down there, marked by boulders, so we can build a fire and brew some coffee as well as water the horses."

"I'm surprised how well you know the trail."

"I ride out sometimes, when I can borrow a decent horse." Judah clicked softly to the Percherons. The left-hand horse was setting rather a slow pace, but the ears of its brother flicked back and forth at the sound.

"I look forward to the day when I can afford a horse of my own," Judah said. "Perhaps a carriage. It's tiresome being a poor man, Nell."

No guesses whose money would buy the horse and

carriage. I smiled in a noncommittal way, pulling the buffalo hide closer around me.

Judah flicked the whip over the left horse's withers. Its skin twitched, and it quickened its pace fractionally. "That one's a lazy brute," he said. "It's ambling along like the lowest kind of mule. Such horses as these should step out more."

"Perhaps it needs a rest?" I suggested.

Judah laughed. "Perhaps. But this journey's a sight easier than pulling a plow or a cart loaded with hogs or wheat. These beasts are bred for hard work. I'll take a look at it when we halt. Something may be bothering it, a sore place or a badly fitted harness."

"Judah, how is it that you're so knowledgeable about horses?" My curiosity got the better of me. "You don't seem to spend an excessive amount of time outdoors."

"I grew up around them." Judah's reply was curt and seemed designed to forestall any further inquiries, but I persisted.

"In Baltimore? Did your family own many horses?" I knew nothing of Judah's antecedents—he had never mentioned father or mother, sister or brother. One might think he had come into the world new minted, an angel fallen from heaven, perhaps. As soon as that thought crossed my mind, it gave way to the realization that a fallen angel was a demon.

Judah merely smiled his dazzling smile, white teeth and violet eyes gleaming in the sunlight.

"You're very curious all of a sudden. I spent a lot of time with horses, and then I became a scholar. I prefer the latter."

His tone brooked no further inquiry, and he looked to the front, presenting me with his perfect profile, but absolutely no answers.

We reached the gully about an hour later. Judah guided the horses skillfully down the shallow incline where the trail dipped, holding the reins with his right hand and leaning on the wagon's heavy brake with his left with practiced ease. He had spent many hours driving before he came to the seminary, I realized.

I wondered, not for the first time, how I had been so blinded by Judah's personal charms that I had omitted to ask who exactly he was. Out here on the frontier, almost none of us had roots or antecedents. Apart from a few families whose parents or grandparents had arrived before the war to scrabble a living out of the plains with only the Indians for company, we were all new inhabitants of a place that was building itself around us. It was easy to ignore the fact that all of us had histories. I thought—as I had many times over the last week—of the letter making its way toward Martin, which expediency had left me no opportunity to read. The clues it contained to Judah's past might help me decide our best course for the future.

A huge yawn interrupted my reverie. Sarah had woken up, and she soon made sure Tess was also awake. Now that we were in the gully, trees lined the trail, and it wasn't long before we came to the group of boulders that indicated the spring, strewn carelessly by the gully wall as if left there by a giant hand. Invigorated by the cold, sharp air and the sunshine—and in Tess and Sarah's case, by a good rest—the three of us cheerfully set ourselves the task of gathering dead wood and making a fire. Judah unhitched the horses and led them to the clear pool, from which I had scooped a potful of water to boil up some coffee.

By the time Judah returned, I had managed—with some difficulty and danger of setting fire to my skirts—to get a small blaze going in the middle of a circle of stones that were obviously there for the use of travelers. He nodded in appreciation at my efforts and took the tin cup I handed him with a word of thanks, but a frown marred the perfection of his brow.

"There's a crack in that horse's hoof—I didn't notice it before. The farmer's a fool to have let that happen to such a valuable beast."

"Is that serious?" The horses looked fine to me. Judah had rehitched them and tied nosebags to their bridles. They were both munching with relish, their ears flicking as they gazed at us with great, patient eyes.

"It could be. If some grit got in—I can't feel a warm spot now, but an infection would need treatment."

"You can't do it?"

"Not if I have to cut into the hoof. I haven't the tools."

"We can do that when we get to the mission, can't we?"

"As long as the brute will carry us that far. I can't drive the wagon with just one horse."

Judah looked up at the sky, which was now invaded by drifts of cloud, mounded white and gray billows through which the sun shone a diffused but still bright light. "It's around ten—let's break camp and get moving. The sooner we get to the mission, the better."

43
CONFRONTATION

"Have we stopped?"

I pushed away the buffalo hide, scrambled bleary-eyed into a sitting position, and began to neaten my hair.

The air had changed, I realized. It had taken on a damp chill with an edge of frost, sullen and portentous. I was stiff from lying on the boards of the wagon with just an Indian blanket between me and the various bumps and depressions that indicated the compartments contained in the wagon box.

A crack of the whip made me start, and I scrambled to my knees. Beside me, Sarah made a noise of complaint and twitched the buffalo hide back over her shoulders. Tess's presence was betrayed by a lump in the other hide. She had burrowed right down under the covers and curled up like an oversized dormouse.

We had definitely stopped. I was able to get to my feet easily, unhampered by the swaying of the wagon. I was just in time to see Judah lower himself down from the bench, an expression of fury on his face. Grabbing hold of the bench, which bounced gently on its springs, I leaned out over the singletree and watched as Judah inspected the hoof the left-hand horse was now holding off the ground.

"Our luck's run out, hasn't it?"

I could see by his face that it was bad news. By the time we had reached the end of the long gully and gotten out of the wagon to make the horses' job easier as they climbed the steep, sloping trail, the left-hand horse was setting a slow and uncertain pace, its ears pinned back as Judah cracked the whip to urge it up the slope.

We had stopped only for the briefest necessities since then and had eaten our meal of biscuits and fried chicken as we rolled slowly onward. Sarah had decided that was a great treat and had been exhaustingly chatty for some time afterward. The last thing I remembered before sleep overcame me was the drone of her penny whistle, which she played in an endless rise and fall of the same two or three notes, over and over again.

"We'll have to make camp here. If I'm careful, I can get down that slope there with just one horse, and we'll have some shelter."

Judah indicated another gully, which ran at a right angle to the trail. It was choked with trees and brush and had no trail through it, but the dirt of the downward slope was packed hard as if worn by the feet of generations of hunters.

"What about the injured horse? You're not going to leave it up here, are you? Won't there be wolves?" I watched, worried, as Judah began unbuckling the straps, muttering under his breath.

"It'll probably follow us once we get far enough ahead. Horses don't like being left on their own. I can't make it move now though—it's acting like it has a broken leg. Infections are painful."

It took a little while to awaken our companions and lighten the wagon's load as much as possible for the endeavor of guiding it down the slope with just one horse. We were all silent as we walked behind the lumbering conveyance. We couldn't see the sun, hidden as it was behind a mass of thick gray cloud, but I knew that day would soon be waning, and there would be no moonlight or starlight. We were stranded, and we could do nothing about it until dawn. It was going to be a long night.

WE MADE OURSELVES AS COMFORTABLE AS WE COULD. JUDAH was right—the injured horse turned up before darkness fell and stood, its head hanging, as near as possible to its hobbled companion.

The mood of our journey had soured. Judah was taciturn and showed little patience with Sarah's and Tess's repeated remarks on the cold, the darkness, and the sheer loneliness of the spot we were in.

At least we were out of the wind, I thought as Judah and I set silently about the task of gathering wood. And while the trees in the gully formed a dense, impenetrable mass that whispered and creaked like a host of demons, they provided plenty of wood for the fire. We arranged the wagon and our camp so our backs were against the gully wall and the fire was between us and the access to the wagon.

"We won't be able to see if anyone—or anything—approaches us." Judah passed a hand over his chin.

"It's impossible to see anything anyway," I pointed out in a brusque tone. Worry and the discomforts of travel were making me cross, and I had the added burden of trying to allay Tess's and Sarah's fears. I felt uneasy in Judah's presence and annoyed with him for being so curt with my daughter and companion. Could he not see they needed comforting? So did I, for that matter, but I wasn't going to let Judah see that.

We had brought more than enough food for a day's journey, but traveling had made us hungry. What remained made a meager supper after I had divided it so we would have some breakfast. And once our morning meal was over, we would have little left.

"You'll have to ride for the Lombardis' once day breaks," I said to Judah once Tess and Sarah finally retired to huddle under the blankets and one of the hides. I had conceded the other to Judah, who planned to sleep by the fire.

"I'm aware of that." There was a note of derision in Judah's voice, and his slanted eyes held an expression of mild contempt.

"I'm sure you are." My own voice sounded shrewish. "I just want to be sure we each know what the other is to be doing. It's safer that way. And I have to explain things to Sarah and Tess, so I want to be clear myself."

"It won't be difficult to explain to them what you'll be doing," Judah said. "You'll be doing precisely nothing while I take the risk of a bareback ride of some two hours' duration."

"Do you think I would not rather take your role?" I retorted, nettled. "If you don't know by now that I dislike idleness and passivity, you don't know me at all."

Judah's lips twitched. "When we're married, you'll find out just how well I know you."

I had spent the day reining in my anxieties about Judah in general, and this journey in particular, for the sake of my daughter and friend. I had spent the week worrying about the letter that may—or may not—hold information about Judah that might, at the very least, give me an unassailable reason for breaking with him. I was tired, my feet were cold, and my stomach was growling. So perhaps it was excusable that I said what I did.

"If you knew me at all, you'd realize you shouldn't be so sure of me."

I knew instantly that I'd done exactly what I didn't intend to do. The alert lift of Judah's head and the gleam in his eyes —more than just the reflection of the fire's flames—indicated that my remark had put him on the *qui vive*. I quailed inwardly. Then, like a steel spring recoiling on itself, my nerve returned to me, and I stiffened my spine against his reaction.

Judah was silent for a long moment. When he spoke, his voice was like the purr of a cat, low and powerful in the dead silence of the winter's night.

"You're having second thoughts." His eyes widened a little as realization came to him. "I thought you were a little distant because—well, I imagined you were making an effort to get that numbskull Rutherford out of your mind. A man who can't stay faithful to his wife in thought but doesn't have the intestinal fortitude to seize the opportunity any truly red-blooded man would pounce on." He sniggered, poking the fire with a stick from the supply we had heaped up.

"Don't say such things about Martin. He's trying to preserve his honor—and mine."

"You have no honor. You're the mother of a bastard child. The only honor you can ever obtain is by marrying it, don't you understand that? Are you so stupid that you'll really pass up the only offer that has come to you in four years? Except that milksop Lehmann, of course, but he hardly counts—and he was pretty quick to change his mind once he found out the truth." Judah flung the stick into the fire, which was now blazing high, the flames sending sparks up toward the clouds.

My hands were trembling, and I balled them into fists by my side.

"I'd rather live without honor than live with you, Judah."

I scrambled to my feet from the flat piece of rock on which I had been sitting. I noted as I did so that a few snowflakes were whirling down from the sky, brushing my face with soft, cold fingers.

"You're tired and anxious." Judah also got to his feet and came to stand between me and the wagon. "Come, Nell, you need to sleep. In the morning, we'll reach the mission, and you'll remember all the good reasons you have for becoming my wife." He reached a hand toward me, the beautiful smile back on his face—but I batted it away and took a step backward.

"No, Judah. Never."

"May I remind you that you are promised to me?" The smile faded. In the firelight, Judah's slanted eyes looked like chips of stone. "Cam Calderwood all but announced our engagement in front of the town. And you went with me—willingly—with only a child and an imbecile as chaperones. That could only have one possible interpretation. If you return from this trip a single woman still, your reputation will have evaporated like the morning dew. Especially if I let it be known that our embraces have, shall we say, overstepped the bounds of propriety. And that would be the truth. If you're intending to jilt a man, Nell, you must not let him kiss you—or put his arm around your waist—thus."

He moved as quickly as a striking snake, encircling my waist with both of his hands and then hooking one of his arms around me so that he had me pinned against his body.

"Of course, I could always make sure of you here and now," Judah murmured, his breath warm on my cheek. "You're practically my wife, Nell. We're meant to be together, and it's too late for you to be capricious. Yield to me now, and I will do you the favor of forgetting the conversation we have just had."

The hand that was not around my waist moved upward, following the line of my corset up to the swell of my breasts.

"No," I said faintly.

The hand squeezed, and suddenly my mind was flooded with the memory of a day in May four years before, when Jack Venton had done something very similar—

"NO."

And suddenly I had lost control of myself and become a kicking, squirming madwoman, my hands flailing desperately as I tried to rake Judah's face with my nails. I could hear myself making a peculiar noise, a sort of sustained squealing mixed with groans and pants as I fought to get free of Judah's hands. I would have bitten him if I could get close enough with my teeth. I rained blows at his face, neck, and shoulders until he let go of my waist in an effort to defend himself and then pushed back as hard as I could so that there was a little distance between us.

But not enough. The blow seemed to come out of nowhere, a lightning bolt through my cheekbone that jarred my head as if I had run it into a stone wall. I reeled, catching myself just in time before I stepped backward into the fire. I snatched at my skirts, checking hurriedly for smoldering patches as I stumbled sideways and back. As I did so, the pain came, an ache so fierce that both eyes began to water, and Judah became a black blur among the shadows of the night.

Nobody had ever hit me before. And certainly nobody had ever called me the name that came out of Judah's mouth. I backed around the fire, trying to put the blaze between me and Judah and yet ensure he was not between me and the wagon.

I stumbled over a long branch that stuck out of the fire. Now Judah was closing on me, and I knew he would hit me again at the very least. I grabbed at the branch, pulling the glowing end out of the blaze and pointing it at Judah. It was long enough to keep him at more than arm's length. I wrapped both hands around it as he tried to dodge it, following his movements as best I could with the red heat that glowed brighter as the wind caught it for a moment.

"Leave." My voice sounded strange to me, calm and cold, although I was blinking desperately in an effort to see, and my legs were shaking. "Get away from us before I push this into your face. You'll never put your hands on me again—and you'll never see a cent of my money, whatever tricks you may try. We're finished, Judah. Utterly finished."

"And where precisely am I to leave to?" Judah inquired, a note of derision in his voice. "We're in the middle of the prairie, and a snowstorm is probably coming. You're terrified of snow, Nell. Do you really want me to leave you alone in this?"

"I'm not alone. And even if I were, I'd feel safer alone in a snowstorm—with wolves into the bargain—than I would with you, Judah. Take the horse if you wish—I doubt I'd be able to make use of it anyhow, and we'd be safer in the wagon than with me trying to ride or drive. Pastor Lombardi will come looking for us—he's probably looking for us now since we didn't arrive at the mission by dark. Tess and I will keep the fire going, and we're not so far off the trail—he'll find us. And when he does, you'd better be long gone. I don't care where you go—return to the seminary if you like and spin a tale about me. See if your precious moneymaking schemes come to anything now."

"A fine speech, my dear Nell." The firelight flickered on Judah's curls. "Keep talking. That branch will soon have cooled down enough for me to grasp, and then—"

"And then I'll shoot you."

Judah whirled around, and I almost dropped the branch. The firelight shone orange on Tess in her white nightgown, a few feet away from where we stood. A log shifted behind us and a flame shot up, reflecting off the barrel of the rifle she held in her hands.

"Don't be ridiculous. You don't know how to use that." Judah took a step forward but then appeared to think better of it and stopped.

"I pull my finger back on this thing, don't I? I watched the farmer do it." Tess's voice shook, but I had the impression it was more from cold than fear. I was horribly afraid for her though. Judah was right—she really didn't know how to use a gun. But she did have the barrel pointing straight at him from a distance of some ten feet.

"If you move, I will try," Tess said. "I watched carefully—pull back and then push this lever forward and back, and then pull back again."

"And when you miss, you'll wish you hadn't been born," said Judah calmly as he took another step forward.

I swung the branch in a wide arc. For a few seconds, time seemed to pass very slowly, and I could see the wood glow as the movement fed it with a rush of air. And then it connected with the back of Judah's head, and he collapsed face forward onto the dead growth on the gully's floor.

Tess squeaked and dropped the gun, which promptly fired, causing the horses—which, luckily, were on the other side of the wagon—to snort and buck with fright. Tess screamed and ran to where I was standing, the branch still in my hands, gaping at the dark shape on the ground in front of me.

"Did you kill him?" Her teeth were chattering.

"I don't think so." Handing the branch to Tess, I dropped to my knees and placed a hand on Judah's back. To my relief I felt the steady rise and fall of his breathing. I scrambled to my feet again.

"He's all right," I gasped as I pushed myself up. "I didn't even mean to knock him out. I was just trying to distract him from you." I winced as pain shot through the left side of my face and tentatively touched my cheekbone with the tips of my fingers. "But it serves him right."

"What a-a-a-a-are we going t-t-to d-d-d-d-do?" asked Tess. What with the cold and the excitement, her stutter was so bad I could hardly make out what she was saying. I looked at her, realizing anew that although she had stockings on, all that stood between her and the freezing wind was a flannel nightgown. How she had climbed down off the wagon by herself, I didn't know, let alone with a rifle in her hand.

Soft flakes of snow brushed my cheek, achingly cold on the bruise. I looked down at Judah, who let out a soft groan, his fingers twitching.

"We're going to get back into the wagon, fast," I said. "You'll freeze out here like that, and he's going to get up in a moment and come after us."

"We have to take the rifle." Tess picked up the gun and pointed it toward the trees, well away from the horses. "See, you do this—" and she worked the lever awkwardly but vigorously, letting out a high-pitched peep of triumph when the spent casing leapt out of the top of the chamber. "Now it's all ready to fire again. I think you should hold it though, Nell—you're stronger than me and your hands are bigger. It's hard to do, you know," she added informatively.

"I don't think either of us should be taking our chances with guns." I watched the rifle warily, at the same time trying to keep an eye on Judah. Literally one eye, since the other appeared to be closing. That whole side of my face felt tight and throbbed alarmingly.

"You don't want him to have it, do you?" Tess thrust the

gun at me and headed back to the wagon, her gait awkward on her cold legs.

I certainly didn't. Cradling the rifle in my arms, keeping my finger well away from the trigger and the barrel pointed skyward, I backed toward the wagon and clambered up, pulling Tess after me.

Tess burrowed into the blankets—I could hear her teeth chattering—before I could advise her to put some clothes on. I sighed and grabbed a spare blanket, pulling it around my shoulders. Of course, I'd left the other hide at the fire, and now that the excitement had ebbed, I was starting to feel chilled to the bone.

I picked up the rifle and lay on my stomach on the floor of the wagon. I cursed the steel rods of my corset, which pressed into my flesh at a most uncomfortable angle. I could hear the sound of Judah rising to his feet—I was almost certain he was muttering swear words under his breath—and in a moment saw his silhouette against the glow of the fire.

"Tess was right, we do know how to fire this gun," I said as calmly as I could as he walked toward the wagon. "We tried it." That wasn't strictly true, but how was he to know? "And now I'm pointing it at you, Judah. I'm not going to let you come near me again. I suggest you get on that horse and ride back to the seminary. You can tell them whatever you like. I know the pastor will come for us soon, and he'll bring the men from the mission. If you're still around by then, I'll make sure everyone knows you hit one woman and threatened another. You're better off leaving. You're a good rider and can be back at Eternal Life before daybreak."

Judah stood still, seeming to consider my words. Finally, he shrugged. "Very well," he said. "I'll need the bridle—it's hanging on the front of the wagon."

"Fetch it," I replied. "But know that I'll shoot you if you step one foot toward me."

I shifted into a sitting position as the dark shape moved toward me. My heart pounded so hard I could feel the pulse throbbing in my injured cheek, but Judah did nothing except unhook the bridle and then step away from the wagon.

"You may not survive this, you know," he said conversationally. "The plains are a very big place and mighty dangerous. A woman, an imbecile, and a child out alone in the middle of winter—the wolves will have you, Nell."

I shivered but refused to let his words sink into my brain. "Get out, Judah. Get away from me and never think to approach me again."

"Oh, we're not done." I could not see his face, but I could imagine the gleam in his beautiful violet-blue eyes. He rubbed the back of his head, and when he spoke, there was a smile in his voice. "We're not finished at all, Nell. I'm looking forward to our next meeting."

I felt my shoulders relax a little as I heard him walk in the direction of the horses, but I kept the gun at the ready. I could hear him talking to the uninjured horse as he slipped the headgear on; a few more minutes elapsed before he rode into view. The horse was unsaddled, I knew, but in the faint light from the fire, I could see Judah was sitting on its broad back with nonchalant ease, straight-spined and almost elegant. He wouldn't come to any harm, I thought, and was glad. I didn't want my actions to be the cause of his death, however much I wanted him gone.

"I'll see you shortly, Nell. If the wolves don't see you first." He turned the horse's head, and then I heard the rattle of loose stones as he urged the animal up the slope, toward the high plain.

Very little snow had fallen—a mere dusting lay between the grass and dead stalks of plants—and the snowflakes were now falling more sparsely. I lay watching the glow of the fire, not daring to compose myself to sleep, but also reluctant to get down from the wagon. So when sleep finally took me despite all my efforts, my last jumbled thoughts were a confused chaos of fire and snow. My dreams were haunted by the image of Judah—wearing the expression I had glimpsed as he aimed a blow at my head—circled in a halo of white light.

44

PERIL

"Nobody."

I had returned from my reconnoitering trip to the top of the gully. I sank my head into my hands, despair washing over me. Outside the wagon, a few flakes of snow floated down to join the others on the ground.

We had managed to rekindle the fire. I had known a moment of terror when I awoke, cold and stiff in every limb, to find the fire out. Far worse was that the injured horse was gone. As useless as the animal had been to us, it might at the very least have given warning of wolves. And it would have given them something to prey on rather than me, Tess, and Sarah, I had thought callously.

"You're so cold, Nell. You shouldn't have stayed up there for so long." Tess pulled the buffalo hide up over my shoulders.

"I'll go stand by the fire in a moment. I just wanted to talk to you while Sarah's still asleep. What are we going to do? We've wasted half the day waiting, and no one has come." I stuck my hands, freezing despite my mittens, back under my armpits. "We have no food—aside from the biscuit I saved for

Sarah—and in perhaps three, four hours, it'll be dark again. I'd be sorry to prove Judah right."

I would indeed. For Sarah's sake, I had tried to make light of the situation all through the long morning. I had kept her busy gathering wood for the fire, telling her I had fallen, and Mr. Poulton had gone to get help. Tess, stalwart, played games with Sarah inside the wagon while I stood a lonely vigil for as long as I could on the trail.

I had hoped against hope to see the moving specks on the horizon that would mean Pastor Lombardi had come for us. But nothing had moved in the frigid air except the occasional bird. Even with the rifle on the ground beside me, I had been in a constant state of terror that a pack of wolves would sneak up on me. Or that they would attack the wagon and I would return to find Sarah and Tess mauled to death—

Or, more realistically, that the snow would fall deep and we would be completely stranded. So far the snowfall had been light. No more than an inch of white powder dusted the ground, settling between the grasses and sprinkling the bare branches of the trees in the gully like fine sugar. But I was certain it was colder than it had been the night before. There was something ominous about the lowering gray clouds that seemed to press down on us from the vast sky.

"If it snows hard, you won't be able to move so fast." Tess's words echoed my thoughts. "Or maybe not at all. I think if you're going to go, Nell, it should be soon."

"I know." The notion of attempting the trail by foot had been on my mind since the morning. Tess had initially opposed it, and she was perfectly correct that the safest course of action was to stay put and wait for a search party. But as the day dragged on and the clouds darkened, the possibility of being stranded in an impassible snowstorm had thrown both of us into a far less certain state of mind.

When we'd been forced to make camp, Judah had estimated we were about two hours away from the Lombardi mission. All I had to do was to walk along the trail for maybe three or four hours—for I was sure the wagon didn't travel all that fast—and I would find the mission and direct the rescue efforts to the right place.

"You must take the buffalo hide, Nell," Tess said. "We have enough blankets. It's a pity Mr. Poulton took the other one though. It was ungallant of him."

"I don't think gallantry was foremost in his mind," I said, gingerly touching my sore face. Handfuls of snow, scraped up from the grass at the edge of the trail, had brought down the swelling at the cost of red, raw fingers, and I could now see out of my left eye again. But the soreness extended from my cheekbone to my ear, almost down to the jawline and up to the temple. I could only begin to imagine what it looked like.

Tess watched me for a minute as I stared out of the front of the wagon, my mind a whirl of indecision. "Make up your mind, Nell," she said. "Whatever you do will be right in my eyes, but if you decide to go, now really is the best time. If you go when Sary's awake, she'll scream and cry. That will be hard for all of us."

I nodded, wincing as the movement sent a lancing pain through my face. We had been over this a hundred times. Now was the time for action.

"I'll build up the fire before I leave," I said. "And you keep a tight hold on that rifle, Tess."

With a longing glance at the sleeping form of my daughter, I hugged Tess tight and then grabbed the buffalo hide she held out to me. "Tell Sarah—tell her I love her and I didn't want to leave her."

I piled the fire high, adding the thickest branches I could find in the hope they would hold the heat for several hours. And then with a last look at the wagon, I shrugged the buffalo hide over my shoulders, its thick, coarse fur enveloping me in its warmth, and set off one more time up the slope that led to the trail.

"Look after me, Mama," I whispered to the sky. "Tell me what to do."

For some reason, memories of my mother had been crowding in thick and fast all that long day. There had been moments when her presence seemed almost tangible. I had sworn once or twice I could smell her lily-of-the-valley perfume on the bitter, snow-laden wind. As I began to walk as fast as I could, my head ducked to stop the keen wind from making my face hurt even more, I clung to her memory. As if, at the end of the trail, I would find my home.

And yet—shouldn't it be my father I sought in this howling cold? For what I was doing now was exactly what he had done all those years ago—gone on a rescue mission because he couldn't wait for help to come. And he had died in the snow and left behind him a child—me—almost the same age Sarah was now. Perhaps it was my fate to repeat his.

WHEN I HAD BEEN SAFELY ENSCONCED INSIDE THE WAGON, THE plains had seemed immense but friendly, a landscape of waving grasses and the ghosts of summer's flowers sparkling in the frosty sunlight. Now that I was alone on the trail under a leaden, cold sky, the undulating landscape took on a sinister aspect.

As my onward march nibbled away at the miles, step by pitifully small step, I began to imagine I was walking along the spine of a sleeping giant, a Gulliver so vast that his torso had no end to it. That the giant was dreaming I had no doubt. It didn't seem possible that the voices I detected, rising and falling like the ebb and flow of a conversation only half-heard, were just the sounds made by the wind. That wind had now turned vicious and whipped along the ground in a roar of speed that flattened the grasses and tossed the seed heads wildly as I passed them.

I had been walking for—one hour, two? I no longer knew—when the clouds darkened to pewter gray. The snow began to fall in earnest, at first in soft, mounded flakes, but soon in stinging ice crystals that assaulted my eyes and forced me to walk with my head bowed in defense. The wind hurled the chips of ice up and under the buffalo hide I had wrapped tight around my shoulders. It stole away the warmth from my legs and midriff so that shivers of cold moved upward to join with the rivulets of icy snow melting down my neck.

My hands, even clad in mittens, would begin to ache if exposed too long to the biting wind. I changed their positions frequently and suffered a loss of heat every time I did so. My feet didn't hurt—from the cold at least—because I simply refused to stop for even a second. I doggedly put one foot in front of another to the rhythm of the tunes I sang in my head to block out all thought of what I was doing and where this could end.

When the wind shifted and the snow turned once more to loose, soft flakes, I raised my head with relief, hoping to soothe my aching neck. Only to find that a new torment had been prepared for me. Now the snow tickled my nose and cheeks, making them itch. Every time I used my hand to scrub at my face, the hide would slip, and a small cascade of snow would join in the assault on the dryness of my clothing.

After a while, I realized I was repeating the same words under my breath again and again and again. "In the sweet by and by, we shall meet on that beautiful shore."

It was my last memory of Mama's voice raised in song, from the summer after Sarah was conceived but before anyone save myself knew of my disgrace. She had taken a fancy to the new hymn they were singing at our church and trilled it as she sewed, arranged flowers, or sorted her correspondence. Without my realizing it, the words had taken root in my brain only to burst forth in this time of peril.

"We shall sing on that beautiful shore, the melodious songs of the blessed, and our spirits shall sorrow no more, not a sigh for the blessing of rest."

There were other verses, I knew, but I couldn't remember them however hard I tried to reach the memory of Mama's high warble, muted by the plush upholstery of our parlor. "You goose, Nell, you have forgotten," I heard her say. Or was it the wind?

I realized that some time had passed without any awareness of what I was doing. Was I still on the trail? My heart gave a sudden jolt of fear, and I looked wildly about me. Yes —I thought I was. At least, I was following a jagged line of clean, blank snow that cut through the uneven landscape of grass stalks and the black dots of sunflowers, their petals long dissolved into the dirt.

I looked down at my boots, which were covered by the merest layer of snow. Why had I stopped? How long had I been standing there? "I mustn't stop," I muttered under my breath. "Don't distract me, Mama, I have to keep walking. Help me to live."

In-the-SWEET—by-and-BY—no, that was the wrong rhythm, it made me stumble. I could not fall now. In-the-swee-ee-eet-by-and-by-eye-eye—yes, that was better, I could move more easily to that.

You would think, with all this walking, that I'd be warmer. It was strange how I didn't seem able to get warm. But it was dark, of course, and the absence of the sun would make everything colder. How long had it been dark?

In-the-sweeeeeet . . . Perhaps I should just let the buffalo hide fall. It wasn't keeping me warm anymore, after all, and it was a dreadful heavy thing. Or perhaps I *was* warm. I had stopped shivering, and that was good. I could go faster without the burden of the buffalo skin—

"And then you will DIE-ie-ie," the wind whispered to me, and I shrieked back in terror, a formless, wordless scream that tore at my throat and left me shaking.

The horror of the night invaded me like a bolt of lightning. I wasn't going to survive, was I? I was alone in the snow, with endless miles before me and endless miles behind. I had made my decision, I had taken my gamble, and I was going to lose.

So be it, I decided, the moment of fear passing. We shall sing on that beautiful shore. I gritted my teeth—at least I thought I did, I could barely feel my face anymore—and did my best to hitch the buffalo hide more tightly around me.

I've never seen the sea, I thought. Or did they mean a shore like Lake Michigan's, all scrub and dead alewives? That wasn't particularly beautiful, but it was the only shore I knew. No, they must mean the sea, I decided. Was the seashore beautiful? I hoped there would be flowers, for Mama's sake. But I would not stop walking, not until I found myself at a shore that was, in point of fact, beautiful. There, I had my resolution.

There was a light up ahead, but I had seen that before. It was a ghost light, I was sure, because it seemed to come from no definite source, just flickers that turned the snow gold but gave no heat. There were voices too, but they were the wind. Keep walking.

"It was a wolf."

"It was a scream."

"Wolves make a noise like that, Martin. You haven't been out on the plains enough."

Martin?

I opened my mouth to call, but only a whimper emerged. "Mama." No, that was wrong, wasn't it? She was on the beautiful shore. I took a deep breath. "Martin!" If only the snow had not decided to begin falling more densely. As dark as it was, if the snow would stop falling, the white snowpack would surely give me something to see by.

The light burst forth in full radiance, like the sun coming out from behind a cloud, and blinded me. I threw up a hand to shield my eyes, and a bucketful of snow cascaded down my back from the slipping buffalo hide. I wailed feebly in protest, like a child who has had quite enough of the day and just wants to go to bed now.

There were two lights, I realized. One hung back and said, "Did you see that?" but the other darted toward me, rocking dizzily from side to side. I was about to protest at the lurching movement when the light plunged to somewhere near my feet, and something wrapped itself tight around me.

"I found the mission," I heard myself saying. "I found the mission, didn't I? Tess—and Sarah—they're all alone—come back with me; we'll fetch them."

My feet went out from under me, and my empty stomach lurched as the giant upon whose spine I had been walking swung me into the air. The buffalo hide slipped completely away, and I gasped at the shock of cold on my chest and shoulders.

"Get that," I heard the giant say, and then the lights began to dance, whirling like the snow. Better close my eyes, I thought, or I'll be sick. I felt the scrape of a button against my cheek, and gave myself up, gratefully, to the dark.

45
CABIN

"Are you completely insane?" Martin asked. "No, don't answer that. Take a sip of this."

I twisted my face away from the nasty smell. "You know I don't drink." Was that my voice, so far away and weak?

"Just one sip, to revive you. Nell, please. Don't faint again. I need you—I need you to live."

I sipped. Then coughed violently as the alcohol stung my throat. I jerked myself upright in Martin's arms and opened my eyes.

"That's better," I heard Martin say.

It *was* Martin. Either that or an extremely convincing hallucination. Would a hallucination have unshaven cheeks and smell quite so richly of horse and sweat? And the other face, the one that was grinning at me like a lunatic—

"Reiner?"

"At your service."

Reiner Lehmann gave a small mock bow. He was thinner than I remembered him, especially in the face, and his hair was somehow different, sparser perhaps under his broad hat. But it was undoubtedly the young man whom I had last seen on the day he had been taken away from the seminary, accused of murdering Professor Wale.

"How do you and Martin—no, never mind. Martin, Tess and Sarah are all alone in a wagon, in a gully full of trees that starts near the trail. We have to go back—*now*—and get them."

At least, that was the essence of what I tried to say. In fact, I had begun shivering so hard that my entire body was vibrating, my teeth were making a sound like marbles clacking, and I could barely string the words together.

"We have to get you warm," Martin said and moved me round so I sat up against what felt like bare boards. "Lehmann, let's get all the wood we can."

"No!" I tried to shout. "Tess and Sarah—"

"I'll get them," Reiner said soothingly. "But you can't travel. You should see yourself. And what did you do to your face?"

He moved to the—yes, it was a door, where on earth were we?—and looked out.

"Snow's slackened off," he said. "I should be able to ride in this. Rutherford, we should bring your horse inside. It won't like it much, but if you're going to stay with her, it won't do to leave your mount in the open. I'd take it with me, but that'll slow me down. Besides, when I find them, it'll be easy enough to carry both of them in front of me."

I saw Martin's nod by the way his shadow moved. We were in a cabin, I realized, a solidly built structure of evenly cut logs with a fireplace at one end. There were some pieces of furniture—two chairs, a table, even a bedstead carved with the letters H.E.—E.E. But the place had no windows and looked abandoned.

Martin moved purposefully around the cabin, grabbing at the debris on the dirt floor and piling it into the fireplace. A noise like the tumbling of ninepins indicated he had broken up one of the chairs and dropped the resulting pieces of wood to one side of the fire.

"But if I don't g-g-go with you h-h-h-h-how c-c-can you find the p-p-p-place?" I managed to ask.

"A gully's not that hard to miss. Land sakes, Nell, what were you thinking? Why didn't you just stay with the wagon? I'll swear you consarned females are more trouble than you're worth—sometimes."

Reiner ducked out of the cabin, and a moment later led in a sturdy gelding, its shaggy winter coat liberally dusted with snow. He unsaddled the horse while the animal and I looked at one another. When Martin struck a match and coaxed a fire into being on the hearth, the horse shifted uneasily and pressed itself into the logs on the other end of the cabin. Reiner produced a handful of something to eat. After a while, the horse stood calmly munching as the fire flared and crackled, plainly soothed by the fact that the humans showed no fear of the leaping flames.

Martin dropped to one knee and slid an arm around my shoulders, another under my legs.

"I can walk," I protested.

Martin's only answer was to press a swift kiss on my lips, and I felt my face flame. But Reiner was preparing to leave—

"Food," I called out to him. "They've had no food all day. Do you have any?"

"Plenty of pemmican," Reiner answered cheerfully. "Don't worry, Nell."

He watched as Martin deposited me on the bare dirt by the hearth, folded his lanky body into a sitting position with his back against the wall, and hoisted me into his lap.

"Improper, but practical. Mr. Rutherford, sir, let me just say I put my trust in you as a gentleman."

"Go boil your head," said Martin laconically, wrapping the buffalo hide around me and using his free arm to poke the fire with a stick. "As long as this chimney doesn't catch fire, we'll be waiting for you. Get back here as soon as you can."

He watched as Reiner disappeared and then pulled off my mittens, turning my fingers toward the light.

"It'll be a miracle if you don't have frostbite," he murmured. "Can you feel your fingers?"

I was shaking so hard I could barely speak, but I managed a nod. I was beginning to feel the heat of the small fire. To be surrounded by the buffalo hide and the warmth of Martin's body was an indescribable pleasure after the freezing wind of the prairie, but my body still felt strangely cold, as if my bones were frozen. And yet I could feel all of my limbs, every digit, almost every joint.

My light-headedness and exhaustion didn't hide a muted buzzing sensation caused by Martin's nearness, his physical presence both comforting and disconcerting me. When he reached around me to tug at the wet laces of my boots, I let out a squeak of protest.

"I can do it." And indeed my fingers were now working, albeit clumsily.

"And your stockings too," Martin said and laughed as I stiffened, his breath hot on my cheek. "As Lehmann suggested, practicality is more important than propriety. The circumstances are hardly conducive to lovemaking in any case."

"Does he know—?"

"That I love you? Yes. That I'm married? Yes. We have discussed—many things. That young man is shaping up to be a pretty good attorney, Nell."

"Hmph. Turn your face away."

Even with Martin's gaze decently averted, it gave me a strange feeling to reach up under my skirts in his presence and roll stockings and garters down my legs. I handed my sodden boots and the damp woolen stockings to him. He set the former on the hearth and draped the latter over a broken chair leg, which he held as close to the fire as he could without scorching the stockings.

I curled my bare legs up under my skirts and leaned my head against Martin's shoulder, feeling immensely tired and —oh yes, very hungry. My stomach growled.

I felt Martin's chest move as he laughed. He fished in the pocket of the heavy coat he wore and dropped a rawhide package in my lap.

"What's that?" I asked, sitting up.

"Pemmican." But Martin's smile faded as he watched me pull at the thick rawhide thongs. He touched the bruise on my face, and his mouth tightened.

"That's a prizefighter bruise. You didn't just fall over in the snow, did you?"

I shook my head gingerly. I was still shivering, but it was coming in fits now, leaving me feeling more normal in between.

"Judah hit me. To be fair, I hit him first."

"Why?" Martin's voice was soft, but one look at his face showed me he was far from calm inside.

"He was trying to—he put his hand—I don't know what happened to me, Martin. I went berserk—I don't think he really would have forced me, but there was something—that made me think of Jack."

I concentrated fiercely on the package I was opening. I knew that my cheeks—or at least the unbruised one—had flushed deep red.

"Nell." Martin put his hand over mine and waited until I looked him in the eyes. "You wouldn't tell me before—did Jack Venton force you?"

"No. Yes. I don't know." Perhaps it was hunger that made the tears rise so easily to my eyes. "I wanted what we were doing—the kissing—and him touching me—so how could he have forced me? I just didn't know—what would happen next. Nobody ever told me." I hung my head, ashamed of my ignorance, then and now. "This time—with Judah—I was afraid."

Martin drew me against him, and I felt his chin rest on the top of my head. "Poor Nellie," he sighed. "And here I am, bullying you to give me an answer that will satisfy my own selfish jealousy while you're faint with hunger. But let me tell you something. Jack Venton should not have gotten an innocent girl—who didn't know what would happen next—alone and done what he did. He set himself up as quite the gentleman, your cousin. But a gentleman does not—not unless he is quite sure the woman is willing. Even then, I have my doubts as to whether he can bed a woman who's not his wife and still call himself a gentleman. I'm not sure about it in my own case. I was a fool, Nell, and I'll pay for it for the rest of my life."

He picked up the package I had let fall into my lap and finished untying the thongs, not looking at me. He unfolded the square of rawhide and held it out.

"Eat," he said. "You're hurt and frightened. It's unconscionable of me to talk of things you can't change and hurt and frighten you even more."

"I'm not a child, Martin," I said but picked up one of the lumpy brown patties and sniffed at it. Finding it didn't smell as bad as it looked, I bit into it. The taste was peculiar, and it was greasy, but I was ravenous, and I managed several mouthfuls without balking, trying not to chew on the injured side of my face.

Martin picked up another of the patties and took several bites in quick succession before handing me his canteen of water, waiting till I had drunk my fill before sipping from it himself. Then he drew me back against him, and I settled my head into his shoulder, my skin tickled by the fur collar of his coat.

"Thank you for coming to get me, Martin."

"I'm angry at myself for not arriving sooner," was his reply. "For taking the time to look up Lehmann when I arrived in Saint Louis—although I must say he's been uncommonly useful. I don't think I could have gotten us equipped for the plains as quickly as he did."

"How did you even know him?" I asked, my voice muffled by the fur.

"I made a point of acquainting myself with him on the way back to Chicago after we left the seminary. I asked a lot of questions at the seminary, you know—particularly of the servants. I knew from what they told me that he had good reason to dislike and distrust Poulton, and I needed an ally. The thought of you with Poulton simply terrified me, Nell."

His arms tightened around the buffalo hide that covered me. "I didn't care what you thought of me—I was determined to get you away from him. I just knew he was wrong in some way. And then I got your letter, and every one of my fears seemed to be coming true. I expect I have some white hairs by now."

I laughed at that, relaxing into Martin's embrace. "How could you tell?" I wriggled a hand free of the buffalo hide and smoothed back a lock of white-blond hair that had fallen over Martin's forehead.

I was quite warm by now, and sleepy. Propriety dictated I should move off Martin's lap now that the aim of warming me up had been fulfilled, but surely five more minutes wouldn't hurt. I was safe with Martin; on that I could stake my trust.

"What was in the letter about Judah?" I asked, yawning on the last word so that it came out as "Judaaaaaaah."

"In short, the man is a liar, a cheat, a seducer, and probably a murderer," Martin replied. "I'll tell you the whole story when you're a little more awake. Do you realize you fell asleep for a moment just now?"

"Don't be silly." I hooked my arm more securely around Martin's neck, wondering how it had gotten there. "I'm not in the least bit sleepy." I blinked, realizing Martin's face was bent over mine, his beaky nose outlined by the glow of the lamp. "Tell me the story about Judah."

"Go to sleep, Nell."

"Good night, Martin."

Perhaps it was a dream that I raised my face to Martin's and kissed him on the lips. Perhaps it was a dream that he kissed me back, long and hungrily, before unwrapping the buffalo hide and laying it on the dirt floor. I felt myself go boneless as he lowered me onto the thick fur and covered me with his heavy coat. The last thing I saw was a brief glimpse of Martin's profile, lit by the firelight, his hair aglow with orange and red light and a strange, bleak expression on his face.

46
REPENTANT

I sat bolt upright as the crack of a rifle shot split the air. It was far from the cabin, but it was unmistakably a shot.

As sleep released me, I became aware of several things. Martin was gone and so was his horse. Its odors lingered, and I was still covered in a heavy coat that smelt pleasantly of Martin and the outdoors. The fire was a small pile of glowing ashes, both chairs now gone. The lamp was flickering, about to expire. My stockings were back on my legs, quite dry—had Martin put them there? My hair dragged at my scalp, causing me considerable discomfort.

I pushed the heavy coat away and began pulling pins out of my hair, sighing with relief as the pulling sensation ceased and the heavy curls tumbled down over my shoulders. I shoved the pins into my pocket and pushed my feet into my boots, which were damp but not intolerably so.

The rest of the pemmican and Martin's canteen lay by the hearth. I gulped a few mouthfuls of water and took half-a-dozen bites of pemmican, swallowing without chewing.

Thus prepared, I stepped outside the cabin. It was not yet

day, but a faint light glowed in the east, and the sky was clear. The snow gathered and reflected the light. I could see well enough to spot the two horsemen galloping toward me on the trail, one in pursuit of the other. The pursuer's rifle cracked again, and I shrank back into the cabin's doorway. Where was Martin?

The answer to my question scared me half to death. As the two riders came closer, there was a sudden movement to my left, a massive body speeding past me so fast I felt the wind of it stir my hair. Snow and dirt flew into my face from the horse's heels, and then Martin was on the trail, riding at an angle to the first horseman and cutting off his escape.

The massive Percheron dug in its forelegs and skidded to an inelegant stop in the snow, causing Judah to lurch forward. He didn't fall, and for a second I marveled at both the speed he had gotten out of the huge carthorse and his skill in staying on its broad, bare back.

He pulled its head around to escape from Martin, but Martin's gelding was far more agile than the Percheron. A burst of speed brought it close enough for Martin to aim a punch that caught Judah in the side and pitched him off his horse in a whirl of arms and legs.

Martin's momentum caused him to fall off too. For a sickening moment, I saw his boot catch in the stirrup, but he twisted it and worked it loose as his animal shied away, unwilling to step on its rider.

The snow softened both men's fall, and they were up in a moment. Judah headed for Martin's horse with one eye on Reiner, the second horseman, who had caught up with the group and was raising his rifle to his shoulder. Before Judah could reach the animal, Martin drove a fist into his middle, causing him to fold up with a sound like a bellows and drop to his knees.

Reiner reined in his horse and slid to the ground, but

Martin needed no further help. He dragged Judah into a standing position and aimed a blow at his face that made me wince with remembered pain. Blood from Judah's nose and mouth spattered the snow, spreading into a pinkish stain.

"No!" I realized I had shouted as Martin hit Judah again, a vicious blow to the ribs, and raised his fist to aim once more at his face.

"Martin, no!" Martin's face was a mask, practically as white as the snow, his gray eyes almost black with rage. He would kill Judah if I didn't stop him.

"He's not worth it." I flung an arm around Martin, putting myself between him and Judah, who was once more on his knees. Reiner stood by watching, his hand curled loosely around the stock of the rifle.

"Unless—" The hair rose on the back of my neck, and I whirled to face Reiner. "He didn't hurt Tess or Sarah, did he? Because if he did, I'll kill him myself." Thinking of Tess and Sarah made my arms and legs weak, and the pemmican rose in a greasy mass into my gorge. I made a huge effort to stay on my feet and not vomit, bracing myself against Reiner's reply.

The young man's eyes widened, and he shook his head. "They're all right," he said. "I found him talking to Tess—who stood in the front of the wagon with her gun at the ready like Davy Crockett himself. I do believe she would have taken a shot at him if he'd come any closer. I could hear Sarah hollering that he was a bad man and he'd better not have hurt her Momma. The fire was out, but they'd obviously survived the night in one piece."

"I need to go to them." The irrational part of me wanted to leap immediately onto the nearest horse and head back along the trail. Instead, I turned to Martin, who had let his hands drop to his sides and was watching Judah with a stunned look on his face. "What are you going to do with him?"

Judah raised his head and looked at us. His upper lip was split and swelling, his nose a bloody mess. His slanted blue eyes were mocking as he looked first at Reiner, then at Martin and me.

"Yes, Rutherford, what are you going to do with me? Now that our darling Nell has saved my life. You can accuse me of nothing worse than hitting a woman. Although ungentlemanly, that's hardly an uncommon occurrence out here on the frontier. If she hadn't stopped you, you'd have been a murderer. You need to watch that temper of yours."

He rose to his feet stiffly and painfully, probing his middle section with care. "I think you've broken a rib or two," he said. "Wherever you take me, I'll be sure to raise that point." He looked at Reiner. "And it's a good thing you're such a bad shot, Lehmann."

"I wasn't shooting at you, you flannel-mouthed swindler," Reiner replied, a sneer on his lips. "I was making sure Rutherford knew we were coming." He looked at Martin. "I'd say best thing would be to get him back to Springwood once we've made sure the ladies reach the mission. That letter of yours should ensure they run him out of town good and for all."

The stunned expression was leaving Martin's face, and his eyes sharpened. "Your uncle should have the copy I sent him by now too. You're right, Lehmann—if we can't accuse him of anything direct, we can at least make sure everyone knows his true colors. And it's possible that when Cam Calderwood knows about his disgrace, he might be a bit more forthcoming on certain points if he wants to save his own neck."

"The hell he will," said Judah. For a moment, he seemed to coil in on himself, and then he sprang, as quick as a cat, and sent Martin flying backward into me with a double-handed push.

I landed on my side in the snow, coming down hard on my hip but without any real injury. Martin twisted around onto one knee to avoid falling on top of me, giving Judah time to leap on the gelding Martin had ridden. He pulled it around, heading not along the trail but across the prairie. The horse's hooves churned out chunks of soil and grass from under the snow as it leaped forward, eyes rolling, the unused stirrups flying around Judah's knees.

Reiner fired, pumped the rifle's lever, and fired again. The horse gave a sort of sideways leap and landed badly, all four legs scrabbling for purchase on the snow. Judah rolled around the saddle so that he was halfway down the horse's side. For a moment, I thought he would pull himself up again —and then the gelding's foreleg buckled, and Judah slid into the snow, the horse landing heavily on top of him.

WE RAN.

Time stretches when something unthinkable happens right before your eyes. It must have been no more than ten seconds that the horse's massive body rocked back and forth over Judah's outflung form as it struggled to get its legs under itself and find a footing, but the scene passed in agonizing slowness.

And there was blood. Fat droplets flew out over the snow and stained it with pink-edged crimson splashes that steamed, just for a second, in the frozen air.

As the horse finally got to its feet, it became clear that some of the blood came from a wound in its flank, a livid gash around six inches long that glowed red against its shaggy side. It sidestepped skittishly as we drew near and regarded us with bulging eyes, as if daring us to approach.

We all ignored it and came to a halt near the broken man who wheezed faintly, his legs twitching. A flailing hoof had crushed one hand, leaving the bone and gristle of the fingers and the knuckle joints horribly exposed. The thumb was almost completely torn away and lay at a gruesome angle to the rest, attached by a mere flap of skin, from which the blood seeped into the mud the horse had scraped up from under the snow.

"What are we going to do?" I gasped, crouching and putting uncertain hands on Judah's shoulders as if I could raise him up. His eyes were glassy with shock and pain, but at my approach, his body gave a convulsive jerk and then flopped back into the snow, heavy and useless.

"Don't touch me."

I snatched my hands back as Judah's lips drew back from his teeth in a long shudder. "It hurts."

Reiner had taken his eyes off the injured man to fix them on the horizon. He stood, gesturing to the west. "The party from the mission is coming. Perhaps they can help."

Judah's gaze was directed at the sky, but his words showed he had heard. "Is the pastor with them?"

"Pretty sure he is."

"Good. I may—have need." The words came out at jerky intervals as Judah fought for breath.

I took a long look at Judah's body, limp and helpless on the snowy ground, and turned my gaze to Martin. He read the question in my eyes and nodded. He too saw that Judah was dying.

"Better if you send the pastor on here and go with the rest of the men to fetch Tess and Sarah," he said to Reiner. "There's not a whole lot any of us can do for him."

Reiner set off at a run, and Martin put a hand on my arm. "Do you want to go with him, Nell?"

"No." My answer came so fast that even I felt surprised. "I'll stay with Judah." Suddenly, I had a strong sense that both Sarah and Tess were safe—safer than they had been for a long time. I had not seen my stepfather die, and it seemed oddly important that I should bear witness now. As if some greater force than myself was telling me that this, for the moment, was where my duty lay.

Judah turned his head a fraction and smiled at me. Despite the bloodied nose and the split lip, there was still beauty in his face, and I felt my breath catch with a kind of sadness.

"You—almost loved me—once, didn't you, Nell?" Judah whispered.

I knelt beside him, feeling the chill of the snow through my skirts, and took his uninjured hand in both of mine as gently as I could. "Almost."

Judah grinned, blood showing between his teeth. The smile turned into a grimace of pain, and the hand I was holding twitched.

"You looked—at me—and loved me. It's always worked. When I—wanted it to."

Pastor Lombardi had come silently up to us, and a look of deep sadness suffused his face as he heard Judah's words. "Don't," he said, shaking his head. "This is not the time for pride. You're about to meet your maker, man. For the sake of your soul, repent now of any sin that stains your conscience."

Judah began to shake, and for a moment I clasped his hand tighter, believing his death convulsion was upon him. But then I realized, with a thrill of horror, that he was laughing—until a spasm of pain seized him so hard his back arched, and he screamed.

The pastor dropped to one knee beside him. "Repent," he whispered again, sounding as horrified as I felt.

"Thought—I had—time." Judah's chest rose and fell rapidly, and he screwed his eyes shut against the rising sun. "Put—the world—right—later. When I had—all I needed."

I felt Martin's hand rest on my shoulder as he came to stand behind me. "Was it true?" he asked Judah. "All those things that were in the letter?"

"Never read it." Judah's legs moved feebly. "Probably—true though. Missed some things, I'll bet."

"Did you kill him?" I had to know. "Professor Wale?"

"Not personally." Judah sounded almost indignant. "Don't—don't go looking for the half-breed who pulled the trigger. He—ugh—he'll be long gone."

He took a few deep breaths before he continued, staring straight up at the pale sky shading into blue.

"I confess to the mercy killing of Hendrik Adema."

The last word came out in an anguished grunt as another spasm of pain took him, and I winced. The movement made me realize how cold I was, and I hugged my arms around my body.

"Martin, he must be so cold. Would you please fetch your coat? I can't—let's ease him as much as we can."

"You're kind, Nell." Judah smiled at me again and licked the blood from his teeth. "Don't bother. Can't—feel cold."

"Did Dr. Calderwood have anything to do with those deaths?" Pastor Lombardi's voice was a thread of sound.

"No. But he—knew. Compromises—lives for his own—glory. His wife—doesn't know."

Judah's whole body had started to tremble. The color faded from his face, leaving it a sickly white against which his bloody nose and mouth showed crimson.

"Repent." The pastor's voice rose to an anguished moan. "For God's sake, man. Your hour has come."

"Of all—these many things and more—I—" Judah's eyes widened. "I—repent."

The last word turned into a gurgle as a small gout of blood gushed from Judah's mouth and flowed down both sides of his face, bright and steaming in the cold air. And then he was still, his beautiful blue-violet eyes open to the azure dawn above.

FOR A FEW MOMENTS, WE WERE ALL SILENT, OUR EYES FIXED ON the still form that lay crushed and broken on the snow. I began shivering, not the violent shudders of the night before, but a continuous trembling due only partly to the cold.

The pastor's eyes were round with shock at Judah's sudden end. His normally genial face was gray, all its lines drawn downward, his mouth hanging open.

And then he took a huge, shuddering breath, breaking the silence. He stooped to urge the eyelids gently down over the staring eyes. He wiped the blood from Judah's face with a clean handkerchief, using a little snow to aid the process. He then settled down to pray for the dead man, his voice steady as he performed the familiar ritual.

I bowed my head and tried to listen to the pastor's prayers until I felt a large, warm hand just above my elbow, urging me upward.

"You're shivering," Martin whispered. "Leave them. Reiner will be back soon with Sarah and Tess, and you won't be much use to them if you're faint with cold."

He led me toward the cabin, briefly draping an arm around my shoulders and then dropping it again, with a backward glance at the pastor. The horses—Martin's gelding and the big Percheron—had made their way to a spot not far from the cabin and were companionably nosing through the snow to find grass. The blood had stopped flowing from the gelding's side, and it appeared untroubled.

Martin ushered me into the dark cabin and draped his coat around my shoulders. Shutting the door, he went back outside, presumably to hobble the horses and do what he could for the gelding's wound.

I sank onto the buffalo hide, reeling with the peculiar weariness that came from stepping indoors after being out in the wind and sunshine. And, I realized, the weariness that stemmed from the onslaught of emotion that had passed over me as I watched Judah Poulton take his last breath. There was relief, sadness, and horror at the terrible sight of his once-lithe body twisted and sprawled on the ground like a discarded rag. He was gone, and he could never threaten me nor anyone else again, but I couldn't rejoice in such a passing.

A rush of air and burst of light told me Martin had re-entered the cabin. He perched on the broken bedstead and removed his hat, raking his hands through his thick pale hair and pressing a hand over his eyes. He squeezed and massaged his forehead, as if he were trying to expunge his thoughts.

"Do you need a fire?" he asked. "I don't suppose it'll be long before Reiner's back, but if you're cold—"

"I'm all right," I assured him. "I've stopped shivering. Martin, you look dreadfully tired. Didn't you sleep?"

"Not much," he admitted and then grinned at me. "You, on the other hand, slept like a stone, which allowed me to pace and fret and step outside twenty times to look for Reiner. And to watch you sleep." His voice softened. "You're turning me into a sentimental fool."

His words trailed off, and he stared at the dirt floor, then at the cabin door, as if he were trying to avoid my gaze. But finally he spoke, and when he did, his voice had a strange sound, bleak and hopeless.

"I need to tell you. Seems selfish in the face of death, but —I may not have another chance. I spoke to an attorney— one who deals with matters concerning marriage. Settlements and so on. Divorce."

I nodded but didn't reply. My heart began to beat faster, knocking at my chest, surprisingly painful. I knew from Martin's face that he had not received the answers he wanted.

He cleared his throat. "The new law makes a divorce possible without special legislation, but it by no means makes it easy."

He turned his hat in his hands, rubbing his thumb along the brim. "The man listed the possible causes so many times I have them by heart: Impotence. Bigamy. Adultery. Desertion. Drunkenness. Malice. Cruelty—or the interesting discovery that you're married to an infamous criminal."

I seized immediately on the one word that jumped out at me. Adultery. "You said Lucetta wasn't faithful to you," I faltered.

Martin looked at the hat he was twisting around in his hands and threw it across the cabin. It hit the wall with a soft swooping sound and dropped to the floor.

"Walters—the attorney—has urged me to engage a Pinkerton detective to follow her around, gathering evidence against her. Evidence that will be discussed in full in the courtroom. At the same time, I must remain above suspicion because if both parties to a divorce have committed adultery, there will be no divorce."

He stared at me as if willing me to comprehend something. When I did not speak, he continued, enunciating each word with precision.

"It is possible, for example, that Lucetta's attorney may

try to procure evidence of my—affection for you as proof that I too am at fault." He pressed the palms of his hands against his temples. "And I have corresponded with you in affectionate terms—sent you gifts—ensured your finances are on a sound footing. It's highly likely that you—your past —would become mixed up in the proceedings, and that I could not countenance. Assuming, of course, that Lucetta is unwilling to divorce me—"

"And she is unwilling," I interrupted. "She made it clear to me she would fight to keep you." I felt a plummeting sensation in my stomach and curled my fingers into the coarse fur of the buffalo hide to stop the world from spinning round.

"It was bad enough to think I'd have to drag Lucetta into such a matter," Martin said. "To bring a scandal down upon any woman—no matter what she had done—is repellent to me. But that it should be you—and by extension, Sarah—is unbearable."

I quailed inwardly, knowing that what was worrying Martin was not the mere thought of dragging my name into court. It was the tide of public opprobrium that would come crashing down upon my head and Sarah's once the fact of her illegitimacy became widely known. Me again. My decisions, my stubbornness, my weakness, my arrogance. The consequences of that May afternoon when I had followed Jack Venton behind a screen of young willows, my hand in his, his laughter hot on my cheek, were still rippling outward in an endless motion.

"My only hope," Martin continued, "is that I can somehow persuade Lucetta to divorce me—for desertion, I suppose. I'm already living in a hotel, Nell, not in our house." He gave a small snort of derision. "She may not have noticed, of course. I was in the habit of spending time away from home wherever I could. What a mess, Nell. What a damned idiotic mess I've made of my life."

I wanted to wrap my arms round him, to give him what comfort I could, but of course I couldn't do that. I drew my knees up under my skirt and stared miserably at the ground, the heavy weight of Martin's coat the only nearness to him I could, in all fairness, aspire to.

It was almost a relief to hear a shout from Pastor Lombardi and to see Martin dart to the door. As I raised myself from the ground, hampered by my clothing, I felt as though I had aged ten years in one morning. Judah was dead, and I was free of him—but for a while I had allowed myself to imagine that freedom might include Martin, and this was clearly not going to be.

47
DEAD END

"You're exhausted," Catherine said as she poured steaming water from the huge pitcher into the small tin tub by the kitchen stove. "Why don't you rest, and I'll bathe Sarah?"

I laughed. "Thank you, but I'm not lying on a bed until I've cleaned myself up as well. Tess and I have plans to take the large tub up to our room and draw lots for who's going first, and I'm so happy you have a laundress we can hire. How one small and quite fastidious child can attract so much dirt is a mystery to me."

I wrapped a cloth around the handle of the pitcher I had put on the floor and used another cloth to tip it so that the water cascaded into the tub. "There, I think that's ready."

"But it's far too hot."

"By the time I've found Sarah, dragged her away from Teddy, listened to her chatter about every animal and child at the mission, persuaded her it's time to come inside and relinquish her overalls for her dress, and actually gotten her to undress, the water will be just about right."

I straightened up, stretching my spine to iron out the

kinks in my lower back. "Poor Teddy. It's a lot to expect of a fifteen-year-old boy, playing nursemaid to a four-year-old girl."

"I expect it makes a nice change from chopping wood, mending fences, drawing water, and running errands." Catherine picked up both pitchers and headed for the door. "I must see to Roderick. He spent far too long out on the prairie with Mr. Poulton's body. Although I do sympathize that you didn't want a corpse sharing the cart, and leaving it —him—alone would have called the wolves, for sure. I'm going to insist Roderick let me apply a mustard plaster, for prevention."

"Where's Martin?"

"Asleep in a chair in Roderick's study." Catherine grinned. "He's kept himself busy today, what with retrieving the body and helping to pack it in snow for the journey back to Springwood. He also oversaw the sewing up of his horse's wound and ensured they tended to the carthorse. It's a shame we haven't found the other one."

I nodded as I held the door open for Catherine. Reiner had offered to take the healthy horse back to the farmer with profuse apologies and enough money—supplied by Martin—to pay for a new team of Percherons. He would leave the next day. Martin planned to wait a day longer and then accompany the pastor—and Judah's body—back to Springwood.

After that he, Reiner, and Pastor Lombardi planned to continue to St. Louis, which would take several days. From there, Martin would begin the journey back to Chicago, Reiner would go back to his desk, and the pastor would begin the delicate process of informing his denomination about Judah's confession and the implications it had for the Calderwoods. Judah's death would not be the only shock they received as a Christmas present. Serve them right, I thought callously.

Catherine was correct; I was exhausted. My legs and back still ached from the long walk through the snow. The very tips of the ring and little fingers on my left hand were white, numb, and tingling by turns. Frostbite, Martin had told me—he didn't think it was serious, but his eyes had darkened as he informed me that if I ever took it into my head to risk a cold and lonely death again, he would personally lock me up and throw away the key.

I smiled at that, but I wasn't foolhardy enough to forget the biting wind and the soft, deadly touch of the snow. Then there was the knowledge that if I'd passed by Martin and Reiner in the night without them seeing me—or if the night had been but a little colder—I would be just as dead as Judah.

It was the thought of Judah that led me to push myself past exhaustion, hoping my reward would be dreamless sleep. I didn't want to stay awake for one minute thinking of Judah, any more than I wanted to close my eyes only to see the snow whirling—

"But I survived, Papa," I muttered under my breath as I wrapped a shawl around my shoulders and went in search of Sarah. "And now I have a much better idea of what your end must have been like. Did you think of Mama and me as you lay down in the snow? Was your head filled with dreams and visions as mine was? I saw Mama and a beautiful shore—and I wasn't frightened, not really. I think I might have lost my fear of the snow, even if I've learned to respect it."

As I shoved my feet into galoshes placed by the mission's front door, I had a sudden memory of my father, one I had never encountered before. He sat in Bet's large armchair by the fire, a favorite haunt of his despite my mother's scolding that it was unsuitable to spend so much time in the kitchen. He had his feet propped on the hearth, and the summer sun set his red hair aflame in a coruscation of copper, auburn, and gold.

He was reading, with the intentness that characterized everything he did. The sun should have bothered him, shining as it was on his face, but he ignored it, his large blue-gray eyes tender as he lived the story unfolding under his eyes.

My memories of Papa had always been marred by the imagined picture of the frozen man under the bush, his lips blue and his hands crossed over his chest. I had overheard Bet's description of him as I played in a corner of the kitchen, my small child's heart still raw from missing him. The tears had run down my face as I built a picture that would never leave me, even as I grew out of childhood. A picture that had haunted my dreams.

There were tears now, pricking at the back of my eyes and moistening their corners so that the bright patch of Sarah's hair seen across the courtyard blurred and swam. But they were tears of joy and relief because somehow—I knew it for certain—I had given myself a new picture of Papa, one that would replace the frozen man in my mind. The snow had lost its power over my father and me.

"So you're free now."

Reiner was holding my hand but in a decidedly brotherly fashion. He had not said anything about Martin and me, but I had seen him glance at us often enough to surmise he understood—and, oddly, given his original reaction to Mrs. Drummond's revelations, sympathized.

"I'm free of Judah, at least." My answer was an admission as well as a confirmation, and he squeezed my hand.

"I should have stuck around to protect you, fool that I was. I always knew Poulton was a bad lot."

"But to die so horribly . . ." My voice trailed off, and I

looked up at Reiner, suddenly realizing that Judah's grisly death was in large part due to the young man in front of me.

He met my gaze squarely, his eyes wide and his expression open. "Don't think I haven't dedicated a nightmare or two to my own guilt in the matter. If I hadn't grazed that horse with a bullet, Judah Poulton would undoubtedly have lived to prey on someone else. I have very mixed feelings about that eventuality."

"If," I said. "If I hadn't provoked him to anger and sent him away—if I'd stuck to my original plan of turning him down here, where I could hide behind the protection of the Lombardis. If I hadn't been so idiotic as to consent to travel with him in the first place . . . You know, Reiner, I think I'll give up traveling across the countryside in any kind of horse-drawn conveyance. I set off in a cart once, and somebody died because of that. I came back to the seminary in a wagon, and there was the professor. And now this."

Reiner's homely face lit up with mischief. "It's a good thing Martin isn't returning with you, then. And it's an even better thing, as far as I'm concerned, that I'm traveling alone."

"So you're not breaking your heart over me after all? Oh—that sounded more flirtatious than I meant it to be." I was abashed but also grateful to Reiner for this lighthearted moment.

Reiner grinned, catching my mood. "I'm in a fair way toward complete recovery from all my traumas, Nell, so don't you worry. A certain Miss Amy Larke has something to do with that. She has magnificent dark curls and deep green eyes. I'm maneuvering a meeting between her and Pop just as soon as I can persuade him to leave his business for long enough. A career and a fine prospective wife should convince him I've finally attained the age of reason."

"A respectable wife—unlike me." I grinned, my spirits lifting even higher as Reiner's face pinkened.

"Land sakes, Nell, you don't have to be so hard on a fellow." The beginning of a frown turned to a rueful laugh. "I should have trusted you better instead of being a barnburner, shouldn't I? I let us both fall into Poulton's hands, and I'm sorry for it." He held out a hand. "Forgive my mistakes?"

"If you'll forgive mine." I put my hand in his, and we shook hands heartily.

"So you like being an attorney?" I continued. "I'm glad you've found a job you can truly believe in."

"You'll be a sight gladder once I'm a judge, then." Reiner smiled, but then his face became sober. "That's no blarney, Nell. Sitting in jail thinking I might hang and knowing the real killer might get off scot-free gave me a whole new set of ideas about justice. The frontier needs proper, organized law enforcement. Right now any man who thinks he's one heck of a curly wolf has plenty of ways to evade the law and keep robbing banks and stagecoaches as the fancy takes him. Look at the James brothers—why, Missouri came close to welcoming them with open arms. It's a flat-out disgrace."

The thought of Reiner taking on the James brothers gave me a momentary qualm. "Be careful," I said. "Don't give Miss Amy Larke cause to regret your career choice. But I think you'll make a fine judge, Reiner."

"And you?" Reiner asked. "I suppose you'll be thinking of leaving the seminary now."

I nodded, looking out of the window where the early morning sun had turned the snow golden. "I don't see how or why I'd want to stay, even after the pastor has made sure the Calderwoods get what's coming to them. Why, they even have a replacement seamstress already. I came to Kansas looking for a new life, Reiner, but I feel like I've reached a dead end."

I SAID AS MUCH TO CATHERINE AS WE WATCHED TEDDY—hindered more than helped by Sarah—unload the last of our boxes from the wagon, which had been retrieved from the prairie. "I may not know where I want to go, but I do know the time has come to leave."

"Yes, it's a wise woman who listens to her heart when it comes to doing what's best for her family." Catherine's face settled into grim lines as she watched her son. "Even if that sometimes means reneging on a commitment."

"That sounds ominous." I stared at Catherine.

She was thinner than ever. Vertical creases had appeared in her cheeks, and when she smiled—which she did a lot less than she used to—it alarmed me to see a molar was missing from her white, even teeth.

"You'll be traveling in the spring, I suppose, as long as the weather isn't too wet. Well, we'll be traveling too—later in the year, when we can. Roderick has finally listened to me."

"Where will you go?"

"Wherever we can find a physician for Lucy." Catherine's mouth thinned into a stubborn line. "I will not stand by and watch my child die, Nell. And even Thea is willing to cooperate with my plans if it means she has a chance—when she's old enough, of course—to hunt for a husband who isn't a farmer or missionary. Teddy might stay on here though. He likes the frontier—and he'll be sixteen in February. Old enough to make his own decisions."

I watched the lanky youth stride toward the house with a trunk balanced nonchalantly on one broad shoulder, Sarah at his heels. "Is this causing strife between you and your husband?"

"Not anymore." Catherine's voice was not entirely steady. "Roderick has conceded that my duty to God might be a little different from his. As a woman—as a mother—I'm entitled to answer the overriding call of my duty to my children. He says he can bear a little disappointment for our sakes."

I put my arm around my friend's waist, obliging her to turn and look at me. "You'll accept a gift of money from me —you won't even think of refusing it. That physician will charge a high fee, and Lucy will doubtless need nursing—nourishing foods—a salubrious place to live. A sanatorium, even. You won't deny me the privilege of helping you."

Catherine did not speak for a few moments, and when she did, her voice was husky. "For Lucy's sake, I will not. After all, I've been praying for a miracle. And God has answered my prayer—through you."

And then a hint of merriment crept into the fine hazel eyes that were now more than ever her best feature. "When you climbed out of the carriage that cold day, I little realized that the disgraced and friendless girl I saw before me would one day be our benefactor. Roderick's always saying the Almighty has a strange sense of humor, and I believe He delights in turning the tables on our pretensions."

"What pretensions do you have?" I asked. "I haven't noticed any."

Catherine smiled, but her eyes turned sad. "I hide them well. But I'll admit to you now that when we came to Kansas, my heart was filled with pride. I was sure our mission would be a resounding success, and we'd be renowned throughout the frontier. I'd been a good matron at the Poor Farm—I knew it well—but it hurt my pride to know that it would be Mr. Schoeffel, not me, who would be superintendent. That the mere suggestion a woman could be eligible for such a high post would elicit stares of amazement if not outright laughter. I thought I was remarkable—and it galled me to realize nobody else shared my elevated assessment of myself."

"You *are* remarkable." I grasped Catherine's hand and

squeezed it. "And I'll make sure you have enough to feed, clothe, and house you for quite a while. Don't see me as a benefactor, Catherine. This is merely a little of the excess from the pile of wealth Martin has built for me. I did nothing to deserve or earn it."

"None of us deserve wealth or fortune," Catherine said. "And you work hard enough, don't you? But Martin—" She stopped short, hesitating over what to say next. I braced myself.

"I believe he's a good man," Catherine said slowly. "But—I worry when I see him looking at you. And when I see you looking at him."

What was it Judah had said? Love and a cough cannot be hid. I felt my cheeks flame, but I refused to cast down my eyes and stared steadily at Catherine as I spoke.

"There isn't—and won't be—any wrongdoing between us, Catherine. I swear it. It appears we can't help our feelings for each other—or hide them—but you're right, Martin's a good man. And I'm not that girl who came to the Poor Farm, not any longer. Yes, I must move on—but it won't be out of the frying pan into the fire."

48
CHICAGO

Always an early riser, on the morning of Martin's departure I was up well before dawn. The weather had warmed a little, and a light mist hung in the air, seemingly lit from below by the snow that nestled between the prairie grasses.

Closer to the house, the snow had mixed with the dirt of the yard to form a viscous, pale mud. It clung tenaciously to the hems of skirts and trousers and splashed the mules that tossed their heads and brayed at the activity around them.

The first item loaded on the cart was a plain coffin of pale wood. The mules caught the scent of—Judah—and shifted uncomfortably, but no doubt they had pulled many a load of slaughtered meat. Would this seem so very different to them? I felt a little sick as I watched the men work, lit by a pale sun fighting to burn away the shreds of cloud that diffused its light.

After a while, I could bear it no longer and headed for the kitchen, sighing with relief at finding it empty. Someone had raked up the stove and disposed of the night's ash, so the flames burned hot and fierce, and it didn't take me long to boil coffee.

I sat sipping the bitter, scalding brew, my mind a blank canvas on which a deranged artist was throwing thoughts at random. Martin—Judah—Sarah—Catherine—Tess . . .

Tess had borne our adventure better than anyone, I recalled with a smile. When the mission's cart finally reached the cabin, Sarah was clingy and inclined to whine, but Tess was positively exultant. She boasted to anyone who would listen of her mastery of the rifle and her success in fending off Judah. They had had to pry the rifle from her hands.

I was still laughing to myself over Tess when Martin entered the room. I rose and poured coffee into an enameled mug, which I pushed across the table to him. He nodded his thanks, and we sipped silently for a few minutes, reassuringly companionable.

It was Martin who broke the peace of the still air, his voice drowning out the faint sizzle of the wood as it burned in the stove.

"You'll come to Chicago, won't you, Nellie? Just for a few weeks. You need time to consider—to make plans—and I'll help you. For heaven's sake, don't give me cause to move to Kansas." The laughter lines gathered at the corners of his eyes as he said that, and I smiled in response, but my mind was whirling.

"But after what you said—about the lawyers—"

"I know. I've been thinking about that."

He smiled again, and my heart gave a funny little jump in my chest. "You'd find it hard to believe how much time I dedicate to thinking about you, Nell. Even before I realized I was in love with you, thinking about you was one of my favorite occupations. Now, you fill my days—and nights."

I blushed at that, and we both looked down at our mugs,

seeking normality in the simple action of enjoying our morning coffee. Martin drew a deep breath.

"I've told you before, the reason I've worked so hard to give you all the money you need, and more, is to ensure your freedom. To make it so you can live your life in a way few women experience—give you horizons too often reserved only for men. I know well enough that you never wanted to marry. If I were free—well, I'd be on bended knee right now asking you to marry me. But if you refused me out of aversion to the wedded state, I wouldn't think you any less womanly because of it."

I swallowed to rid my throat of the lump that had grown in it. "Don't talk of what might have been, Martin. What good does it do?"

And it did no good to tell him that if he were on bended knee before me, my aversion to marriage might just collapse like a castle in the clouds. That the notion of spending the rest of my days—and nights—with one man, running his household and having his children, didn't seem nearly so bad if it were Martin's face I would see smiling at me when I awoke. If only I'd realized that sooner.

"No. Well, the money." Martin spoke briskly now, as if resolving to stick to practical matters. "Isn't it time you took your place in society? Or are you going to hide from it forever because of Sarah? Chicago isn't a small gossipy town like Victory. There are women—and mark you, I'm not trying to draw a comparison—there are women of ill repute who arrive at my store in elegant carriages and order their gowns with the manner of a duchess. With wealth, a woman can be anything she pleases. Lucetta knows that well enough."

I looked up in time to catch the wry twist to his mouth, the fleeting cynicism that told me better than anything what his marriage was doing to him.

"I don't want to stay at the seminary," I admitted. "I've been thinking about where we should go. Don't forget that Tess and Sarah will have opinions about that too."

"Then use Chicago as your starting point," Martin said. "I want to introduce you to your banker. He'll instruct you how to draw on your funds and decide on investments if you want to handle your money yourself. I'll make other introductions—I can give you access to a vast network of people who have interests all over the country. Be a society dressmaker if you wish, or a society grande dame, or travel the length and breadth of Europe—it's all open to you. Let me help you get started, and then—if we have to part, we'll do so as friends who each have a place in a wider world."

"So you'll accept whatever decision we arrive at?" I asked. "If I decide to leave Chicago after a month, you'll not prevent me from going?" I wrapped my fingers tight around my mug to stop their trembling.

"I'll cling to the hope of a future with you until the very last shred of hope is gone," said Martin soberly. "I'll work to free myself from Lucetta, whatever the cost may be to myself—as long as it is just myself, and not you, who is harmed. But I will hope. And yet if you tell me, with absolute conviction, that we're finished—I'll let you go. Your freedom is yours, Nell. It was your money in the first place —I simply made it grow. Yes, I'll suffer—from anxiety on your behalf, from jealousy—I admit to that. But I will let you go."

He spread his hands in a gesture of release, and I squeezed my fingers tight against the urge to capture his.

"Supposing I meet another Judah?" I asked softly. "One I want to marry?"

Martin clamped his palms over his eyes so only his mouth and nose were visible. "Eleanor Lillington, if you get yourself mixed up with a murderer for a third time, I will disown you altogether. First Hiram and then Judah—no, it's not possible it could happen again."

He slid his hands down his face and opened his eyes wide. Suddenly, we both dissolved into laughter, our hands reaching out and locking with each other in acknowledgment that all we had been through in the last two days was over. We were alive, and Martin was right—the unknown future held boundless possibilities. I felt a tiny bubble of optimism expanding inside me into a buzz of excitement.

I gave Martin's hand one last squeeze and then let it go as shouts from the yard outside penetrated through to the kitchen.

"It's full dawn," Martin remarked. "Time we were going. Give Sarah and Tess a kiss from me." They had said their good-byes the night before, as Tess and Sarah were so tired from all their adventures it was unlikely they'd rise early.

"Good-bye, Martin." I didn't dare say any more. I leaned over the table and kissed his cheek, newly shaven and smelling of soap. Picking up the mugs, I moved around the table, heading for the scullery.

Martin stood up, clearly resolving to leave—but as I passed him, he reached out a long arm and pulled me in close.

He kissed me thoroughly and at length, and despite my reservations about being kissed in a kitchen where the pastor might walk in at any moment—and a slight awkwardness occasioned by the mugs in my hand—I reveled in the feel of him. We seemed to fit together as if we were two halves of a whole person. His mouth moving on mine awoke my entire body, making it crackle with a delicious, yearning energy.

"Chicago," he said a little hoarsely, releasing me and reaching for the hat that lay on the table. "Promise me, Nell."

"Chicago," I said. "Be—be careful, Martin."

I wouldn't tell him I loved him. He knew it anyway, and

to voice the words would make our parting worse—or impossible.

I waited several minutes before making my way to the front of the house, doing my best to compose my face into its everyday shape.

"Secrets and lies," I told my reflection in the tiny mirror that hung near the kitchen door. "They don't suit you, do they, Nell?"

The face that looked back at me had dark smudges under the eyes, the result of a night spent thinking about the moment now before me—yet another separation from Martin—and about the coffin that would be one of his traveling companions. The straight auburn brows looked a little more disordered than usual. The white skin of my face still bore traces of the cold wind that had scoured it for hours on end, and my bruises were fading to a dull purple ringed in green. My eyes—were they really windows to the soul? Could the fear and longing and the tiny core of hope and joy that Martin's love kept awakening be read there?

"No, they don't suit me. But they're what I've got." I turned resolutely on my heel and held my head high as my boots clacked along the bare wood of the hallway.

And there was Martin seated already on the bench, examining the reins and waiting for the pastor, who was kissing his wife good-bye.

Catherine joined me on the porch as the pastor hauled himself up into the cart, seating himself next to Martin and greeting me with a cheerful wave. "A fine day for traveling! We'll have sun later."

I looked at the mist and up at the struggling, pale sun and tried not to shrug. "Your husband is an optimist," I said to Catherine.

"Always." There was a note of amusement in her voice

that was not quite wholehearted. "He loves the beginning of a journey."

Martin clicked to the mules, and the cart wheeled slowly around, its wheels churning the mud. From our vantage point, I could see the coffin.

"Good-bye, Martin. Good-bye, Judah."

And when Catherine noticed the tears on my face, I was at a loss to explain exactly why I was crying.

PART V
1876

49
CHANGE

February 28, 1876

Dear Martin,

You asked me to let you know as soon as we'd fixed our date of departure, and I finally have a date—March the twentieth. As I received no answer to the last letter I sent you, I presume you're traveling as you said you might once the coldest weather had passed.

I won't hold it against you if you're not in Chicago when we arrive given the uncertainties of travel at this time of year. Our wait for winter to end has been made all the worse by having little to do except fret. Jane Holdcroft is firmly in charge as seamstress now, and I don't suppose you'll be surprised to hear I miss my former role.

With the Calderwoods gone—no Judah—Eliza Drummond dead—and the seminary returned to its former modest sobriety under Dr. Spedding, I finally have the peaceful existence I craved when I first arrived here with a baby in my arms. I don't want it.

I want Chicago and a new challenge and—well, other things I can't have. I know what the pitfalls are of moving to a new place and am determined to do better this time, even if that means I have to be more deceitful than is natural to me. For Sarah's sake, I'll do it.

Only three weeks until I stand on the doorstep of the Eternal Life Seminary for the last time, Martin. It can't come soon enough.

Yours,

Nell

THE BREATH OF THE PRAIRIE ENVELOPED ME AS I PUSHED OPEN the heavy doors and stepped out under the recessed arch that sheltered them. After a week of mixed rain and sunshine, the breeze carried a sharp edge of cold, a memory of winter's frost to remind us that the season was yet early.

The horizon I could see from the seminary's front door was gray, tinged with the faintest pink. As I watched, a spark of golden light appeared at the point where sky and soil came together, highlighting a few shreds of cloud that drifted, wraithlike, across the dawn sky.

The golden fire grew, bringing the yellow stone of the seminary's facade to life. The light, I knew, would reflect off its rows of windows and make tiny specks embedded in the stone scintillate with minute rainbow-hued sparks.

I faced east, and the frontier was behind me. I was retreating back whence I had come, sobered by the experiences of the last four years, but a little—perhaps a lot—more prepared for what the great world had in store for me. I had the means to survive on my own now—if I could not have Martin.

Wanting Martin was the greatest change of all and held untold implications for me, my child, and my dearest friend.

A light step sounded behind me, and a small hand curled itself into mine.

"Momma, the cart is all loaded up in the yard. We can go now, can't we?"

I picked Sarah up, marveling at the weight of her in my arms. She was still slim and dainty, not particularly tall for her age, but there was a strength of muscle and bone in her that spoke of health and vitality. I remembered the plump baby I had brought to the seminary and hugged her tighter for just one moment.

"Are you sorry to be leaving Kansas?" I asked.

Sarah squinted against the growing light, looking out over the plains. The sunlight turned her irises into deep wells of jade green, in which swam small flecks of black, like fish frozen forever in a tiny pond.

"Not really," she said. "It's so big and pretty, but there isn't much to do, is there, Momma? We can have a lot more adventures in Chicago. And as long as you and Tess are there, I'll always have home with me, so it doesn't matter where we go."

I kissed her soft cheek. "How did you get so wise?"

"Well I *am* five now, Momma. And Tess says reading books makes you smarter, and you know I like to read."

"Tess is right." I couldn't help grinning as I smoothed back her copper curls, crisp and springy under my fingers.

"Are we going to go now, or do you want to stare at the prairie some more? I can tell Tess to wait a bit longer."

"You don't have to." I kissed Sarah again, put her down, and took her hand. "I'm ready."

Nell's story continues with

The Shadow Palace

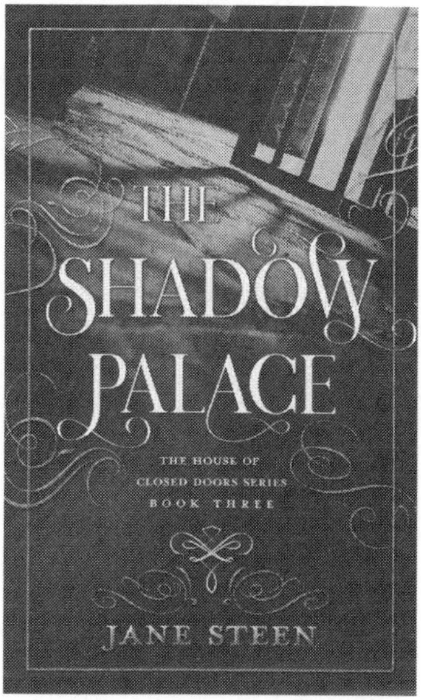

There was no prospect of reconciling my conflicting desires, which all seemed to center on Chicago.

Available as an ebook, in paperback, and as an audiobook at all major outlets

The Scott-De Quincy Mysteries

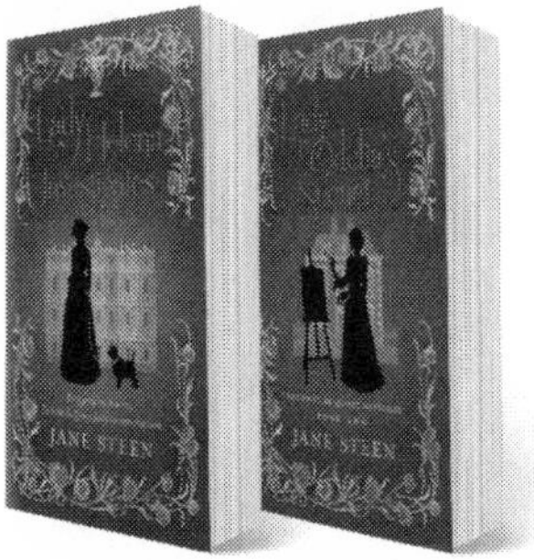

Lady Helena Investigates
Lady Odelia's Secret

A reluctant lady sleuth finds she's investigating her own family.

As the sixth daughter of an Earl, Lady Helena Whitcombe has grown up not to expect much from life. Yet widowhood leaves her with a fortune, a grand mansion in Sussex, and a friendship with French physician Armand Fortier—and her discoveries about her family's past ensure that her position as the baby of the Scott-De Quincy family will not remain her lot in life.

"I can't say enough in praise of Jane Steen's worldbuilding, the immersion into Helena's world, and her character"—Coffee and Ink book blog

FROM THE AUTHOR

Dear Reader,

I hope you enjoyed reading *Eternal Deception* as much as I enjoyed writing it. I'm an indie author paying bills by doing what I love the most—creating entertainment for other people. So my most important assets are YOU, the readers, without whom I'd just be talking to myself. Again.

My promise to you is that I'll do my best. I'll research to make the historical background to my stories as accurate as I can. I'll edit and polish until the book's up to my (high) standards. I'll give you a great-looking cover to look at, and I'll make sure my books are available in as many formats and in as many places as possible. I'll keep my prices as low as is compatible with keeping my publishing business going.

What can you do for me? If you've loved this book, there are several ways you can help me out.

Let me know what you think. If you go to www.janesteen.com, you'll see a little envelope icon near the bottom of the page. That's how you contact me by email. Or you can use the Contact page on the website. I'd love to hear what you thought of the book. Or find me on Facebook, Twitter, or Goodreads.

Leave a review. An honest review—even if you just want to say you didn't like the book—is a huge help. Leave it on the site where you bought the book, or on a reader site like Goodreads.

Tell a friend. I love it when sales come through word of mouth. Better still, mention my book on social media and amplify your power to help my career.

Follow me on BookBub to be informed about deals on my books or new releases.

Sign up for my newsletter at www.janesteen.com/insider. That's a win-win: my newsletter is where I offer free copies, unpublished extras, insider info, and let you know when a new book's coming out.

And thanks again for reading.

AUTHOR'S NOTE

My inspiration for the setting of *Eternal Deception* was an old photograph of the Virginia Theological Seminary, a wedding cake of a building surrounded by small trees. I had sent Nell off to Kansas, not Virginia—yet this is not a novel about Kansas in any way, shape or form, and is certainly not a novel about Virginia.

The point was to give Nell the isolation she thinks she needs in order to bring up Sarah far from gossip, and for her to discover that her Garden of Eden has a few snakes in it. The seminary setting was ready to hand because as the frontier pushed out into the vast central plains of the United States, so did the religious communities. People whose primary resource was determination erected huge buildings in the middle of nowhere on the assumption that a town would eventually grow up around them, and many of those buildings still exist at the heart of colleges dotted around the United States.

I wanted to remind the reader that the westward expansion wasn't just about the homesteaders, cowboys and indians, and saloons filled with gun-toting prospectors that we see in film and TV. During the latter part of the 1800s America was under the influence of a strong temperance movement that sought to restrict the use of alcohol (and eventually succeeded.) The Third Great Awakening swept parts of the country with evangelical fervor, and the sabbatarian movements fought to enforce a regimented Sunday rest.

At the same time the churches were being challenged by scientific discovery and secularism, not to mention a large number of new religious movements and experiments in communal living. And the frontier received news (and goods) faster than you'd think, thanks to the burgeoning railroads, enterprising merchants like Montgomery Ward and Marshall Field who sent their salesmen out into the wilderness, and communications companies such as the Western Union telegraph and the Wells Fargo mail and banking services.

The Eternal Life Seminary and its satellite town of Springwood exist only in my imagination, and the denomination that supports it is left deliberately vague. I feel I should make it clear that I had no intention of criticizing any particular denomination or even Protestant Christianity in general—I was simply interested in the idea that an isolated location could easily come under the control of people whose underlying motives had nothing to do with religion. The narrow-minded, venal, grasping Calderwoods were great fun to imagine, and were based on no historical model.

Judah has an entire backstory that never made it into the final version of the novel, and if you're frustrated that the contents of the letter were never explained, rest assured that the writer of that letter didn't know the half of it and accept my apologies for the decision not to slow the story down by explaining Judah. I do love my villains, and am hoping to write a Judah story one of these days. The fact that he bears a slight resemblance to Benedict Cumberbatch as Sherlock Holmes is a gift to my critique partner, Katharine Grubb. And while I'm on the subject of actors, I would like to apologize to Meg Ryan and Billy Crystal for Chapter 9.

The dresses that Nell makes in the course of the four years covered by the novel are all inspired by real historical gowns, and I'm grateful to all of the museums, research institutes and nineteenth-century enthusiasts who make original photos and costumes available on the internet. Go to my Pinterest board at https://www.pinterest.com/janesteen/eternal-deception/ to see the originals. This is probably going to be the most dress-filled Nell novel because it's where she really develops her skills, so thanks for indulging me.

ACKNOWLEDGMENTS

This novel has been so long in the making that I'll almost certainly forget someone who has been instrumental in helping it see the light of day. Particularly since the writing of Eternal Deception took place during a stage of my life where we (the adult generation) were adjusting to our children's transition into adulthood and seeing our elders move into a quieter, less active stage of life. But I'll never forget receiving the first draft back from my critique partner Katharine Grubb, covered in orange pen—a sight that led to the extremely fruitful decision to rewrite the whole thing from the beginning and keep rewriting until I got the story right. I'm grateful for her honest and rigorous assessments of my work and her creative insights about my characters.

Several other writers (and one reader!) had the patience to read through one or more versions of the manuscript and give their opinions about what was and was not working. Thanks in particular to Maureen Lang and Judy Knox for their detailed, knowledgeable assessment of the last version but one, and thanks in general to Sherri Gallagher, Myra Wells, Tonja Brice, Megan Krizman, Tracey Stewart and Mary Walter for being wonderful readers and critiquers who are all responsible for some vital change or the other.

Few writers are talented enough to produce a book as well as write it, so my thanks go out to my editor, Jenny Quinlan, for patiently correcting my wayward punctuation and pointing out quite a few instances where I used a too-modern term even though I thought I'd eliminated all of them.

Many thanks to designer extraordinaire Rachel Lawston (lawstondesign.com) for the gorgeous cover, although I'll never forget the original design by Derek Moore and photography by Steve Ledell.

And, of course, thanks to my family for putting up with being neglected while I tended to my fictional loved ones. Love and eternal thanks in particular to Bob, for supporting my writing, never putting any stumbling blocks in the way of my various ambitions, and generally being a wonderful husband.

ABOUT THE AUTHOR

The most important fact you need to know about me is that I was (according to my mother, at least) named after Jane Eyre, which to this day remains one of my favorite books. I was clearly doomed to love all things Victorian, and ended up studying both English and French nineteenth-century writers in depth.

This was a pretty good grounding for launching myself into writing novels set in the nineteenth century. I was living in the small town of Libertyville, Illinois—part of the greater Chicago area—when I began writing the *House of Closed Doors* series, inspired by a photograph of the long-vanished County Poor Farm on Libertyville's main street.

Now back in my native England, I have the good fortune to live in an idyllic ancient town close to the sea. This location has sparked a new series about an aristocratic family with more secrets than most: *The Scott-De Quincy Mysteries*.

I write for readers who want a series you can't put down. I love to blend saga, mystery, adventure, and a touch of romance, set against the background of the real-life issues facing women in the late nineteenth century.

I am a member of the Alliance of Independent Authors, the Historical Novel Society, Novelists, Inc., and the Society of Authors.

To find out more about my books, join my insider list at www.janesteen.com/insider

facebook.com/janesteenwriter
twitter.com/JaneSteen
bookbub.com/authors/jane-steen
goodreads.com/janesteen
pinterest.com/janesteen

Made in the USA
Columbia, SC
14 December 2022

73764325R00286